THE AURORA'S
PALE LIGHT

E. W. DOC PARRIS

MAGIC
GENIUS

MAGIC GENIUS BOOKS

A MAGIC GENIUS BOOK
Magic Genius, LLC
Warrenton, Virginia, USA

Trade paperback:979-8-9873889-5-2
Kindle ISBN: 979-8-9873889-6-9
eBook ISBN: 979-8-9873889-7-6
Mass-market paperback:979-8-9873889-8-3

THANK YOU FOR SUPPORTING MICRO-INDEPENDENT PUBLISHING. WE BELIEVE THE FUTURE OF PUBLISHING LIES IN THE VISION, COURAGE, AND TALENT WORKING EVERY DAY TO PUSH INDEPENDENT PUBLISHING FURTHER INTO THE MAINSTREAM.
IF YOU ENJOY THIS NOVEL PLEASE LEAVE A REVIEW WHEREVER YOU PURCHASED IT.

For Dominick, Daniel, and Jacob.

ARGUMENT

The Aurora's Pale Light is the second volume of a longer history of humanity's future—collectively referred to as *The WalrusTech Universe*. This tale begins in the first volume, *The Dent in the Universe*, which takes place in the very near future, a time when most of the technology and cultural references feel comfortably within reach. This book picks up essentially where that story left off, though where time machines are involved, *when* one enters a story can be tricky to pin down. What follows is a synopsis of that novel for those whose memories have faded.

But first, a word of caution, it would be better for everyone involved if you read that first story before peering further into this one—honestly, the difference between experiencing the thrills and chills of that tale and catching up with a slip-shod synopsis is hard to express. To be fair, the first volume gives the reader a far more rich understanding of the vagaries of time machines with all of their quantum strangeness. But... we've all been stuck in a beach house rental with only the second volume of a series to read and no nearby library. It is for you, sunburned reader, that I chose to add this cramped and withered summary of *The Dent in the Universe*.

That said, the following is one big spoiler. Turn back now. You. Have. Been. Warned.

In 2030, decorated African American war hero, Fire Chief John Banks receives a video call from an old army pal, notorious tech billionaire Stephen Lucas. Stephen appears to have aged, and his face shows scars that are new to Banks's eye. Stephen bets he can accurately predict the play-by-play of the next ten minutes of a live baseball game. The stakes? John must consider an unusual job offer. Winning the wager, Stephen begins his recruitment pitch by predicting John's imminent death in a fire.

Two weeks later, Detective Julia Swann, investigating John's mysterious death in a wildfire, finds a clue connecting Chief Banks with famous One Corporation CEO Stephen Lucas. She interviews Stephen after his keynote address, introducing a new faster-than-light, sub-space gaming network. He testifies he knows nothing about John's death and hasn't spoken to him in years. The business icon and the detective share a mutual frisson of attraction. Unbeknownst to the couple, the unknown subject of Julia's other case, a serial killer that's eluded her for years, has observed their meeting.

Six years later, in 2036, Stephen's sub-space gaming network hasn't panned out. When a freak accident causes a crash of their global gaming network, One Corp's board calls for his ouster. Stephen is ready to sell his soul for a new hit product when his hardware guru, Walrus Roberts, discovers the crash was due to IP traffic arriving *from the future*. Extrapolating that bug into an instant gratification device that allows impatient shoppers to receive purchases immediately, Stephen works in secret with Walrus to hammer the glitch into the hit he so desperately needs. While they work, Julia discovers gruesome evidence in her serial killer cold case, tying the murders to a One Corp employee. After reaching out to Steven for information, they rekindle their previous attraction. This time, they begin to date.

Stephen demos the prototype—Oneiri: the time machine for the rest of us—to his beta testers, including Cliff Price, lead designer of gothic horror hologames. After the beta test begins, Julia's partner discovers evidence that Cliff is their serial killer and stumbles onto his torture dungeon. When her partner goes missing, Julia raids One Corp with an arrest warrant. Cliff magically escapes. Stephen dismisses Julia's evidence and expertise, convinced Cliff is incapable of committing such atrocities.

Exploiting Oneiri, Cliff plays past financial markets, generating unlimited wealth. He dials up the past to fund a bogus defense research project to bioengineer a horrific virus for release in the present. The infected develop violent behavior, a thirst for blood, and keratinous horns—like the demons of Cliff's hologames. As the pandemic spreads, stock markets crash, world governments destabilize, and wars erupt across the globe. All that after less than a week of Oneiri beta testing.

As demons roam the streets, and the world mirrors Cliff's games, Walrus suddenly goes missing. Convinced Cliff was responsible, Stephen hatches a scheme to bargain for Walrus' life. With a preproduction prototype of a new mobile Oneiri, he charges in to confront Cliff. Stephen sets a timer on the new device before Cliff overpowers and tortures him. The timer goes off, texting Julia his time and location. She leads a team, battling through fire and demons to rescue Stephen. She shoots Cliff repeatedly, but he escapes with the new Oneiri—unaware Stephen has sabotaged it. With Julia showing signs of infection, a desperate and humbled Stephen abandons her to use Oneiri one more time to save her life and set things right.

Back in 2030, Stephen completes his story. John has trouble swallowing it all. Stephen tries to enlist John to help prepare the world for the coming apocalypse. They argue, and John refuses Stephen's mission. He hangs up, leaving to oversee a nearby wildfire, but he's surprised by a sudden wind change. Precisely as Stephen predicted, John wrecks his truck, fleeing the fire. He's rescued at the last possible moment by a team sent by Stephen. Stephen makes John understand the point of his long tale— Stephen is the *villain* of the story. He needs John to be the *hero*, ready the world for the apocalypse, find a cure for Julia, and prepare to lead humanity back from hell.

ROBERTS' RULES FOR TIME MACHINES

1. Information can be sent backward in time.
2. Information sent into the past cannot alter the sender's observed reality.
   A. The sender's observation of the present collapses the wave function of the past.
      i. The wave function of any observable event represents the probabilities of all possible outcomes, no matter how unlikely.
         - Once the sender observes an event's outcome, its wave function collapses and cannot be altered through the use of the time machine.
   B. The sender cannot alter the present. The sender _can_ alter the future, including the moment immediately following the present moment.
   C. What *has* happened is immutable. What is *yet* to happen remains mutable.
3. Attempts to alter the sender's current reality will always fail.
   A. How failures manifest is outside the sender's control and is subject to the combined

probability of all the things that
can go wrong.

   i. The total probability of all
things that can go wrong equals
100 percent.

   ii. Generally, the thing that is
most likely to go wrong will,
but small odds sometimes
pay off.

4. The timeline cannot generate
information spontaneously.

   A. As a result, the sender cannot
provide their earlier self with
any information about the future.

   B. Nothing prevents the sender from
providing information about the
future to others so long as that
information can never reach the
sender's earlier self.

      i. Attempts to provide future
information to the sender's
earlier self will always fail
(See Rule 3)

PROLOGUE

JULIA

YOUR MEMORIES ARE COMPLETELY WORTHLESS.

But you aren't a special case or anything. Far from it. Even the most disciplined mind can no more rely on subjective memory than they can on the accuracy of the tenth day's outlook on a ten-day weather forecast. Memory is not a mechanistic recording of facts and metrics. It's not rigid data stored on a trillion-dollar corporation's rapacious cloud server. It's not even cuneiform impressions in a clay tablet hardened by the sun. At best, our view of the past is an impressionist painting. Our memories, imprecise daubs of oil paint dappled on the canvas of the mind, swirl with the tints of our emotions. Our fears, our hopes, our carnal urges, and our petty hatreds muddy our every recollection. Memory and emotion weave together in our simian brains—cementing some connections and shredding others into tatters.

So it was with the memory of Julia Swann, onetime detective, in the Madre Pueda Police Department. An outpatient in the psychiatric arc of the Nunavut Technology Center's H-Dome, she was a source of hope for all who met her. Julia had survived *the cure*—an anti-viral cocktail to combat the effects of stage three GGB-Z infection. She had regained her humanity and reacquired her soul; and if *she* had survived, there was hope for so many down there below the Arctic Circle. That was what the Nunavut Technology Center was all about. Hope for all of humanity.

Or so she'd been told.

She closed and locked her apartment door and stepped out into the massive domed structure that was A-Dome, a beautifully designed, climate-controlled habitat nearly two miles across. Her apartment was on the third of six levels, which wrapped the circumference of the pristine structure, and her door opened onto a spacious multi-use promenade that was part sidewalk and part autonomous delivery vehicle highway. As she looked out at A-Dome's Central Park, small robotic go-carts filled with reusable bins of groceries whizzed past at a sane but speedy clip. She turned to walk clockwise toward the eastern ramp to the park.

She had no memory of arriving here at the NTC. No memory of the last three or maybe four years. Her memory was an unreliable jumble of images, sensations, and feelings. From time to time, a smell—like that of Ring 3 cafeteria's peanut butter and jelly sandwiches—delivered a torrent of memories that spilled into her mind and sloshed chaotically for a few minutes or a few hours. Julia had no control over these memories.

The aroma of that peanut butter and jelly sandwich on white bread transported her to Braddock Elementary's cafeteria in 2008. She'd been in first grade when she caught a glimpse of Carl Hanlon picking his nose, pulling out a gelatinous booger, and popping it into his mouth. She was helplessly carried by her memory like a raft on whitewater. The echo of that ridiculous grade-school memory played in stunning, unwelcome detail as she strolled off the ramp and onto the Central Park pathway.

Her brain was healing, and she was just along for the ride.

The Park was a study in happy, controlled chaos as NTC apartment dwellers made their ways hither and thither mostly on foot, though some rode elegant little e-scooters and others queued up for the maglev subway. Every detail of A-Dome—of the entire NTC community—had an architectural style that showed the hand of a skilled designer. Central Park's amphitheater featured a ring of twelve ivy-covered arches that stretched up nearly to the top of the transparent inside surface of the dome. It was high enough that its furthest details were muted by a faint haze. She'd watched a documentary on Stephen Lucas when she was in college. The imagineers that dreamed up this little dreamland had cribbed their design language from him.

She stopped for caffeine at the Park Barista's station. The line was winding down from the morning rush. The teenager behind the counter poured her a chai as she approached and wrote *Julia* on the cup. She smiled and nodded at the young man and headed for H-Dome. Now that she'd been released and settled in her new place, it was time to begin the next phase of her recovery.

She dreaded it.

All cops had a fear of the psych evaluation. But then, not all cops had done time as a demon. She took a sip of her chai and headed down the hill that dipped beneath the curved walls between A-Dome and B-Dome.

An air gate enveloped her at the bisection of the two massive structures. B-Dome was larger than A by, she guessed, a half a mile, but that's not what anyone noticed as they moved through that air gate. While the air was pleasant enough in the apartment dome, B-Dome's air was rich with smells, from floral fragrances to the whiff of fresh horse apples. Plants grew almost everywhere around the outer rings of the dome in hydroponic stacks that stretched as high as the dome's ceiling would allow. Within these rings were concentric circles of grazing lanes each about 100 feet wide. Bright green Bermuda grass in some, duller, more ragged-looking switchgrass in others. And each lane had a team of cows or goats or some other livestock marching about the circle, munching away on their front end and dropping fresh manure out the back.

It never ceased to make Julia smile.

The psychiatric arc of H-Dome's top ring—Ring 6—overlooked the circular plaza below. Julia peered down from a session room as she waited for her mystery guest. Dr. Wilson had scheduled a few of these meet-and-greets with people from her past. The first had been Frankie Lazlo, her former partner in the Madre Pueda Police Department's Detective Division. Frankie was not someone she had any trouble recalling, and they fell right back into their comfortable bullshit after a few good hugs and a few good cries. Exactly who was on the menu for this morning's session was, per doctor's orders, unknown.

She waited and watched the busy community beyond the window. Though it was not as lively as M-Dome with its military exercises, nor as lovely and fragrant as B-Dome's botanical garden, H-Dome's plaza provided a reassuring hustle and bustle of doctors, nurses, lab techs, and EMTs. In many ways, it felt more like the pre-Downfall urban world Julia Swann had called home than the NTC in general. She sipped her chai, a tea that felt nostalgic and familiar—though, as yet, she couldn't put a finger on the memory that made it so.

She was a coffee drinker. Always had been. She couldn't remember switching to chai. Chai was a drink for rich boy poseurs. But since those dim, dreamlike days of her awakening, she'd been drawn to chai. It reminded her of something vital and urgent and... what? It was literally a memory on the tip of her tongue. The taste made her want to swirl it across the seam of her closed lips, to feel the soft underside as if she could French kiss herself.

Was it a kiss? A French kiss? With whom?

Can you kiss me more?

That was a song from the year the first Covid pandemic was terrifying everyone. Doja Cat and SZA. Sharon used to stream it in their flat as everyone struggled to adapt to lockdown. Junior year at Fresno State. She'd been killing it in all her criminology courses before everything went remote and online.

Sign first, middle, last, on the wisdom tooth… Taste breakfast, lunch, and gin and juice.

She felt a heart tug as she thought of Sharon in her underwear and a Fresno t-shirt belting out the lyrics. They'd been like sisters in crime. Sisters in Criminology. Sharon, a cute, smart, Black sophomore from Cleveland, teasing Julia for her California white girl crush on SZA.

She remembered *that* well enough, goddamn it.

She took another sip. Her eyes misted over as she tried again to find some fresh aspect of memory associated with the chai. Before she could produce a result, the door opened, and the largest Black man she'd ever met—or, more accurately, could currently remember—popped his head into the waiting room. His was a face she recognized but couldn't place: handsome and fit, though he looked a little gaunt and thoroughly bone tired. He carried it as if he was on the road to recovery from a task that had worn him raw.

On the mend, she thought. *Like me.*

His face was thoughtful, empathetic, and cautious. He asked her permission to enter with a simple, humble raise of his eyebrows. She nodded and took another sip of tea. The man entered and closed the clinic door behind him. He eyed his choices of seating—a large, overstuffed armchair, the couch on which Julia was curled, or three wooden chairs against the wall. He dragged one of the latter to the edge of the braided rug, turning it so he could sit on it backward with his large arms folded over the back as he looked at her and smiled. The cool, blue light of the dome's high apex cast a glint off the scar that ran the length of his cheek.

John Banks, she thought suddenly, and a wealth of information flooded her mind. She couldn't remember last summer, but instantly she could recall infinite details about his case: Holding his photograph in her hand—that pirate-like scar—his green MPPD file folder—she and Frankie, pissed that they had to shelve the serial killer case they were working—a fire that burned an old pizza restaurant she'd visited with Kenny Loomis before COVID-28—the Branch Fire—the cinder-sculpture remains of a man—Banks' townhouse, abandoned—the line of Frankie's finger on the dust-covered credenza—A DNA report—dental records.

Banks saw the look on her face and smiled again. She attempted to ease the brakes on her out-of-control memories.

"Hello Julia," he said. His voice was deep, but gentle.

His magnetism was everything her witnesses had said. She remembered Stephen Lucas had said he was a born leader, a mensch. She could believe it. The Governor of California had said the same thing.

Wait! When had she met Stephen Lucas?

"Hello…?"

"We've never met," he said. "Dr. Wilson asked—I understand your memory is returning. He thought I might help on that front."

Julia nodded. Her brow pulled into a frown as her eyes narrowed. Her memories were playing games. She remembered something that was clearly impossible. She closed her eyes and shook her head.

The torrent of her memories chose a bad time to start raging into rapids: Stephen Lucas, the hologaming billionaire she'd fangirled since she'd seen that PBS documentary back at Fresno—the memory of meeting him—standing in the immaculate One Corporation parking garage—white epoxied concrete—a choir of angels—seeing the panoramic atrium of One Flat Circle from the C-suite on the tenth floor (an architectural kissing cousin of A-Dome's Central Park)—interviewing Lucas—finding him just as dynamic as she'd imagined—shorter and younger—Frankie accusing her of flirting a little.

But she'd been there because she was working a case.

"Your name *is* John Banks, right?"

"Guilty as charged."

Her frown deepened as she fought to keep her focus on the here and now. Her head shook slowly as she questioned herself.

"Is there a problem, Julia?"

She looked at John with confusion in her pale blue eyes. Those eyes still had thin, red outlines from the hemorrhages. Her golden blond hair was growing out, but was still less than an inch long. Her skin was still marked with the rough patches where the demon horns had erupted. She was on the mend, but her face looked vulnerable, unsure, and lost.

"My memory is fucked." She shook her head and looked away. "Well, I mean... more than I thought."

"Why do you say that?"

"Because." She bit her lip and looked back into his clear brown eyes. He was a handsome man, no doubt. "Because I remember investigating your death. I remember kneeling next to your corpse." The impact of that image cast a shadow on her face. "You died in a fire."

John nodded.

"I did. Yeah."

They sat in awkward silence for a few seconds before John stood and moved to the couch next to her. He sat on the opposite end, lit by the large bright dome outside the window. There was a sadness in his eyes she hadn't noticed before. He sighed and then held his hands out with the fingers spread wide.

"I'll tell you about that, but the story began earlier. You need to know everything. It's not a tale most people down there know." He gestured to the busy NTC citizens below. "We haven't eliminated the need for secrecy yet."

He thought a second longer, trying to decide where to begin. "There was a period where the game board was being set up and the pieces were being placed. White and... black. The game was already underway by the time I was..." He trailed off. "Let me tell you what I know, what I *can*. It's been six years, and I haven't told this story to anyone from start to finish. Maybe it will help me to tell you. Maybe we can be a little therapy group of two. Does that sound all right?"

Julia nodded, sipped her chai, and thought briefly of the moment Lucas had pressed his card into her hand at the end of her interview, his hands so strong and coarse for a tech geek.

If you need anything…

BOOK 1
DOOMSDAY PREP

10-31-29, 12:00 AM EDT:
MONSTERS

THE SOLID BRICK home sat within the moon's shadow of the Holy Trinity Catholic Church. Autumn had turned cold early, and all the trees were barren. Entangled branches wove black spiderwebs along the cobblestone sidewalks of Georgetown's N Street. The cold muted the Halloween nightlife down on M. Revelers in costumes ill-suited for the chill kept to the canal and the riverfront. Two blocks north, it was quiet but for the crisp, rustling, wind-torn leaves skittering across the pavement.

Melissa Jones' EV expertly parallel-parked between two similarly upscale black sedans. The car's magnetic pad clunked onto the charging disk in the street's rubber composite surface. Her dash confirmed the charger's mating with a lightning bolt bisecting the battery icon. She checked her makeup and ran a brush through her dark auburn hair. With blood-red talons, she scratched lightly at a dry patch on her pale, freckled forehead, then stepped out into the slicing breeze. She didn't look around. She'd been here hundreds of times.

She found the cast-iron gate's clasp in the dark and proceeded down the alley. A few of the townhomes had Halloween lights and decorations. The trick-or-treaters were long abed, but their parents were still in their cups. She turned into the first walkway lit by two spherical sconces, down three steps, and knocked on the black door with five sharp raps.

The peephole darkened.

The door opened, and a small, intense man looked reflexively up and down the alley before guiding her in with a gentle clasp on her shoulder. His home, as always, smelled of old books, garlic, and cloves. She continued into the parlor without waiting for her host, removing her black trench coat and green and silver-gray scarf. The man's wife appeared from the kitchen.

"Hello, Number Three," she said and gestured to take Melissa's coat and scarf.

"Hello, Four," Melissa said. "It's decided to skip right past fall and plummet into winter."

"So it seems," said the older woman as she walked up the adjoining stairwell with Melissa's things and out of sight. She returned with her arms free. "We're just waiting on Two."

"Tonight's Number One is already here?"

The old woman nodded as she headed back to the kitchen. "Already downstairs with Six. You know Six likes to prepare them. I don't know why…" her voice trailed off.

"I'm sorry, you don't…?"

"I don't know why Six feels the need to *prepare* them." Four raised her volume. "I think it weakens them. I think the ceremony requires that moment of… that feeling that the supplicant has gotten in over their head. That loss of control is vital."

"Six runs this Pentaculum, Mother," her husband said, finally making his way from the mudroom. "He's been very successful in establishing new pentacula over the years."

"Of course, Five. Of course."

Melissa smiled falsely at the couple's meager efforts to refrain from bickering. She was saved from a full-tilt passive-aggressive non-argument by five sharp raps on the door in the mudroom. Five turned and shuffled to answer as Four rolled her eyes.

Five returned with a handsome young Arab man in an expensive suit.

"Where's Six?" he asked without greeting.

"He's already below," Five said with a touch of apology. "We're ready to begin."

He opened the basement door, and an ancient memory crept out into the parlor—an emptiness—an old and familiar smell. Melissa's mind flashed to her grandparents' root cellar in the late spring of her childhood. The fungal smell stirred memories of abuse, helplessness, and loss. In all the years she'd been part of this Pentaculum, she had never been able to steel herself to that dank, subtle perfume. It was as much a part of the ceremony as the blood of the One.

The four members followed their host down the old stone steps that revealed the age of this home that predated the very idea of America. It had been quietly passed from mother to daughter for 350 years. The Pentacula had been carried here from old Europe. Four, when she spoke of it, humbly bragged that her family still held the third position in the Pentaculum in Istanbul, the original Pentaculum—formed before the city was christened Constantinople when the Thracians called it Lygos.

The Pentacula were older than the Nazarene, older than the Baptist, older than Rome, and perhaps older than Moses. True, it was an organization at odds with the Christian church, but it was so much more than that. It was a shaper of civilizations, an underlying network whose mark could be seen across the millennia. They were the hand of Satan, according to the moralists—the Magicians, the Witches, the Wizards, and the cults of darkness depicted by so many writers and artists through the centuries. So misunderstood.

In reality, they were an enlightened few who gathered to promote themselves and their ideas. They recruited the brightest minds, the most skilled artists, the best humanity had to offer. Certainly, recruitment demanded blood, but it offered meaning, purpose, and a clear path to real power.

Upon reaching the bottom of the stone staircase, the four members separated by gender—the men turned left, the women, right. Melissa and her hostess removed their clothes and donned light teal hospital scrubs. Melissa supposed in the early days the congregants wore robes, but the network kept up with the times. Scrubs were much more practical, and the ceremony was no religious act of fake thaumaturgy.

The ceremony was the summoning of purpose. It was a simple exchange. The supplicant surrendered their vulnerability, their innocence, their conscience—and received payment, something that had genuine value and meaning. It was a deal, freely entered, fully documented—even though few, if any, read that document in its entirety. But this wasn't so different from any End User License Agreement. No one ever regretted it if they survived. It wasn't a deal with a devil. Melissa had the research to prove it. Human minds, pushed beyond a certain threshold to the brink of madness or death, almost inevitably find enlightenment on the other side.

The women walked through another door to leave the dressing room. They emerged into a circular stone room. Two small cast-iron wood stoves stood with metal chimneys rising up through an arched ceiling of old brick. White tiles covered the floor with a black, five-pointed star mosaic in the center. Each point had a Roman numeral at its apex. In its center was an altar —roughly shaped and pitted—that looked older than the rest of the stonework. The pores of the stone were dark with centuries of stains, though Melissa knew Four meticulously cleaned the thing after every new induction ceremony.

A naked man, perhaps forty, olive-skinned, with copious amounts of black body hair, was lying naked on the altar, talking quietly with Six, a tall, gray-haired elder statesman. Six was, Melissa thought, incredibly magnetic, attractive, even sexy for his age. He was the reason they were all here. Six was the reason they had a One nearly every Pentacula Eve. His charm was seductive, and he was a natural marketer for the benefits of the deal. He was also, in Melissa's opinion, a bit of a rat-bastard. He looked up as

Melissa moved to the number three spot, and Four took her place beside her.

"You see, One? Our Pentacle takes shape." Six smiled gently.

The hirsute, naked man raised his head slightly. He showed no embarrassment or fear, only the slight anxiousness of a new bridge partner. Melissa thought he looked dull and stupid. But then, all the Ones did. Six had a keen talent for finding dull, meaningless lambs that lead idiotic lives at the mercy of random, external events. Six could see the hidden spark that might be lit by the ceremony. One actually smiled and waved.

The other men emerged. Five looked flustered and agitated, as if Two had begun an argument.

"Everything al lright, gentlemen?" Six asked.

They took their places and nodded. Six raised an eyebrow. Everyone, besides One, was dressed in identical scrubs. The room had the air of an operating theater with Six as the head surgeon. He spent a few quiet seconds arranging a set of gleaming utensils on a table against the stone wall. The sounds of fine metal tools scraping against each other echoed off every stone surface. Six turned his attention back to the One.

"All right then." Six lowered his head and closed his eyes as though about to pray. He had no prayer, only a well-worn path through the ceremony. Melissa wondered, could it be the thousandth time for him? Ten thousandth?

"Thank you for gathering on this important night. There are only a few such nights in our calendar, and we only gather when the One is found. It is an honor, of course, but also a profound responsibility. When the stars and the moon are in their place, those marked must join the Pentaculum and witness. This allows the Pentacula to continue, grow, and replenish itself. It provides meaning to those who wander blindly in the world, their eyes sewn shut by trauma, ignorance, and fear."

He raised his head and acknowledged all the congregants. "Let us begin."

Six stepped to his place at the head of the Pentacle, his feet on the black tile VI. From there, the One's head was within easy reach. The hairy man's eyes only now started to reveal any anxiety.

Six leaned over and whispered, "There, there." He straightened and spoke more formally to all. "We gather according to the Wheel of the Year. This gathering of the Six on Samhain's Eve is a particularly potent aspect of the Wheel. So, we gather here, when the veils between the worlds are thin, to aid the One, to bring him to the one, pure, white light." He leaned down and retrieved a leather strap attached to the underside of the ancient altar. Six gently strapped the One's head to the altar as the other congregants stepped forward and found straps beneath the altar as well. They quietly and gently secured each of his limbs. Melissa's position as Three gave her the right leg to secure, and a view of the One's groin, which was so hairy that his penis was shrunken from view.

There was no escape now. The One's breathing increased in speed and volume. The reality of his situation was becoming clear. It was at this moment that Melissa often felt the need to stifle a laugh. She remembered this point in her induction, remembered the panic rising. What happened next was less clear. Her ceremony had lasted nine hours, they told her later. She had needed three months to recover physically.

Six turned from the altar and selected something from the table near the wall. He turned back, holding a twelve-inch blade. It was not wavy or serpentine or overly theatrical; however, any casual observer could see it was sharpened to perfection. The One began to pant hoarsely.

"No. Nope. I've changed my mind," he said. He sounded like a dreamer, talking in his sleep. "I didn't think it was real, I thought—"

Six slid the blade into the trembling flesh just above the One's pectoralis major, entering the skin below the collarbone and moving toward the navel, between the muscle and dermis. Blood poured out of the wound and matted the black chest hair. The

One howled, and his mouth filled with spittle. Suddenly, he was crying and struggling against his bonds. With an experienced hand, Six plunged the knife in to its hilt and removed it while the One convulsed.

The congregants felt the first rush of adrenaline as they each remembered their own trauma. None of them felt an ounce of sympathy or pity. Their eyes shone with wonder, fascination, and joy. Their hearts beat almost audibly in unison.

Six turned to wipe the blade on a rag. The One caught his breath.

"You know who I am, Baxter. You know me." He tried to turn his head as Six moved to his right side calmly, deliberately, without menace or even much thought. He moved as if he were listening to an internal symphony. He slid the knife into the skin above the right chest. Again, the One howled and arched his back. Six wiggled the blade to separate the skin from the muscle, then withdrew it and turned to clean the blade.

"I have money, you mother-fucker! I have MONEY! I don't need your help!" the One barked hoarsely. Adrenaline was thickening his vocal cords and forcing him to struggle with verbal communication. No longer the dull, idiotic, doughy nothing Melissa had seen earlier, the One's pain filled him with rage, which made him more interesting. He made eye contact with her. His eyes widened with mad anger. "You think this is funny?! You fucking bitch!"

Melissa turned to the small wood stove and chose her implement, an iron rod tapered to a point, hot and red as a ripe cherry. She had been called out, so it was now her duty to guide The One. She pushed the searing point into the flab, where his belly met his quadriceps. The room filled with the odor of burnt hair and fat and flesh. The One arched his back and snarled oaths against all of them and their mothers.

Melissa was starting to believe that Six had chosen a winner again.

The ceremony lasted until half past seven in the morning. Five and Four tended to the One as the rest said their goodbyes. Pentacula network medics would arrive within minutes via a tunnel system established during the waning days of the slave trade to return freed men to their masters. Discrete access was a feature of all Pentaculum sites because, sometimes, the congregants got carried away and the inductee became a sacrifice. It was another way to find one's meaning.

Tonight's One would be moved to a secret rehab facility in Maryland. From there, he'd return to his life and find a place in another Pentaculum, forever bound to Six's Pentaculum.

As Melissa walked to her car in the gray morning light, Six called out to her.

"Melissa!"

She winced at the use of her name. She looked up and down the street.

"Dr. Baxter," she replied.

He, too, grimaced slightly at the use of his life name.

"Are you going into work today?"

"I planned to take PTO."

"I was wondering if I could buy you breakfast and discuss an opportunity."

"I'm pretty happy where I am, as you know." Indeed, Baxter had been instrumental in helping her land her mid-level analyst position at the Defense Intelligence Agency. Her Ph.D. in quantum mechanics, Master's degree in applied mathematics, and his Pentacula connections opened all *sorts* of doors.

"Certainly, certainly. But this is extraordinary. I've—" He hesitated. She'd never seen a chink in his confidence. "I've received a message from a protégé of mine. He's a loner… not a congregant, at least not formally. He's something of a *savant*, really—a wild-born. Something like you, actually." Baxter paused and cast a sideways glance at her blood-red nails. "He has something only you could verify, at least of all the congregants I trust. He's fallen into some tech that could be important…if what he says is true. I thought you might take a look."

"Some tech? What are we talking about here?"

"He says he has a working *time machine* at his disposal."

Melissa wasn't a fan of eating in public. Her appetites aside, she was never comfortable with the process, the biting and chewing, the noise, the mess, and the inevitable need to eat and talk simultaneously. She considered feeding to be a private observance. The idea of doing it in daylight on a Georgetown bench while those around you did the same? Horrible.

She ordered a plain bagel with lox and light, whipped cream cheese, and a tall coffee with cream and sugar. The food truck chef seemed petulantly unchallenged as she handed over the order. Melissa pulled five napkins from the dispenser and found Baxter at a secluded cast-iron picnic table. He smiled and pulled his mobile from his breast pocket as she sat opposite him. The cast-iron was as cold and hard as she'd expected. Melissa took a small bite of her bagel and covered her mouth as she chewed.

Baxter flipped to the message app, found a thread, and opened it. He scrolled to the start of the conversation, handed the device to her, and took a ravenous bite of his ham and egg sandwich on white toast.

The message conversation was between Baxter, and someone tagged *Cliff P.* She looked up at him, but he was sipping coffee and watching several young boys playing on the jungle gym. She turned back to the device and read.

> Sir, I have not been in contact with any Pentacula congregants in years. However, when convenient, I have some important new information that will interest you, the congregants, and the Pentacula. ~Cliff P.

Sorry to keep you on read for so long, Cliff.
Meetings all day. You have my undivided
attention. ~Dr. Baxter

> From my timeframe, there was no delay. ~Cliff P.

> That is part of the information I need to
> communicate. You know I hold a position within
> One Corporation as Senior Game Design
> Director. ~Cliff P.

Indeed.~ Dr. Baxter

> As such, I am often pulled into guerrilla testing of
> new products. I was asked to participate in a
> demonstration of a new product two days ago.
> The product is called Oneiri, and it is a simple
> time machine. ~Cliff P.

Metaphor?~ Dr. Baxter

> Accurate description of the product. I can
> provide more technical details, though much is
> beyond my understanding. But a simple proof is
> that I am contacting you from 2036. September
> 14th, 2036, at 1:12AM PDT, to be precise.
> ~Cliff P.

Melissa dragged the screen to the left slightly to see the time
stamp. The conversation started on October 28th, 2029, at 6:00PM.
She squinted, frowned, and kept reading.

> I am sending my side of this conversation from
> six years in your future. ~Cliff P.

That is an astonishing assertion, Cliff. ~Dr.
Baxter

> Truly astonishing. You are the reason I am in any
> way affiliated with the Pentacula, and I respect
> and trust you. ~Cliff P.

I propose a simple demonstration. I can provide you with knowledge of future events. Information that you can verify within 24 hours. Would that suffice as a first confirmation? ~Cliff P.

Sufficient. I will pick the info? ~Dr. Baxter

Yes. ~Cliff P.

Provide the NASDAQ, DOW, and Nikkei index at closing time tomorrow. Provide the final scores in three MLB baseball games. Provide a piece of international news that breaks tomorrow morning. ~Dr. Baxter

NASDAQ: 22,432. ~Cliff P.

DOW: 52,333. ~Cliff P.

Nikkei: 49,345. ~Cliff P.

Reds 8-7 Diamondbacks. ~Cliff P.

A's 6-4 White Sox. ~Cliff P.

Rangers 6-2 Twins. ~Cliff P.

Moody's will drop Australia's credit rating to AA. ~Cliff P.

That was fast. I strongly doubt that last one, but "time will tell." ~Dr. Baxter

My response took 30 minutes in my timeframe. I'll await your reply after you have confirmation. ~Cliff P.

Holy Hell, Moody's dropped the Aussie's credit rating! ✔~Dr. Baxter

That last was time-stamped the morning of the 29th. Baxter had stopped watching the little boys and was now watching her.

His gaze was disturbing in its predatory intensity. He was smiling.

"Keep reading," he said and sipped his coffee.

The subsequent texts had timestamps that spread out across that morning and afternoon.

Nikkei: 49,345 ✓ ~Dr. Baxter

Reds over Diamondbacks 8-7 ✓ ~Dr. Baxter

Rangers over Twins 6-2 ✓ ~Dr. Baxter

NASDAQ: 22,432 ✓ ~Dr. Baxter

DOW: 52,333 ✓ ~Dr. Baxter

A's over White Sox 6-4 ✓ ~Dr. Baxter

That was a genuinely remarkable 24 hours, Cliff.
~Dr. Baxter

> Truly magical. ~Cliff P.

I have a trusted advisor who could vet the technical aspect, help me evaluate the validity, the possibility of this before I commit fully. I assume you have plans? ~Dr. Baxter

> I have plans. ~Cliff P.

You are consistent if nothing else, Cliff. ~Dr. Baxter

Can you provide any technical specs regarding this Oneiri? ~Dr. Baxter

> ONEFTL_SCHIP.pdf~Cliff P.

> ONEIRI_DEMODECK_pdf~Cliff P.

This should be sufficient for now. I will be in touch. ~Dr. Baxter

Melissa popped open the two PDF docs. The first covered One Corporation's upcoming OneFTL Network and the sChip currently under development. She was already aware of it only because she worked for the DIA. Her office kept track of all new and emerging tech that might have intelligence gathering value or disruptive potential. You wouldn't need a time machine to provide those specs. She dug more deeply. They were dated 2034 right up to 2036—six years from now. If it was a con, it was oddly specific. She'd need to dig into those more closely.

The other was a briefing deck. She flipped through the cards and got the gist. The idea was sound in theory. It would take a genius to pull it off. Walrus Roberts *was* a genius.

"Is it valid?" asked Baxter.

"I'll need to read more, but I can't immediately debunk it from what I've skimmed." She tapped a few times on the screen, then scrolled and tapped a few more times.

"Bottom-line the tech for me."

"I'll need to read more." She continued to tap and scroll.

"Melissa."

"It appears legit," she said sharply as she handed his mobile back. "We know Walrus Roberts found a way to use quantum tunneling across an Einstein-Rosen bridge between entangled network chipsets to send IP traffic instantaneously. Faster than light communication. They use these new chips that use quantum tunneling tensor arrays to pass signal between devices—no matter the distance—with no lag. They're leveraging this tech right now to launch a hologaming network at One Corporation's upcoming 2030 developers conference, OBFDC. That has already been confirmed by multiple DIA HUMINT and SIGINT sources." She left Baxter wondering about her acronyms for Human Intelligence—spies—and Signals Intelligence—electronic eavesdropping. She bit her lip and gazed at the brightening clouds above the park. "Their demo says they found a way to send signal into the past. The deck says three weeks. 2036 is more than 3 weeks away. Maybe they'll find a way to overcome that limitation?"

She looked back at him.

"There would probably be some serious causality issues they'd need to reckon with. I need to read more. There was a slide on *Roberts' Rules for Time Machines*, so it looks like they've hammered some of that out. You're going to want me to analyze that at the bare minimum. This guy, Cliff? He needs to get me more and you need to forward a copy of these docs."

"No," Baxter said firmly.

"What do you mean?"

"I mean, you've verified that it's even theoretically possible." Baxter put his phone back into his jacket pocket. "We're going to make sure you're in a position, when the time comes to acquire one of these Oneiri devices, to help us analyze it." He wiped his mouth almost daintily with his napkin and stood.

"This is a big deal, Baxter."

"Oh, you have no idea. I'll make sure you're kept in the loop. The Pentacula will know of your contribution." He shook her hand with a dismissive smile, gave five quick sharp raps on the cast-iron table, and walked away.

The absolute fucker.

A scathing autumn breeze whipped around the food truck. She looked at her barely-touched bagel with disgust and tossed it into a nearby bin.

5-18-30, 8:36 PM PDT: THROUGH
THE FIRE

LT. ROBIN MERCER, ad hoc commander of the Borealis 1st Division, closed his eyes, leaned his head against the Whisper-Pod's bulkhead, quieted his mind, and tuned out everything but his senses. The carbon fiber, monocoque airframe purred with the eerily smooth vibration of a dozen computer-controlled, brushless outrunner motors that powered the asymmetrical hexagonal array of ducted fans. Everything was engineered with triple redundancy, from the tuned toroidal props to the motors to the fly-by-wire computer control system. The LT plasma power supply was physically incapable of failure. The whole flight system was integrated with AI monitors looking for ten million ways the craft might drop out of the sky every thousandth of a second. Flying along at 200 knots, the thing was as stable as a rock on solid ground.

Robin knew it was the safest ship he'd ever flown in, but the sensation took some getting used to. The fucker was unnervingly quiet—just that purr, a hint of a hum, and even that was only noticeable if you leaned your skull back and pressed it against the frame. He'd flown 145 missions in these Borealis ships. His first was when he and two of his squad had been resurrected themselves.

But this job was special.

"LT, says here Banks was in 10th Mountain? You two serve together?" PFC Christopher "Murph" Murphy asked at a conversational volume. His eyes had the glazed, unfocussed look people got when gazing at their Aurora feed.

They'd have been shouting to be heard in a conventional chopper, even with headsets. Absent bone-to-airframe contact, Robin couldn't hear the WhisperPod's motors at all, only the rush of the wind outside the window. Without opening his eyes, he replied, "Before my time. Chief Banks was in Afghanistan from '11 to '19. I was still in boot his last year. It's in the report, Murph." Robin opened his left eye, raised an eyebrow, and said, "Read more, talk less."

"Yes sir, I read it, sir, I'm just—"

"Yeah, me too. Wildfires take some getting used to." Robin leaned forward, placed his almost delicate hand on Murph's, and then pressed it against the bulkhead. "Feel that vibration?"

"Barely, LT."

"Yep. It's faint. Focus on that. Let it fill up that overactive noggin of yours." He smiled. "That's what I do."

He looked around at his team. Sgt. Kevin Liu, a stocky jarhead with black, serious eyes, had the look of calm detachment that belied a coiled-steel readiness. Specialist "Oz" Osunyemi, tall and lithe, wiped down his fire axe as though it were a medieval weapon.

On the cabin floor between them lay a long, black, vinyl body bag from the Borealis med bay morgue, still damp with condensation. The body inside, a big Black male, had been thawing for three days in their walk-in fridge.

Robin leaned forward to look out the cockpit windscreen. The fire was already on the horizon. The pilot, Warrant Officer Jackie Maurais, saw his reflection in the dark glass. Without turning, she said, "Eight minutes out, LT."

Robin nodded, turned to the men in the cabin, and raised his voice to command mode. "Jackie says eight minutes." He waited till they all made eye contact. "Target is hauling ass down

Manson Bridge Road toward Elks Branch at Clarksdale Cross-roads. He will not make it. History will record that Chief John Arthur Banks will perish in the fire this evening. We will ensure we have no beef with the timeline, but *we* have other plans. Stay chill, do your jobs, we all come home, and we give Chief Banks a new life. No guarantees with this. If we miss him, he dies. If we don't execute according to the timeline, we all die. He's probably going to be terrified, he may be irrational and he's a big man. Six foot four. We've been there before—"

"Not in the middle of a forest fire, LT," Liu said.

"Yeah. That part will be new." He impaled his sergeant with his best no-shit glare. Fire scared the shit out of Robin, and he knew the rest felt the same. You could plan all you want, but fire has its own ideas. "We've trained for this. We follow the plan, we get a new addition to our happy family." He banged his chest twice with his fist and shouted, "LOST BOYS!"

"BANGARANG!" his team shouted back, mimicking his chest thumps.

He turned and tapped Maurais' helmet. She reached down and flipped a switch on the dash. As quiet as the WhisperPod had been, it suddenly became completely silent as she commanded the CCS to tune the motors to a greater precision and feather the 12 toroidal props. Now, they were a hole in the sky with no lights, holographic camouflage, and absolutely no sound, racing toward a spreading California wildfire.

"Remember your drills. No improvisation. Tick tock. By the metronome. In and out with our man," Robin said, loud and clear, as the WhisperPod dropped to the treetops and followed the terrain. Ahead, a gout of flame rose before them, filling the cabin with baleful red light. Robin watched as his team's eyes widened in awe at the sight. He knew they were all tasting the copper bite of adrenaline now.

Maurais was not fazed in the slightest. She'd flown water drops in the US Army Corps of Engineers for wildfire contain-ment. They were lucky to have someone like her for such a mission; then again, Borealis had a strange relationship with luck. Oracle's Oneiri device made certain of that. For a moment, he wondered at the elaborate temporal mechanics that placed Maurais' butt in that pilot seat on this mission, but he'd learned long ago that the physics made him cross-eyed.

The WhisperPod crested a stand of tall pines and passed the fire line. Treetops spun and danced in the chaotic wildfire fueled winds. The dark thread of Manson Bridge Road stretched off to the east. The landscape below was a mad gradient, black to red to blinding orange, with sharp spikes of charcoal—pine trees throwing long jagged shadows—as the fire rampaged through the old-growth forest. It looked like a scene from an anime, high contrast blacks breaking up the harsh, blood-red light of the fire. Their target's truck lights appeared on that long, dark ribbon. Jesus, he was close to the oncoming fire. Robin jabbed his finger at the headlights in the distance.

"There!"

"Yep. There's a clearing. I can make that," Maurais said matter-of-factly, as if she were eyeing a parking spot at the mall.

Again, Robin felt the thrill of panic, that dryness in his throat and mouth, that nagging need to flee. They were going to be too late. They didn't have enough time. Yes, they had a time machine to help them plan, but this time—this time, no matter what the Oneiri device said—they were going to fail and history would play out exactly the way it appeared from Oracle's timeframe. His mind was just making shit up now. He nodded to his team, showing not a shadow of his internal doubts.

Robin estimated Maurais' landing would be 15 yards from where Banks' Jeep had ground to a halt, wedged in a drainage ditch at a thirty-degree tilt. The pod lowered to the pavement as trees less than 30 yards away started to pop and shatter from the heat. Liu slid the door open, and the blast of radiant heat hit the entire team. As Robin steeled his nerves, grabbed the door, and pulled himself out, he got his first look at John Banks.

He was big. Robin knew that from the file, but he was the kind of big that struck you differently in the flesh. There stood Banks, like a stone wall, on the far side of a steel culvert wearing a flame-retardant suit, mask, and helmet with a SCBA air tank strapped to his back.

"He doesn't look like he's terrified to me, LT," Murphy shouted as he tugged on the cadaver bag.

"He does not," Robin shouted in confirmation.

As they streamed out of the cabin and jumped into action, Banks didn't move, didn't react to the sight of his rescuers or their sci-fi-looking aircraft.

Robin sprinted to his side.

"Chief Banks, I'm going to have to ask you to take off your clothes very quickly, sir," Robin shouted as he watched the fire line approaching behind Banks.

The tall man stripped without a pause to consider this strange request. Robin helped pull off the air tank as Banks started peeling off his reflective mylar suit. Sweat drenched his civilian clothes underneath.

"I'm Robin Mercer, sir. I'm honored to meet you, sir." He took John's clothes and said, "You can keep your skivvies. History didn't record what underwear you were wearing, sir." Banks squinted in thought, then nodded. "If you'll go ahead to the WhisperPod, we'll finish up."

"I've got men, a team from the Butte CAL FIRE team—"

Robin nodded. "I'm sorry to have to inform you that they perished twenty minutes ago, before you left Jamison." Banks looked like he'd been punched. In the fire's light, Robin noticed the shrapnel scar running the length of his face. "Please, sir," Robin gestured to the black rotorcraft. Banks ran to the open door in his boxer briefs, passing Murphy, Liu, and Oz hefting the cadaver bag out of the cabin. Banks watched with calm interest as he grabbed a hand strap and pulled himself onto a jump seat. In the middle of a wildfire, faced with serious shit, Robin noted Banks projected stillness.

The team delivered the cadaver to the culvert and unzipped

the black vinyl bag. Robin handed Banks' shirt and fire-retardant jacket to Liu, and the jeans and fire pants to Oz. Murphy tugged at the corpse, a close physical match for Banks—tall, Black, solid —to help Liu dress it. Then he turned to help Oz. They worked quickly. Robin slid the fire boots on. His skin was baking in the massive infrared of the approaching fire line as Murphy turned the body so he could strap on the air tank Banks had been wearing moments before—the aluminum tank was hot to the touch.

A two-foot diameter pine, one hundred feet inside the fire line, exploded.

"Holy shit!" shouted Murph, but he kept working.

As they'd practiced, the four of them hoisted the body by the tough fabric of the suit and slid it into the steaming culvert as far as they could. It was good enough. The fire would do the rest.

"Go!" hollered Robin, but no one could hear him over the steady, explosive roar of the fire. It didn't matter. No one needed to be told to flee back to the WhisperPod. Robin was bringing up the rear, and Maurais yanked on her stick as his feet hit the skid. The down forces made him land in his jump seat hard.

"Hold on to your knickers, ladies!" Maurais shouted as wind shear twisted their flight-path, rocking the team and Banks hard. She worked her controls to gimbal the turbines and found steady air as they rose above the treetops to see the devastation beyond. Robin leaned out to survey their work. The corpse's boot-covered calves were just visible in the Jeep's headlights before the fire line covered them both. An instant later, the lithium-ion batteries in the truck popped like a series of mortars. The pyrotechnics display flashed so brightly it bathed the drop zone with a circle of pure, white light and left Robin dazzled, blinking, and belatedly shielding his eyes. The force of the rapid staccato explosions lifted the truck's frame 15 feet before it collapsed onto its side beneath a rushing ocean of flame.

Robin slid the door closed and looked at their target. The wind was already drying Banks' perspiration. He was going to get cold and risk going into shock. Robin reached for a go bag held to the cabin wall with webbing.

"Once we clear the fire, it's going to cool down to a normal Madre Pueda spring temperature, sir." He handed Banks the bag. Banks opened it to find a Borealis uniform—dark gray shirt, black dungarees, black boots.

"Thank you," he said, then observed, "You've done this before. This appeared routine."

"Yes, sir." Robin nodded. "146 for me." He smiled sheepishly. "First time in a wildfire."

Banks looked like he wanted to ask a follow-up but held his tongue. His face was still, but his eyes, dark brown with expressive eyebrows, reflected a keen mind wrestling with enormous information. Despite what Robin knew to be the cognitive whirlwind that accompanied every resurrection's aftermath, Banks's eyes didn't look like those of a man in shock. Most of the resurrected went nearly catatonic. Some required a week of sedation in the med bay.

Robin Mercer was impressed by John Banks. He would remember that night for the rest of his life, tell boastful stories about it while attempting to appear humble. He and his team resurrected Commander John Banks back-when, six years before Downfall. Yes, he did. I shit you not.

The craft's moon shadow played on the thin, silvery layer of clouds beneath him. The low din of Madre Pueda street traffic below rose above the rush of the rotors as they skirted Thorne International Airport-controlled airspace. Low-power RGBLED/LCD holofilm sheathed the craft, generating a convincing illusion of the empty night sky. Mostly carbon fiber, Its stealth and the lack of running lights meant Maurais had to be exceptionally vigilant. Her eyes glinted with internal light. All her instruments were virtual, projected on her retinae by Aurora. Her eyes darted between the flight path and night traffic invisible to Robin.

Robin's ears popped as they descended through the gauzy mist, meeting their looming shadow and passing through it. It always felt like a dream, the silence, like Peter Pan flying Wendy to Neverland.

Springdale, a forgettable suburb to Madre Pueda's southeast, rose beneath them. They lowered to the rooftop of a nondescript complex of industrial park structures. Maurais set the craft down with a kiss on the skids. Rotors clicked off, and the hush of their downdraft stilled. Robin nodded to his team, and they slid open the door and bounced out. Banks watched as they walked away, evaluating the men. He looked back at Robin.

"Are you assigned to keep me under control, LT?" Banks asked.

"No, sir," Robin responded with a deference that Banks recognized.

"No, sir? You act like I'm your commanding officer, son."

"Yes, sir."

Banks frowned. The rest of the team headed for the steps leading off the helipad. They passed a forgettable man with light brown hair in his mid-thirties to mid-forties. Banks looked like he recognized this beige man. Robin smiled. SDS staff had a look. They were all drab, professional, and nondescript—no one in particular. Banks looked again, clearly unsure if it was the same guy or another forgettable white dude. Robin almost laughed.

The beige man walked behind a white woman of average height, with light brown hair, in her mid-fifties, wearing a mauve pantsuit. She walked out to the WhisperPod to greet Banks as he stepped onto the roof.

"Chief Banks, a pleasure." She offered a prim handshake. Banks' large hand surrounded hers, and she gulped softly. "We've been so looking forward to meeting you. I'm Mary Allan. You've met Greg Rumsfeld." She turned and nodded to beige man.

"Welcome to The Borealis Foundation," he said as he extended his hand.

"The Borealis Foundation?" Banks asked. "I thought this was Standard Data Systems."

They walked together at Mary's prompt toward the few stairs down from the helipad.

"That's correct. The Borealis Foundation is collocated here with the offices of Standard Data Systems. One big happy family. SDS is a management and human resources organization while Borealis specializes in recruitment, relocation, intelligence, and special operations."

The WhisperPod's rotors powered up. Robin looked back to see Maurais wave a salute and lift away, bathing the departing passengers with a rush of spring wind as she went. Banks marveled at the thing as it sailed into the night sky. Within moments, they couldn't see it, though Banks strained to do so.

"I'm sorry, you were saying Borealis specializes in…"

"Recruitment, relocation, intelligence, and special operations —essentially, saving the world. Your resurrection and recruitment as the head of Borealis has been a priority since Stephen first theorized that we could pull off these little magic tricks on the timeline." Mary said as she gestured for John to follow her toward a pair of doors at the base of the steps.

Banks stopped. "Wait. Did you say *head* of Borealis?"

Mary smiled as if she was used to this sort of confusion. "I did indeed, Chief Banks. The Borealis Foundation is at your disposal. It has been tailor made to support your mission. We're all energized to have you finally at the helm, where you belong."

They passed through the double doors and proceeded down a small flight of stairs to emerge onto the floor of Borealis' ultramodern hospital facility. Dozens of patient rooms were arranged like spokes around a central nurses' station hub. It had the quiet ambiance of an ICU after dark. Greg continued down the stairs to the lower floors. Mary, Banks, and Robin walked in silence until they emerged on the other end of the unit through glass automated doors.

"Borealis is a medical facility?"

"Resurrections often require medical assistance. Our medical team was on standby should you require any intervention." She led him out of the Med Bay, past an executive office suite that was dimly lit. "This area is all SDS headhunters and logistics specialists."

There were several dozen cubicles adorned with personal pictures and decorations. The staff were all gone, and the lights were subdued. It was just past 9:00 PM, long after regular work hours. Four 72-inch flat panel holo-displays along the back wall showed an intricate, multi-dimensional Gantt chart in beautiful colors against a black background. Mary continued beyond the open-plan office down a hallway that circled back almost to the exits to the helipad. She stopped at double doors with a small placard that said simply, *BOQ*.

As she opened the door, Banks found himself in a familiar setting: a large common room divided into a small kitchen, a fitness area with resistance and cardio gear, and a media center with a massive gaming holoscreen. Hallways led off to the bunks and showers. It looked like any Bachelor Officers Quarters on any military base anywhere, though a bit upscale. Oz sat on the couch playing One Corporation's latest hologame, *The White Horseman*. The hallway to the right echoed with the sound of showers.

Mary pointed to the alcove hidden along the back wall by a row of ficus. "You'll find your private quarters back behind the forest. All the books from your home library have been stocked on your bookshelf, and if that isn't enough, we have everything in print on a tablet in your quarters. Lt. Mercer will be available to answer questions or not, as you require. Settle in. We're here to assist. I'm available on *@Once* on your tablet until you're established on Aurora. Then that's generally more convenient. You're scheduled for that procedure in the Med Bay at 6:00AM."

"Aurora?"

"It's an upgrade to, well, *everything*. Our utopic device-less future," she said glibly. "We've left literature about the Aurora implants and the medical procedure in your tablet for you to read. Everyone on the Borealis team has undergone the procedure, even Lieutenant Mercer here."

Robin nodded.

"But you've had a day full of new information and dramatic events. I'm sure you'll want to rest, recover, and acclimate. So good to meet you in person, Chief Banks." With that, she turned to leave.

"Hold up," John said a little too loudly.

Mary and Robin froze.

"Sorry, Mary? It's Mary, right?" Banks said as he rubbed his eyes. Ms. Allan turned. "I am tired. I am overwhelmed. It has been a hell of a day. I mean, I just watched these guys—" He motioned to Robin and Osnunymi. "—stuff my body double into a wine-country culvert like it was just another day at the office." His large, muscular body radiated subdued, managed nervous energy.

Robin and Mary exchanged awkward glances. He had their attention.

"So. Stephen Lucas wants me to run an operation that saves the goddamned world. He's probably sold me as this larger-than-life heroic man of action, right?" He wiped moisture from his palms with one thumb and then the other.

Mary and Robin nodded.

"We have six years before the whole of human civilization collapses. Do I have that right?"

Mary nodded. "Five years, 8 months, and some days."

"And, according to my old army buddy, we have something like 3 billion people who will die if we—"He made a large circle in the air between the three of them. "—don't bust our asses to save them?

"So. If you'll pardon my French—fuck rest, fuck recovery, and fuck acclimation." He wasn't smiling now. "It looks like I've been tasked to save James—" He paused and shook his head. "To save the world." He looked at them with every ounce of inborn leadership he could muster after a plainly terrible twenty-four hours. "My every urge, other than to run screaming into the night, is to get to work, to dive in, to take action. But sometimes, the only action you can take is to get smart about the problem. Sometimes the best thing for a heroic man of action to do—" He paused and smiled a thousand-watt smile. "—is to schedule an impromptu mission briefing, lasting as long as it lasts."

He furrowed his brow.

"Three hours of conversation with Stephen in a bar over bourbon and ribs is not enough for me to know what the hell we're up against. I'm going to need a briefing—and I mean right now. Can we do that? Let's get people out of bed if we need to."

Robin watched as Mary, silently and without ego, recalculated her organization's entire power dynamic. Her eyes had the momentary lack of focus of someone interacting with her Aurora. She turned and opened the door to the hallway.

"We'd be better off in the conference room until you get your implants. I've just put the department heads on standby. We can start with the three of us, cover the 50,000-foot view, and decide who to bring in as we go?"

If nothing else, Mary Allan knew how to pivot.

"Perfect," Banks confirmed. He barked like a Commanding Officer, "You coming, Mercer?"

"Sir, yes, sir."

"Who can show me how to make coffee around here?"

INTERLUDE 1

"THE BODY WAS A PLANT? *What about the DNA we collected at your home? What about the dental records that matched the corpse?" Julia seemed insulted that her investigation had been corrupted.*

"*Borealis agents have a backdoor into CODIS and NDIS systems,*" *John shrugged with a smile, "and MPPD's labs use the same three California government contractors for processing DNA results. It's pretty easy to swap records in a dentist's office. Paper records and digital. It's not exactly Fort Knox. I mean, we're just talking about a file cabinet and a CloudBox server.*"

"*For fuck's sake!" Julia said, wondering if any of her police work was valid. "Could* anyone *just spoof the entire criminal justice system like that?*"

"*Anyone with a working time machine and an unlimited budget,*" *John said. "It's not a problem anymore." He shrugged again as his smile faded. He gestured to the dome outside the window. "Beyond these domes, there is no criminal justice system, no laws, no police, no DNA labs, no dentists.*"

Julia looked out the window at the busy plaza below. Downfall, they called it. She'd slept through the fall of human civilization and awakened in this science-fictional, engineered, and designed community. She'd missed the collapse—but that wasn't actually true. If she could only remember.

"I interviewed Stephen Lucas when I was investigating your death."
She looked down at the cup of chai. Once again, she thought about how
she'd always been a coffee drinker, but now it was chai—every morning,
a cup of chai. "I visited One Corporation's Campus in the Braintree
Hills. I still have… I had the slick titanium business card from the guy."
She looked out at the massive clean curves of the dome structure. "This
place looks a lot like that place. I see the design similarities everywhere."

"Stephen's hand is everywhere in the planning and design of this
place." John nodded. "All the people, too. He was involved in all the
recruitment and the rescue ops. Behind the scenes, of course."

"From his vantage point in the future?" She squinted and shook her
head. "With this time machine he invented?" She was skeptical; but
still, if anyone could invent a time machine, it would be Lucas. Stephen.
She wanted to refer to him as Stephen, inexplicably.

John nodded.

"All these doctors and scientists and brilliant minds. You can't
swing a dead cat without hitting a genius of one kind or another."

John smiled. "I know, right?" He shook his head. "I don't fit in
exactly."

Julia looked at him suspiciously. Was he really that modest?

"No. I think you fit here, Commander Banks." She pointed her
thumb at her chest. "But I'm just a cop, a detective. Don't get me
wrong, I'm a good detective. But I don't really know how I ended up
here. What made me so special?"

John looked pensive. Observational skills honed from almost twenty
years of police work told her he was holding back. He knew the answer to
her question.

"I feel like I'm a sleepwalker, and you've been warned of the dangers
of waking me up," she said.

John smiled, and his physical tension eased. He laughed gently. "I
was told what a capable detective you were."

"By who?"

His tension reappeared.

Julia nodded. He knew why she was here.

5-18-30, 11:00 PM PDT: ALL NIGHTER

JOHN WAS ALONE in the conference room when Mary arrived with hard copies from her office. He was doing his best to find a footing. His brain felt like a bag of angry cats. He recognized this energy from his work with refugees, people displaced by war, fire, or just shitty political circumstance. He was now roiling with it, the urge to return to a place that no longer existed. The flight-or-fight response crept up his spine like a cluster of spiders.

He poured a cup of coffee from the glass pot. He'd made it the way firefighters make coffee—strong.

"I'm guessing you like your coffee black?" John asked.

"That's perceptive," Mary said with her prim smile.

"You lead enough organizations, you learn to size people up quickly." He offered her the cup with a steady hand and turned to pour another. He added enough cream to turn it from black to light tan and offered it to Mercer as he, too, entered with folders of material. Mercer tasted it as he found a seat and nodded his appreciation. John added a touch of creamer, from black to rich brown, and a half teaspoon of turbinado.

Mary's eyes took on the unfocussed look John had seen a few times since his arrival. She made a gesture as if she were tapping a button just short of arm's length in front of her. The 100-inch holo-panels that wrapped the room came to life. John raised an eyebrow at the magic remote control as he sat. He made a note on an old-school yellow legal pad he'd scrounged up during his coffee preparations.

"Let us start at the end," Mary began; clearly, this presentation was well-trod ground for her and Robin. She swiped in mid-air, and a deck of slides popped up. A bright red banner marked the top and bottom of the first slide. SDS-BOREALIS FOUNDATION TS - TOP SECRET - LEVEL ZERO EYES ONLY TF-ALL. John gave it a cynical appraisal. All classification systems were arbitrary, unenforceable, and essentially made-up—and this classification seemed doubly so. John recognized the TS classification—Top Secret—but the TF-ALL was a mystery. Mary spoke to the bullet points without glancing at them.

"In August of 2036, One Corporation's Vice President of Hardware and Software Design, Walrus Roberts, will discover a quantum tunneling phenomenon allowing him to send IP electronic data into the past. A simple, functioning time machine. Roberts and Stephen Lucas will develop that technology into a prototype consumer product codenamed Oneiri over the next month. One week of guerrilla user testing of the device will begin on September 11th with ten Oneiri cubes and ten testers.

"The initial time horizon for the technology will allow internet orders to be sent into the past up to three weeks, allowing instant delivery of anything—product or service—available on the internet. Oneiri will work flawlessly, and as the test proceeds, improvements will be made to allow IP data to be sent further back—six years—to our current timeframe." John was taking notes, but showed no indication that Mary had told him anything he didn't already know.

She swiped to the next slide. "Our future will be threatened, however, when Cliff Price, One Corporation's Senior Director of Game Design, will be revealed as a prolific serial killer and a dangerous psychopath. During the test, Madre Pueda police will identify Price as the subject of a multi-year investigation. Taking advantage of Oneiri's capabilities, Price will elude them until

Stephen devises a way to trap him, allowing the MPPD to intervene. Price will be cornered by the MPPD per Stephen's plan, but not before Price captures him and tortures him for the better part of an hour. Though mortally wounded, Price will escape once again."

John frowned but continued to jot notes. "And there's nothing we can do to stop this mother—" He bit his tongue. "To stop Price before he does his dirty work? The nature of time prevents us from doing *anything*? Do we have any in-house Oneiri experts? Someone who can explain the tech and the... what did Stephen call the rules?"

"Roberts' Rules for Time Machines." Mary nodded. "We have a handful of physicists on staff with quantum mechanics backgrounds. They're helpful, but bear in mind, Walrus Roberts is a once-in-a-generation mind."

"I'm not looking to know the physics. I'm just looking for someone who can make me more comfortable with the whole collapsing-wave-function bits of the Oneiri device." He pressed his eyes shut as if trying to remember. "Stephen called it—spooky temporal enforcement." John squinted. His upper body showed nothing but calm, focused engagement. His legs, however, were coiled like steel springs, and he gripped his chair arm to prevent himself from fleeing. He was teetering on the brink of a panic attack, managing it, keeping it from erupting. It was a skill he'd learned in Afghanistan.

"So, let me summarize my understanding of how this Oneiri works and—more importantly—doesn't work," he said with his hands over his eyes and his head tilted back. "With Oneiri, you can send messages back in time on the internet. You can order a pizza, per Stephen's story, and send the order 30 minutes into the past to get it delivered—in your reference frame—instantly."

Robin and Mary nodded.

"Okay. So, that's how it works. How it *doesn't* work is if you send the message back ninety minutes and order for delivery an hour ago." He pulled his hands from his face and opened his eyes. "Since I don't see a pizza—and if I did, why would I order one? But since there's no pizza here, we know the order will fail. We don't know how. We don't know why. All we know is there's no pizza here—and we can't change that reality with Oneiri."

Robin and Mary, with less certainty, nodded again.

"I need to understand that better. It makes my brain hurt," John said, looking at the two of them.

"You and me both, sir," Robin added.

"That makes three of us. Moving on." Mary swiped and returned to her presentation. "After his encounter with Price, Stephen will disappear. To avoid collapsing the wave function of the fates of all of his friends, coworkers, and loved ones—of everyone, really—Stephen will flee everyone, everything, and every place he has known. He will establish himself beyond the failing civilization in a location he's chosen to keep hidden from us," John wrote furiously for a few moments. He completed his thought and looked up to find Mary waiting for him.

"Price's mastery of the Oneiri device will prove to be... considerable," she continued. "He develops—*will* develop—an expansive organization beginning in this current year or, possibly, in the last few months of 2029. We know virtually nothing about that organization or its leaders here in this timeframe. He will, we know, sanction the development of the bioweapon GGB-Z, a virus engineered to mimic the demon virus we see in the current One Corporation hologame, *The White Horseman*."

"Life imitates art imitates life." John shook his head. "It's a feedback loop."

"We further know his followers will sow the seeds of terrorism that will culminate in the destruction of most of the Haber-Bosch fertilizer factories across the planet, ensuring a global famine that Stephen estimates could last a decade or more. And, though this is less clear, it's presumed he will have a hand in laying the groundwork for the fear and mistrust between Russia and the US that will lead to the use of tactical and strategic nuclear weapons." Mary turned to the final slide. "That's our 50,000 foot overview."

John flipped to a new page and wrote for half a page.

"Okay. That was a great summary," he said. He tapped his pen onto his notepad with a manic intensity. "You condensed the end of the world into fifteen minutes and 10 slides. After Stephen heads for the hills, what do we know?"

"Our critical path ends at Downfall for a reason. The World Wide Web, writ large, goes offline September 18th, 2036," Mary said without looking it up. "Beyond that, there will be no historical record that can be relied upon. History stops, and we're into the world of rumor, myth, and legend."

John stopped tapping his pen and thought for a long beat. "But that works for us, right?"

Both Mary and Robin looked perplexed.

"Stephen shot some figures and facts at me rapid fire last night. I don't recall all of them, but this one stuck in my head. By summer 2037, the population will be down to 2 billion—from 8 billion."

"Those are the numbers he's quoted to me as well." Mary nodded. "I'll admit, I don't know where he gathered that intelligence."

"I mean, the wave function can't be collapsed if the observer's quote-unquote *facts* are unreliable," John persisted.

They stared.

"The observation of reality in the sender's timeframe collapses the wave function, right? Maybe I misunderstood, but the wave function can't collapse unless the sender's perceptions of reality are true. In our current civilization, the reliability of our facts is pretty high—fake news notwithstanding. We can count on our observation of a news report, for example, effectively collapsing the wave function with certainty. But in a world without news, with just word-of-mouth gossip, we'll have much more freedom to game the system. If Stephen's sources are unreliable, we might be able to save a lot of people."

They looked at John with the dawning awareness that he was more than a military commanding officer. It was becoming abundantly clear they were dealing with a first-rate intellect as well.

"I will schedule an appointment with you and our physics team at their earliest convenience." Mary looked like she was jotting a note in mid-air. "It sounds like you understand the wave function nature of time machines better than most."

A little after 1:00 AM, John instigated the ordering of pizza. While they waited, he took the opportunity to escape, to wander the darkened halls of SDS. As he left the conference room, he felt, or *imagined*, that Mary and Robin were hesitant to let him out of their sight. That was probably wise. The primal instinct toward flight was clawing at him. When he wasn't scrambling in his mind for a framework that would allow him simply to *believe* he could return to his life, his thoughts swirled like the flames of the wildfire that had nearly ended him.

To tamp it down, he strolled the halls, looking at offices and kitchenettes. He stopped and examined the bulletin boards. He discovered the Borealis section of the SDS office. There was something familiar and comforting about the way a military outfit's decorations differed from the Northern California look of SDS. The complete lack of taste or design sense made him feel a bit more at home.

Wanting to be alone with his thoughts, he walked down to wait for the pizza delivery. He wanted to walk outside, get some fresh air, and look out at the night sky. As he stepped onto the broad sidewalk circling the entrance, he found the stars weren't visible with the industrial park's light pollution. But the evening was cool, the humidity was low, and he felt less—what? Like he'd been kidnapped? These people had saved his life. Yet, that's not how his limbic system was responding.

He turned and looked at the beige brick building with blue

mirrored windows. The conference room's lights were the one touch of warmth on its icy facade. It looked like any industrial park office anywhere in Northern California. Anywhere in the country, really. He'd grown up in Madre Pueda, played football for MPHS. He couldn't be sure he hadn't driven past this place back in the day in a minivan full of beer-soaked varsity jocks.

He had a moment's thought about his parents. His father's sudden stroke and his mom's slow death by heartache had left him detached from the world. Stephen, though crass and insensitive, had been right. He'd been isolating himself for almost three years. Only his career and the relationships with his CALFIRE team gave him a reason to get up in the morning. He pictured his home, a neat, tidy, empty, boring townhouse—a place he could never set foot in again. Suddenly his mind filled with the flames of the wildfire swallowing a pine tree as big around as his chest.

The spring breeze blew against his bare forearms, and a patch of gooseflesh rose on his dark skin.

The fire had ended John Banks. Now, he was dead to the world. He would have died in truth if it weren't for that time machine of Stephen's. He thought he *would* die, but here he was. Resurrected. The gooseflesh rose again at that thought.

"I've never seen anyone adapt so fast to all of this," Robin said from behind him. John didn't jump.

"You sure you're not here to monitor me, LT?"

Robin shrugged imperceptibly and smiled. It was not a denial this time, at least. "I've walked a mile in those shoes, sir."

John felt his shoulders relax. He'd almost forgotten that others here could understand what he was going through. "How was it for you?"

"I was one of the early resurrections. I was in an HH-60 crash at Fort Liberty back in November. Jensen and two others were with me. Night operation. We were in pretty bad shape. I snapped my collar bone… the, uh, clavicle. Broke my arm and the wreckage had me trapped with avgas leaking everywhere. I knew I was a goner, sir. Jensen was worse." He shrugged again. "SDS was still working out the kinks in the process, using merc opera-tives. But they pulled us out of the chopper and swapped us out with cadavers. Then the medical team patched us back together." He hitched up his black knit sleeve to show a long, raised scar that crossed his elbow. "35 stitches and a custom 3D-printed, carbon-fiber-fortified, ceramic pin. Better than new."

"Did you ever…"

"Get the urge to bolt? To run for home?"

"Yeah."

"Sir, everyone does. That's what I was just saying. You seem to have adapted and jumped into the life." John could feel the muscles in his jaw and neck ease. Just talking with Mercer was easing his stress.

John watched as the pizza store's autonomous, electric go-cart approached the curb. He felt his palms. They were wet and cool with perspiration. "Mercer, my plan is to fake it until I make it." He tapped a code onto the hood of the small, red and blue fiber-glass vehicle and it popped open to emit the smell of grease, salt, sausage, and cheese. Removing three hot boxes, he turned back to the SDS front door.

"It helps to hear I'm not a special case. But I've known Stephen Lucas since the shit. Fifteen-plus years. We're literally blood brothers. I've seen him happy, sad, drunk, sober, annoying, hysterical, poor, and rich beyond imagining. I have *never* seen him wracked with guilt the way he was earlier tonight—uh, yesterday evening."

They walked to the elevator, and John pressed the button for the top floor.

"I always figured Stephen would be smart enough to get himself into some kind of trouble he wasn't smart enough to get himself out of. That man *still* exceeded my expectations." The elevator doors closed. "Son, I'm mostly just fooling the public, but if it looks like I'm adapting to the facts on the ground quickly, I guess it's because I trust Stephen. I believe his story. You and Mary reinforce that with every detail you add."

They took a break from the knowledge transfer as they ate. John encouraged Robin to tell stories of previous resurrections. Robin, though somewhat shy, had a gift for understated humor. His stories were just what John needed to feel at home. They were the stories every soldier tells, full of hair-brained plans, inevitable screw-ups, and all's-well-that-ends-well outcomes. Even Mary Allan, whom John had trouble getting a bead on, joined in and told a few tales of recruitment misadventures.

John worried about being a bull in a china shop, showing up, following his take-charge approach, and stepping on Mary's or Robin's toes. Robin seemed overtly glad of his new leadership. With Mary, it was less clear. He reminded himself that her boss had offered him this command. He decided he'd move forward, bull and china be damned, and sweep up afterward as needed.

As they spoke, as John bent his mind away from the insanity of Stephen Lucas' expectations, away from the madness of time machines and impending apocalypse, he fell back on his practiced habit of bonding with the new coworkers.

After the pizza remains were stored in the fridge and the paper plates had been bussed, Robin took his turn presenting. His eyes took on that unfocused aspect before a deck appeared on the display that could have been from any army briefing John had ever dozed through.

"Hold up," John said. "When you all pull up briefing materials, you do this thing with your eyes. Mary did it, too. Then a hand gesture." He imitated their pantomime mid-air gestures.

"That's Aurora." Robin nodded.

"I mentioned it earlier. You're scheduled to receive your Aurora tomorrow morning." Mary glanced at her watch and raised her eyebrows. "*This* morning. It's a procedure to implant personal computing and networking devices. You'll never need a computer or display again."

"Everyone at SDS and Borealis has Aurora?"

They nodded.

"And it requires surgery? Implants?"

"Yes, Sir," Robin smiled. "Best thing I ever did. I don't have to equip a mobile device or a laptop."

Mary nodded. "People get artificial lenses every day of the week, Commander. I was a little intimidated at first, but nothing —no device ever—has made me more productive."

"Alright. I guess I'll see tomorrow." He shrugged. "Carry on, Lieutenant Mercer."

"Yes sir. You can call me Robin, sir. I'll start by saying it's an honor to work with you, Chief Banks. We're all fully briefed on your background, your time in Afghanistan, and as head of CALFIRE."

John waved away the praise.

"And let me also assure you," Robin continued, "that every single aspect of the Borealis 1st Division, even that appellation, is preliminary pending your approval." He swiped left. "Borealis 1st is obviously tiny for a division, barely a platoon, but Oracle has set us up to grow as the need arises."

"Oracle?"

"That's our call sign for Mr. Lucas."

John smirked and shook his head. "I can tell you with all authority that Stephen Lucas would approve of that call sign. Oracle! For f—" He paused.

"Don't bite that tongue for my sake, Chief Banks." Mary smiled and took a sip of coffee.

"Noted. Carry on, LT."

Robin grinned and continued. "You referred to me as LT and, yes sir, that's the rank that I've assumed; Sargent Jensen and Sargent Liu report to me. They've each got a complement of two corporals and eight privates. We're bivouacked here at SDS head-quarters when on specific missions, and Borealis office staff operate here, but we're based northwest of San Jose. Borealis has 300 acres in a valley outside of Henry Cole State Park. The base is called Saint Norbert's. It's an old, abandoned vineyard. That's where we do our training and drills."

"Mercs?"

"No, sir, SDS hired mercs to start, but Borealis troops're all Lost Boys now."

"Peter Pan? Or late 80s vampires?" John tilted his head.

"Dealer's choice, sir. You're one of us now. We pulled all our recruits from the timeline when history wrote us off as dead."

"Resurrected," John mused.

"Yes, sir, all twenty-four. It's easier to recruit military folks because we're always doing stupid, life-threatening shit, sir."

"Spend time with some firefighters, LT."

"Yes, sir. Most of us have been on board since February. Our missions have been exclusively resurrection runs. So far, we've performed our magic tricks in thirteen different countries. Oracle says you'll be expanding our portfolio, and we're eager to see that."

"Count on it," John said as he finished a few notes. "Magic tricks."

"Sir?"

"Nothing, LT. I'll circle back to a thought I had, but I don't have any notes. I'll want to meet the troops soonest." John squinted and frowned. "As far as my rank is concerned. If this were the Army, I guess it could be anything from captain to general. But this isn't the Army. I don't want to disrespect the Army or ape it in any way. Also, we may need to be inclusive of other services. I'm not Chief anymore, that's for certain."

"Stephen left all of this up to you," Mary said with her hands raised.

"All right. I'll go with Commander Banks. Any objections?"

"No sir, Commander."

John smiled at the ease with which Robin accepted and adopted the new ranking system. "Okay. I want to come back to that thought before it gets away. You called the resurrections *magic tricks*. That seems right—part magic trick, part con. It's like three-card Monty. But now, the mark is the future. I keep coming back to something Stephen said on our call. He said, 'We've got hackers, even a few magicians, and second-story cat burglars.'"

Mary nodded. "That's absolutely true. We've paid three magicians to create illusions to fool surveillance cameras into seeing what history recorded, they…recorded."

"And that's the trick, right? That's the whole ball of wax on this project. If we can fool the future, we can save anyone. Maybe we can save everyone."

Mary frowned. "We can't create an illusion that civilization is collapsing. That's too widely recorded in the future historical record."

"No, you're right." John agreed. "But going back to our earlier discussion. Suppose we can identify Stephen's sources of intelligence and game them? Muddy the waters for the sender's observed reality. We might prevent the wave function's collapse. There's nothing we can do to prevent the big events of mass destruction."

"The virus pandemic," Robin added as the most significant example.

"Right," John said as he pulled a page from his notepad. "But we have six years to find a cure, develop a vaccine, or otherwise mitigate the plague." He wrote on the pad, "#1: Cure GGB-Z" and placed it on the table between them.

"Or the nuclear weapons," Mary said.

"Anything we can do to mitigate those?" John asked. The room fell silent. "We'll need some help figuring out what that even looks like. What's the fallout radius or—I don't have the expertise to know how bad that is compared to, like, Hiroshima or Nagasaki or Chernobyl. There may be nothing we can do. But let's get some experts to inform our preparation."

"Doomsday Prep," Robin said, almost to himself.

"Well, that's the job, isn't it?" John nodded. "Exactly. Our jobs are to prepare the world for Doomsday."

"That's a big fucking job, sir," Robin said with a dubious smile. "Are we up to that?"

"Not yet," John agreed. "But we have six years. Thanks to Oracle, we have nearly unlimited funds. And we have a boss in the future with a time machine."

"We also have the world's population as a staffing pool," Mary added. "Anyone, any expert—with Stephen's financial resources—we can onboard in days. With Oneiri, we can onboard them instantly. I've put together a req for nuclear weapon preparedness technicians while we've been talking."

John nodded, pulled another page from his pad, and wrote, "#2: Doomsday Prep."

"There's no better word for it. For the pandemic, the nukes, the terrorist attacks on the fertilizer plants—we need a worldwide effort to place supplies for the survivors to keep them alive. Food, water, weapons, gear."

"All the shit doomsday preppers have been squirreling away in their basements since the 50s," Robin chimed in.

"We can't do anything that makes the news, or we set ourselves up for a Roberts' Rules violation," Mary said. "We've suffered through a few of those. They can fail in simple ways or dramatic ways. But they always fail."

John nodded slowly as he absorbed that. "I'll need our physics guys to walk me through a solid day of real-world demonstrations of that. If I recall from Stephen's story, Walrus ran almost a full week of tests to confirm that time won't allow a change in the Oneiri sender's perceived reality." He blew out a puff of air. "Boy, that's a mouthful." He continued, "So we need to prepare in secret. We need to stash our supplies—our post-apocalypse provisions—in places no one notices, places that will seem unremarkable, to protect Stephen's perception of his current reality?"

Mary and Robin nodded tentatively.

"We may need to draw on those staff magicians for that," John said.

"How did Cliff Price do all this damage without violating Roberts' Rules?" Robin asked.

"That's a great question. Whatever we're going to do, his team is out there right now doing the same—or the opposite. They have to be doing their work without drawing attention," John mused. He dashed a note on a new page, "#3: Uncover Price's Agents."

"That will require spies and intelligence staff." Mary was making notes on an invisible keyboard. "It's possible Stephen has already set up resources for that sort of tasking."

"Price may have had other plans that failed," John posited. His muscles had unbundled, and he sat in his chair with his legs and arms spread wide. His earlier anxiety was gone. "There may be other schemes out there that require *us* to foil them."

Robin made a gesture, a pantomime of his head exploding.

John laughed. "Yeah." He shook his head. "It's hard to fully imagine how bad it could get. We all rely on the backstop of civilization. In the US, we count on clean running water, on electricity, on paved roads, emergency rooms, grocery stores. We count on being able to leave our houses without the high percentage risk of being raped or murdered." His voice dropped into the lower register of the relaxed but sleep-deprived. "I've served in places where none of that could be counted on. But even there, they had the good old US of A, the American soldier, backstopping them—showing up to help, as imperfectly as we often did."

"But take that all away. Most Americans lose their shit when the power's off for two days. Take it all away, and they'll lose their fucking minds. It's going to get terrible. Cliff Price may have engineered some monsters, some demons—but he also knew that people without civilization can become monsters, too."

It was quiet for a while. They were running out of steam. The sky was brightening outside.

"But they can also be amazing," Robin said quietly, with a

genuine smile. "I served in Ukraine once they let us in there. Mostly, it was mopping up and Army Corps of Engineer projects. But I saw the strength of those folks. People picked themselves up from a years-long battle with a much larger foe. Folks helped each other and lifted each other." He shook his head. "If we give people a chance, they can be a force for good that we couldn't possibly plan for."

The sunlight cracked through the conference room window and splashed the long table. John pulled a last page from his notepad and wrote, "#4: Empower the Good." He placed the four sheets in a neat row in the golden sunlight.

"Cure the virus, prepare for the downfall, foil the bad guys, and empower the good," John summarized. "Looks like we earned our pizza for the night." He yawned. "I guess that's a good start. Now, I think I will take that rest and catch a few hours of shuteye."

"Oh, no!" Mary said with some sadistic glee. "No rest for you. You're due in surgery in thirty minutes. Time to get your implants."

JOHN IS DREAMING. *Submerged, looking up at the sunlight shafts, sinking. He is four.*

Wait.

Rewind.

He is barefoot. Lots of kids. Cousins. He's on the sun-warmed dock at the cabin in North Carolina. It's summer, and Dad has brought them all to Grandma Lucy's. But they're staying down at the river in the cabin. The cabin is a long walk up the hill for a four-year-old boy. It's also a fast, out-of-control run down that hill to the water.

They're on the dock looking at the fish Uncle Bill has landed.

"Look at the size of him!"

"Is that a bass?"

"Sure is!"

"He's a GI-ANT!"

The thing thrashes the surface, splashing all the kids with sparkling droplets. The girls and some boys squeal. Then they laugh. Some drop to their hands and knees on the rough planks and peer down into the holding cage, a submerged pen made of galvanized wire. Its top is just above the surface, its bottom resting on the muddy river floor.

Then, the grown-ups come to see Bill's monster. Bill is tall, taller than Dad, and younger. He smiles more. He stands on the shore as Aunt Sally, Aunt Lucille, Uncle Ronald, and Uncle Benjamin hurry out onto the dock. With the kids, there are now ten looky-loos peering down at the fish.

"Well, I never…"

"No, you never…"

"How many pounds, you say?" Benjamin hollers back to Bill with a smile a mile wide.

"22 pounds and 3 ounces."

"That's gotta be a record, don't you think?" adds Aunt Sally.

Bills smiles, shakes his head. "The record for North Carolina is sixty-six pounds."

Bill Banks is a fireman. He doesn't have a wife. He's a bachelor. To John, it seems that makes him free. John likes him. John likes that Bill is his father's brother, and they have the same last name.

John is four.

Four.

Aunt Lucille maneuvers to get a better look. She leans over and plants her hands on her knees in her yellow dress with white flowers. Her behind, enormous, yellow, and white, pushes John back. The dock is narrow. John is four. He backs off the edge of the dock and drops into the river. His eyes never close as he sinks below the surface. It doesn't occur to him to swim.

He is four.

He sees the sunlight through the brown-green water. He sees the shadow of the dock and minnows darting away from his face. He sees the monster bass eying him coolly. He sees bubbles, large, half-round mirrors, rising from his open mouth as he sinks into the loose, muddy bottom. He hears the sound of voices: troubled, panicky, shrill women and low, rumbling, unsure men.

Voices without consonants.

A large brown arm, muscled and strong, reaches down for John and snags his collar. As fast as he fell in, John is elevated more quickly. Sputtering, coughing, he's in Bill's arms. Bill is laughing and pounding him on his back as water pours out of his mouth. Bill carries John, bounding up the hill to the cabin with the looky-loos now looking at him.

The giant bass is forgotten.

John is saved.

John is dreaming.

A whisper tells him he's sedated, anesthetized, submerged.

That makes sense, since he's in a snow globe.

It's Christmas break. This time at Grandma Millie's in Minnesota. Millie and Ed have a cozy cabin on Sandy Lake. They're clearing her driveway. Dad and John have shovels. James, John's idiot younger brother, is driving the 4-wheeler with a snowblower on the front. Fuck-a-duck, it is cold. Dad is a southern man. Mom is a northern girl. He's not made for this. John's okay. He's seventeen. Big for his age. Tall like Uncle Bill, everyone says. Football and basketball all-star. John wants to be a fireman like Uncle Bill.

John knows every fucking thing.

John is seventeen.

Dad's folks are all dirt poor growing up. Mom's are well off. Millie and Ed own 500 acres of poplar forest among the mosquito-infested lakes between Duluth and Hibbing. Millie is a northern Negro who met and married Ed in college at the University of Minnesota in Minneapolis. Ed is half Swede, half Finlander, and all pale, pale pinky-white. They both worked for 3M, Ed developing magnetic storage media., and Millie developing new synthetic polymers.

Retired now.

Summers in Mississippi, where being a Black kid meant you had to be careful. Winters in Minnesota, where people treated you politely but really didn't know what to make of you.

James is hot-dogging, carving donuts in the snow. James is twelve. Dad is blowing into his gloves for warmth when he looks past John at James with the look. James is out of control. Headed for the lake. Sandy Lake. The 4-wheeler is picking up speed. Only now does John hear James screaming.

Dad goes sallow.

John runs.

His long legs have never run in snow. It's eight inches deep or more. He sees the blank, flat plane of the lake ahead, the wide open. John runs faster. He gains on the 4-wheeler.

"I'm stuck, John. My boot is stuck. Help!" James shouts.

John feels the snow change beneath his feet. They've passed the shoreline. He catches up to the thing, grabs hold of James' parka, and yanks him sideways. The two of them tumble over and over in the snow. The 4-wheeler races away another thirty feet and then crashes, sliding, sinking beneath the ice. James' eyes are wide with fear as the ice tilts back and covers the hole like it was never there.

"Holy shit, John! You saved my life!" he says.

Did he?

Dad runs up, out of breath. Leans over and puts his hands on his knees, wheezing. When he finally gets his wind, he looks at the two of them as they stand up and dust the snow off vainly.

"I thought I was going to lose both of you." He pants as he hugs them both.

"John saved me," James says and starts to cry for no good reason but that he's twelve.

"You're a hero, John. You saved the day."

John feels euphoric at the approval from his father, but also ashamed. Terrible.

Why?

For no good reason but that he's seventeen?

The thought of his uncle Bill dances in his head. Those thoughts shred and tatter in the tide, in the wind, in the water. John is dreaming.

A far-off voice says, "That's not how it happened."

Swirling in the snow. Submerged. Sinking in the arctic water. The bubbles rise to the surface.

Rising to the light.

John is in a dust storm. The snow and cold are gone, replaced with sand and heat, stink, and sweat. Sargent Lucas, Stephen, is just a kid. Stephen is nineteen. Stephen reminds him of James. Look at him. Just a kid, and he's fumbling with his helmet in the middle of the dirt road in Asadabad. The dream is so real it makes John fear it's not a dream.

This. Was. A. Bad. Day.

John has dreamed about this day hundreds of times.

Lucas is pissed off beyond reason.

"I got one of those god damned bugs in my hair, LT!" he shouts as he tugs at his chinstrap.

"Sergeant, DO NOT take that helmet off!" John yells at Stephen as he runs to him to help. "You can get dead real quick, motherfucker, if you take that helmet off."

Oh shit, John thinks in his dream, this is when… a flash of light, a reflection in Lucas' eyes. Stephen turns. Woods and Zebrowski are ahead on the road patrolling when John sees a glint of light, a tripwire for an IED.

"Hold up!" John shouts, but the IED blows—a shrapnel bomb. Time slows down. John turns and tackles Stephen. Woods and Z turn into a blur of fire and red and then, gone. A piece of metal speeds toward him, flies right between them as they fall, slicing John's face.

Then Stephen is on the ground beneath him, covered in blood. Lucas looks up at him and smiles. "This is all on you, John. World War III, Hell on Earth, the future of humanity… it's all on you. Save everyone! Everyone you can!"

John is under, submerged, the waves have him spun around and he's unsure which way is up, which way to the surface. He panics, then sees the light and rises to it. He has tears in his…

5–19-30, 6:17 AM PDT

"There he is. Hello, John. How are you feeling? Any pain?"

He shook his head, felt some stiffness behind his right ear, froze, and winced. He became aware of irritation, a crusty dryness in his eyelids. It was something like a bout of pinkeye. "Maybe I spoke too soon."

"Pain behind your ears? Redness in your eyes?" the doctor asked. She offered him a paper cup of cold water and a pill. "Way ahead of you. Ibuprofen. You're up a bit early. If you want to just lie back and close your eyes, that would be fine."

He washed the pill down and handed the cup back.

"Thirsty? Like some orange juice?"

He nodded.

"Okay. I'll be right back."

John felt gingerly behind his right ear, then his left. Small pads of gauze were taped securely behind each. He closed his eyes and lowered his head gently back into the pillow. A small Borealis Foundation logo, a stylized polar bear, glowed in the lower left corner of his field of vision. He opened his eyes, and the elegant logo was still visible, though it had faded to 40% opacity. It was superimposed on everything his eyes beheld. If he turned his head, it moved with him, but when he moved his eyes, the graphic stayed put in the lower left. When he looked directly at it, it highlighted slightly. So this was Aurora, a ubiquitous visual interface. He wasn't sure he liked the idea, but he could see the possible benefits.

The doctor returned. "Here you go; a little vitamin C and blood sugar boost." He took the juice bag and sucked from the straw.

"Thank you," he said. He *was* thirsty. She pushed a small tray table closer so he could place the juice on it and pulled a small brown bottle of medicine with an eyedropper from her pocket.

"This will help with your eyes' roughness," the doctor said. "Look up?"

He followed orders, and she dropped cool liquid into each eye. He wondered how long the implant procedure had taken. Anesthesia, commotion, and fatigue distorted his sense of time. He still smelled faintly of wood smoke.

The doctor screwed the top on the medicine and looked above him as if checking displays that weren't there. "I'm going to ask you a few questions to assess your post-implant status."

John nodded and said, "Fire away."

"Great. Let's start with memory. Do you know today's date?"

"2030. May 19th."

She smiled. "Okay." She reached forward with her right hand, and pantomime tapped an interface in her Aurora. "Who's the President of the United States?"

"Janelle Morales."

She tapped again. "Do you know why you're here at Borealis today?"

John nodded and smiled. "Because I died in a fire last night?"

The doctor smiled and tapped the invisible floating interface once more.

"So far, so good. I'm going to turn down the light, and *you* are going to close your eyes and rest for 30 minutes. Doctor's orders. I'll just be down the hall." As she spoke, "Rest for 30 minutes," appeared as text in the upper right corner of his field of view. *30 minutes* was highlighted in bold. The text blinked and then faded.

"Works for me, Doc. I can use a power nap. I was up all night."

"Even better." She tapped a switch, the lights went dark, and she closed the door behind her. He was asleep within two minutes.

Precisely thirty minutes later, John rose to consciousness from a restful, dreamless sleep. The type of sleep peculiar to sleep-deprived refugees. For a moment, he was unsure where he was, or when. Somewhere to his left, a pleasant guitar chord strummed repeatedly at an increasing volume. The little polar bear logo was pulsating light blue in time to the guitar chord. Next to it was a blue word balloon in that read, "Rest for 30 minutes—auto timer."

"I'm up," he said groggily to no one. The strumming stopped, and the auto-timer balloon popped. He opened his eyes and looked for the guitar player in the darkened hospital room. His eyes didn't hurt anymore. He blinked a few times to test that he was pain-free until he noticed a tiny woman in the Borealis uniform of black knit shirt and black dungarees who appeared to be waiting for him, standing casually on the tray table. She was well lit in the darkened room. She was, John estimated, about one foot tall.

"You are clearly a hallucination," John said.

"Good morning, Commander. I am Zoe Chandra."

He closed his eyes. He opened his eyes. She persisted. He moved his head around enough to ascertain that she was clearly a three-dimensional manifestation. He placed a hand over his right eye, obscuring the room and the tiny woman, who smirked at his experimentation.

"Good morning, Zoe?"

"I'm guessing you didn't have a chance to read the literature."

"Literature?"

"The surgical procedure and the Aurora Users' Manual?" She was a little miffed and clearly unimpressed by his new, made-up rank in a made-up, imaginary military organization.

"I *skimmed* the part about the medical procedure," John said as he moved closer. Her body was a little taller than his head.

"Do you often undergo elective eye and brain surgery with this level of cavalier disinterest?"

John didn't have an answer for that. He supposed he *could've* elected not to get the procedure, but the thought, among all the whirlwind of madness that was the day before, honestly never occurred. He took a moment to regard this holographic pixie. She was slim of build, fit, and objectively beautiful—enhanced, he thought, by the slight imperfection of what might have been a badly healed broken nose. He estimated her age to be late twenties or early thirties. He guessed she was second generation Asian-Indian-American, judging by her dark complexion, silky black hair, and accent—American, maybe a southern state like Georgia, with a hint of British formality and an occasional sing-song lilt.

"It was a weird day yesterday."

"Did you literally *just* complete the procedure?"

John nodded.

She didn't smile. "Yes, I *can* tell when you're nodding, by the way. Thanks for wondering."

John felt a familiarity from Zoe, the type of familiarity that brings with it a whiff of contempt.

"Have we met?" he asked.

"Not officially," she said. "Would you like to read the literature later, or would a briefing now work for you while you're resting?"

"Now works. The doctor said…"

"I'll text her to leave you to rest until we're done."

"Okay."

"Your eyes are crusty and dry, and the back of your right ear is sore, yeah?"

"Yes, ma'am."

"That's typical. The dual surgeries you just survived were both relatively simple, minimally invasive procedures. The procedures only take 40 minutes, in case you were wondering how long you were out. With MAS, micro-automated surgery, the total recovery time is less than two hours. The audio and processor implants are the more routine. By the time you woke up from the anesthetic, you had essentially healed."

She pointed behind her ear. "Bone conduction audio. Those are tiny ceramic discs implanted behind your ears. That's how you're hearing my voice and Aurora audio UI affordances. The CPU and GPU make the right ear unit a little larger. They 3D print that unit to fit the individual skull. The ceramic will bond directly to your bone within a week."

She humorlessly waggled a finger as he reached to touch the bandage.

"The eye surgery was a bit more involved, but still mostly routine. The Med Bay team replaced your natural lenses with accommodating intraocular lenses that also house a trio of ultra-high-definition, ultra-low-power RGB LEDs—LPLEDs to be precise—that can paint images directly on your retinae. That's how you're viewing me."

She walked a few steps in a circle on his tray table. The illusion of dimension was hard to deny.

"As you can see, the resulting three-dimensional representation is better than holopanels. The surgery cured your existing astigmatism, which was slight but would have worsened over time."

John closed his eyes one at a time to witness the improvement. "So, it's a Heads Up Display?"

"Aurora is a complex, fully networked computing platform, and a fully integrated audio-visual display solution." She gestured to the Borealis bear in John's field of view, proving she could see it as well as he could. It highlighted, and a dock menu slid open along the bottom of his vision. John recognized the *@Once* app and a few other old standards from One Corporation's app suite like *oneBooks* and *oneMail*. But the other twelve icons were a mystery.

"Heads Up Display, or *HUD*, is simply one app available to you. This app, the point-to-point conferencing app we're meeting with, is called *realTime*. You can see me, I can see you. AI generates this full-body representation from *my* Aurora, which captures my voice, head position, and facial data and infers the rest. That is sent to your Aurora, which generates a full-body representation of you for me to see and interact with. Every time someone with Aurora looks at you, Aurora's AI updates your avatar in the cloud to continue to improve 3D verisimilitude."

"My avatar looks like what Mary and the Lost Boys have gathered in the past day?"

"It also scrapes the internet for images and video of you." She tapped an unseen interface, and a miniature of John stood next to the miniature Zoe on the tray table. He assumed it was to scale. If so, Zoe was about five-foot-six or seven because his avatar towered over hers. The likeness, dressed in the black Borealis uniform, was more realistic than a video game, but less authentic than Zoe's. His avatar looked a little freaked out, to be honest.

She gestured again, and his avatar vanished with a spray of pixel dust.

"The various apps are similar to productivity apps you've used. Note that the interface stays where you place it in your three-dimensional space. As you move your eyes to look around, the interface stays in its relative position. If you turn your head, some elements will track with your field of view, while others, like my avatar, are pinned to the 3D space."

John experimented. The menu bar along the bottom and the Borealis Bear panned with his vision when he turned his head while Zoe's miniature avatar stayed pinned to the tray table.

"Using apps is the same as on a mouse-driven platform. You simply look at an icon and tap it with your fingers to open it." The @Once app popped open and showed a rich community of hashtags, channels, and users. "It's so much like using a mouse or a tablet; you'll forget about it within an hour."

She closed the app and said, "That's about as far as the literature goes. The rest we'll cover once you've had the opportunity to play around with it a while."

"Now that I know how to open the dock and apps, I can explore. File system?"

"Old school, Commander," Zoe said. Again, John felt he was being roasted—as though she harbored a slight passive-aggressive grudge. She pointed to the icon of a black folder emblazoned with the Northern Lights. "*AuroraDrive* is at the base of all the apps. That's where you'll find files and directories. Most of the Lost Boys use the file menus embedded in individual apps and eschew the *AuroraDrive* file system."

"Children!" John said disdainfully. "I guess I'll cop to being old school. Okay, I'll do some spelunking on my own."

"As you wish."

"Pleasure to meet you, Zoe." He smiled and nodded to the avatar. "Will I see you again?"

Zoe nodded. "Oh, certainly. I've been assigned as your

handler, Commander. We'll be working together day in and day out," she said with a joyless, professional edge.

He thought, *she'd be more attractive if she smiled*. He instantly shook his head, wincing at his own caveman cliche.

"Well, I'm looking forward to meeting you face-to-face."

"Right. You haven't fully been briefed," she said. "Handlers never meet our agents. To perform our logistical magic, we are ahead of your timeframe by a safe margin. As such, we can use Oneiri to arrange for immediate availability. Anything you want, anything you need to do your job, we can order it in your past, and you'll have it instantly."

For the first time since the surgery, John felt that rising vertiginous feeling of panic rising from the pit of his stomach. Something about the new reality of a world with time machines made his head swim.

"How far in the future are you?"

"That is classified," she demurred. "Oracle has instituted a timeframe-aligned classification system to protect all our activities from spooky temporal enforcement."

"So different timeframes are privy to different info?"

"Correct. In fact, all our handlers are sequestered from our current timeframe to some extent to prevent unpredictable outcomes."

That explained the TF-ALL classification on the briefing deck. John was talking to a woman in the future. Somehow, his conversations last night with Stephen were less reality-shaking than the fact that this overly serious, strangely attractive woman with an inexplicable grudge was somewhen in the future.

"I'm still struggling to wrap my head around little details like that, Zoe."

"We have all the time in the world. As I said, we'll be working hand in glove for the foreseeable future." John smiled at her unconscious puns. Zoe didn't notice. "I have access to your *oneCalendar*. I'll know when to drop in. You can reach me as needed on *realTime*. Or you can program Aurora to contact me with a quick double-tap behind your ear. I'm already in your contacts list, along with everyone on Aurora that you've met."

John nodded.

"Well then. Good morning, Commander. I'll let you get back to your healing. We'll speak soon." The miniature woman blinked away, leaving a trail of glittering particles.

First, the Lost Boys, now Tinker Bell. John closed his eyes and wondered if, sometime in the past 24 hours, he'd experienced a psychotic break influenced by the works of J.M Barrie.

FOR ALMOST ONE HUNDRED YEARS, until the 1940s, when the I-80 connected Northern California to the rest of the country, Saint Norbert's Abbey had been a working vineyard run by Benedictine monks. During the Spanish Flu of 1919, so many monks died that their order's primary source of income ground to a halt. The surviving brethren, some aging and infirm, stuck it out stubbornly for another twenty-two years before the order put the plantation and its fertile land up for auction. It continued on as a commercial winery until another pandemic in 2020 closed its doors once again. Now, the secluded abbey was a barracks for the Borealis 1st, and the outbuildings were their training grounds, meeting space, armory, and live fire range.

Though summer had arrived early in San Jose, the twelve-foot stone walls and cavernous lofts of the abbey's barn kept its interior cool. For a few years, it had been leased out for rustic, upscale weddings. The dark, cavernous, dusty space was the perfect counterpoint to SDS' high-tech, overly air-conditioned facility. No holodisplay panels in sight.

Thirty-five men and women, the Borealis 1st and their SDS support staff, wearing casual uniforms of light gray t-shirts and black cargo pants, found their seats and murmured quietly in curious anticipation. Another twenty, their handlers, participated virtually via Aurora from their classified timeframe. Zoe helped Commander Banks organize, schedule, and map out these three final days of training.

The Commander entered from the rear of the barn and walked to a twelve-foot wide, old-school chalkboard mounted on sturdy maple legs. The soldiers and staff quieted as he picked up a piece of chalk and wrote in large block numerals.

744

Dusting chalk from his fingers, he let that sink in.

"Seven-hundred and forty-four. Does anyone know what that number is?"

No one ventured a guess. No one cracked a joke. After their silence grew awkward, the Commander gave them the answer.

"Seven-hundred and forty-four. That is how many people die every minute that we waste. The math is simple." He turned to write the numbers on the board for them to see. "We have less than six years. Twenty-eight hundred days. Sixty-seven-thousand and two hundred hours."

He wrote his final number out as large and bold as the first.

4,032,000

"Four million, thirty-two thousand minutes. In that amount of time, our mission is to save three billion lives." He was silent for a few seconds. "Every minute we squander, for the next six years, the human race will lose 744 human souls."

John listened to the wind rustle the hay in the rafters.

"And we just wasted another one." He had their complete attention. "Next week, I'll be joining you on missions to evaluate our resurrection process. To get a feel for what we're up against. We're planning out our longer-term intelligence operations and identifying key milestones in our Downfall Prep efforts.

"Up to now, I've been getting the lay of the land. I've been getting to know you all." He faced his soldiers and staff squarely, standing proud and tall. "I am honored and proud to lead you. Every single one. Next week, we, as a unit, are going to kick it into a higher gear."

Someone shout-whispered, "Yes!"

"Before we do, we have some schoolwork to do." John wiped the chalk number away with an old felt eraser in broad strokes.

After two weeks, he was finally beginning to understand why Stephen had chosen him, beginning to see the faint outline of what he could pull off. He'd started to recall many a late-night, bourbon-infused barracks philosophy debate with Stephen in Bagram, Delaram, and Kandahar. Two kids with BFAs: John from UCMP, Stephen from UCB. They both had an undergraduate understanding of philosophy, enough to form the basis of hours of drunken arguments. Stephen knew John could see the philosophical underpinnings of their mission.

John wrote in big letters…

EPISTEMOLOGY

He turned back to his troops. "Everyone stand up."

They all stood.

"Sit down if you never went to college."

Roughly two-thirds sat.

"Sit down if you never took a philosophy course."

Four SDS and three Lost Boys remained standing.

"Sit down if you failed that class."

One more Lost Boy sat.

"What is epistemology?" John asked PFC Maria Ramirez, a standing Latina soldier.

"It's the examination of knowledge, sir!"

"Go on."

"It's an exploration of how we can know anything beyond the existence of our own minds. Descartes stated, '*Cogito, Ergo, Sum,*' 'I think therefore I am'—proving our minds exist. But beyond our thoughts, how do we know our senses can be trusted? Sir!"

"Check out the big brain on PFC Ramirez!" a sergeant in the back row shouted.

John smiled and nodded. "Good job, Private. That liberal arts education finally paying off." The soldiers laughed. He motioned for them all to sit. "How do we know what we know? *What* do we know?" On cue, Zoe discretely posted the *Roberts' Rules for Time Machines* in a window to the right of John's field of view.

"According to Roberts' second Rule for Time Machines, information sent into the past cannot alter the sender's observed reality." He wrote this out in cursive on the left side of the large printed term. He moved to the right side and wrote,

Rule Two-A:
The sender's observation of the present collapses the wave function of the past.

"The sender's observation of the present collapses the wave function of the past," John repeated. "The sender's observation of the present. Put another way, the sender's *knowledge* of the present collapses the wave function of the past." He pointed at PFC Ramirez. "Maria, what does epistemology tell us about our *knowledge* of the present?"

"That we can't be certain we know anything, Sir!" she said with a wide grin.

"That we can't be certain we know anything!" John shouted back.

The soldiers, those who understood, all said "Aaah!" in unison. The rest just frowned, though hopefully.

"So, taking epistemology into account, Roberts' Rules are like the Pirate Code: more what you'd call guidelines than actual rules." John smiled. "Stand up if you understood all of that."

Ramirez and three others stood. John noticed a few who'd never gone to college.

"Okay. Good. Sit down. Stand up if you've been briefed on the Oneiri device and Roberts' Rules of Time Machines."

They all stood.

"Stay standing if you have a complete working understanding of it."

They all sat.

"Thank god almighty!" John shouted at the rafters. "*I've* been briefed. I have. Oracle himself walked me through it over barbecued ribs and bourbon. I have to tell you, there isn't *any* part of it I can fully wrap my head around. A lot of it I'm taking on faith." His soldiers and many of the SDS staff laughed and nodded.

"That's not good enough," he snapped in a quick change of tone. "Our understanding of these concepts is our only weapon, our only tool in a fight we can't hope to win and we dare not lose. There are three billion people on the planet whose lives depend on how well we learn, understand, and exploit Oneiri and Roberts' Rules." Again, he faced silence. "744 people every minute of every day of every week of every year, for the next six years." He left them to stew on that.

"We are in a no-win situation, my friends. We are playing out the Kobyashi Maru for the next six years, but this is no simulation. Success is not an option!" He stopped and dusted chalk from his palms. "We are going to lose billions even if we do everything right. But, if we're smart, if time permits, we may save billions too.

"So. For the next three days, we are going to train. We're going to learn to think differently. We're going to have sessions with physicists, philosophers, magicians, con artists, special effects gurus, and specialists in human perception and apperception. We're going to learn how to fool people, lie to people, and alter their observed reality. We'll listen, we'll talk, we'll brainstorm, but by God, at the end of this weekend, we're all going to understand what time will allow us to do to save as many people as we can.

"I want you to identify your doubts, your concerns, and your ignorance early. I want you to acknowledge your lack of understanding without fear of judgment. These are mind-bending, reality-twisting concepts. I can say with certainty most of your comrades will share any question or misunderstanding you have. Maybe not PFC Ramirez, here." He smiled warmly.

"I can also say with *certainty* that many of our experts will, at the end of this weekend, have their minds blown once or twice, too." He smiled and pointed to the big word on the chalkboard. "Epistemology. In a world where an observer's knowledge can collapse the wave function of the past, epistemology might save more people than anything else we do."

"That's enough out of me, for now. Pay attention. Ask questions. Dig in. Our first speaker today is Professor Adeeb Adawati, and he's going to be talking about Quantum Subspace theory."

Professor Adawati, a handsome young academic, stood and walked confidently to the chalkboard. John handed him the chalk and eraser.

"Okay, we're going old school with the chalkboard." Adawati smiled and gestured to the unfamiliar interface of actual black slate. "I like it. Let's start with the basics. How many of you are familiar with the concept of *quantum tunneling*?"

John walked to the rear of the barn, leaned against the cool stonework next to Robin Mercer, and watched as the professor proved two things to be true: He was an excellent teacher, and The Lost Boys were mostly bright, attentive learners. John tapped his feed to Zoe and texted her, "Thanks for the assist."

She texted back a thumbs-up emoji.

She was still stiff and overly formal in their meetings, but over the last two weeks of his subjective time, he thought he could feel a warming of her initial cold shoulder. Lately, it felt like she was lowering her guard, if only a fraction. He wondered what Zoe's age was. Her Aurora avatar looked like a woman around thirty, but her timeframe could be years in the future. That meant, somewhere out in the world, a younger version of Zoe was just living her life. Five years? Ten years? More?

It was easy to go down rabbit holes in his new world. John wasted far too many thought cycles on questions about his handler's attitude. He shook his head to clear it and turned his attention to Professor Adawati.

"So! What does Commander Banks mean when he talks about this weird concept, 'collapsing the wave-function'?" Adawati asked as he turned from the blackboard to blank stares. "Exactly the look I get from every first-year student in my university physics classes!"

The soldiers smiled in relief.

Adawati pulled a silver dollar from his pocket and flipped it in the air, before slapping it on the back of his left hand. "Heads or tails?"

The troops shouted out a nearly perfect mix of heads and tails.

"Right now, that coin could be heads up or tails up, correct? We don't know! It is, like that famous old cat of Schrödinger's, in a state of heads and tails at the same time. We can write its state out as an equation. It has equal odds of being heads or tails, so we can think of it as both until we peek under my hand and see. It's a trick we can play with math to help us reckon with other things— other problems we want to solve. We call this a superposition. It's both. A magical state of duality." He peeled his hand back and said, "Now? I see it. It is heads!"

Soldiers who'd shouted heads crowed their genius.

"What are the odds that it is tails now?"

"Zero!" a voice shouted in the back.

"Correct!" Adawati nodded. "And what are the odds it is heads now?"

"100%," someone said confidently.

"Also correct." Adawati smiled. "What just happened there? The odds were fifty-fifty before I looked and those odds 'collapsed' to 100 and to zero simply because I moved my hand an inch!" His eyebrows sprang upward in astonishment. "That's what we mean when we say collapsing the wave-function."

"It's not that simple!" a voice shouted.

Adawati held up a hand and nodded. "Also correct. When it comes to quantum mechanics, it can get more involved, but for our purposes—" He pulled out a die from a Dungeons and Dragons game. "If I throw this twelve-sided die onto the floor, what are the odds of getting a six?"

"One in twelve!"

"8.3333 repeating," the professor agreed. "The same odds as each of the other twelve sides." He threw the die, and it landed with nine facing up. He walked to the blackboard and wrote:

$$8.3-8.3-8.3-8.3-8.3-8.3-8.3-8.3-8.3-8.3-8.3-8.3$$

Under that, he wrote:

$$100-0-0-0-0-0-0-0-0-0-0-0$$

"When it comes to the future, the odds of anything happening fall somewhere between zero and one-hundred percent—never exactly zero nor exactly 100. When it comes to the past, the odds of any event happening have collapsed to either 100%—it happened—or zero percent—it didn't happen. All the shades of gray dissipate, and we're left with immutable facts. That is what collapsing the wave-function means when we talk about Roberts' Rules."

The soldiers all seemed to pick up what he was laying down, but John was certain they would need drilling to commit it to common sense. They had three days, but this was a good start.

5-30-30, 3:30 PM PDT

The team spent the morning of Day 2 playing with time. The

physics team developed an Aurora game, per John's orders, that would simulate the effect of using an Oneiri device to send a message into the past. It was a simple game similar to those they'd all grown up playing in school. John thought it would be more effective than lectures and less dangerous than actually using their handler's Oneiri systems to commit Robert's Rules violations.

The game was easy enough: the player had free use of a simulated Oneiri cube; they could adjust their simulated timeframe, and they could interact with a virtual world through a web browser, video call, or various applications. As their characters went through their days, they were presented with problems that could be easily solved by adjusting their devices' timeframe and ordering products or services in the past for immediate delivery. So long as those orders called for delivery after the player's current timeframe, their deliveries were successful.

If they ordered anything for delivery in the past—an order that would, if it were successfully fulfilled, alter the player's perceived current reality—they would witness a simulated Roberts' Rules failure. The game provided instant feedback, informing the player exactly how the experiment failed and showing the odds of that failure among a list of all the possible other causes. It was often a long list.

The Lost Boys sat in rows of folding chairs in the dark barn. The air was warming outside, and the large barn doors were open to allow the breeze to keep the players comfortable. They were all lost in their Auroras, intently playing through their games. John, the instructors, and the game's developers walked among the rows to answer questions. Every few seconds, a soldier would groan, sigh, or curse as their virtual character banged up against a temporal wall. Then, a mentor would discuss the Rules failure with the soldier before they began the game again. Simple shipping delays or products selling out caused most failures. Some deliveries failed due to more interesting random events: flash floods, traffic accidents, or, as one soldier shouted, because "there's hamburger all over the highway in Mystic, Connecticut!".

But one example made John especially grateful they were testing with a simulation. He was about to end the exercise, but as he walked to the chalkboard, he passed a soldier whose reaction to failure was loud.

"Holy shit!" the young, blonde private shouted as John passed.

"Is there a problem, Private?"

"Sir," The girl's eyes focused back on him and the real world. "My game ended. My Roberts' Rules violation destroyed the world! It... it was an asteroid strike on the outskirts of LA. The shockwave arrived just after I placed my order! Game over!"

John's eyebrow raised, and he looked over to an instructor from the Borealis physics squad.

"That is a very remote possibility, but it has a non-zero chance of happening," the instructor, a serious-looking woman with wire-rim glasses, said with a nod. "And it effectively prevents the sender's past reality from being altered. The order never arrives after the message is sent. The cause of that failure also causes the sender's obliteration."

"I thought that the failure had to be directly caused by the senders' message from a future timeframe," John said.

The instructor smiled as she took off her glasses and cleaned them. "Oh no, that's a common misapprehension. The list of things that can prevent a change to the sender's perceived current reality is nearly infinite. They are, in fact, the same things that could cause any internet order to fail. This list includes simple human error like forgetfulness, circuit breakers blowing, things like that—right up to whole electrical grids blowing, tornadoes, earthquakes, and even—" She pointed at the private. "Meteor strikes of any size. The sender's message from a different time frame is irrelevant to the causation of events that produce the temporal enforcement of the rules."

There was a moment of silence as the instructor repositioned her glasses.

John nodded slowly, looked down at his soldier and said, "Don't do that, Private."

The private nodded. Her eyes were as big as goose eggs as she restarted her game.

5-30-30, 8:30 PM PDT

They'd been inside the barn since dinner. Everyone was tired and reaching the end of their attention spans. John waited for a few minutes for the team to settle before he stood, walked to the front of the barn again, and paced slowly in front of his audience. He kept his eyes on the floor and concentrated, thinking his words through before speaking.

"Two days in. Two days of training and talking and playing. I'm hoping you are feeling more comfortable with time machines, the seriousness of Roberts' Rules violations, and the way reality responds to protect your perception of your current timeframe." He turned his gaze to his soldiers. "Yeah?"

Murmurs to the affirmative and a chorus of "Yes, sir" at various volumes and levels of confidence.

"I hope so." He turned to stand before them. "Now we're going to put your understanding to the test. You'll notice that Warrant Officer Jackie Maurais is not among us."

The troops swiveled their heads in all directions to confirm.

"I sent her back to SDS in her WhisperPod this afternoon after we played video games. I needed her to prove a point." John gestured to a petite woman dressed in Borealis casual gear like the rest. She had a big smile and a bigger stage presence. "If you haven't met her," John said, "I'd like to introduce one of Borealis' most valuable consultants, Sally Goldstarr."

Standing beside Commander Banks in a dusty barn sans her gold lamé outfit, stage makeup, platform shoes, and extravagant hair, she was nearly unrecognizable as the world-famous Vegas headliner magician.

Sally did a delicate curtsy to the audience.

"Sally is going to be our last instructor for the day," John said. "I want you to pay very close attention to her and *I order you* to do exactly as she instructs."

His sudden change in tone caught them all off guard. Each and every soldier straightened in their seats and sat at attention. John nodded to Sally and walked to his seat.

"Oooh! *You* have to do as *I* command!" Sally said with a huge, shit-eating grin. "I like that. If you're wondering how Commander Banks got me to work for Borealis for less than my standard eight-million-dollar retainer—imagine what a Vegas magician could do with access to the Oneiri device."

The soldier's eyebrows all raised in unison.

"Nuff said!" Sally said with a sudden clap. "Here's where I usually ask for a volunteer—but fuck that! For the moment, I have his permission—" she jerked a well-manicured thumb over her shoulder at John, "to do with you as I please." She walked up and down the aisles, appraising her subjects. When she came to Robin, she said, "You'll do nicely." She smiled with a manic, evil glee. "You, stay put. Everyone else, stand up."

The soldiers stood.

"Grab your chairs and move them into a horseshoe around— who are you?"

"Lt. Robin Mercer."

"Lt. Robin Mercer!"

Sally walked to the closed barn door as the troops moved chairs and reseated themselves. She tugged one side open along its metal rails and then the other. She returned to Robin, who now sat in the center of the barn dirt floor, alone.

"Lt. Mercer, what do you see out those barn doors?"

"I see the vineyard. I see the path from the barn to the helipad. I see the helipad. I see that it is night. I see—"

"Got it. You are a very observant guy, Lt. Mercer. That's good. Is there a WhisperPod on the helipad?"

"No, ma'am."

"Call me 'ma'am' again, and I'll cut you right here in front of God and everyone."

"Yes… Sally."

"So, no WhisperPod. Warrant Officer Maurais flew hers back to SDS this afternoon, according to Commander Banks over there."

John nodded.

"Here's what I want you to do. Contact your handler—I think his name is Jeremy, right? I want you to tell Jeremy to order Warrant Officer Maurais to hightail it back here."

"Yes, ma—okay."

"Hold on! I want you—" she paused and turned to the crowd surrounding them, "to order Jackie to arrive *thirty minutes ago*. Make it 8:00 PM."

The barn went silent.

"I can't do that," Robin said with a smile.

"Why not?"

"It would be a Roberts' Rules violation. It would put Jackie at unnecessary risk."

"But I just *ordered* you to do it."

"You're not my CO." Robin shook his head, and his grin became more of a grimace.

"Your CO," Sally said as she pointed to John, "ordered you to follow my exact instructions not five minutes ago. Didn't he?"

"Yes, but—" He looked to John.

"Do as she says, Lieutenant!" John shouted.

Robin frowned, but then his eyes focused on his Aurora. His mouth did that slight motion that indicated he was subvocalizing, and he placed the order with Jeremy. He looked out at the empty helipad.

"You had Jeremy order Maurais to land at that helipad?" Sally asked loudly.

Robin nodded.

"You ordered Maurais to get here at 8:00?" She looked at her watch.

He nodded again. Concern for his pilot was growing in his eyes.

"Well, where is she? Does she disobey orders? What happened?"

"That's the point of our training, ma'am!" Robin was pissed. "We can't know what went wrong. She could have crashed, she could have had a stroke, or… or…"

Sally turned to John and laughed. "Oh, Commander Banks, I like this one. He's a keeper." She turned back to Robin. "Go, take a look at the helipad. Go on. Follow this one last order from me."

Robin stood and looked at John.

John nodded.

Robin raised his eyebrow and started walking toward the barn doors to get a better perspective. As he got to the edge of the barn, he laughed.

Sally arched a perfect eyebrow.

"Holy shit! That is a *big, god-damned mirror!*"

He leaned back to look up.

The rest of the troops, at Sally's beckoning, rose and rushed to the barn door to see what he was gawking at.

Robin laughed in wonder and relief.

Sally walked out of the barn, her reflection entering from the right, and rapped her knuckles against a massive sheet of tensioned, mirrored mylar. As she did, the whole reflection, all fifty-by-thirty-five-feet of it, bounced in slow undulating ripples. She invited them to walk out of the barn and touch the mirror surface. The flexible mirror sat at forty-five degrees to the entrance. It reflected a scene ninety degrees to the left that looked precisely like the compound's helipad in the distance. While they had trained, someone, or a team of silent someones, had reworked the compound grounds to mimic the view from the barn's doors, solar-powered lights along the path, and everything. In this post-dusk light, the vineyards beyond were sufficiently similar to the rest of Saint Norbert's' fields. It was identical.

But in this scene, there was no WhisperPod.

They walked to the edge of the mirror and looked past it. There was the aircraft, and walking toward them was Jackie Maurais, carrying her flight helmet.

"We fooled time," Robin said and looked at John.

John nodded, then walked to inspect the magician's equipment.

Behind the mirror stood an enormous, retractable frame mounted on an elevated platform. Sally gave the rig operator a nod. With the whine of an electric winch, the frame collapsed and retracted into a black fiberglass cylinder as the platform lowered to the ground. The gaffer popped a top on the cylinder and packed it into a waiting truck.

"Ninety percent of illusion is perspective. The other ten percent is buying really expensive shit like that mirror rig," Sally said with some professional pride. "And doing the work. The hard work of magic—what we do to earn our fans' ticket money —is taking the time to do stuff no one would ever think *anyone* is willing to do.

"That can mean putting in the hours to practice a card move every day for months until I can do it without thinking. That can mean all the time spent engineering an illusion, working with groundskeepers to stage a fake helipad, and drilling over and over till you work out every bug and get it right every time."

Commander Banks spoke up. "Although we don't have any to waste, *time* is something we have on our side."

5-31-30, 10:30 AM PDT

"I've always hated trust falls," John said as he donned his mask and pulled down his goggles.

"This isn't that, boss," Robin said with a delighted smile. "Besides, it's a Lost Boys tradition."

"Yeah, yeah, LT." John shook his paint gun hopper with a smack of his hand to make sure his ammo was free of jams. This was the last event.

Robin looked up at his Aurora's timer app. "We'll give you a one-minute head start. Starting in—"

John grinned. Without warning, he shot Robin in the chest and sprinted off into the vineyard.

"Ow!" He rubbed the yellow-green paint into his sternum and yelled spitefully after his commander. "FINE! That's THIRTY seconds now!"

Ten of the fittest of the Lost Boys crouched at the starting line, ten yards from the stone vineyard gate. Robin watched the timer.

"TWENTY seconds!"

John turned at the end of the alley of overgrown grape vines. His pursuers watched.

"Left," Oz said. "He went left."

His teammates nodded and limbered their legs.

"Ten seconds!" Robin shouted.

He listened to see if he could hear John running. He heard nothing but the wind. It was warming up. The hunters were just starting to sweat. They shook their paintball hoppers like rattlers preparing to strike.

"Five…Four…Three…Two…One!" Robin hollered as he traced the welt rising on his chest with his fingertips. He fired a flare into the early summer sky. "BANGARANG!"

The hunters leaped, tearing away at a ferocious speed. Each of the four men and six women had a maniacally wide grin as they passed Robin at the gate to the vineyard.

John's goal was to make it to the bell tower of the abbey's ancient stone chapel in the center of the vineyard. It was a simple, probably unwinnable game of Capture the Flag. If John reached the top of the bell tower, achieved the Lost Boys flag, and escaped the chapel without a single paintball stain, his drinks for the first year of duty were on his men. If he failed to gain the flag or had even a single mark on him, drinks for the Borealis 1st were on him for the night.

"Commander, I feel we need to discuss our working relationship." Zoe's disconnected, serious voice, conducted through the bone as it was, had a distinct feel of being his own thought.

He ran to the end of a row and found a particularly large tangle of vines to hide behind.

"I am a little busy," John said as he tried to get a bead on his pursuers' locations.

"Precisely," Zoe said stiffly. "*You* are busy trying to evade hostiles, and *I* am sitting idle, an observer, reduced to the role of spectator. Your handler is meant to be your partner in solving tactical problems *such as this*."

"You want to talk about this *now*?"

"If we don't talk about it now, you will lose and owe the Borealis 1st free drinks for the night," she said.

"How can *you* help me win a game of Capture the Flag?"

John could hear the other team closing in now. He was exasperated that Zoe chose now to challenge him.

"That is a question you could have asked last night when Lt. Mercer told you of this tradition."

After running the maze of the vineyard, John was only now realizing he didn't know the way to the bell tower from his current position.

"Do you have a map of the vineyard?"

His HUD blinked on showing a top-down map of his surroundings. The hunters appeared as red circles.

John smiled.

"Could you highlight the bell tower?"

The tower lit up in green, and the shortest path appeared as a thin green dashed line. He popped his head up to see over the row and get a bearing on the tower.

Okay.

He studied the hunters' formation. They were forming a kill box.

"Can I outrun them?"

"You are fast, Commander, but you will never outrun Osun-yemi, Klein, or Hussein."

If they closed the kill box, he'd come out looking like a Jackson Pollack.

"Who's slower than me?"

"Burris, Nguyen, and Cullen. But they're only a few tenths of a second off your pace."

"Highlight them, please?" Zoe colored their dots orange. "Are their handlers feeding them the same map?"

"I trained them all," Zoe said with stiff pride. "And they've been preparing with their agents for several days."

"Why didn't we do that?"

"I put it on your calendar, and you rescheduled it. To prevent giving away our position, might I suggest you subvocalize as I instructed you two weeks ago?"

John sighed. He *dimly* remembered reshuffling his schedule in the run-up to the training weekend. He also hadn't practiced subvocalizing—the act of speaking without actually speaking and letting Aurora's AI interpret his lingual pantomime into speech— and she knew that perfectly well. He was the Commander. He was busy.

Okay, John subvocalized—ineptly.

The orange dots were two rows over and behind him.

In retrospect, that was a mistake.

Zoe didn't comment. John now understood the purpose of the tradition. It wasn't a test of *his* abilities. It was a test of *their* ability to work as partners. Was that the reason Zoe had a stiff response to him? Had he been ignoring her importance? He sprinted toward the kill box's base. All three of the slowest hunters were formed up in that line.

Zoe had carried an attitude from day one, though. Or maybe

she just suffered from resting cranky face. John didn't know. It was a shitty time to remedy the situation.

Yeah. Well. I guess I should apologize. I didn't realize this was a joint exercise, John subvocalized clumsily. Okay, maybe he should have practiced.

"What was that, Commander?"

I should apologize. I didn't realize this was a joint exercise, John subvocalized again.

"It is our first test as a working team, Commander," Zoe said.

It sounded like she was done biting her tongue.

Well. Let me take out their back perimeter, and if I survive that, we can make up for lost time? Could you analyze the other columns and see what you think?

Other than administrative assistant duties, it may have been the first time he'd asked her to actively collaborate with him.

"Fine." She was enjoying giving him the business. He was nearly certain of it.

Confounded by her perfectly neutral response, he rested at a giant bramble of vines. He tucked in to wait for the approaching hunters. Brian Nguyen rounded the row, and John clipped him with a paint round on his mask's yellow-tinted visor, blinding him.

"Fuck!" Nguyen shouted, dropped his weapon, and sat down with his fists balled.

John shifted and ran to Brian's position. "One down."

"Yes, sir." Brian pulled off his mask. "Only *nine* more to go, *sir.*" There was anger and bitterness in his voice. His black hair was streaked with goopy yellow-green paint, and a welt was rising on the side of his head where the mask had met his cheek.

John laughed and made a mock sad face at him before turning up the crossing row. Jenna Cullen appeared a few rows ahead of him. He fired three rounds, and the third hit her in the hip.

"Goddamn it!" she shouted.

John heard a pop from behind him and dove behind the nearest row. Jenna was taking her mask off as she sat.

"I'm out!" she called to Burris.

"Where is he?" Burris whispered.

John rolled into sight and shot up at him, hitting him dead center of his torso.

"Jesus Fucking Christ in a crosswalk!" Burris screamed.

Now, the kill box was more like a couple of loosely organized columns. If he sprinted up the center alley, John had a straight shot to the bell tower. He smiled as sweat dripped off him. This was fun. When was the last time he had fun? He grabbed an unripe grape off a vine and popped it into his mouth. He winced at its unbearable tartness.

Okay, Tinkerbell, what have you got for me?

Zoe paused before responding. "They are moving slowly as they approach the tower. If you time it correctly, you could sprint past them as they all are shielded by the vines in these rows." She highlighted the last two rows between him and the tower. "If you go too soon, they'll see you. Too late, and they'll have the tower blocked. Go now!"

John followed her command and took off like a short-track sprinter. He focused on running and let Zoe track the hunters. As he got to the last alley before the tower, he could see the hunters through the sparse stretches of vines.

"He's right there!" shouted a hunter on the right.

"Close in! Close in!"

He heard the beat of their footfalls as they hustled to the tower, but John was already past the end of the row. He half ran, half leaped the twenty feet to the tower. As he made it into the tower's dark doorway, he could hear the *pop-pop-pop* of splattering paint pellets hitting the stone. They were close on his tail.

"Right! Up the stairs!" Zoe shouted.

He didn't hesitate. He jogged right and found the spiral staircase. The hunters breached the entrance. John climbed three steps at a time, and paintballs exploded at his heels. He could hear them hitting the stairs now. They didn't speak, only grunts and pants. He made it to the top room, just below the bell platform. In the center of the room stood the Borealis 1st flag in a brass mount. Three open windows in the stone walls looked out over the vineyard. He grabbed the flag.

"Now, you need to escape!" Zoe said. "Jump out a window!"

"What? Are you nuts? I'm three stories up!" he shouted aloud.

"You're going to have to *trust* your handler, Commander!"

The heavy footfalls of the hunters were steps away.

"Which one?"

"It doesn't matter. I'll catch you!"

He hesitated. A paintball hit the opposite wall, missing him by an inch.

"*Go!*" Zoe shouted.

He gritted his teeth, shook his head, ran, and dove out the window to his right.

Pop-pop-pop.

As he self-defenestrated, he heard a series of loud but muffled explosions. He caught the window with his boot, and it shattered into a thousand bright, spinning shards. A massive shape expanded below him, and he crossed his arms instinctively over his face. He fell toward a giant black surface with a bullseye. His arms flailed. The flag streamed behind him. He was going to hit, and he was going to break his fucking neck. As he fell, he managed to somersault onto his back.

Then he was engulfed in the thing like a giant down pillow. It cradled and slowed him. He could feel it deflating and could hear fans pushing air into the thing. Bouncing to his knees, he held the flag over his chest as the entire division and all the staff erupted in applause and cheers. He was dead center of a vast, inflatable cushion. The team surrounded the deflating arrestor and shouted their praise for their new commander. Even the hunters looked down from the window above, covered with his paint shots and grinning from ear to ear.

He heard her laugh in his head. Zoe. It sounded to him like

music. Had he never heard her laugh before? How was *that* possible?

"Excellent job, Commander."

"How—"

"I paused your feed once I knew what window you were headed for," she said with a voice that sounded like she was smiling. "I dialed my Oneiri timeframe back two weeks and ordered the placement of the arrestor. They're filled with gas from an explosive, like an automotive airbag. It's an old Oneiri magic trick, but a good one." She laughed again.

He decided he truly liked her laugh as he bounced to the edge and slid to the ground. His feet never touched the soil, however, for the Lost Boys hoisted him on their shoulders and carried him back toward the barn for the start of the celebration.

Thanks, Zoe, he subvocalized. *I'll try to do better at the collaboration thing.* He looked down at the crowd of happy soldiers. *This is a good team.*

"Agreed," Zoe said.

Tonight, we celebrate. Tomorrow, we get moving.

"Yes, sir."

We have so much to work to do.

6-02-30, 8:40 PM HKT: SAMEDI

DR. KENNETH BAXTER took *nothing* for granted. Of course, he appreciated the finer things. Always had. That his position as the prime representative of Cliff Price, The Black Empty, afforded him nearly unlimited wealth was merely one perquisite of service. The Black Empty could, after all, perform miracles. His aircraft, for example, had, at one point, served as Air Force One. It had languished on the grounds of the Reagan Library until the MAGA party burned the library to the ground in '28. It was a simple matter for Baxter's benefactor to procure the aircraft and refit it to suit his dark purpose.

Baxter had always done well, always. Even as a young boy serving in the Bahamian brothels of wealthy conservative hypocrites, Kenneth knew how to get what he wanted. Some of his success was due to connections made through the Pentacula, some because he was a psychopath. But Baxter liked to assure himself that the lion's share of the credit belonged to his recognition of talent and his ferocious, rapacious intellect. The truth was that it was mainly down to his whiteness and his undeniable good looks. While bright, he was only about 70% as intelligent as he believed. The remaining 30% of what he called intellect was just confidence born of privilege. That 30% did most of the lifting in his life.

His jet touched down at Chek Lap Kok at midnight, Hong Kong Time. His internal clock was on Eastern Daylight Savings Time, now yesterday afternoon. Time was a funny thing. June, the flight attendant, appeared with an espresso on a silver tray as if sensing his flagging energy. He sipped the delicious bitterness as the VC-137 taxied to his private hangar. Three limousines waited, holding Chan Qi Caiping and his entourage. Baxter finished his espresso as his stately black aircraft came to rest.

"See our honored guests to the conference suite, please, June."

"Of course, Doctor Baxter."

She headed toward the cockpit and closed his office door. The last seven months had been nothing short of miraculous. There was no other word for it. During their daily stand-ups, the Emptiness transferred compressed Dow, Nasdaq, and Nikkei data for over seven million publicly traded symbols, along with international bond market data, forex rate changes, and upcoming IPOs. It was a day trader's dream. Baxter had known just what to do with all that information and had all the necessary contacts to maximize its earnings potential. Cliff Price was a savant, absolutely, but his understanding of investing was abysmal.

Price, who had lately insisted on being addressed as The Black Empty, could not be convinced to release more long-term info. Not yet. He dangled the data as a carrot and threatened to revoke Baxter's status as his prime representative as a stick. Baxter was not content. Oh, the limited data was enough to establish an empire. In seven months, Baxter, representing the Emptiness, had acquired unimaginable wealth, power, and respect—beyond even his status as sixth of most of the influential Pentacula. Still, he bristled at the feeling of subservience.

He wanted Price's black box for himself. He imagined what he could do if not limited by his mad patron in the future. He imagined what he could do with a time machine of his very own. Then he'd have enough power to run the table. The *whole* table.

June popped her head in. "They're ready for you, Doctor Baxter."

"Thank you, June."

———

"Doctor Baxter, we are very grateful for the guidance you have provided regarding the High Sun investments. Our organization has seen returns in the billions of yuan."

"Sir, respect demanded that I come to Chan Qi Caiping with these data. You will have, by now, verified that the Samedi Organization is offering our insights only to the High Sun."

Chan bowed very slightly.

"Our intelligence operatives are extremely curious about how your data is so accurate."

Baxter did not move. He waited for Chan to apologize.

"I have told them that your sources and methods are to be respected."

Baxter still did not move a muscle.

"And I apologize for their failure to show you due honor."

Baxter nodded and blinked slowly.

"I appreciate your restraint, and as further evidence of Samedi's appreciation, I bring you a new opportunity," Baxter said quietly.

Chan bowed again, very slightly.

"We are looking to form an exclusive relationship with a player in the biomedical or biopharma space. The Samedi Chair knows that no organization in the Pacific Rim controls as many laboratories outside of state oversight. The Chair offers his most favorable and high praise on the High Sun for their abilities in this space."

Chan was motionless.

"Our needs cannot be met by any other agency, and we would be in your debt if your help were made available for the appropriate reward."

"We will discuss rewards another day. Samedi has proven your value one thousand times over."

The two men had reached a state of equality in their respect. They could now speak as peers.

"The Chair wishes to develop a bioweapon. The wielder of this weapon will be more powerful than the nuclear states. We have acquired intellectual property from a lesser-known biomedical facility in the US. Their initial work was with a mutation of the rabies virus. They worked on this for the US Defense Advanced Research Projects Agency. They failed to secure a final round of funding. We found that decision short-sighted. It shows great promise for organizations with courage."

Baxter placed a 20-terabyte data card on the high-gloss mahogany table.

"We can fully fund an adequately staffed BSL-4 bioweapons lab for six years." Baxter bowed slightly.

"We would have a problem with bandwidth in our Wuhan operation. But we operate many labs that could accomplish this work."

Chan thought momentarily and spoke in Mandarin to a young man in a black silk suit identical to his. Baxter folded his hands while they spoke in low tones.

"Our bioweapons facility in Ulsan, South Korea, will be made available for this." He nodded to the young man, who bowed, picked up the data card, and put it into his breast pocket.

Baxter bowed appreciably.

"The data provided contains the précis, but the play is for the vaccine. High Sun will have distribution rights in the Pacific Rim. Samedi retains those rights globally. The aim is to produce a global pandemic that will terrify the general population, make worldwide headlines that soften the market organically—and then supply the preventative and the cure at a price point that upends the current global dynamic in our favor."

"Exclusive Pacific Rim distribution."

"Well…"

Chan remained motionless.

Baxter smiled. "Done."

Chan spoke to the serious younger man and then nodded at Baxter.

"The Chair requests quarterly updates and progress reports. Otherwise, as with all our dealings, Samedi Organization counts on High Sun's impeccable record of success." Baxter bowed a full three inches.

Chan Qi Caiping stepped into his limousine and looked back at the black jet. His dealings with the Samedi Organization had been lucrative. Dr. Kenneth Baxter was as careful a negotiator as any American Chan had ever dealt with. He understood the Triad's ways, and he was clever. But that didn't explain how he came by the bond market data he'd provided High Sun for the last five months. A few prophetic statements would make him worth the attention. Baxter's information was correct in *every* aspect, day after day for months. Still Chan bristled at the feeling of subservience.

He wanted the source of this information for himself. He imagined what High Sun could do if not limited by his American patron. He imagined what he could do with the wealth Baxter commanded. Then High Sun would have enough power to run the table. The *whole* table.

Chan could not allow the Samedi Organization to hold the source of that information secret from him. Soon, High Sun would be so subservient to Baxter and his mysterious Chair that other Triads would withdraw their respect.

No.

Chan's path was clear. He needed to eliminate Baxter and deal directly with whoever he was taking orders from. The only way would be to identify that mystery man and meet. Luckily, High Sun controlled several manufacturers of mobile device components. There was always a backdoor he could exploit no matter the make of the phone.

One way or another, Chan Qi Caiping would know who controlled Samedi.

6-17-30, 6:30 PM PDT

"Samedi?" John asked in confirmation.

"Samedi Organization, Hong Kong. Yes, sir. It's a good news, bad news situation, sir."

"Walk me through it."

The conference was Aurora audio only on a redundantly secure FTL channel. Still, even John was kept in the dark when it came to the participants. Oracle hired and managed the players directly and, to protect them from Roberts' Rules infractions, their identities and whereabouts were redacted. While there were four others on the line besides John and Zoe, only one agent spoke.

"Oracle established our DarkInt group back in October. He reached the same conclusion as Borealis Actual that our priority was to develop a counter for the bug—GGB-Z. He had no details as to how Cliff Price achieved the final virus when Downfall occurred. His only option was to flood the zone," the Agent said.

"And the zone, in this case, is what? All the bioweapons labs around the world?" John asked.

"Oracle went wider. He looked at all BSL-3 and above."

"BSL-3?"

"Sorry. Biosafety Level 3. Labs capable of working safely with biologics that can cause serious illness and can be spread through aerosols. TB, SARS, West Nile—bad bugs. Above that, BSL-4, are the *big* bad bugs like Ebola, 1918 Influenza, and Hemorrhagic fever. Shit that even the scientists are afraid of. GGB-Z, the final shipped product, qualifies as...*will* qualify as the worst of these."

"So Oracle flooded that zone? Humint?"

"Yes, sir—human intelligence gathering. SDS, as an emerging human resources company, has had good success in partnering with medical staffing firms throughout the world. With access to their systems, we could identify and groom low-level agents in every single state-approved BSL-3 & 4 lab. These operatives are lab workers, administrative assistants, even janitors. It turns out that all the non-state labs—the shady ones that are not licensed—all hire from the same pool of talent."

"Makes sense."

"For the past six months, they've been on the lookout for an incoming project that matched the GGB-Z profile."

"And we got a hit when?"

"Monday morning in Ulsan, South Korea. The Mindful Joy Limited Partnership Research Facility. Mindful Joy is headquartered in Seoul. The lab is BSL-4, headed by Dr. Phillip Sun. We were alerted by Sun's assistant, who tagged the project when she logged a two-terabyte redacted data card provided by Mindful Joy's CEO. The kickoff contract is with Samedi. Samedi also had our interest. Are you familiar with *Baron Samedi*?"

"Bond villain?"

"Yes sir, also a deeper background. Baron Samedi is the mythical master of the dead in Haitian Voodoo. The Bond character was based on that. His mojo is responsible for the earliest incarnations of zombies. Price named the evil terrorist organization in his hologame, *The White Horseman*, after the same character though a different name. *Baron Simitye*. Depending on who you ask, Samedi and Simitye are brothers, or they're just different dialects. The Simitye Faction creates the zombie apocalypse in the game."

"Stephen said he was rebooting the game with Oneiri." John's mouth was dry. "This sick fuck."

"Yes, sir."

"Did we get a dump of the data?"

"We did, sir. And here's where the bad news comes in."

"Okay."

"The data we received shows that Samedi has had two other teams working the problem. They have records showing a total of twelve years of effort on the bioweapon. Oracle calls it multi-threading."

John was silent for a good long time.

"And by knowing that we've collapsed that wave function. We can't stop *those* efforts. We *didn't* stop those efforts." He frowned. "So we've got this data card, two terabytes of data. Y'all have skimmed the surface. No way you've had time to deep dive yet, right?"

"Correct. We had an LLM parse through it. But we've only actually read through bits and pieces highlighted by the AI."

"Okay. I want you to be very circumspect in your analysis from a wave function collapsing point of view. LLMs can halluci-nate. I doubt an AI review will constitute an actual observation, but I could be wrong. Anyway, I want to know where those other labs are, and I want to get our people in those doors. We can't stop them from developing the thing, but we can become experts. We can know this virus better than they do, and—who knows—we may be able to build a hidden Achilles heel into the thing."

"There are also the vaccine considerations, sir."

"Clearly, we want their vaccine work."

"Also, if I may, sir?"

"Don't hold back."

"There may be a further net positive outcome on that front."

John was all ears.

6-18-30, 2:00 AM PDT

The Commander's quarters at St. Norberts were in a century-old cabin atop a hill overlooking the vineyard. In the summer moonlight, John could see the rows of vines in subdued detail. He tapped Zoe's contact icon. She answered immediately, as always.

"Commander?"

"You up?"

"I'm always up."

"What did you think of the intel brief today? I didn't have time to circle back with you after."

"I thought your insight to preserve the wave function and maximize our ability to affect change was good." She didn't ask why he was still awake at 2:00 AM. He knew she knew his local timeframe. She knew he had trouble sleeping.

"I'm still getting my sea legs with managing our efforts across different timeframes. Please feel free to yank me up short if you see me making any missteps."

"'Yank me up short.' Is that a military or a firefighter expression?"

"Well…could be?" He tried to remember where he'd first heard it. "It could be a southern Black thing? Maybe a horse-riding thing."

Zoe laughed.

John smiled.

"Commander, I only have a year of familiarity with the Oneiri device and all the 'spookiness' that it engenders," she said sooth-ingly. "I come from an intelligence background, but time machines were never part of our standard kit. I would venture to say that no one is an expert. But I think you have shown remark-able aptitude in understanding the peculiarities of this brave new world. You have taught all of us new ways of conceiving of our approach to it already."

John was silent for a moment as he looked out at the vineyard and felt the summer breeze flow over him in the darkness.

"When a wildfire burns through a woodland environment, everyone sees the catastrophe. There is a *lot* of it to see. Trees that took decades to grow, forests centuries old, homes, roads, all of it brought low in the worst way imaginable." His voice was soft and low, as if he were dreaming.

"I can't imagine."

"I have no need to imagine. I've seen it. Dozens of times a year." He tilted his head and stared out at the horizon. "But most people don't see what happens the next day, or the next week, or the next year. I have. I'm lucky enough to be in a job that lets me see the rest of that story." He caught himself. "To *have been* in a job —I got to see the forest recover over weeks and months and years. Watched the fungus and lichens grow on the ash, watched the new plants cover the forest floor, watched the seedlings sprout. Pretty soon, the birds are back, and the other animals follow. Within a few years, what was a wasteland becomes so thick with life you can't hike through it without a machete."

"That's amazing."

"It truly is."

"We're going to go through that, Zoe. Humanity is going to go through that. This virus is going to burn through us like wildfire. We won't be able to save everyone."

Zoe was silent.

"I want to make sure, when the fire comes, we save the right people. If the fire takes the rest, if it burns away some of the bad in the world… that's not terrible, right?"

Zoe was silent a bit longer. When she spoke, her voice was trembling with feeling.

"You know you won't be able to save all the good." She struggled to find the words and the emotional balance. "It is still going to be a catastrophe. I don't think I am collapsing any wave functions in saying that. Success—" Her voice caught on the lump in her throat. "Success is not an option."

And suddenly, John was certain. Zoe was in a time beyond the Downfall. She was a survivor. His imagined future was her lived experience. In her voice—her lovely, lyrical voice—he could hear a tragedy, a trauma that she carried.

"Success is not an option. Roger that," he said, unable to think of anything more articulate.

There was a long, unbearable silence. John wanted to find the words to soothe her, to make amends for dredging up whatever he'd touched in her.

In the end, all he had was, "Good night, Zoe. Thanks for listening."

"Good night, Commander."

"SEE, *this* is why I like a manual!" John said as he barreled through a yellow light on the dark road. "Sure, it's a pain in traffic, but with plasma powered…"

"JOHN! There is a truck to your right—" Zoe said , the anxiety clear in her voice.

John imagined her covering her eyes. She was, in fact, thanks to Aurora, looking through his.

John tapped the clutch, downshifted, swerved behind and clear of the panel truck, and jerked into the right lane. "Thank you, Zoe."

He jammed his foot to the floor. The Camaro's brushless high-torque motors whined, and he veered around the truck.

Despite the issues the two had in the early days, they now, after nearly a year of missions, worked like hand in glove. John had learned to rely on Zoe in the planning of every Resurrection Op, every Counterintelligence strike, and every spy-versus-spy encounter with the agents of Cliff Price. Zoe's use of the Oneiri device in her time frame showed true genius. He was often surprised and delighted by her ability to save his bacon while keeping him clear of any Roberts' Rules infractions.

According to Zoe, in her reference frame they'd been working together for over 18 months. She'd told him on more than one occasion that she found his behavior undeniably courageous, but it came with a streak of foolhardiness. She felt he was insufficiently risk averse. Guilty on all counts. She was a good check on his ego. Without her, he couldn't have managed the growth of Borealis. From one division, they'd expanded the covert military to seven, a true global force.

"Turn on my HUD for me, please?" John asked. "I'd like to keep my hands on the wheel."

Zoe activated the feature so he wouldn't lose track of their targets. The two cars—now outlined for his benefit—were half a mile ahead. A black Lincoln was chasing after the light blue minivan. The minivan was underpowered and outmatched. However, the driver seemed motivated and showed a bit of genius using other cars on the road as obstacles and shields.

Neither driver paid attention to John in his gray Camaro a half-mile back. "It sure would have been nice if we had better intel as to where this was going to happen," John said as he raced to keep up.

Zoe said, "I have access to everything available. The database is filtered to your timeframe so I won't collapse any wave functions ahead of you. It's unclear where they go off the road. Police arrived after their Mazda5 had exploded. You'll have to keep up if you want to be the first on the scene. Robin and the bus are waiting nearby for your word."

John nodded. "Okay, it has to be any time now." As he spoke, the Lincoln made its move, lunging forward and clipping the minivan in its left rear quarter panel. Angular momentum tugged at both vehicles unpredictably. The Lincoln launched into the air at almost a forty-five-degree angle. It sailed up and over the guardrail and then crashed horribly into a flood control spillway. The minivan started doing something like a canter, skittering and bouncing on different wheels as the driver tried to keep it under control. It was a valiant but losing effort as the vehicle slid off the road and down an embankment. Its speed made it uncontrollable, and it flipped onto its side and then the roof, skidding several hundred feet into the shadow of an overpass.

John, under better control, followed it off the road. He pulled to a complete stop. "Okay, you've got my position and time; get that bus here."

Zoe disconnected from him for a moment to do the Oneiri shuffle. The ambulance team appeared within seconds, approaching from the opposite direction. Zoe's breathing returned in John's ear.

"You should see them now."

"Yep." He ran to the minivan and dropped to the ground. "They all look okay. Banged up, but okay." The driver, a thirty-something redhead, struggled with his seatbelt and reached for his wife. John put a large hand on his shoulder through the shattered window. "Brian. *Brian*. She's okay. Stay calm, and we'll get your family out." His voice was gentle but commanding.

Robin ran to the overturned vehicle as his team pulled out four backboards. Each board had a black body bag strapped to it. The bags were occupied.

Robin sliced through the seatbelt webbing with a propane hot blade and removed the unconscious woman from the front passenger seat. He checked and reported, "She's got a strong, regular pulse."

Four EMTs from his team arrived, unstrapped their loads, and carefully transferred the wife to the board. Robin tossed the hotblade to John.

John held the trigger down, and when the blade glowed red in an instant, he sliced Brian's belt. He was able to scramble out on his own after the belt retracted with a snap. "Watch the glass, man. It can cut your hands. Okay. I'll get your daughter. Is this Janet?"

Brian nodded, confused how John knew his daughter's name.

"Okay, you go with the tech. Go with Robin there. He'll get you checked out."

John held the trigger down and sliced the girl's belt. Another pair of Borealis EMTs pulled the other girl free, placed the limp bodies on the transfer boards, and double-timed it back to the ambulance. With the minivan empty, John followed them back to the ambulance.

The mother had regained consciousness, but she was still strapped to her board. Her wrist looked swollen. The EMTs set the girls gently on the other gurneys. Brian was being assessed for brain injury.

John said, "Okay, Brian, we'll get you to a secure medical facility. The bad guys chasing you, we don't have to worry about them. But their bosses will be checking hospitals. So, we're getting you someplace safe. Okay?"

Brian nodded and said, "Are you guys FBI?"

John smiled, looked him in the eye, and didn't answer his question. "Goodnight. I'll be by to discuss your case in the morning." John shut the ambulance door and pounded on its fender. The driver pulled away gently.

The remaining techs were busy pulling cadavers from the vinyl bags: a man, a woman, and two pre-teen girls. John hated this part. Zoe said in his head, "The police are inbound and will arrive in twelve minutes."

John sniffed the air. "We have less time than that. This gas leak could go any minute." He helped the technicians wrestle the bodies into the minivan's seats. "They don't have to be perfect. They just need to be in the right place and orientation," John advised as he finished getting the "father" in place. He felt the coolness of gasoline dripping onto his supporting hand. "Robin, you good over there? We have a lot of gas on the ground."

Robin responded, "Good here, Commander."

They backed away from the vehicle as they folded up the body bags. The smell of gas was strong now. John motioned for them to move further back. He'd seen his share of gas fires. They waited.

Zoe said, "Four minutes."

John said, "Yep. I wanted to see if it would go up on its own.

He struck a single match, lit the book, and tossed it into the nearest visible puddle of fuel. The flame raced back to the minivan and found enough vapor to catch with a *woof*. The night filled with light, and their lungs felt the wallop of the pressure wave. They should have been further away, and they all staggered back two steps with their arms shielding their faces. They finished folding the black vinyl bags, walked back to the Camaro, and slowly drove away past the burning wreck.

3-14-31 9:35 AM CST

Brian Cosgrove and his wife, Celine, shared a room in the Chicago, Illinois, Borealis medical facility. Brian noticed that the place was small but incredibly well-staffed and equipped. As an engineer at Tesseract, he knew high tech. The number of wireless medical devices was beyond anything he'd ever seen at Holy Cross. When John arrived, the doctor was providing some parting hospitality. They were fine, apart from a scratch on Brian's forehead and Celine's fractured wrist. Brian was fascinated with Celine's 3D-printed purple soft-cast. They both seemed cautiously grateful for their rescue and care. John exchanged a few words with the doctor, clapped him on the shoulder, and laughed. John had come to know everyone on staff at most of the Borealis Med facilities over the past three years.

He entered their room as the doctor continued on his rounds. "Hello. How are you two doing this morning? How's your wrist?"

Celine smiled but held her arm close. "We're fine."

John smiled. "But you have some questions." They nodded. "What's Borealis? How did we know about you and your daughters?" He looked around. "Have you seen your daughters today?"

Brian smiled. "Yeah, they're fine. They've found the hologaming room. We may never get them to leave."

John laughed. The couple relaxed a little when he did so. His warmth was a natural anti-anxiety treatment. "Yeah, it's popular with the kids all right—and the doctors and nurses—my agents too, for that matter. But the kids are okay?"

"Yeah, they're fine." He paused and looked uncomfortable. "How did you know we were going to crash? You—"

"Okay." John grabbed a chair. "Brian, you have been doing some pretty impressive work in 3D printing at Tesseract, right? Pretty groundbreaking stuff? The folks running this place have noticed your work, and they became aware of your troubles with…." He let Brian fill in the details.

Brian looked at Celine. He spoke quietly, "We got into some trouble making ends meet. A guy I knew asked me to design a better printable ghost AK-47, one that they could get past a metal detector. I was working with ceramic printing and carbon fiber printing. I got to where I could laminate layers of Bucky Tubes. You know what Bucky Tubes are?"

John smiled. "Carbon fiber with really high tensile strength. And there were some guys your guy knew who wanted that technology."

Brian nodded. "Bad guys. Political assassins and worse. I took their money, but I wasn't going to give them what they wanted. I bricked my personal computers, drives, and printers. Then we made plans to leave town."

John said, "And that's when we showed up. To answer your question, we've been watching them and you pretty carefully, looking for an opportunity like this. They are not going to leave you alone unless they think you're dead. The police, the FBI, they could protect you if you were on their radar. But you're not." John looked at the couple as they gravitated toward each other. He said, "You *were* on our radar. This is what Borealis does. We identify good people in bad trouble and give them a fresh start. We're part private witness relocation, part human resources, part miracle workers." John looked around. "I'm sure it's not lost on you that we have some pretty high-tech gear here."

Brian nodded. "Some of this stuff looks like it's from the future."

John laughed again. "Well, funny story—Anyway, our staffing folks identified you as a perfect candidate. We'd like to offer you that fresh start you were looking for. This fresh start will allow you to keep working in your field, collaborating with some of the smartest people on the planet. I will tell you, it's a bit of a move, relocation-wise. But they have elite schools. It's a friendly community. A bit out of the way. It's up north."

Brian looked hopefully at Celine. She smiled hopefully back. "I'm from Northern Minnesota. Duluth."

John laughed. "Duluth? Yikes! I know Duluth! I think this might be warmer than Duluth in the winter. It's in Nunavut. In Canada, there's a big technology center they've been building for three years, the Nunavut Technology Center. You'd like it, Brian. They have all the toys. The Center's foundations were laid with Tesseract foundation drones."

Brian's eyebrows crept up his forehead. "I designed those!"

John nodded. "I know you did. Well, think it over. I'll send you some links to the NTC community site. Meanwhile, rest up. Heal. I'll be back once you've made your decision."

With that, John said goodbye and left them to consult with one another. Their anxiety had evaporated. They could see a future for themselves and their girls. It felt like a miracle.

3-18-31 6:23 PM EST

The only thing visible from the twin-engine Otter was the cluster of domes and the runway lights. They entered the pattern of NTC field just as daylight turned to dusk. According to the website, the construction crews had only completed the largest of the domes last October. Brian couldn't imagine such a massive structure could exist out here amidst the emptiness. The smallest dome was almost half a mile in diameter, the largest over two miles. In the arctic scene, they radiated warmth from within like some sort of candy-land, fairy tale village. The girls marveled at how the edges glowed through the several feet of snow.

What wasn't on the website was the origin of the Nunavut Technology Center, how a state-of-the-art community so rich in science, engineering, and research came to be built twenty miles north of the Arctic circle. There was no history page to document how, in 2029, a shell company created by Stephen Lucas had negotiated with the Canadian government to build a modern industrial hub here on the island the Inuit called Aaffaffak Qaqqaq—the literal translation was "Walrus Rocks." Certainly no record existed of how pleased Stephen Lucas was with that name and how much it influenced his decision to place his boondoggle there. But he'd chosen it because, honestly, who even knew the island existed? It was a place with no history beyond the tribal histories of the Inuit, and that suited Stephen just fine.

The website *did* cover the partnership between the Borealis Foundation and the Walrus Rocks Island Inuit Business Council and the valuable contribution of the residents of Walrus Rocks' largest community, Broad Harbour. The whole venture was made possible due to a First Nations clause in all the documents— leases, easements, building permits—required before a single shovel was pushed into the frozen earth of Walrus Rocks.

Brian peered down at the flat, white nothingness below. He knew the Center was on an island, but there was almost nothing to inform an observer on final approach this time of year. Only the runway lights made it clear where they were going to land. He turned and looked at the expressions on Janet's and Barb's faces. They were thrilled, wonder-struck. He turned to Celine. Her eyes, too, were round with wonder, but her brow held worry.

She looked out at that emptiness and feared they had made a mistake bringing their girls here. Brian nuzzled near her face as they looked out the small window. "Look at those domes. Inside, they say it's like San Diego. You'll be able to work in their arboretum."

She laughed, "I'm not afraid of the snow, silly." She reached up and grabbed his chin. "I'm worried about the wilderness. I like my shopping, Brian Cosgrove."

He smiled. "Anything you need, we'll *print* it, lady."

The plane crunched to a stop on its skis in front of a fleet of twelve snowcats shuttles with wide rubber treads. The pilot and snow-cat driver moved baggage from the planes's storage to the cats. Passengers, including the little Cosgrove family, boarded the well heated shuttle and were soon hustled through the cold to the airfield terminal's door. It still had that new-terminal smell. It appeared to be designed to handle thousands of passengers, but they were the only new arrivals this evening.

Unmanned kiosks pointed their way to a small, electric maglev subway that sped them to the residence dome. As they hurtled through the short tunnel, Brian noted the trademark layering pattern in the concrete foundations. The curved concrete walls looked like they'd been deposited by some giant mollusk. He was thrilled to see such large-scale use of 3D printing. Previously, he'd only seen it used in small projects like farmhouse yurts. The subway opened up into the Central Park of A-Dome. Celine smiled at the look of awe on her girls' faces. It was as if they were suddenly in California and over-dressed. The dome was held aloft by air pressure and an intricate carbon-fiber structure which Brian suspected was printed as well. It was hard to tell since the top was nearly 800 feet above them. It felt like the evening sky if you didn't look right at it.

The concierge met them as their car hushed to a stop. She informed them that their apartment was ready for occupancy and installed the security app on their mobiles. The app allowed them access to the public spaces and the rest of the community. It provided security permissions for their apartment to them alone. The girls were given necklaces with RFID pendants. This opened the doors they had permission to and provided instant location information for them. The concierge concluded by telling them that their luggage had already been delivered and that their meeting with 'Mayor' Shaw would be the following morning.

They followed the map to the southwest elevator, rode up two levels, and found their new home. Brian unlocked the door to the apartment as the girls burst past him to explore. Janet declared the middle bedroom to be hers. Barb did not protest. Celine draped herself around Brian in a loving embrace and said, "*Oh. My. God.*"

03-20-2031 08:05 AM EST

"*Good morning!* For those I haven't met yet, and there are quite a few, my name is Athena Shaw. I'm the Vice President of Operations here at the Nunavut Technology Center. You can think of me as the mayor of our little 'town.'" Mayor Shaw was a born politician. Despite her diminutive size and her age—Brian doubted she'd yet to see thirty-five—she inspired confidence in the NTC's management.

"If you have a problem with anything, my door is always open. There aren't so many of us yet that I can't get to know all of your names and the names of your families. In a few years, I expect our community will be too large to know every single one, but for now, I cherish that smallness." She swiped her tablet, and the enormous holopanel behind her showed a three-dimensional model of the Center's six domes with a ring of outbuildings surrounding the smallest. "And by small, I mean, our current population is just shy of twelve-thousand citizens. This is where we are today."

She swiped again. "And this is where we're headed together

in the next 18 months." Six new domes appeared, hopscotching northward and inland from Broad Harbour. "By May of 2034, we expect upwards of 120,000 resident scientists, engineers, and technicians helping to build the future."

She looked out at the group and smiled.

"Why, in this little group alone, we have experts in viral biology and epidemiology, sub-space mechanics, 3D printing"—she looked directly at Brian Cosgrove, who blushed a bit. Athena continued—"electrical engineering, computer science, and nano-materials research."

The small group chuckled at how impressive they all appeared to be. Brian wondered how many had been as lucky as he, rescued from a life spoiled by bad decisions.

Athena explained their technological roadmap, a multidimensional Gantt chart that looked incredibly ambitious. All the timelines lead to an obscure date in the third quarter of 2036—September 17th. She swiped her tablet to zoom the schedule to the near term.

"Three months from today. We hope to be completely self-sufficient in terms of food and supplies by this summer's solstice. That means we'll have sufficient food production, energy generation, materials, and manufacturing to cut the cord with the world outside Walrus Rocks Island. That is our goal, and all of you will help us reach it." The small group chattered a bit at the possibility. Miss Shaw smiled.

"I see some skeptics out there. That's good. *That* makes you scientists. But keep your eyes open. NTC is going to make believers out of you! Okay. We're going to take a short break for biology and bagels. We'll reconvene in fifteen minutes when Abe Akkilokipok will walk you through the NTC floor plan so you know where you'll all be working. You'll be roughing it a little more in your labs than in your apartments. We prioritized your families. But Abe will cover all that. So, thank you for your time. If you ever need anything, drop by my office. Mayor Shaw's door is always open. Once more, welcome to the NTC."

Brian's buddy for the "noob tour" was Adeeb Adawati, a young Palestinian man whose specialty was applied sub-space theory. Adeeb spoke the king's English and humble-bragged about his years as a professor at Oxford. He was responsible for conducting Brian's real estate tour of the center. They began at the center of the main dome in the open quad known as Central Park. The circular park was broken into three grassy areas arranged around the central amphitheater. The central dais was ringed with tall, elegant arches that sloped inward and touched at their apex, two hundred feet below the dome's ceiling. Ivy had grown about a quarter of the way up the arch supports. It would reach the top in another few years, completing the picture of a natural and academic space.

Adeeb called Brian's attention to the apartment ring that formed the dome's base. Three stories of elegant, variegated curving concrete walls swept the entire circumference of the enclosure.

"I like how they've incorporated plants into the design. It becomes a challenge to imagine what it's like outside." Adeeb quickly looked at his mobile. "Outside the domes, it's twenty-five below zero, Celsius. Don't worry. You won't be completely insulated from the arctic up here. Wait till you see the lab ring. Athena always calls it 'roughing it.' That's quaint, but… well, let's not get ahead of ourselves."

Brian pointed out his apartment. "That's us over there. 3224A."

"The A designation is the Dome. This is A-Dome. Botany is in B-Dome. C-Dome is the smallest. It's for the administration offices. So 3224A is Dome A. Level 3. Apartment 224. There are 350 apartments per level." He pointed to an apartment about 45 degrees clockwise from Brian's. "We're in 4342A. Still room to grow, but we've doubled in population since I arrived late last year." They walked past the concierge desk across from the subway exit. "If you ever need to go in town, down to the port in Broad Harbour, there are Snow Cats or snowmobiles free to use in the winter, scooters, or cars in the summer—all LT plasma electric. Some members like to go down to Broad Harbour for breakfast or drinks at the Blue Caribou. Lots of members never leave the domes, though."

They continued along a walkway that took a dip beneath a low arch, and the air suddenly smelled of peat, manure, and freshly cut plants. Brian looked up and saw they'd entered B-Dome.

"Oh man, Celine is going to fucking die." His bride was booked for the afternoon orientation to allow Brian to pick the girls up from their first day at school. "She's a molecular biologist... plant biologist."

The arch on this side was covered with flowers. The air was noticeably more humid. B-Dome was visibly larger, and its design was very different. This was workspace—no public square. The outermost ring was covered with green pasture. Small herds of livestock grazed quietly while walking in a vast circle. Australian sheepdogs kept the cows, sheep, and goats organized as they munched on the grass.

Adeeb pulled Brian's elbow to keep him from stepping in a fresh cow pie. "Manure is valuable in here." Inside the grazing ring, arranged in a radial pattern, hundreds of rings of hydroponic towers, *stacks* as Adeeb called them, reached halfway to the dome ceiling. The air was thick with organic smells and tastes. Brian found his smile was irrepressible.

He turned to Adeeb, who was also smiling like a child. "I believe that this place *could* be self-sustaining. It's like a prototype for a Mars mission or something."

Adeeb nodded, "Certainly. You are not the first to see that potential. It would explain a great deal, chief among them being why build this beautiful facility in the Arctic circle of all places. A lot of happy hour debates have centered around that very idea.

There are rumors that *Stephen Lucas* is an investor—that this is his run at a Mars colony. *Maybe*."

They walked directly through the center of the dome. It took several minutes to bisect the broad circle. A particularly grumpy-looking older Asian woman handed them each a fresh carrot unexpectedly, as if it was their job to taste it. Brian snapped a bite of his and looked astonished. "Oh, my god! It's so sweet." The woman laughed before returning to her harvest. The two of them munched on their carrots like happy horses as they walked. "Celine is going to fucking die," Brian repeated as he turned to take in the view from the opposite side.

They approached another low arch with a slight dip in the walkway. Almost instantly, the Botany Dome's organic fragrances were gone, replaced with the smell of an office building. It was an oddly nostalgic smell to Brian, who had worked remotely in his garage for the last decade. It smelled like paper, toner, deodorant, cheap perfume, and deadlines. While C-Dome was smaller than the other two, it was still a cavernous space to fill with open-plan cubicles. "What do they even *do* in here?" Brian asked.

Adeeb laughed, "Everyone asks that. I have no idea. I'd rather die than work in this dome."

They followed the outer ring past conference rooms and cubicles filled with people in front of displays filled with spreadsheets. Adeeb led the way to an exit airlock. He said, "Get ready. It's a little chilly out this door.

He pushed out as a shot of cold air hit Brian. It wasn't the full, raw arctic air, but it was brisk. They emerged into a spacious, plastic-sheathed igloo. It was, in fact, a giant inflatable ring that wrapped around C-Dome. The ring tube was sixty feet in diameter, and the snow outside had drifted to cover it entirely. The snow, backlit by the morning sun, turned the light slightly bluish. A pair of pale-eyed huskies ran to them, tails wagging. Adeeb kneeled down to offer them some love.

"The local Inuit raise them as sled dogs—real workers, these. Very good boys. Magnificent boys." Adeeb scratched behind their black, fluffy ears. Brian was happy to join in roughing up their thick, dense fur for them. He looked up from the happy pups.

Arranged around the ring were trailers. Brian could see fifteen of them from where he stood. The rest arced behind the dome in either direction. He frowned, puzzled.

Adeeb said, "Welcome to the trailer park. This is where they've got us working. This is where the science lives."

Brian laughed. "Well, that's fucking typical."

Adeeb laughed at that and nodded. "Want to see my favorite lab?" He jogged down five trailers and waved for Brian to follow. The huskies kept up. The sign on the trailer said *Protein Sequencing*. Adeeb turned to the dogs and said sternly, "Stay." Once they each sat politely, he pulled open the door, and the smell of Moroccan food poured out. Brian's eyes grew wide as he followed. Inside, he found five researchers standing around a grill. Distributed around the backside of the trailer were large cylinders filled with liquid. Something was suspended in each of the cylinders. None of that mattered. The smell of charred lamb was all that did. Adeeb said, "I'd like you all to meet Brian Cosgrove. He's a 3D printing genius."

The researchers, munching on kebab, grunted hello.

Adeeb grabbed a kebab and handed it to Brian. "This is the protein sequencing team. Charlotte, Sanjay, Betty, and Daphne." Brian waved and took the hot wooden skewer. He followed their lead and took a bite of the lamb meat.

They all watched his reaction. His knees went a little soft at the taste. Daphne smiled and said, "I don't think we have to do anything to the enzymes. I think this is as close to real lamb as we're going to get. It's time to move on to improving our beef."

Sanjay shook his head, readying a rebuttal, but Brian spoke with his mouth full. "What do you mean 'as close to real lamb?'"

Charlotte pointed to the cylinders. "We grew that in our mad scientist lab. One hundred percent sequenced protein. No animals slaughtered to make these kebabs."

Brian carefully ripped another cube of meat from the skewer.

It was straight-up *delicious*. His eyes fluttered. Daphne said, "See? We are *so* done."

The team erupted in debate. Adeeb and Brian said their good-byes and escaped into the igloo with their kebabs. "Oh my God," Brian said.

Adeeb laughed, "See? That is why it's my favorite lab"—he tossed a kebab to each of the patient dogs—"and theirs! C'mon!" He waved. "It's time I showed you your kingdom."

They hustled in the chilly air down another ten trailers. Brian smiled when he saw the sign. 3D printing and fabrication. There were four trailers in a row devoted to that specialty. Beyond the last trailer, he saw a Tesseract 400 pressure concrete foundation drone. His patents were all through the innards of that model. It was factory fresh with a custom white paint job. On its side was a logo of an Inuit walrus with the name Akkilokipok underneath. Adeeb showed him into the first trailer. Five researchers nervously stood up when he entered.

Adeeb whispered, "They've all been dying to meet you." He said more loudly to the room, "I'd like you to meet your new technical lead, Brian Cosgrove."

Brian blanched. No one had said anything about being the lead of anything. The researchers all rushed forward to shake his hand and introduce themselves. "Hi, Mr. Cosgrove, I'm a big fan. I'm Julian Beulle."

Brian shook his hand and noticed Julian walked on a pair of elegantly printed artificial legs. "Just Brian. Nice to meet you, Julian."

"Brian, I'm Theresa Kaplan."

"Theresa."

"Big fan of your work, Brian. I'm Josh Schmitt."

"Me too, I'm Glenn Kwok."

Brian smiled and said, "Josh, Glenn. I'm going to forget all of your names. Don't hold it against me. Julian, Theresa, Josh, and… Glenn. Okay." He looked around the room and saw ten of his open-source designs printing away. He winced. He'd made crucial improvements to those designs in the last month to fix embarrassing shortcomings.

Adeeb said, "Brian, it looks like you're home. I will leave you to explore it. Give me a shout later, and we'll get together for a happy hour, right sport?"

Brian nodded, "Thanks, buddy. I will, Adeeb." And then he turned to his team. "Okay, show me what you all are up to."

"DR. BAXTER, THE SENATOR HAS ARRIVED."

"Thank you, Adrienne. He can wait," Baxter said as he gazed down on a stormy afternoon in Washington.

Baxter's K Street offices were the envy of the cadre of Washington lobbying firms. The building's facade was original 19th century Second Empire, constructed of black granite, and had significant historical value in a city that was the *center* of American history. Aaron Burr himself had maintained offices on the first floor during his declining years. That facade was all that remained of the original historical structure, however. The interior was all 21st-century glass, stainless steel girders, three-inch tensioned cables, and polished hardwood.

Baxter, Dante, & Milton employed 1,200 of the most ambitious, cut-throat, and charming psychopaths in the nation's capital. Their one overriding mission was to control everything the Federal Government of the United States did. Even before The Emptiness had provided Baxter with the means for unlimited wealth, BD&M was gushing with cash. The Citizens United decision in the early teens had opened the floodgates to more money than Baxter's minions could stuff into the pockets of the country's elected representatives. It was so much sheer cash that no virtuous, civic-minded, naive do-gooder could stand long against its corrupting temptations.

But now, The Emptiness had made that entire model obsolete. The scale of capital available to Baxter through the investment data provided by his benefactor made it pointless to wait for governments to move. When distributed through the Pentacula, that data turned the centuries-old community into a supremely powerful multi-level marketing scheme. All those congregants scrambling to achieve wealth were willing to do *anything* to gain access to the merest crumbs of that data. And the beauty of the Pentacula was, once a congregant had been inducted, endured that torture—anything meant *anything*.

"Adrienne, please see the Senator in." Baxter sighed.

This miscreant, for example. He wasn't even a member of the Pentacula, merely a wannabe. He'd sniffed around since his election by the yokels in South Carolina. The Senator was like a half-blind truffle pig snuffling out the moldy, musky odor of political power. His ambition led him right to the leaders of the Pentacula. He was certainly too idiotic to recognize it as a single, contiguous organization, but he'd traced out its shape by dumb luck and persistence.

Adrienne opened his door, and Senator Donald P. Rand entered with a sly grin and his hand out. His hair was, famously, a messy mash-up of bedhead and boy-band-era product-laced curls.

"Kenneth!" he said with unearned familiarity. "I've been waiting to meet with you for a decade. Big fan."

"Thank you, Senator Rand. You are too kind. I hope your trip from the Capitol wasn't too wet."

"What, this?" Rand asked as a bolt of lightning lit up the room. "Neither rain, nor snow, nor…" He clearly did not know the whole motto. "Bah! I wouldn't let a little rain slow me down."

"Of course not. Please, have a seat."

"It sure is coming down, though, isn't it? I've got a meeting with my constituents after this, but fuck that. You know what I mean."

"I do. You are *term-limited*, are you not, Senator? South Carolina voters passed term limits in—"

"Yep. SCOTUS overturned Thornton in '27. South Carolina was the first in the nation to impose 'em on their reps."

"A remarkably stupid move on the part of South Carolina voters," Baxter said without hesitation.

Rand frowned. "We were pretty proud of it."

"If you limit a representative's term, what leverage does the voter hold on him to assure he actually meets with them ever again? You yourself are going to 'let a little rain' stop you from meeting with the voters who put you here." He raised an eyebrow. "Or am I misreading something?"

"Maybe I got off on the wrong foot—" Rand sputtered. "Maybe—"

"You are term-limited by your state, in your final year as a US Senator, and demonstrably unsuitable to run for President." Baxter narrowed his eyes. "What can *I* do for you?"

"What do you mean, demonstrably—"

Baxter cut him off with another raised eyebrow.

"Baxter, Dante, & Milton are Washington's premiere power brokers, Senator. We make kings. We make queens. We mold leaders from straw, wet clay, and desert sand. You are here to be crowned when you are barely fit to muck our stables. Am I putting too fine a point on it?"

Rand looked like a possum caught in a truck's headlights. Like a possum, his initial shock began to turn to feral, idiotic rage —his nostrils flared and his eyebrows twitched.

"But there is some good news for you, Senator. Due to recent expansion in our operations, we have more opportunities than credible people to fill them. If you have a pulse and can tie your own tie," Rand involuntarily tugged at his hastily tied Windsor, "BD&M has a position for you. How does that sound?"

"I, I—"

"Good. Are you familiar with One Corporation?"

"The hologaming company?"

"The very same. We'd like to get a man on their board. A retired US Senator would do nicely."

"Stephen Lucas might have something to say—"

"Oh, he will. We have been shuffling pieces on the board for years to create this opportunity. He'll be eager for you to join with your conservative voting record and your vocal opposition to violence in gaming."

"One makes some of the *most* violent games."

"And *you* will run interference for them, allowing them to make more. The Senate is looking to pass legislation for hologaming. You will strangle that legislation in committee."

"I—"

"And when you step down in 2033, you will be named to One's board of directors. It will burnish your reputation as a pro-business conservative, and when the time is right, you will oust Stephen Lucas and take control of the company."

"How?"

"Have you seen One's stock performance this last year?"

"No."

"It has been sluggish and trending down due to the desultory performance of their new OneFTL network. BD&M will lead an effort to further devalue the stock until shareholders demand new leadership."

Rand grinned. "Now we're talking."

Baxter shook his head at the idiot's delight.

"See, Doc? I knew you and I could do business." Rand preened. "Member of the Board of One Corporation. That'll do! That'll do! In a few years, I'll be running the place? That will fill my campaign coffers for a run at the President. The voters eat that shit up."

"Senator, you use the word *voter* as if it's interchangeable with the word *sucker*." Baxter sighed. "No matter. You will do *what* we tell you to do *when* we tell you to do it. No more, no less. We will manipulate the stock valuation, and you will time the coup d'état per our exact instructions. Understood."

"Sure thing, Kenneth." Rand smiled.

With Rand in place when the Oneiri device was developed in 2036, Cliff Price would find himself unnecessary. Perhaps they could arrange to have Rand participate in the Oneiri beta test. Instead of Price feeding into his bizarre delusions of grandeur, Rand, a puppet of the Pentacula, would acquire the McGuffin for them. Which meant Price could be eliminated at any time. Baxter had already set those contracts in motion.

"Hey, Doc? What about now, though? Can you do anything to get me on Ways and Means? Those guys get all the good bribes," Rand said with his over-practiced, aw-shucks drawl.

Baxter thought it might be worth inducting him into the Pentacula simply for the opportunity to torture him to death.

1-14-32, 3:20 AM EDT

Arnaud's relationship with Baxter was long, respectful, and lucrative. He was one of six assassins that Baxter relied on when a key individual stood in the way of history. Arnaud was everything Baxter admired in an associate; he was punctual, polite, discrete, and a perfectionist when it came to the work. He had been a Pentacula congregant since his sixteenth birthday, three months after his first contract kill.

In those early days, Arnaud was like an over-eager puppy. He delighted in the killing, and the most challenging part of the work for him was refraining from bragging about his victories with the local girls in the suburbs of Levallois-Perret. An elder statesman of Le Milieu, and a congregant, discovered him and guided him to the Pentaculum of his induction. Arnaud had been in the hospital for a month recovering from the wounds. But he *had* found his meaning. He had become more than a man. The fictional John Wick had nothing on the reborn Arnaud. It was likely Wick was based on him.

The current assignment was a simple one. His target was a holographic game designer in Madre Pueda, California. Cliff Price. According to Dr. Baxter, Price was also a wild-born serial killer, unaffiliated with any Northern California Pentaculum. Price had been raised by a family of sisters, apostates from the Pentacula that diverged in the mid-19th century. While Price had been raised in the tradition of the congregants, he was clearly an undisciplined rogue.

Regardless, Arnaud's target stood athwart history and Baxter wished the obstacle removed.

Arnaud had been in Madre Pueda for twelve days and had developed a feel for Price's routine. In Arnaud's experience, serial killers were usually not very imaginative. They were not world travelers, well-read, or sparkling conversationalists. They were usually just good at the one thing. Arnaud was superior to them. He was a citizen of the world. He was fluent in five languages, he maintained homes on three continents, and he could write restaurant reviews of fine cuisine around the globe. He, too, was an expert at his trade, but he had a wider aperture on life. His work did not define him. He bore no label.

Price was little different from most serial killers. He held a day job that was quite creative, Arnaud had to admit. His work in hologame design was impressive, complex, and showed true genius. Arnaud felt some sadness at the thought of removing that from the world. But outside of the day job, Price was disappointing. His life was an endless repetition of sameness. His only variety was the location of his targets. The targets themselves were homogenous—small, dull, zaftig blonde girls, sometimes effeminate boys. During Arnaud's period of getting to know Price, he had seen him stalk two subjects and cull one. He was on a second this evening. Tonight, Arnaud was in place to finish his assignment. The only question was whether to end him before he took another life or after. Arnaud didn't care overmuch either way, but he considered his options as a matter of logistical efficacy.

In the end, it was a simple solution. Price had a unique method of disposing of his victim's remains. A city built on rolling hills, Madre Pueda's sewage system employed large, macerating impellers to liquefy solid waste before pumping it to the level of the next treatment plant. They were very effective in turning human remains into a smooth froth in the effluent. Arnaud respected Price's ingenuity in this matter and planned to add it to his own toolkit in the future. It made a perfect opportunity to dispose of Price as well.

Price arrived at the sewage substation at 3:14AM, and Arnaud waited across the street in the shadows for him to move the two large, gray, watertight containers from the back of his mini-van. Price had a passkey for the substation and entered with the first of his containers. When he returned with the obviously lighter container to retrieve the second, Arnaud readied his syringe and walked across the street. Price entered the substation and closed the door behind him as Arnaud reached the edge of the street-lamp's shadow.

Arnaud did not see the open manhole in the center of the street. The cover had been stolen by three art students from the Braintree suburbs. Open manholes on a dark side street are visually identical in tonal value to an old, rusted manhole cover. Arnaud stepped directly into the center of the hole and plummeted silently from street view. His trailing leg snagged briefly on the hundred-year-old hand holds, but his momentum and body weight snapped his femur into a compound fracture and ground his face into the concrete on the opposite side. The hand holding the syringe, filled with venom extracted from an inland taipan snake, spasmed inward and up such that the impact with the bottom of the sewer drove the needle into his neck below his right jaw. The force of the impact collapsed the syringe's plunger. Arnaud was dead before the pain impulses from his horribly broken leg had time to reach his brain.

On a chart of possible ways for his mission to fail, the odds of this particular outcome were below .00004%. But that was the nature of spooky temporal enforcement. It was a numbers game.

When Cliff Price exited the substation with his second empty container, there was no sign that Arnaud had ever existed. He closed and locked the substation quietly, placed the containers in the back of his SUV, and drove away.

Arnaud's body was not discovered for another three weeks. As he had no wallet or ID and matched no missing persons report, his body was cremated as one of several John Does that Madre Pueda PD processes in any given year.

———

3-21-32, 6:15 AM EDT

The Georgetown Pentaculum's Ostara gathering of the Six wound down. The inductee's breathing was ragged and shallow, but his pulse was steady. Her blood loss and shock would leave her unconscious for the time it took for the support team to arrive. The Hamptons (Four and Five) waited to welcome them at the access passage of their basement tunnel.

This morning, the inductee had been resilient, almost stoic in her tolerance of the torture. It had taken some effort to bring her to a place where she could cast her pride aside and be broken, as all congregants must.

As they parted, Baxter again called out to Melissa Jones. The last time had been on a Halloween over two years earlier. Melissa closed her eyes and frowned.

"What is it, Baxter?" She had lost whatever fondness for the man she might have once kindled. He had clearly benefited from his contact with the man with the time machine while she had been in career purgatory at the Defense Intelligence Agency.

"Could I buy you breakfast?"

She wanted to tell him to fuck off. She wanted to stab him in the eyes and carve him like an Easter ham. She wondered how marbled his tenderloins would be.

"Sure, Baxter," she said.

The late March weather was not that different from October weather in Georgetown, and they stopped by the same food truck. Melissa ordered a plain bagel, lox with light, whipped cream cheese, and a tall coffee. Baxter, a ham and egg sandwich, toasted. She felt a strong sense of déjà vu.

"Do you have another time machine for me to vet?"

"No."

She watched him now, and for the first time, she noticed something she'd never seen before. Baxter looked shaken and unsure.

"What is it?"

"The man I told you about with the, um—"

"The time machine?"

"Yes." He paused and shook his head. "I do not believe in the supernatural. My participation in the Pentacula has always been from the vantage point of solid Jungian psychology."

"Right. Jesus, Baxter, what's got you spooked?"

"I believe Cliff Price has achieved divinity."

She was about to say something flip, but he was completely serious.

"What do you mean?"

"The time machine has proven enormously powerful in generating near unlimited wealth."

"I understand you've done very well for yourself—"

"Not just for me. Not just for my partnership. For the entire Pentacula system. At Cliff Price's direction, we have… It's not hyperbole to say we have taken organized crime to new levels of power and potency."

"That doesn't sound like a sign of divinity, Baxter."

"He appears to be immortal!" Baxter hissed. "Price is using it, all the money, all the power, to destroy the world. He's set things into play that frighten me. Insane things." He took a sip of coffee and looked around at the park. They were alone. "He's bankrolled a bioweapon. He's working with terrorist cells, financing them, gaining their loyalty, and convincing them he has a direct line to God, or Allah, or Satan. He's developed dark networks deeper than anything I ever cultivated. I initially helped him to gain power for my own ends, but he's outstripped my network and outgrown me."

And there it was. Baxter was being cut out. He was less worried about Price destroying the world and more worried he wouldn't have the chance to rule over the ashes. Melissa was not displeased to hear this. Fuck Baxter. He deserved it. She decided her best response was to patronize him.

"You're still the most powerful man in Washington. You're still the leader of the American Pentacula."

He smiled at her kind words.

"I'm still not hearing proof of divinity. What do you mean he's immortal?"

His smile evaporated.

"I decided I wanted to get this time device for myself." He hesitated. "So I set out to kill him."

This made Melissa's eyebrows raise. Baxter was not the type of person to kill someone and *admit* to it. She was certain he'd ordered dozens of assassinations—maybe thousands—but for him to talk about it openly was not in character. He was also not a person to blanch at the prospect of chaos and mayhem. She knew the Pentacula had prospered during the worst of times, down to and including the Black Death. She didn't doubt Baxter wanted *The Black Empty* dead, but he was playing her. He wanted the source of power, the McGuffin, Oneiri for himself.

"Bottom-line this for me, Baxter."

"He can't be *killed*, Melissa." He shook his head and took on a thousand-yard stare. "I work with a half dozen contractors for such… wet work. I assigned them one after another over the course of three months. All of them had impeccable track records and near-perfect success rates. All very expensive. Every *single* assignment was a failure. Three of them are dead, one is in a coma, and another is in a burn ward clinging to life. The last, a boy I groomed personally, hasn't been located yet. No word. No body. Not a trace. It is as if he fell into a black hole!" He shook his head again.

"Price killed them all?"

"No! That's the *madness* I'm dealing with. The way they all died. One of them was electrocuted while shaving in his hotel room. Another was in a traffic accident. Another was in a building that collapsed during an earthquake. The man in the burn ward? He was walking to the terminal from his airplane when a Cessna dropped out of the sky and crashed into a jet fuel truck 200 feet away. The explosion roasted him like a Sunday goose."

Melissa suppressed a laugh. Baxter was so shaken.

"These are acts of God. Force majeure. You see why I believe he's achieved divinity?"

"Why are you telling me all this, Baxter?"

"You are my last hope. If anyone I know might understand the powers this time device affords Price, it would be you." He met her eyes. He was desperate. "You have a degree in physics, correct?"

"I have a PhD in Quantum Mechanics and a Master's in Applied Mathematics. You should know this."

He waved away the details. "If you can't explain this to me rationally, I will be forced to change my worldview."

"Ahhh."

It had been two and a half years, and she'd skimmed the docs attached to Baxter's text conversation for ten minutes. Her eyes drifted upward.

"I'd need to see the documents he sent you. You only let me skim them... Wait." She froze with a slight squint, as if she could actually see the PowerPoint in front of her again. "Wait. Hold on."

Baxter took a bite of his breakfast and sipped some coffee.

"In the deck, there were rules for time machines, sort of like Asimov's laws of robotics. *Walrus' rules for Time Machines* or something. Huh." It was coming back to her.

She laughed out loud.

"Okay, Baxter. How much is your worldview worth to you?"

Baxter didn't blink.

"My conditions: I want all the documents this Black Empty has sent back through time. I want all the intel." She looked him directly in his piercing blue eyes. "And I want to get my hands on this device as soon as Stephen Lucas and Walrus Roberts begin user testing it in—what is it? Three-and-a-half years from now?"

Baxter frowned, was silent for a moment, and then nodded.

"The good news is, I think I can prove Price isn't immortal." Melissa smiled. "The bad news is you can't kill him until 2036."

"ALL I'M SAYING IS... it's not exactly a guy movie," John said as he waited in the dark alley. He heard no reply from Zoe; he wondered if Aurora had sent his audio. "Hello?"

"Oh, I can hear you," Zoe said curtly.

John grinned. She was pissed. "This is that important to you? *The Princess Bride?*" She was not speaking to him. "I mean, I get women like it. It's romantic." Silence.

A Seoul police cruiser drove past the alley entrance with its lights flashing. "Don't look down here. Don't look down here," John said.

His shoulders eased down a bit as they continued on their way. A lone, six-foot-four Black man was an unusual sight in Seoul any time or place. But in a dark alley, leaning against a tricked-out LT Plasma Mercedes, he looked like a poster boy for organized crime.

"Zoe?"

Silence.

Silence.

After a few seconds, she relented. "Not every movie has to be a *guy* movie, John. Not every movie has to have action heroes and superpowers and explosions. *'Cheeseburger! Cheeseburger! Bang! Bang!'"*

John laughed. She wasn't letting him off the hook.

"I'm sorry. You are an *amazing* man, John Banks. I know how smart you are. I know how well-read you are. I've spent four years looking through your eyes. But you—"

Silence.

Silence.

His face showed genuine concern. "What?" he asked.

Silence.

She was truly upset. He'd only been playing.

A black Jaguar eased into the alley and turned off its lights. John lit a cigar with a silver zippo lighter bearing a dragon enameled on its case. He made sure their car's night vision enhancements could see that logo before he snapped it closed. The Jaguar rolled to a stop, and two Korean men stepped out of the back passenger doors. They looked back at the main street and walked toward John's glowing cigar.

Zoe eased up the infra-red gain on his lens implant. John could now see the alley as if it were noon. She ran facial recognition on the two men, confirming they were kkangpae working for the Yang-eun faction. Po's men. They looked with suspicion at John's tall silhouette. He raised the flame again to his cigar, flashing the dragon emblem in the flame's light once again for good measure. The two men exchanged a glance and a nod. The younger of the two pulled a data card from his jacket pocket. "Mister Po says thank you for the sChip lithography files. He is satisfied with their authenticity."

John smiled. "Mister Po is most welcome. We may have other products he might find valuable in the future. A happy customer is a repeat customer."

The police car drove past the alley a second time. John's face was visible in the red and blue light. His customers only saw the scar that ran across his broad cheek. John saw fear in their eyes.

"Our business is done for now. We should be on our way," the young man said.

John nodded, turned, and opened his car door. They returned

to their vehicle. John pushed the drive into the card reader in the dash and uploaded it to Zoe. "Is that what we were looking for?"

Zoe went dead silent for a few seconds, then replied, "Our team confirms. These are the complete plans and specs for all Samedi Organization-funded bioresearch facilities." John could hear the difference in her voice and wondered how long, in those brief seconds in his timeframe, her teams had scoured the data to establish its authenticity. A week? "Yang-Eun must really have beef with High Sun. We should be able to retrieve what we need with these documents."

The Jaguar made its way into traffic and was gone. John started his Mercedes and pulled out after it. As he navigated to the hotel, he said, "Okay, *Princess Bride* it is."

Zoe emitted a short squeak. "Really?"

John smiled. "Really. Have some microwave popcorn delivered to my room. You have popcorn there?"

Zoe laughed. "Always. I love our movie nights."

John shook his head. "I may cry. I'm warning you now."

Zoe was silent for a moment. "You are such an idiot. Don't you know? That's one of the reasons I—" She fell silent.

John sniffed. "I knew that. 'Course. It's one of my most endearing—"

"John."

"Yeah?"

"Shut up."

Zoe disconnected, and John drove through Seoul in silence.

What was this? What had this become? Where could this *go*? The questions that always arose when Zoe's voice wasn't in his head, when he was alone with his thoughts of her. It was now four years since he resurrected and joined The Lost Boys as their leader—four years since he and Zoe became partners in every sense of the word.

They spent so many nights together in the early years, waiting for some event to occur in her history book and his future. Waiting to swap a briefcase while a businessman was

distracted for that one blink of an eye. Waiting for an unforesee-
able car accident on a lonely highway, miles from nowhere.
Waiting to rescue another genius or poet or engineer or math-
ematician bound for Nunavut. As they waited, they talked.
They grew close… and then closer. He could see her in his
Aurora when he closed his eyes at night. She could see him
through his own eyes in the foggy mirror when he shaved in
the morning. Her voice was inside his head, *literally* in his
bones.

And her voice was—her voice, her laughter still thrilled him.
Late at night, purring into his implant, or waking him with a
whisper in his ear. The audio felt so intimate he could hear every
pop and sibilance—it was almost as if she was here with him
right now.

But she could never be here. *She was not now.*

He couldn't touch her. He was afraid to ask *when* she was
exactly, and she likely wouldn't be able to say. They'd danced
around it coyly but never crossed that line. He knew she was
beyond Downfall, beyond 2036, but how much further? He'd
never been able to tie that down. If she were in her mid-30s—he'd
done the math over and over. Zoe, the current Zoe, was out here
in the world right now. But she was how many years younger?
10? 20? Was she even born yet? With his line of work, would he
still be alive in her time?

Tonight, they would watch *The Princess Bride*. Together.
Forever apart in time and space. She would pipe her video feed
through Aurora. Her avatar would sit on the bed next to him.
Aurora's stereo simulation would make it feel like their own
private theater. They would munch popcorn in each other's ears
and laugh at Vizzini and Montoya. *Inconceivable!* They would sigh
at the fate of the young lovers. They would cry at the happy
ending.

Together.

Then, as always, they would say a slow, lingering good night.
John would drift to sleep with a smile, and Zoe, at some other

time and some other place, would drift off to sleep and dream of him as well.

He parked his car and rode the elevator to his floor. Saturday night party people joined him from the lobby to the mezzanine. Then he completed his ride in silence. He entered his room with a quiet click to find a package of popcorn, placed on Zoe's orders by housekeeping, atop his microwave. He smiled and tapped on her icon in his Aurora.

"Hey, you."

TIMESTAMP CLASSIFIED

"You are in position. You should go." Zoe looked out of John's eyes at the lights of the Seoul skyline.

Warrant Officer Laura Roth maintained the horizontal position of the WhisperPod so expertly the thing looked like it was bolted to the sky. She had engaged the holofilm before entering Inchon International airspace. They were invisible from the street and virtually silent as they hung above the Mindful Joy Limited Partnership Research Facility. Robin and John stood on the aircraft's skids. Robin positioned the hefty swivel arm supporting the arresting gear. He turned and nodded to John. In black from head to toe, he was strapped into a harness attached to the overhead decelerator.

John looked back at Robin, gave a quick thumbs-up, and said, "Okay. Away we go." He stepped off the transport's skid and dropped toward the rooftop below. Zoe marveled at his rocksteady heartbeat. He fell twenty stories, and his BPM never rose above seventy-five.

Robin monitored the diamond fiber filament as it unspooled. John arched his back as he dove, gracefully guided by the invisible black line. As he neared the rooftop, the decelerator exerted the right amount of continuous force to slow him to a stop. He pivoted with the grace of a dancer, stepped onto the roof, and unclipped the tether. The invisibly thin line retracted skyward. "Laura, you better get some altitude."

The pilot responded, "Way ahead of you, boss. Climbing. This thing flies like a rock without electronics."

John gave the WhisperPod time to get clear before shutting down his Aurora and triggering his pocket EMP. There was an audible pop from a service panel on the roof behind him, and the building went black. The rush of HVAC units slowed to a stop. He knelt, clicked open the hatch at his feet, and climbed into darkness.

Zoe could now monitor John only via his shielded audio implant—and only if he initiated contact. She could only sit and monitor the WhisperPod's position and the Seoul police's status in the area.

The available surveillance sources saved to the cloud from 2029 to 2036 facilitated her ability to assist John. That is to say, she usually had more sources than she could use. In every major city of the time, she had access to thousands of state LEO cameras, business security cameras, and even doorbells and dash-cams. She could direct dozens of American NRO satellites to peek down at John in a pinch if no one had them tasked. All of these were sending a continuous stream into the cloud via fiber, ethernet, Wi-Fi, cellular, and even old-school twisted-pair copper wires in some cases. At Oracle's orders, all of it had been meticulously and covertly crawled and scraped by an SDS IT team numbering in the tens of thousands aided by deep machine learning and LLM AI.

All of it was available to her. The analysts in C-Dome and their array of AI tools had been at work since 2029, before the establishment of the NTC, cloning this information, tagging it, and organizing it for missions like these. Thousands of missions and hundreds of agents across the six years from 2029 to 2036. Zoe often marveled at how dreadfully boring that work must have been. Sorting the overwhelming pile of bullshit that was the internet in the the first third of the 21st century was a monolithic task. She knew that much of it was processed by AI, but even with machines sorting and sifting, human minds had to add the final context because machines made shit up sometimes. All of it was at her fingertips instantly as she worked with John Banks on these missions.

But John's pocket EMP knocked out all the surveillance systems in a roughly one-hundred-meter sphere, creating a bubble of data shadow.

She hated being in the dark like this. It would have fried his Aurora if he hadn't powered it down. She was far happier being John's miracle worker, the angel on his broad shoulder. She loved it when she could use Oneiri tech to put a rideshare vehicle right at his elbow as he turned a corner in time to evade a pursuer. She loved helping John disappear like magic, or be in the precise right place at the precise right time to foil a criminal conspiracy years in the planning. They were a team.

Partners.

She had seen how resilient he was. She had seen him place his life in her hands and monitored his vitals as he did—his heart was as steady as a metronome. His faith in her was gobsmacking. It was absolutely vital to their mission, but that didn't make her heart swell any less every time he demonstrated it.

She had fallen in love with him. Desperately, bone-deep in love.

It was absolute madness. It made no sense from any point of view in *any* timeframe.

He was aware that she lived in some vague future. He didn't know, however—and she could never tell him without creating a Roberts' Rules violation—that they had actually met in her lifetime, not yet in his. It was years ago, and he was years older than her John, perhaps thirty years her senior. They'd met in the worst of human circumstances. He had made terrible choices. Necessary but terrible. Though she'd resented him in the early years, she had sorted through those feelings. She saw him now as *her* hero, plain and simple.

She couldn't reconcile her feelings for a man who lived in another time and another place. But she could also not deny them.

John reestablished his connection, suddenly shouting. "Zoe, a little help?"

She could hear gunfire. She pulled up the schematics of the research facility. "What floor?"

"I'm on the 12th floor, west side. Um. Office number…" A gunshot ricocheted near enough that Zoe ducked at the sound. Her eyes widened. "Office number 1245A."

"Did you just stick your head out to look at the office number?" Zoe heard John fire three rounds.

John said, "Well. You know me."

"One second." Zoe set the time frame to a few minutes earlier and contacted Robin. "Get the transport to the west side. Drop the cargo web and be prepared to take a load. I'm sending him your way." She monitored Robin in that timeframe and coordinated with his handler Jeremy while continuing to speak to John in his, multi-threading her Oneiri device. "Okay. I need you to shoot out the west side window and jump out."

John paused. "You want me to jump out a twelfth-story office window?"

Zoe shouted. "It's just like our initiation! Robin will be there. Do it now!"

"That was three stories! And they were only shooting paintballs!"

"Trust me!"

"I hate this idea." She heard his Glock firing—once again, his life in her hands. The sound of glass shattering was followed by traffic sounds below and the rush of air as he shouted, "*Aaaas Yoouuu Wiiiish.*"

She heard automatic weapons fire following him. Wait. Did he just quote *The Princess Bride?* She laughed suddenly then…

Then she heard silence.

She shouted at Robin. "Do you have him? Robin, do you have

John?" Her ears filled with a rush of wind. Zoe's hands balled into fists.

Silence.

Silence.

"I got him," Robin said. "Fuck if that guy doesn't weigh a ton. We dipped down two floors before the rotors compensated. Those NTC nerds make tough little flying machines."

John's Aurora rebooted. He clung to the cargo webbing hanging beneath the electric flyer. He pulled himself into the cabin and laughed as Laura gained altitude. "Zoe?" John asked, "You still there?"

Zoe shouted back, "AM *I* STILL HERE?!"

He laughed again. "I'm all right, Tink."

She was angry. She felt helpless. Tears welled up in her deep brown eyes.

"Good news!" John laughed. "I got the research on the final release of GGB-Z. Let's get it to NTC."

She wiped her eyes and dragged a sweater sleeve across her wet nose. Intellectually, she knew he wouldn't die in that time-frame. He couldn't. That wave function had collapsed. None of that mattered. In the moment, she was terrified of losing him.

She heard John laughing with Robin as they sped away toward Inchon International. By the time they arrived, she was laughing along with them.

"*JAMES!*"

John bolted awake with sweat pouring off him. His motel bed sheets were drenched. The AC unit beneath the window was cranked up; the room was uncomfortably cool. He tossed the sheets aside and stood in the dark, walking by feel to the bathroom. He shivered once, a tremor of tension releasing. He heard a ping in his head. He tapped accept, and Zoe was there.

"Are you all right?" she asked.

"I am."

"I almost broke in. Your vitals…"

"Please don't monitor my vitals while I'm sleeping."

"That is literally part of my job."

"Yeah. Haven't we moved beyond that, Zoe?" he asked tersely.

He could use the excuse that he wasn't fully awake. Sure.

"Is it the same dream?"

John didn't answer.

"I've known you long enough to know you wake two or three times a week with a—"

"Yeah. It's the same dream."

"They're getting worse?"

"Worse?"

"More frequent?"

"Yeah."

John turned on the light and stared at himself in the mirror. The perspiration was already dried. He poured himself a glass of water. He was only marginally sensitive to the fact that he was naked, and whatever he saw of his body—his dick—she could see as well. In over five years, she'd seen it before.

"Do you want to talk about it?"

He drank the water in three deep gulps and set the glass down.

"You going to be my therapist now, Zoe?"

"I'm trying to be your friend, John."

John walked out to the bed, propped the pillows against the headboard, and sat back. He closed his eyes.

"My brother James. The dream is about my brother, James. We were up in Minnesota. My grandparents had a cabin in a little town called Silica. One time, my folks decided we should see what winter was like in Northern Minnesota. It's not that different from Nunavut weather, honestly." He looked at his reflection in the mirror opposite the bed.

"My father, my brother James, and I decided we'd do my grandfather a solid and shovel his driveway after an early snowstorm dumped eight inches of snow on us. I'd never seen anything like it. My dad was probably what? 42? James was twelve. Stupid. Funny. Smarter than me by a mile. Pain in the ass. Heart the size of the sun. I was seventeen. I was at the peak of my self-centered jock phase. I was a big boy even then, and I could play any sort of sportsball you could throw at me. Football— Varsity All-Star. Baseball—Varsity All-Star. Basketball—Varsity Team Captain."

"Impressive."

"Yeah. I sure thought so." John didn't brighten at her teasing compliment as he usually did. "Well, we were out in the cold. My dad and I had shovel duty. James got a chance to drive my grandfather's four-wheeler. It had a snowblower fitting, and he's having the time of his life. Shooting fountains of snow twenty feet in the air. I mean, after a snowfall in Silica, the sky is so blue, and the sun is so bright, you think *nothing bad* could happen."

He went silent. When he started again, his throat was constricted.

"Well. James. He finished the driveway while we were still only halfway done with the walkway. So, he started spinning donuts."

He went silent again. His eyes shimmered.

"Somehow—I guess his foot got stuck—They said his foot got stuck on the accelerator. He panicked. He raced past me and Dad, screaming. I thought he was fucking around. James was a— anyway. It wasn't till he was halfway across the flood plain headed toward the lake that I realized he was in trouble. I tore off after him. Running—in brand new snow pants and snow boots my mom got us for the trip—but I ran. I caught up to him, I did. I had my hand on him as we hit the ice."

John stopped talking. Zoe let him. After a few seconds, he continued.

"I caught up to him, and I could reach him…" He was breathing heavily now. Tears were falling from his staring eyes. His heart rate was elevated. He bit his lower lip. "But when we hit the ice—"

The lump in his throat made any further speaking impossible. His tears were flowing in sheets now.

"Oh, John."

John wiped his face roughly with a sheet corner and sniffed.

"It was a long time ago, Zoe," he croaked. "A long time."

"It was ten minutes ago."

"What?"

"You just dreamed about it ten minutes ago. It's that fresh."

"Yeah." He felt purged a little, spent. "I guess."

"Why do you think you're dreaming about him now? Why more frequently?"

"Because I'm not the hero Stephen Lucas *thinks* I am."

"What?"

"He built me up in his head as a big, goddamned, world-saving hero." John sniffed again and wiped the last wetness away. "I'm not that guy he needs me to be so he can sleep at night. He has me trying to put the world back together after he knocked it over like… like a cat pushing a snow globe off a shelf."

"But you have done so much!"

"Zoe, it's not something *anyone* can do. The world was trying to destroy itself long before Cliff Price finished the job. It's out there right now, trying to end itself. The Oneiri device isn't the first time humanity built something to knock it back to the Stone Age. I can't be the hero—"

"John. Stop."

"Stop what?"

A window popped up in John's Aurora. It was a video of the last orientation day at NTC. Central Park in A-Dome was at over-flow capacity as Athena Shaw welcomed them.

"You have been responsible for saving all the lives, all those families at NTC." She switched to an aerial shot of the eighteen completed domes and the nine newly poured foundations stretching northward. "There will be well over a million taking refuge after Downfall hits."

"It's not enough."

She threw pictures of shipping containers stacked in empty lots, hundreds of pictures, each stamped with their locations around the world. She showed a map. Pins of all those containers blotted out every landmass.

"Provisions for survivors. It was your idea to place the doomsday prep provisions in shipping containers all around the world. Anonymous, invisible shipping containers. They're every-where, in vacant lots in every city and town around the world, and no one wonders what's inside them. No one looks twice at them. History will ignore them. It was your idea to place provi-sions in plain sight of history—ready when they'll be needed. MREs, medical supplies, clothing, canned goods, water."

"Zoe!" He shouted into the dark, empty room. "It's not *enough*."

He was quiet for a while, and she closed the windows in his feed.

"We've done everything we can, Commander Banks."

"I know." He sighed. "Tomorrow, we come face to face with the real enemy. I've been dreading it. I don't think I admitted it to myself. Up to now, it's been all fun and games. Lost Boys playing in Neverland. Magic tricks and sleight of hand." He frowned. "Tomorrow, we begin the real war. Y'know? I've been through one war."

"John. I love you."

He was shocked out of his concerns. His eyebrows lifted from their frown, and his eyes widened.

"What?"

Zoe laughed sweetly. "You heard me."

"I—"

"Shut up for a minute. No. I've never said it out loud before." She now turned silent, and he waited for her. "I have worked with you and watched you. I've seen your courage, your strength, and your compassion with everyone in your command. I've seen the intelligence you bring to bear on the impossible problem that Stephen Lucas has given you to solve. *You're right*. It isn't enough." He could hear her smile. "But I can't imagine anyone else doing anything more, anything better." They sat in silence for a moment. "I don't know Stephen Lucas. I watched his interviews back in the day. He seemed like a spoiled, egomaniac brat."

John smiled. He loved it when she was on a roll.

"Sure, he seemed like a genius, but the *only* thing I like about him is that he was *your friend*." She was quiet for a moment. "But here's the thing: I can't imagine anyone I'd trust to accomplish this task more than you. I agree with his assessment. You *are* that hero."

"But, I—"

"You aren't going to be able to save *all* the good people, John," Zoe said. "No hero can. It took me far too long to realize—"

"I love you too."

"I know."

John smiled.

Zoe's avatar disappeared. In its place, a window of her Aurora feed appeared. She stood in front of a full-length mirror in what John guessed was her bedroom. This was not an avatar, but Zoe in the flesh, seen in a mirror through her own eyes. It was a first for John. The lights were low, candle light. She was wearing a black negligee. She was so beautiful.

"Hey, you," he said.

"Hey."

10-10-35 1:00 PM EDT

Robin shoved a hot dog into his face faster than he could chew. John glanced at him as he pulled up to the red light.

"What?"

"Is it good?"

Robin finished chewing and wiped a bit of mustard from his lip. "It's the *best*. I haven't had a street hotdog in three years. The protein-sequenced hot dogs at NTC are *not* hot dogs. I figure we're a year away from no more actual hot dogs."

He and John were both dressed as local Miami EMTs. Their ambulance was an exact match to those of the Florida Mercy Hospital. John was tired, but his stress level was rising again.

"Zoe, how are we doing on time?"

"You're fine." Zoe's audio was routed to Robin's feed as well.

"Did Ramirez and Oz intercept the other ambulance?"

"They did. Their EMP did the trick. They'll be late on the scene. You'll be right on time."

"Okay." He smiled and forced himself to ease his grip on the steering wheel.

Robin looked back at the crates in the back of the bus. He rubbed his arm unconsciously, the arm he'd been injected in when the Lost Boys all received the GGB-Z mRNA vaccine. It had been eighteen days. Any immunity they might have would be at its peak effectiveness. It had not been tested yet because exposing anyone to the actual real-world live virus would be unethical. How do you ask volunteers to risk becoming a soulless, blood-thirsty demon in the name of science?

The decision had been made to only test against a real-world threat. He, John, Ramirez, and Oz were the lab rats. Robin leaned his head back and rested it on the back wall of the cab to feel the engine's vibration.

The light changed. John turned onto Rickenbacker Causeway, and Robin sat up. John flipped a switch, and the lights and siren screamed to life. He accelerated and pulled out to pass the slower traffic headed for Key Biscayne. They headed out over the bay, and John floored it. Flying over Virginia Key and through Crandon Park, they passed golf carts and overly-tanned elderly women walking their cockapoos in the summer heat. A right on Harbor Drive and the ambulance screeched to a halt in front of the Yacht Club. Tennis players rubber-necked as John and Robin pulled backboards from the rear of the bus and ran into the building to find two demons rampaging in the club's overpriced dining room.

These were the first two in the hemisphere. Before this, there had only been a handful of infections worldwide. They doubled every two weeks. First one, then two, then four. This week, there would be eight. Next week sixteen. The inexorable, exponential pattern that would end next September with infections all around the world. But today, they had these two.

Karen and Chad Davis, members in good standing of the Biscayne Yacht Club and self-described world travelers, had been feeling poorly for two weeks. Nothing life-threatening, they were sure. Just a touch of the flu, or so they told everyone they had shaken hands with or sneezed on since their Hawaiian vacation.

Karen and Chad did everything together. They sailed together. They golfed together. They were soul mates and best friends after twenty years of marriage. Twelve minutes ago, during their lunch of battered and fried soft-shell crabs, they had collapsed together, too.

John had been hoping to arrive while they were still seizing and immobile. But there had been video rolling, sending the live birth of America's first GGB-Z demons out to millions on social media. Karen had risen first in a halting, bizarre series of jerks and spasms. The kind-hearted waitstaff, a young Cuban-American girl and a pimple-ridden white boy, scrambled away from her as she lunged, desperate to get her teeth into them. Kevin joined Karen within a minute as the patrons struggled to process what the fuck was going on.

"On your left is the source of our video feed," Zoe said, and sure enough, a cute teenager stood rapt with a journalist's zeal to capture the action. John accidentally knocked the phone from her hand with his backboard, and the girl's mobile made a satisfying *zzzipt* as it hit the marble floor.

"And that explains why the video stopped short," Zoe said.

The rush of patrons exiting the dining room into the Yacht Club lobby concluded, leaving demon Karen and demon Chad alone among the overturned chairs and empty tables. John and Robin rushed in, both thinking only one thing.

"I sure hope this vaccine does the trick," Robin said.

"Yeah." John smiled.

Robin couldn't figure out what had cheered him up overnight.

The demons noticed them and began to sniff the air in their direction. Robin thought the term *demon* was an apt one. They didn't look human anymore, didn't move like people.

"Their eyes," John said, and Robin nodded.Karen and Chad's eyes were ruined, black and blood-stained animal eyes. Robin dropped his backboard, reached down, and unclipped his holster. He raised a dart gun as Chad tilted his head like a dog listening to a Slim Whitman single. John raised his dart gun, too.

"Put on your red shoes and dance the blues," Robin said.

John smiled, and they moved in toward their targets.

Karen's hand found a chair and dragged it behind her. Then she lowered her head, her mouth fell open, and she roared. It was a horrible, alien, god-awful, guttural noise. Chad, focused on Robin like a laser, followed suit, joining his animal howl with hers. They sounded like rhinos preparing to charge.

Then they charged. Robin and John fired and fired and fired again. Each of their darts found a home in the Davis's chests, the orange fluffy feathers reminding Robin briefly of clown hair.

The demons screamed louder and pawed at the darts. Two of Chad's darts fell away. It didn't matter; the drug was delivered. The question was, would the massive dose of blood thinners, anti-virals, and elephant-dropping sedatives get their job done?

Karen continued her charge.

Chad suddenly looked directly at the overhead chandelier. He emitted a strange whimpering creak. Then his knees buckled, and he collapsed.

Karen sprinted for John. Robin watched as John dropped his gun, leaned down to pick up the backboard, and swung like a pro baseball player going for a home run. The sound of Karen Davis' head as the board hit it echoed in the dining room. She sailed back and to John's left, then struggled to her knees with another roar. John raised the carbon fiber and resin board again.

Then the drugs finally kicked in, and she dropped into a nearby chair and gurgled into unconsciousness.

"And the crowd goes wild," John said.

Robin turned, grabbed his board, and knelt beside Chad as Ramirez and Oz arrived. Within a few minutes, the team had the GGB-Z victims strapped in and transported to their ambulance. Each demon was deposited in their custom transport crate, which cooled their bodies to 72°F and fed them carefully controlled doses of another cocktail of drugs. The crates were closed, sealed, and prepared for their nine-hour flight to Nunavut. The two teams raced off, sirens blaring, for Miami International.

John turned to Robin.

"Okay, two demons down," he said. "V-Dome has the development data. Now they have some live subjects. We have a vaccine. Maybe a cure will follow."

Robin leaned his head back against the back of the cab and felt the vibrations of the road.

"Two down. Two *billion* to go. Easy peasy."

"How hard could it be?"

5-1-36 7:30 PM EDT: THE MASQUE

BAXTER'S HELICOPTER landed at dusk. He was feeling chipper. His home was already filled to bursting with the world's most wealthy, most depraved, and most beautiful individuals the human race had produced through four billion years of evolution. These were the apex predators, the survivors, and soon they would rule openly and mercilessly. Baxter smiled radiantly as he stepped out of the aircraft and walked across the inlaid stonework of his helipad. Gone were any of his fears and doubts from a few months earlier. His pewter hair was unruffled by the slowing downdraft of the rotor.

Inside the forty-foot-tall picture windows of his ballroom, he could see his guests whirling in dance and sparkling with lively conversation. This was the first Pentacula Masque in over thirty years, and Baxter intended to return the events to their former costumed glory. The last Masque had been on the eve of their most tremendous success, the 9/11 missions to tilt the world's power dynamic away from the masses and back toward their betters. This Masque celebrated an even more impressive victory.

A new world order was coming and they would be its rulers.

Baxter's new understanding had been brought about through the instruction of Melissa Jones. Her series of presentations on the rules that govern time machines cleared up his own doubts that perhaps the world was governed by a true supreme being. She convinced him that the works of Cliff Price, The Black Empty, were not miracles, but they *were* immutable. His actions in the future could not be changed. Baxter could no more stop what was coming than he could stop the setting sun.

Though it had taken some time to wrap his head around The Black Empty's vision of Hell on Earth, Baxter had come to accept the inevitable logic of it. It was only when he realized it was, in its essence, the induction of the entire human race into the Pentacula in one orgiastic ceremony of meaning Baxter could fully align himself with The Black Empty. His only regret was that he had arrived at that enlightenment so late in the process. But, though his faith had been lacking, his performance as The Black Empty's agent had been equal to the remuneration.

"Good evening, Dr. Baxter," his head butler shouted from the edge of the topiary separating the helipad from the Roque court.

"Good evening, Robert," he replied, handing him his briefcase and coat. "It looks like everyone is here."

"For the most part, sir. Mrs. Baxter demanded the dancing begin at seven."

"And the medical staff?"

"They are set up in the parlor and have been administering the vaccine since five."

"Excellent." He stopped momentarily as he admired the view of his guests reveling in the warm lights of the ballroom's four enormous fireplaces and the crystal chandelier. "So much power under one roof. So much fabulous power."

"It is inspiring, sir."

"It is indeed."

———

"Darling." Melania Baxter leaned close to smack air kisses two inches from each of Kenneth's ears. "I thought you'd abandoned me to the mob."

"This is the furthest from a mob you could get, my dear." He looked around the main floor of the ballroom, up to the mezzanine filled with lively conversation, and finally craned his neck to the balcony, lined with a quieter cohort observing the dance. In keeping with Pentacula tradition, all were dressed in elegant 19th-century suits and gowns, and all wore elaborate and expensive masks of every shape and size. It was a shame to hide their supreme, undeniable beauty but, Baxter thought, hiding that beauty made it, perhaps, more intriguing.

"You *know* what I mean, Kenneth," Melania whined, already showing signs of boredom.

As the dancers whirled to the band's whimsical, harpsichord-rich tune, Baxter noticed the black Band-Aids marked with the silver pentagram on most of the women's upper arms.

"I see the vaccination is proceeding as planned."

Melania nodded and lifted her toile shoulder decorations to show her Band-Aid. "Yes, Dr. Baxter."

"Excellent. Excellent." He lifted a fluted glass of champagne from a nearby waiter and gave Melania a quick air kiss. "I'm going to get my shot before I fully join the festivities. We should dance."

Melania rolled her eyes at his retreating back.

Baxter skirted the dance floor, nodding and smiling at his guests. He knew each of them, what they wanted, what secrets they kept hidden from the world, and what crimes they committed to attain their positions. As he walked, a hand would jut out every few seconds and he would shake it firmly as he passed. He was the only one without a mask, but it was his party, his house. Soon, it would be his world.

He had finished his champagne by the time he reached the back doors of the ballroom and handed the glass to a waiter before turning back to watch the crowd. His eyes were sparkling with the firelight and the joy of knowing that all these beautiful, ambitious creatures were beholden to him in thousands of ways. There was not a one he couldn't destroy utterly.

He continued down the hallway to the parlor. The vaccination line stretched almost to the foyer. Entering the massive mahogany double doors, he nodded to Dr. Mengel, a dark and severe man. Mengel's four nurses worked quickly and efficiently, moving from the small refrigerators with trays of black glass ampules and disposable needles. Each guest took their turn in the red leather Eames chairs and bared an arm. They endured a few questions, an alcohol swab, and a quick jab from the black vials of vaccine.

Baxter walked to the head of the line, and the young man he cut in front of bowed his head slightly with a smile. In a moment, he was injected, bandaged, and back on his feet. Now, he was immune to the coming plague that would burn the world away. They all were. The demons had been appearing for months, if one knew what news sources to trust—first in South Korea, the Caribbean, and London. Just a few individual cases at first. So far, the frequency of the outbreaks had been sporadic and random. It would be months before the Stage Three infected became common enough for anyone but paranoid fantasists to connect the dots. By then, the world would be burning and nothing would stop it.

Baxter thanked the nurse and nodded again to Mengel. Mengel's team had coordinated the simultaneous distribution of the vaccine to each and every Pentaculum and assured that each house medical team had the proper orientation materials. Before the morning light, every major and minor house, and their agents and familiars, would be properly proofed against the coming wave of demonic plague.

His four primary pentaculum congregants, all male, waited for him as he emerged from the parlor. They'd dropped their masks but, dressed in their tailcoats and cravats, they looked as Baxter imagined the conspirators of John Booth might have looked, preparing for a night at Ford's Theater.

"How was your jab, Dr. Baxter?" the taller of the four asked.

"No worse than the latest Covid booster," Baxter said as he walked to his elevator. "I was just going up to change into something more…Victorian." He gestured to them all. "Come, you can brief me on our progress."

Baxter pressed the button, and the doors opened to reveal an interior of black marble with ivory buttons and dark brass fittings. He entered, and they followed. Their various colognes combined and competed in the ride to the top floor of Baxter's home.

"Two, how goes Project White?"

"Distribution vectors have already shown the anticipated effectiveness. Infections continue to double every 19 days. Incubation periods vary from one month to up to three months—exactly as our friends in Seoul guaranteed. Using flight attendants and concert venue staff as initial viral hosts was more effective than any other category. With an R-naught value of six, we expect to see an infection rate worldwide of 60% by the end of the summer and as high as 95% when school begins in the fall."

"So, on target."

The car arrived, the doors parted, and they entered Baxter's bedroom. They'd each been there before in various combinations for various activities. Baxter proceeded to remove his twentieth-century garb as the four younger men watched.

"Three? Project Red?" Baxter dropped his trousers.

"The misinformation campaign has been solid. U.S. Intelligence agencies have swallowed that Russia is developing a bioweapon and a vaccine. There is some chatter of a research presence in northern Canada, but we've coopted that chatter and diverted it to finger the Russians. Our operatives have been back-washing the intel to the Russians to increase their general state of anti-Western paranoia. We've got a few former Soviet scientists working to reinvigorate their aging nuke sites. We'll be ready."

Baxter sat shirtless on his four-poster bed and removed his socks.

"With that crusty old badger Morales appointed as her DNI, your team has an easy row to hoe, it seems. The Director has always seen the Russians behind *every* global catastrophe. I've placed Melissa Jones in his office. She'll provide the proper push when needed. She's also our best analyst of the Oneiri device and its peculiarities. She's with one of my lower echelon Pentacula. Not a major house."

He stood, letting his red silk boxers fall to the Persian rug, naked and unabashed before them.

"I'm going to take a quick rinse. Just be a minute."

The four men sat patiently while their host entered the bath and turned on the shower.

"95% by September?"

"Yes."

"That's terribly good, isn't it?"

"Those South Korean biotech firms are top-notch."

"Truly. Terribly good."

Baxter emerged, still toweling himself off.

"Four?"

"Project Black is on target as well, Baxter. The terrorist cells are putting the funding to good use. Recruitment is up across the board, but the fundamentalist religious factions are going gangbusters. The entire operation is self-perpetuating now. I daresay we could all be hit by a bus and the operation would still go off without a hitch at the appointed time."

"Excellent. Suicide bombers are never in short supply among the faithful," Baxter said as he pulled his cream, fall-front trousers over his silk socks and made the lower buttons fast. He threw on his white, high-collar shirt and nimbly buttoned it up.

"And Five?"

"Senator Rand believes he has the votes for the next board meeting in August. That makes him the CEO of One by September."

"That strikes me as optimistic," Baxter said as he tied his cravat. "Donald Rand is an idiot. It disturbs me that we couldn't get anyone better in that position."

"I agree, sir. In any case, he *will* be in position to acquire the MacGuffin when the development is complete."

"That man could fuck up a perfectly good wet dream. We should have contingencies for everything. Once The Emptiness topples the current world order, we have a very narrow window. *Hell is coming to Earth, gentlemen.*" He pulled on his tailcoat and secured the last button of his vest. "I intend to be the *ruler* of Hell, and I intend you to be my vassals."

"Yes, sir."

"Good job, everyone." He patted his upper arm. "We are immune to the coming evils. Let's enjoy the delights of this night and put our long-term plans on the agenda for tomorrow."

He pressed the elevator button, and Two straightened his cravat lovingly. Three handed him his ebony cane. They entered the car, and Baxter pressed the button for the ballroom balcony.

They emerged men of power, with a swagger denoting their privilege. Baxter walked to the balcony rail and surveyed the dance floor. As if encouraged by his presence above, the band launched into a spirited waltz with a dizzying leitmotif of piccolo and strings.

The dancers appeared choreographed, cutting swirling, spiraling patterns across the parquet floor. The waiter appeared, and the vassals each snatched a glass. They toasted Doctor Baxter silently as they donned their ornate masks. The band's music continued to pick up pace and took on a sinister, primal rhythm that compelled the dancers to pick up speed. Baxter's pulse skipped a few beats. And he felt a strange flush as he sipped his champagne. Someone below dropped their champagne glass, and a titter of laughter erupted above the harpsichord.

Baxter's vision blurred but then returned to normal. He gripped the railing until his balance returned. Perhaps a slight side effect of the shot. His arm *was* sore. After a moment, his discomfort passed. He gazed down at his guests as the harpsichord and three violins took up the spiraling motif and accelerated it. Melania took to the dance floor with a man in a red jacket and a black mask. In a moment, they had become lost to his eyes among the crowded dancers.

A waiter arrived. Baxter downed his champagne and handed him the empty. Suddenly, his underlings were gone. He felt parched. His teeth found the inside of his cheek and began to chew on it absentmindedly.

He owed Melania that dance.

He took a deep, cleansing breath, stood up straight, and nodded to a young couple nearby as he made his way to the spiral staircase.

Around he went, around and down to the Mezzanine. The guests there seemed quiet and self-absorbed. No one was talking. They just stood and stared into their own infinity. He continued down the staircase to the main floor. For a moment, his spiraling steps matched the hypnotizing beat of the harpsichord, and he nearly stumbled. He caught himself before he fell with a hand on the marble rail. He'd had too much to drink, perhaps.

Wait.

He'd only had two glasses of champagne. His arm really did ache. He regained his balance as the music increased its manic tempo. Then, from the ballroom, sounded a dreadful crash and a shriek. This time, there was no laughter. Only gasps and then stunned silence. Even the dizzying harpsichord and the band halted in uncoordinated, clumsy disharmony.

"Call 911!" a man shouted.

"Where's Dr. Baxter?" another shouted.

Baxter hurried from the stairway and found the crowd surrounding the dance floor.

"Here I am!" he shouted. "What's wrong?"

The crowd turned to look at him, then they parted, and he saw the dance floor emptied. In the center of the polished parquet, a man's body lay face down in a heap, its right arm twisted backward at an angle that was hard to look at. Baxter rushed forward.

"Get Doctor Mengel in the parlor." He felt for a pulse and found one. It was slow and arhythmic. There was almost no blood. The guests were murmuring and looking up at the mezzanine. "Did he fall from the mezzanine?" He looked up and saw the guests looking down from the floor above and the balcony above that. They didn't look right. Most had removed their masks or pulled them to the side. They stared blankly at the commotion on the dance floor. But there was something strange in their eyes. It must be a trick of the light.

"Does anyone know who this is?" Baxter asked, afraid to roll him over. As he looked about for an answer, the body of the fallen man began to quake. It startled Baxter, and he jerked his hand back. The man's body heaved again. Then the poor man jolted, kicked and flipped onto his back, the twisted, broken arm flopping sickeningly. His eyes were wide open, and they were shot through with blood. His diaphragm clenched and squeezed a roaring gurgle from his lungs. Baxter kicked back away from the injured man.

He had clearly landed face-first. His nose was crushed. *That explains the hemorrhaging eyes*, Baxter thought dully.

"He's seizing!" Baxter shouted. "Where's Mengel?"

The injured man spasmed into a sitting position. His broken face turned to Baxter, and his jaw, tilted at a mad dislocated angle, chomped the air lazily. He took a deep, rattling breath, then explosively lunged to his feet and scrambled toward Baxter.

Baxter screamed like a child. He jumped and shoved and elbowed his way to safety behind the crowd. The injured man did not care. He leaped onto the nearest guest, a woman with green hair and enormous silicone breasts, and sunk his teeth into the soft tissue of her neck. The broken jaw frustrated his effort, but his body weight, momentum, and animal desire got the job done. Baxter watched a fountain of red blood spout up and over the crowd as he recoiled and fell backwards onto his ass.

The crowd gaped for half a second before losing their fucking minds.

Scuttling backward like a crab, Baxter reached the leg of his 100-year-old Jacobean buffet, a stout, hand-carved monstrosity. He found refuge under its six-inch oak legs as the guests scattered for the exits, any exits. Had he not clung to the thing, he would have been trampled under their blind flight to safety.

He looked up at the curiously sedate gathering on the mezzanine as a few leaned over the railing with dull looks of what? Hunger? As he watched, three of his guests scampered onto the railing and leaped into the panicked, fleeing mob. What the *hell* was going on? Baxter shook his head, felt a strange twinge in his left eye, heard an odd little *pop*, and suddenly he was seeing double. My god, he was feeling thirsty. His mind felt like it was wrapped in steel wool.

He crawled out the backside of the buffet and found a place to stand against the wall as the crowd dissipated. The three new jumpers were finding their way to their feet. The first man, the one who had tried to attack him, was hunched over the green-haired woman and was ripping his head back and forth. Blood flowed over him and onto the polished wood floor. The other jumpers dove for the growing puddle and lapped at it eagerly. It did look *delicious*. It did look…

Baxter shook his head again. He was aware of a ruckus by the large picture window doors leading to the helipad. The guests that swarmed there struggled with them.

"The doors are locked! The doors are locked!" a woman screamed.

Her shout drew the attention of the jumpers, and they rose, blood-drenched with those queer, blackened, ruptured eyes. They scampered toward the guests in a stuttering, crazy sprint. They each found a dance partner and tackled them as the rest turned and pounded on the doors.

Good luck with that, thought Baxter. *Those doors are bulletproof 3/4 inch acrylic.*

Or did he say that out loud? His thinking was clearly affected by the champagne. He grabbed another from a tray on the buffet and made his way to the stairwell. The sound of screaming, flesh tearing and blood gurgling was, to his ear, a different sort of music.

"Where is that *harpsichord?* I paid good money for a *harpsichord!*" he shouted as he staggered up the spiraling stairs. He passed several of his guests; some were weeping, some were seizing, and some were making out... or were they feeding? Baxter was losing focus. The champagne was hitting him hard, but it wasn't quenching his thirst.

On the mezzanine, the guests who had fled the ballroom had found no escape. It was a different kind of dance up there. Plenty of screams and feeding there.

Screams and feeding.

He made it to the balcony and found Melania crouched near the railing. Her dress had been torn away, and her breasts were exposed. He had paid serious money for those perfect breasts. He walked to her, placed his hands on the railing, and looked out at the ballroom.

All of his guests were turning into something exciting. There were still a few runners, a few screamers. But most had turned in the last few minutes into monsters, well, a more authentic *form* of monsters. He laughed and again felt a sickening *pop* in his eyes. He lifted Melania up and held her trembling, perfect body for a moment. Then he set upon her soft blood-filled neck and tore and drank and tore some more.

5-1-36 9:00PM EDT

John watched from across the Potomac. His troops formed a perimeter to keep any guests on the Baxter estate, but Baxter's mansion was a fortress. Borealis hackers had no trouble triggering the security system and locking the various exits as tight as a hummingbird's sphincter. By morning, nothing would be left to do but mop up the stragglers.

All their intelligence and all of the NTC medical research showed the same thing: GGB-Z had broken containment and was spreading precisely as predicted. The R-naught numbers Samedi had engineered held true in the real world. They may have been low-balled. Since the first contact with the couple in Miami, Borealis teams had collected over thirty stage-three subjects. Their numbers were increasing with an inexorable, exponential acceleration that fed John's enormous self-doubt.

The centralized command structure of the Samedi Organization and their reliance on the shadowy Pentacula network, a sort of pyramid scheme for psychopaths, made its membership easy to target. And Baxter's need to be seen as the great benefactor of the conspiracy—to take credit for himself that rightfully belonged to Cliff Price—made it even easier to arrange a single red wedding to decapitate the operation that had facilitated the end of civilization.

The vaccines Mengle had received were *not* what the doctor ordered. Borealis operatives inside Mindful Joy had maneuvered their way into the fulfillment production lines. While the Borealis team at NTC had developed a working mRNA vaccine for the GGB-Z virus, the vaccine produced by Mindful Joy had been shoddy and ineffective. Still, it provided slightly better protection than a placebo. At John's instruction, the scaled production run of the vaccine was sabotaged. Instead of the vaccine, the ampules shipped to the Samedi Organization were an earlier, pre-release strain of GGB-Z.

Borealis moles, via the Samedi Organization, had delivered to each and every Pentacula congregant a virus that produced the same outcome as the final GGB-Z but was not transmissible through water droplets and had an incubation period that was measured in minutes, not weeks. The only way to be infected was through direct injection or through the exchange of bodily fluids —snot, semen, blood, saliva, or vomit. This version had been rejected as unsuitable to produce a global pandemic—the infected would manifest symptoms too quickly to hop on a plane and transport the contagion to new breeding grounds. But it was well-suited to the confines of Baxter's estate.

Roberts' Rules had prevented them from stopping the spread

of GGB-Z, but no collapsed wave function protected Samedi or the Pentacula, the true source of Cliff Price's power in this time-frame. Dr. Kenneth Baxter and his secret society were fair game. By hiding from history, they made Borealis's job unusually straightforward.

John had accepted early on that he and the NTC Steering Committee had been charged with saving humanity. Along with that awesome responsibility came the task of deciding what the makeup of that surviving population would look like. No matter what came next, no matter how many good people he couldn't save—weeding out the monsters only made the world better. Their net wouldn't catch them all. There would certainly still be bad guys in whatever humanity made it through. John was real-ist, or cynic, enough to believe that was inevitable. But the rule of these elites had come to an end.

There was now one final psychopath for John to target and *he* was protected by Roberts' Rules until after Downfall. It was a loose end John intended to resolve personally.

INTERLUDE 2

HIS REMORSE WAS CLEAR, *though he tried to cover it with a thick veneer of "practical necessity," "just sentencing," and even "karmic backlash." It didn't take a detective to see that John didn't buy any of it. He wasn't proud of his actions even if he felt that they'd done the right thing. He had doubts fueled by his constant companions, guilt and self-recrimination. Julia was no shrink, but it didn't take a skilled detective to get that read on the Commander. After relating his tale of the mass murder of the Pentacula, John skipped a few of their meetings.*

John and Julia met thirty times for their late afternoon group therapy sessions à deux. It wasn't every day, but nearly. Julia came to welcome John's deep, gentle voice telling his tales of adventure and magic. She realized over the weeks how desperately he needed to tell his stories, how burdened he was by the weight of the task that had been laid on his shoulders. They were broad, strong shoulders, but... Jesus Christ. Atlas carried the weight of the world. John Banks carried the lives of two billion souls. He had borne that load admirably, but it was more than anyone should have to.

It was also clear to Julia that John had been broken long before this responsibility began to crush him.

She wondered if all heroes were so damaged inside. What makes a man or woman decide they need to save the world? Is heroism a harvest that rises from the fertile soil of guilt? In Afghanistan John had saved

Stephen Lucas, but it was the deaths of Gerry Almirez and Mike Zebrowski that he still carried with him. Julia didn't recall when she'd heard the story of John's heroics in the army; it was, like many of the facts she carried in her head about the man, locked up in the tangle of her memories that were obscured by her time as a demon.

John's friendship had become a nagging question—and a clue.

Why was Commander John Banks, Hero of the Borealis 1st, spending his time talking to a recovering demon detective from Madre Pueda? What was she to him? How did she end up being the first to recover from the plague that burned across the planet?

It was all tied up in Stephen Lucas.

When they began their sessions, she couldn't recall any part of 2036. A whole year, gone. But as they'd talked, as she'd recovered further, she could recall the winter, then the spring, and the beginning of summer of her lost year. Her hair had grown three inches, her keratosis scabs had softened and showed hope of fading back to her normal complexion. But as spring was approaching at NTC, as the sun was lasting longer each day outside the domes, she was starting to recall that summer of '36. She had a memory of a crime scene, a ghastly one with the remains of multiple victims. She'd dreamt about it first, but over the past week, she'd become confident that it wasn't just a nightmare. It was a break in her serial case.

And buried in that vein of memory was a tiny, loose thread that connected to John Banks. She was infuriatingly close. If she could get a grip on that thread and pull it gently, it would unravel to reveal... everything.

If you need anything...

John arrived at his appointed time with a cup of coffee and a cup of chai. He offered her the chai and sat, as he always did, on the far end of the couch. He took a sip of his joe and looked out at the sunlight filtering through the dome.

"I'm sorry I missed our last two sessions," he said. "But I've been

enjoying these mornings and we're coming up to the hard part of the story."

"The fun and games are over?" Julia tilted her head and watched him.

He nodded.

She sipped her chai and tried to tug at that loose end in her mind.

"When the world tipped, it tipped hard, and it tipped fast. We thought we were ready. We weren't." He paused for a moment and then began to talk. Their session went long, through that whole day and into the evening, and John talked nearly the whole time.

BOOK 2
THE ALBATROSS

WORLD ON FIRE. World on fire.

A family fled on foot, running south on Santana Ave in Madre Pueda, California, on the city's last day. There were four of them: a mother, a father, and two boys. The oldest boy was maybe twelve, the youngest perhaps ten. Their eyes, all of them lined with soot, were thrown wide by panic and terror. Their teeth were all bared, and their tongues wagged in their mouths as they ran with mindless, grim determination. Seventy demons were on their blood trail, a relatively small swarm as things go. The demons had caught the scent of human blood from three blocks away. The family had been running now for the better part of three hours. The father lifted the youngest and ran ahead, looking for a refuge, a hiding spot, anything.

John raced past them, going north. There *was* no place to hide. In fact, as John watched, an even smaller swarm rounded a cross-street intersection, caught sight of them, and made for them as well.

"There's nothing we can do," John moaned as he pushed his foot harder to the floor. He hadn't thought through how hard it would be to keep to a timetable as he watched innocents fleeing the monsters. If they failed in their current task, if they missed their deadline, all of their planning would be for nothing—their six-year mission might stretch on forever. "There's nothing we can do," he repeated as he saw the demons rip the younger boy from his father's arms and bury them both under their dark, flailing, tearing bodies. The mother and the other son froze, gaping as their loved ones were torn apart before them. John turned on a crossing street as the other swarm caught up and piled on top of them too. The fresh blood stood out against the demon faces, black with soot and ash, and caked with dried viscera.

John and Robin pressed on.

They'd stopped counting the demons, stopped counting the innocent dead. They saw the infected now, all the teeming millions of them—perhaps billions now *(what day was it?)*—not as individuals but as a single contiguous whole, an insect colony, a conceptual unity, a force of nature. Indistinct, identical drops of water become the river. To John, the demons were a fire that burned through humanity. A fire that would never *stop* burning, that couldn't be extinguished. As long as there was fuel, the fire would spread. Where there were people, the demons would burn through them. The more people, the more blood, fear, and terrifying death. Life fueled the fire.

Two demons had become twenty, twenty became a thousand. A thousand demons? When was the last time they'd seen only a thousand in one place? Was it last month in Korea? Last week in Mumbai? The days had begun to blur *(what day was it?)*. Buenos Aires, he concluded. There had been only thirty in the outbreak group they'd corralled in that crowded *villa miseria*. Since then, the numbers had veered straight up, accelerating from a few isolated communities to uncontrollable, unstoppable, worldwide outbreak.

The horror had also grown exponentially right before his eyes. Initially, it looked like civil unrest, if you paid only glancing attention to the US news feeds. In North America, GGB-Z hit like a dam breaking. On Tuesday morning *(what day was it?)*, people were flipping each other off in rush hour, vying for a good parking spot at the mall, walking their dogs and bagging the poop in colored plastic bags. Life was still proceeding according to the rules that governed Tuesday mornings.

By Wednesday night, however, those same people were running until their muscles cramped, screaming until their throats went raw, and hiding with quivering breath, eyes wide with shock. Every city on Earth was now awash with demons, death, and fire. Every last one. In the end, it no longer mattered what day it was.

The clock had stopped. The calendar had burned away.

Stephen Lucas and the billionaires in Madre Pueda's Braintree Hills must have been profoundly isolated from the world to not see this horror breaking around them. Then again, John's mission had given him a front-row seat.

His mouth was parched and sour with the taste of copper.

He'd driven through wildfires hundreds of times on three different continents. It always felt like he was driving through Hell itself—surrounded by all-consuming flames, bombarded by invisible infrared energy that baked your skin, illuminated by the unholy blood-red of the inferno. It was terrifying enough when it was in a forest or unpopulated wilderness. To see a city like Madre Pueda burn felt like Dante manifested. John had always maintained the illusion that Stephen's description of Downfall was hyperbole. *Hell on Earth*, he'd said in that barbecue joint six years ago. It wasn't a metaphor.

Somehow, a hopeful corner of John had nursed the quiet delusion that all their work could prevent this. He'd occasionally pictured a happy ending. Though he struggled against it, he'd unconsciously bought into his status as a hero. A part of him believed his own press, believed on some self-deluded level he could save the world. But what man can even hold the world in their mind? The world is too big, its problems too vast, and a man's mind is too small to picture it.

The image of that little boy's eyes as the demons ripped him from his father's arms—that look of confusion and shock—filled his mind, blinding him to the world beyond his windshield. His whole body shook with a violent tremor of remorse.

"There was *nothing* we could do!" John heard himself saying and knew it was the thousandth time he'd repeated it in the last week.

He raced his Camaro through block after block of burning row houses. This was once a historic neighborhood. Nothing would be left by morning. He took it personally. He was Stephen's chosen one. He was supposed to stop all of this.

John sped into the turn onto Field Street in a wobbly drift. He glanced over as Robin grabbed the oh-shit handle above his door. Robin's eyes widened, and John looked forward quickly enough to see a flaming, four-story brick storefront collapse onto the road ahead. He rode his anti-lock brakes and spun the wheel, sliding into a howling 180. The Camaro's back wheels came to rest on smoking rubble.

"Zoe?"

"There isn't much I can do. Surveillance is going down like dominoes all across the city." Her voice was calm as she rifled through her database, looking for a path to their target.

The surveillance state was crumbling along with the rest of human civilization. Washington and London were already dark, off the grid forever. The source of the Borealis handlers' data was being strangled by the plague. Soon, it would blink off for good.

"Wait." Zoe said, "There's a police helicopter streaming video. Okay, continue north on Field, two blocks. I've got contemporaneous video. Three blocks up, head east on Brookings Ave. That will get you where you need to be by 12:15. But you'll need to step on it, or he'll get away again." Zoe was squeezing the last dregs from Lucas' massive data warehouse.

"Hold on, Robin" John said as he floored it, tires screeching in a cloud of burnt rubber.

"Holy shit, Batman!" Captain Mercer said.

This was a date he couldn't be late for. After six years of knowing exactly what would happen, exactly when, and exactly where—John, Zoe, and Robin were beginning to fumble in the dark. Their epistemology games were done. Had they succeeded in fooling the future? They might never know. John had his doubts. The future, the next few hours and beyond, was no longer mapped on a pretty, holographic flow chart.

Now, they were making the future up as they went.

He drifted again onto Brookings Avenue. John noticed a severed leg, ragged flesh, and a hip joint above its fishnet stocking leaning casually against a fire hydrant in the light of a rare working street lamp.

In the distance, the Gallows district of Madre Pueda looked like a wall of flame. A mile ahead, he could see the flashing lights. A siren was barely audible above the raging fire and the rhinoceros-like thunder of the rampaging hordes of infected. John leaned on the gas and overtook the unmarked black ambulance with ease. He passed on the left, spun the wheel, and skidded to a stop. The ambulance was forced to brake as John and Robin jumped out with double-barrel shotguns cocked, at the ready.

John pointed his barrels at the driver as he walked to his door. The reflection of burning buildings multiplied the look of mayhem in his eyes. "Get out. Don't do anything dumb."

The ambulance driver killed the siren, put the transmission in park, opened the door, and raised his hands. Robin opened the rear doors and convinced the EMTs in the back to exit. John held up a key chain. "See that Camaro? Classic '28. LT Plasma. It's all yours." In the distance, a victim of the demon swarm wailed in terror. "Go. All of you get in the car. Or you can take your chances with the rabid. Limited time offer." He dangled the keys again.

The driver nodded. John tossed him the keys. He looked in the Camaro's driver-side window and turned to the EMTs. "Have you ever driven a manual transmission?" An older EMT raised his hand.

"There you go," John said and pointed the shotgun at the driver's face again.

The EMT got behind the wheel and his co-workers joined him.

John fired a blast in the air. The driver shifted the car into first and pulled away before the lead shot rained down on them. John and Robin climbed into the black ambulance.

Zoe said, "You have four minutes."

John looked up and pointed at the silhouettes of the macabre towers of Grady Castle, two blocks away. According to future history, right about now, Stephen Lucas was being quietly tortured by Cliff Price in the Castle's Penthouse.

"It won't take that long."

He flipped the siren back on.

———

Heat lightning crackled as John pulled the ambulance past the burning cedars lining the main entrance. He pulled through the construction gate, barricaded off from the main parking area by a quarter mile of chain-link fence. A swarm of infected demons gathered at the base of Tower One. John looked up, following the red line of a garbage chute to the Penthouse. Up there, *right now*, Stephen Lucas was strapped to a chair, his face flayed. John had finally caught up to his old army buddy. A large window shattered, and black curtains blew out into the night. The Penthouse lit up with gunshots that were muted and faint by the time they reached John's ears. As he watched, a figure, barely visible but for his garish red pants, jumped from the window into the construction chute a mere foot below.

John pulled the ambulance to the construction dumpster in time to watch the chute rattle and sway for almost fifteen seconds before the mortally wounded body of Cliff Price shot out of the end as if he were exiting a water slide. Though the container was full of chunks of shredded foam, Price's body tumbled and slammed into the steel floor, dislocating his shoulder. *This* was the evil, fucked-up monster that turned the world to Hell? John looked at Robin with a cocked eyebrow.

"There are easier ways to escape from a building." He looked at the heap that was Cliff Price and said, "I don't think you fully thought that through." He knelt and looked at this broken, torn-up body clinging to life. Price's eyes rolled randomly in their sockets, his breathing rattled, and his right arm stuck out a crazy angle. John wanted to start punching Price and not stop. Instead, he got to work.

Robin grabbed the backboard. John pulled the gurney out of the back of the bus. They strapped Price to the backboard—roughly. They moved the backboard to the gurney—roughly. Price gurgled back to consciousness as they shoved the gurney into the back—roughly.

"Be careful, you idiots! That hurts!" Price slurred.

John leaned over and looked deeply into Price's eyes. Price smiled. The fucker smiled at him. John leaned in closer, nearly touching noses, and smiled back.

John met the Ridgeback 6x6 patrol vehicle at the corner of Gallows and Minaret, in the heart of the burning slum. Every building in sight was on fire. He parked the ambulance. Robin got out as John stepped into the back to talk to his patient.

"Cliff Price."

"We don't use that name any longer." His trip down the chute had fractured his palate, and his voice sounded wispy and incomplete.

"We are the Angel of the Black Pit. The Black Empty." Price eyed John with a growing sense of confusion and indignation.

John smiled back. "Oh. *The Black Empty*!" He chuckled. "Why is it crazy people are always so grandiose? Always Lucifer, never Uriel or Raphael, or some lesser seraphim?"

Price squinted at him, befuddled. This was no way for hired help to speak to the master.

John wiped sweat from his face with the back of his hand. The ambulance was getting warm.

"You are Clifford Price, and you had a shitty mom and dad. You were powerless to defend yourself, so you invented a big imaginary friend who did terrible things to people. Some people buy comic books; *you* went another way. There's nothing supernatural about it." John leaned over to look more closely at Price. "You've been a bad boy, Cliffy Price. You've been a busy boy this last week. Famine and Pestilence and War and Death. Yeah, yeah. I know."

Cliff giggled from deep inside that destroyed body.

"I've been cleaning up your mess for six years," John continued. "I expect I'll be cleaning up the mess you made for the rest of my life." John inhaled deeply and sighed it all out. He was tired. "Here we are, at the end of civilization, the end of the world." John opened the back doors and let Price see the burning city. Price's eyes lit up at the sight of the overwhelming destruction. In the distance, a horde of demons was ravening through the streets, baptized with fire. Many continued to charge along, though their hair and clothes were aflame. "There it is. Hell on Earth, your magnum opus. You were thinking you were going to start a new project. Thought maybe you'd rule in Hell? Well, that's not going to happen." He shook his head. "That is not going to happen, Cliff."

John counted down three outstretched fingers. "The Samedi Organization? Gone. The Pentacula? Gone. All your evil little tentacles have been amputated. They're all demon fodder."

"Are you sure?" Price asked with sickening confidence.

"Pretty sure." John smiled back. "It's just you, and frankly, you look like sledge-hammered dog shit. Oh, you ended the world. But you know what that means?" John asked. He answered his rhetorical question with slow seriousness. "No judges. No laws. For the moment—it's *your* world, Cliff." John looked out the left window. Robin had climbed onto the back of the troop carrier. He looked out the back doors. The horde had seen them or smelled them. Even John could smell Cliff's blood. "We *are* going to have a trial though. I'm going to leave your fate…" John gestured to Price's wounds, "… and your medical needs… up to a jury of your peers."

Cliff started laughing in liquid, bloody, gurgling guffaws. With his working arm, he fumbled in his blood-stained, red velveteen sweatsuit pockets and found what he sought. John watched the approaching demons picking up speed, growing more frenzied. He turned to see Price fumbling with a thin, black mobile device. Along its thin edge, a blood-smeared LED twirled and danced. John smiled and let Price fumble one-handed with the Oneiri Mark 2. Its sapphire display screen and tungsten body had survived the trip through the chute without a scratch. Quality build.

John fired off two blasts of his shotgun as he stepped onto the asphalt. This drew the attention of two more swarms of demons who might have passed on by without noticing the ambulance. John hopped onto the six-wheeled vehicle, as the two swarms converged 20 yards from the ambulance.

Cliff turned on the device and opened the Oneiri app. He set the time frame to three days in the past and opened his video conference app. A small modal window appeared. The dialog box said in white, 14 point, Avenir Ultra Light:

Unable to establish a OneFTL network connection.

There was a single button labeled *Okay*.

Cliff whimpered, then whined, then he screamed until he was hoarse, until his bloody saliva spattered the display of the Mark 2.

John watched the jury deliberate from the safety of his perch atop the Ridgeback. He scanned the burning neighborhood for any last-minute rescuers. Had Cliff thought far enough ahead to cover himself with a tail, a failsafe team to pull his bacon from the frying pan? It's what John would do. But John and his team had been at this for six years and Stephen had the advantage of more time with the Oneiri. Stephen would be working to cover their asses for decades into the future.

Cliff had only had his one week.

The infected swarmed over the ambulance. It rocked on its

wheels as the demons scrambled to enter the back compartment and consume the body and blood of their lord and maker. When he was certain no one could save Cliff from his death sentence, John banged on the hood with his fist and they drove away through the fires of Hell, leaving the city to burn.

———

09-19-36 5:45 PM PDT

"What's in the box?" Private Scott Dominguez asked Corporal Jillian Cho.

She looked back at the white, insulated container strapped to the fuselage of the Airbus A400AM. It wasn't going anywhere. The med team had fastened it to the airframe of the medical transport with nylon webbing and ratchet tensioners.

Cho said, "Don't worry about the cargo, Private. Keep your eyes on that taxiway. Commander Banks wants us to keep that taxiway clear. That's what we're going to do."

The white box shook and trembled a bit. Dominguez looked back into the transport's cavernous open bay. "Is that a casket or a fridge? It looks like a fridge, or a freezer, or some shit."

Cho slapped the private's helmet and pointed at his eyes. "I want your eyes on that *taxiway*."

Dominguez cracked his neck, shouldered his weapon, and turned his eyes to the taxiway. In the distance, the main terminal was ablaze. An Avgas refueling truck had gone up near three 747s. That was at 7:00 AM, after the evacuation teams had headed out for their last rescue ops.

CSAR ops were ongoing around the world. Borealis-led NTC fighting teams had been dispatched to locations that dotted the globe. When Cho was resurrected, there were only a thousand Lost Boys. Now there were nearly ten times that many under the Commander's Western Forces alone. Each of the four Borealis forces, led by their own colonel nearly as impressive as Commander Banks, had their list of priority targets to recover from the ongoing collapse of human civilization. The Borealis 1st started arriving in Madre Pueda a week earlier.

There were now four of the big NTC Airbus heavy birds aligned, wingtip to wingtip, at the tarmac's far southern end, a defensible corner of Thorne International. Two of the A400s were retrofitted with two decks of passenger seating for the evacuees. It was cramped, but it was livable. Most of the high-priority individuals on C-Dome's lists were onboard and waiting for the Commander. After a day of waiting on the tarmac for more passengers, Cho was glad she wasn't riding in *that* plane.

One of the transports was for the military, Cho's team, and three others. It was the First's home away from home in Madre Pueda and the command center for this op. It was gutted and stripped to carry forty-eight soldiers, a twenty-ton Ridgeback 6x6 patrol vehicle, a seven-ton command vehicle, and enough room left over to scratch your ass if you were lucky.

The medical transport was the mystery to Corporal Cho. Their team had a military escort wherever they went but didn't seem involved in rescue ops. Their transport was filled with a mobile medical lab, filled with gizmos and computers, and V-Dome *mad scientist* shit. The empty insulated container had flown in with the med transport. A priority evac team had taken it with them on their first run into MP at midnight after the shit had gone primeval. When they returned, it wasn't empty. There was something alive in there. Whatever, whoever, it was, it was the highest priority of the mission.

Commander Banks and Lieutenant Mercer had led sorties into the city and out to the Braintree Hills and Crofton for the last three days. They were on their final run. That's why Dominguez was jumpy. Everyone knows shit always goes sideways on the *last* run.

"Mister Ray, at three o'clock," Private Dominguez said.

Ray was short for Rabies. The use cases were endless: Ray Charles, Ray Bans, Ray Ray, Ronald Raygun, X-Rayted. Grunts on the ground had lots of time to kill.

Cho turned and spotted half a dozen infected shuffling off about half a klick to her left. They seemed to have found something to chase. Those fuckers loved to chase shit. If it was moving fast enough, they'd chase after blowing newspapers. Ray-Ray weren't bright. She alerted the other security teams on their shared Aurora channel. "We're seeing Ray at about half a klick to the east. Our eleven o'clock. Anyone else seeing any other action?"

"Nothing here. We Roger your eleven o'clock Ray."

"Roger that." The white box trembled. She looked back into the shadows of the transport. That thing got on her very last nerve.

"Corporal!"

She turned to follow what Dominguez was clocking. The handful of infected on their left had swollen to several hundred.

"Hanks? Godley? You seeing this increase in Ray action?"

"Affirm."

"Roger."

"Okay, double-check that your shooters are suppressing." Cho glanced at the suppressor on her rifle and Scotty's. "Let's not start a party. But be prepared if the party comes to us. They might walk on by." She pulled her weapon up and viewed the swarm in her scope.

Dominguez joked as he trained his scope on a high-school-aged demon, "Yeah, I'm fine. I think it's only the flu, Mom."

The horrible sight in her scope was so at odds with how the virus started. These weren't human any longer. Perhaps three days ago, they'd all had a case of sniffles. Now, they moved in unnatural jerks and spasms without sense. She watched a man in a blood-soaked business suit and tie stop and snap at the air with his teeth for several seconds before turning back to follow the swarm. He was wielding an opened, empty briefcase. They all had their weapons, baseball bats, two-by-fours, and branches. It seemed the virus directed them to have something in their hands at all times. Something to swing. Something to attack with. Not that they couldn't kill you with their teeth and nails alone.

She flashed on a memory from two days earlier when she witnessed an infected beating in the skull of a twelve-year-old girl with a rolling pin and lapping up the gray matter. Cho had only hoped, over and over for the last two days, that demon wasn't the girl's mother.

Dominguez tapped her shoulder. While she'd been wool-gathering, reliving her trauma, a new one was developing. The hundreds on the east side of the tarmac were now thousands. They were threatening to block the taxiway Commander Banks had ordered her to keep clear. "Suppressors on, let's have headshots only, please. Fire at will!" Cho barked.

In the distance, she could hear the cracks and pops as human heads exploded. Two dozen shooters dropped two hundred infected at the edge of the tarmac in under twenty seconds. The swarm kept surging forward, tripping over the fallen but making progress. Cho tilted her head as she received a message via Aurora.

"Commander Banks is inbound. ETA three minutes. They have the final eighteen evacuees. We need to make sure these birds have a taxiway to get to the runway for takeoff. Let's clean up!"

She started firing. In her scope, infected after infected stopped and dropped. Not every shot was a clean headshot. Their erratic motion made tracking a challenge. She looked from behind her scope. The swarm was becoming a mound of corpses, and yet the rabid kept coming, scrambling over the dead. She had that metallic taste in her mouth, her throat turning to cotton.

Dominguez was shouting, "*Yeah! You love it! Is that good for you? What? Do you need some love too? How about you?*"

She looked at the taxiway slowly being choked off from the runway. She was not getting it done. The sky was growing toward twilight. She was feeling panic as the swarm pressed forward.

The world brightened for a moment. An RPG arced past from her four o'clock. The RPG hit the swarm where they encroached on the taxiway. The explosion knocked the bodies back twenty feet and obscured them behind black smoke.

The Ridgeback armored transport pulled onto the tarmac with soldiers hanging to the roof and sides. Lieutenant Mercer stood in the following command vehicle, shouldering the rocket launcher. Behind them were four up-armored white commercial Humvees that looked like they'd been playing demon demolition derby for a month. The soldiers on the transports jumped off and began engaging the swarm with an overwhelming show of force. The Humvees' passengers were hustled into the VIP birds. The drivers pulled the Borealis vehicles into the back of the open A400 cargo bay.

Looking eight feet tall, Commander Banks strode out of the command vehicle and clapped Cho on her shoulder. "Good job, Corporal. Get your team onboard and strapped in." He looked out at the swarm diminishing in the distance. He didn't even acknowledge that he'd saved her kimchi. Cho watched him for a moment as she stowed her weapon and collected her gear. He stood there like an onyx statue. After a moment, he spoke as if to himself, "I irrationally hoped we'd evacuate Stephen before we were done."

He fell silent, and Cho realized he was listening to his handler's voice in his Aurora. Cho noticed a look of sadness in her commander and something else. It was as if he was talking to his wife or girlfriend. It felt intimate. He wouldn't be the first to have an intimate relationship with his handler.

"Yeah, I knew it intellectually," Banks said. "Roberts' Rules. But I couldn't shake that hope," he said, then listened for a moment.

She felt like she was eavesdropping, so she was about to turn away and head toward the transport when he nodded and looked out at his troops.

He spun his finger in the air and shouted, "All right, you

primates! Let's pack it up and get on our way. We'll be fighting the Nunavut winter if we don't make it out soon."

He turned and looked at the large white insulated box. The first big bird was starting its engines, blanketing the tarmac with prop wash.

"Jillian, hold up," he shouted. He knew her first name! She turned, and he pointed to the medical transport. "I need someone to escort that cargo. It's important. Can you ride in the medical bird on this leg?"

Cho nodded. "Sir, yes, sir!"

Commander Banks grinned one of his incandescent grins. "Go on. I'll see you in Nunavut."

She turned to Dominguez. "Make sure our *special delivery* gets tended to, right, Dominguez?"

"I've got it stashed in the big ride, Corporal. Sandy Hoyt ain't gonna die if I have anything to say about it." He never looked away from his rifle site. "Go follow the Commander's orders. We're good."

She clapped him on the shoulder and ran to the cargo hold just before the aft ramp lifted off the hardtop. As she strapped herself in next to the big white box, it trembled again. She remembered having jumping beans when she was a kid. The subtle movement inside the insulated box reminded her of that. Something was alive in there, something the Commander thought was important, or maybe dangerous? Either way, he trusted her to keep an eye on it.

"That's it, that's the last Madre Pueda video surveillance source in our records," Zoe spoke in his ear. "What happens from here is all un-collapsed wave functions." She paused, and John could hear her weigh a decision in her silence. "John. I'm not supposed to tell you. There are details I've had to withhold from you."

"I know, babe. I know." John fell silent as he strapped himself into the jump seat. His troops were packed like sardines in-between the chocked-and-locked vehicles.

"John, I just wanted to say—" She hesitated. Her voice was choked with emotion. "I'm risking a Roberts' Rules violation, but I need you to know. You and I will—" There was a loud screech in his head. "*I forgive you for my parents*—" Her signal was breaking up in his Aurora. He looked around; all those with implants looked like they were having issues.

"What?" he asked. "What about your parents?"

"*—forgive you.*" Another bone-shattering screech in his audio. "*You'll find m—*"

John waited for a few seconds—nothing.

"Zoe?" He tapped behind his ear. He clicked on her *realTime* icon in his Aurora. No window appeared floating over his field of vision. "Zoe?" He shouted to Robin, "Mercer! Can you reach your handler?" The sound of the four engines starting drowned out his voice. John waved, trying to get Robin's attention, but he just leaned his head back and closed his eyes. John tried and failed to reach him through *realTime*.

The four props chopped the air into a palpable roar as the pilot tuned their pitch for takeoff. Hydraulic pistons groaned as the flaps extended. The first of the enormous planes pulled away and headed for the taxiway. Soon, all four of the NTC craft were rolling. John looked out at the burning terminal as they passed. He tapped the spot behind his ear again — no response.

A plume of black smoke rose from Thorne ATC tower. The four planes were on their own. John knew their pilots would be monitoring CTAF, and the co-pilots would look sharp for traffic in the pattern. The first passenger transport began its takeoff run. As it rotated and started to climb out, the second followed.

As the third bird accelerated, their aircraft made the slow arc to align with the runway. When the medical transport was climbing into the gray-blue sky, John felt their engines revving and the gear rolling across the rumble strips. He looked over at Robin and saw him looking back. He didn't bother shouting, but gestured to his ear. Robin tapped behind his ear and looked puzzled. He tapped again and looked back at John, shaking his head. Both their coms were out.

John looked into the cockpit as the co-pilot pointed dramatically at something below and in front of them. The pilot saw it too, added power, and pulled back on the yoke. John had only a fraction of a second to wonder what they'd seen when their plane hit *something*, pivoted forward hard, and a sound of tearing, grinding metal could be heard—no, felt—above the roar of the engines. It felt like the landing gear was ripped away. The plane yawed and rotated over on its nose. John looked forward and saw a blur of tarmac out the front window.

The pilot was working the problem as they continued to skid, sparks flying in the shattered window. He managed to shut down all the engines as the gear crunched hard again, and the plane dropped. John felt like he was inside a blender. He looked back, grateful to see the troops, and the vehicles had been secured properly. Though the plane was whipping and bouncing, that 20-ton Ridgeback stayed put. If it broke loose, half of his soldiers would be crushed.

There was a sudden molar-jarring vibration, and John turned as the cockpit was demolished—the aircrew was gone. Through his window, John could see the right wing's leading edge was now on the ground. Its props were mangled, their blades bent or sheered away. He turned and tried to see through the opposite windows. The left wing was angled skyward, with its props freewheeling, as the plane continued to skid. Tarmac flashed by the gaping hole that had been the cockpit door. They hit a patch of grass, probably the divider between the runway and the taxiway. Sod and soil were thrown up and into the cabin. John was pelted with handfuls of black dirt. Finally, the motion stopped. The plane came to rest, and everything was suddenly, sickeningly, silent. John tapped behind his ear again out of pure habit.

"Zoe!"

Silence.

No time to worry about her now.

"Anyone injured?" John shouted as he unstrapped.

His soldiers' heads swiveled. An unsteady chorus of responses indicated they were more-or-less whole. John turned to Robin.

"Okay. I'll take the lack of screaming in pain and bleeding as a good sign. Cap, pop your head out of that door. See if we're going to explode." He asked the obvious, "What the hell did we hit?"

He looked at the cockpit passageway. It was a nightmare of blood, sod, shattered glass, and shredded aircraft aluminum. He thought he saw the asphalt of the taxiway through the darkened wreckage. Robin popped the side door, climbed out, and stood on the side of the canted aircraft.

"Commander, there's a lot of jet fuel on the ground. No flames or smoke," he hollered back down to John. "We should get everyone out, just in case."

John nodded. "All right, you primates. Let's get the hell out of here and regroup on the tarmac. Get those doors open." His soldiers unstrapped and bent to their tasks.

Robin looked into the distance. "There's a herd of infected about a quarter mile back and a lot of blood. Looks like we hit a ground support baggage shuttle. Maybe they were trying to escape a swarm and drove onto the runway."

"Your coms are still down?" John asked as he climbed up.

"Roger that, Commander," Robin confirmed as he helped him out.

His mind reached for Zoe, a woman who was now how many decades away? He'd never felt more abandoned and alone.

"Well, shit." He watched the other three birds vanishing into the towering northeast clouds. "We're on our own."

09-20-36 9:00 PM EDT:
ARRIVALS

THE SMELL OF HUMANITY, of fear, was hard to ignore. Right on schedule, the world was ending as forecast; and, though the Nunavut Technology Center was purpose-built as a life-raft for humanity, the influx was proving to be a rigorous pressure test of all of Stephen Lucas' plans—and all of Athena Shaw's efforts to realize them. The NTC terminal, not a small building, was filled to overflowing. Though the Nunavut autumn had turned to heavy snow outside, inside the terminal, the musk of thousands of bodies made the atmosphere feel hot and humid. Outside, on the tarmac, it was looking like a mob scene. The sound of A400s touching down was a constant cadence of tires screeching and braking thrust. Downfall refugees were coming in from all over the world, shepherded by the thirty-eight divisions, Four regiments of Borealis's finest. According to C-Dome, it would be the largest influx in NTC's timeline—past, present, and future.

Borealis troops worked diligently to help the G-Dome teams process the refugees and get them aboard the subway cars. The terminal had been designed for this, but it was still bursting at the seams. The crowd was loud and their tone was frustrated, confused, and showing signs of a sudden phase change to hostility. These were people who had, in the last 48 hours, learned the danger of being in large crowds of human beings. As far as they were concerned, every one of them was a time bomb.

"Mayor" Athena Shaw, the Director of NTC operations, trailing a coterie of assistants, made her way through the crowd to the terminal door carrying a shiny white megaphone.

"Can I please have your attention?" The crowd, indoors and out, took a few seconds to quiet. "I wish I could welcome you to the NTC under better circumstances. Our team is processing new arrivals as quickly as humanly possible, but you can hear the planes landing for yourselves. More refugees are on their way." The crowd murmured. Athena spoke quickly to stave off the eruption of a question-and-answer free-for-all. "I know you were all briefed by the Borealis teams while you were on your planes. They showed you all a quick video about NTC and our rescue operations. That video should have answered the lion's share of your questions. I *know* you will have more."

She stopped and smiled sadly. "My God. *Of course* you have questions. I can't imagine what you have been through, each and every one of you." She nodded as she took in the entire crowd. "All I can say for now is this. We are here to serve you and keep you safe from what is happening *out there*." She pointed vaguely to the world beyond Walrus Rocks. "We have prepared for this, and we have prepared to welcome all of you. Once you are situated in your new homes, you will have access to our intranet and the answers to all of your questions. You will have the help you need to adjust to all of this. But first, we need to get you processed and out of this snow." She nodded again. "Our medical team will be working their way through the crowd. They are going to be giving shots. *Everyone* gets a shot. Some of you received the shot on the plane—based on risk assessment, some got a shot before you boarded. We are struggling to keep up with the demanding situation. But *everyone gets their shot!* It's a multivalent vaccine and a cure for early-stage GGB-Z virus."

The crowd erupted in applause, then cheers. There were tears in the eyes of men and women alike. Eyes that showed the strain of unspoken terror giving way to sudden inexpressible relief. Being in a large crowd would never be the same to anyone who'd witnessed a demon outbreak.

"That's one worry for yourselves and your families that you can leave behind. So, look for the medical teams bearing needles. Roll up your sleeves when they ask, despite the temperature." She smiled, nodded, and turned to go back into the terminal, then thought and turned back to the crowd. "On behalf of the Nunavut Technology Center, I'm Athena Shaw, and I'd like to welcome you to your new home. We still have so much work to do. All of you are welcome and so, so valuable to our efforts."

The crowd applauded, and she clicked off the bullhorn. As she turned, a big, shaggy-looking character caught her eye. Out on the tarmac, in the light of the crisp LED lamps, ignoring the crowd, enjoying the snow, and actually trying to catch flakes on his outstretched tongue, was a large man with graying brown, bushy hair and beard. She appreciated his ability to find childlike joy in the moment and headed back into the terminal.

She surveyed the scene to determine what part of the intake process was holding people up. It looked like a line of subway cars was forming. She shook her head. The registration counters were taking too long. She headed in that direction but was stopped by a delayed recognition. Athena triggered an alert with her Aurora immediately. She twirled and headed back out the door.

It took some struggling to wade through the crowd, but they were at least cordial after the vaccine news. She lost her attendants in the process, but made it to the edge of the walkway and approached the man she'd spied earlier. He was now surrounded by half a dozen kids, all spinning in circles, trying to land a snowflake in their mouths, all laughing, all seemingly unaware that civilization was ending.

"Excuse me," she said as she tried to get his attention.

The man was at least as tall as Commander Banks, but chubbier, softer, and furrier.

"Oh, I'm sorry." He smiled and turned to her, his eyes trying to adjust to a non-spinning world. She'd been correct; he was on her list of VIPs. His picture was on her bulletin board of The Most Wanted.

"Mr. Roberts!" she exclaimed.

His eyebrows raised, and he laughed a deep, infectious belly laugh.

"That's me!" he said. "But please, everybody calls me *Walrus!*"

09-20-36 11:12 PM EDT

Alina Sapru waited in the airlock for the attendant to complete her forms.

The attendant said, "Okay, we're going to take your temp." After a moment, "97.9. Dr. Sapu, you are thermally regulated like a fine Swiss watch." They giggled together. "Okay, now for the fun part." She uncapped the nasal swab. Alina leaned her head back, and the attendant gently inserted the swab until it felt like it would scrape Alina's brain. Alina was a pro and had done this every day for the last four years, but she still teared up *every* time. The attendant removed the swab, popped it into the container, and popped the container into the suitcase-sized device on the desk.

Now they waited. Few citizens of NTC knew about V-Dome. There was no subway or walkway to or from any other dome. It had been built ahead of its alphabetical ordering system in secret. It was now the smallest of the domes, smaller in diameter even than C-Dome by several hundred feet. The device beeped, and the attendant read the screen. "You're all set."

Alina continued to the airlock door, waited for the attendant to release the lock, and entered the secondary airlock and suiting station. She swabbed her hands with antiviral, anti-fungal, and anti-bacterial solutions, then held them beneath a UV lamp as she counted to thirty-six. Then she moved to her suit and scrutinized it for any abrasions, lacerations, or *anything* that could compromise its integrity.

Inside the small dome, trailers that had once served the engineering labs were now spaced in a radial pattern, each with its own life support, air, water, and sewer. Surrounding each trailer were inflatable tents with individual environmental controls. In an emergency, all the air inside any tent could be evacuated through a venting system lined with high-intensity UV LED panels before venting into the frozen plain to the west. To date, only one of the trailer labs had broken protocol in a way that required this procedure. Thankfully, no one suffered a compromised PPE, though the doctors and tech were all quarantined and tested for three months before they could return to work.

V-Dome was the home of NTC's virology lab. Twenty-four double-wide trailers, operating in complete physical and temporal isolation from each other, all working to understand the GGB-Z virus and its engineering. All one hundred and fifty virologists, biologists, and epidemiologists were working to find a vaccine and a cure.

Dr. Sapru completed donning her suit, grabbed her positive pressure suitcase, and plugged it into the socket at her waist. The suit ballooned up, and she moved to the airlock door and passed her card in front of the reader. The door puffed open, and she entered the dome.

These labs and the doctors and scientists who worked here were isolated from the rest of the community and from each other to protect the sanctity of their timeframes as much as to prevent the spread of the disease. In the other public domes, the GGB-Z vaccine was already available to protect the community. Inside eighteen of the trailer labs, the vaccine had *yet* to be developed. In their sequestered timeframes, the vaccine was a goal they worked toward. Each lab had been handed a file of research and information from a previous lab. Each had four years to work on their puzzle pieces before handing the file to the NTC administrators in C-Dome.

Using Oneiri, the administrators pushed their data findings back to the next lab four years in the past. The process was called temporal multi-threading, and it allowed NTC scientists to accomplish nearly a century of research and analysis—all in under four years. Lab 1 began its work in 2032, when the dome was completed, with files obtained from the Sunlight Joy Limited Partnership Research Facility in 2034. Lab 2 also began their work, isolated from Lab 1, in 2032, with the data and findings from Lab 1's completed efforts from 2036. When Lab 2 completed its contribution in 2036, the busy bees in C-Dome pushed their work back to Lab 3 in 2032, and on it went. V-Dome represented a little over 92 years of continuous, rigorous scientific research directed toward one goal—the cure for GGB-Z.

Last August, the vaccine was completed in Lab 18. A new facility had been established offsite for producing the messenger RNA vaccine at scale. Since the pandemic had happened, since *that* waveform had collapsed, they knew they couldn't prevent Downfall from occurring out in the world in 2036. However, they could protect their people, and they could work to find a cure if one was possible. Alina followed the branching path to Viral Lab 20. She entered the trailer to find Bill Watkins and Sunny DeAngelis busy preparing to open the package they had received the night before.

Sunny said, "Hey, darlin'. We waited for you. Didn't want to open our present without you."

Alina smiled. "You are too thoughtful. Good morning. Good morning, Bill."

Bill waved and approached with a hex driver. The large insulated white box was about the size of a home freezer, though a bit taller. "She's settled down overnight. We've been pushing coolant all night. It's 62 degrees in there. A lot less of the tremor behavior this morning," Bill said as he carefully unscrewed three hex bolts from the left side. He moved to the right side and removed those three as well. "A little help, Sunny?"

Sunny moved to the foot of the container and said, "Careful not to take the plexiglass seal too this time."

Bill laughed. "Yep. Make *one* mistake, and..." They lifted the insulated foam top off.

Alina peered in. "Okay, let's have a look at you."

Inside the box was a woman in gray pants, a black shirt, and a blue blazer. Her clothes were black with freeze-dried blood. Her hair was matted with blood as well. Only a few dried tufts were identifiable as golden brown. Her hands and feet were bound with black plastic zip ties. Alina tapped a switch on her helmet to start a recording. "Female, 35—in good physical condition. Subject is infected with the GGB-Z virus, stage three" Alina tilted her head to see a med delivery patch adhered to the subject's neck. The skin under the patch had been hastily washed. "An NTC-V BetaTrank dermal dispenser has been applied to the subject's left carotid area. Good. Looks like she's only been hibernating for less than forty-eight hours."

Alina and her team had been the first to discover one of the unanticipated side effects of the GGB-Z virus. The known change in metabolic processes made the victims easy to freeze. That viscous blood was the reason. As the infected's temperature dropped, their cells shifted to a mode similar to the diving response in healthy humans, but much more dramatic. Breathing could drop to one breath per minute. Heart rate could be almost undetectable.

"Let's get an O2 sat on her. Can we get her cleaned up and moved to a recovery pod?"

Bill nodded.

Alina's gloved hand patted the plexiglass safety barrier. "Let's see if we can make you better."

Bill and Sunny removed the subject from the insulated box. They moved her to the hygiene station for Sunny to rinse her down while Bill broke the container down and removed it from their small lab. Sunny removed her clothes and began the meticulous process of shaving and cleansing her.

She trimmed her nails nearly to the quick, inserted a mouth-guard, and attached a face shield. No one operating in a moon suit wanted a fingernail or a tooth to tear or puncture their PPE— not when they were working with the demon virus. While they were vaccinated, until they completed their work, there was no verified cure. Perhaps the current cocktail would be the one.

They worked together to dry her.

Sunny said, "She's beautiful."

Bill said, "I'm not big on the whole bald chick, punk vibe."

Sunny shook her head. Even bald, their subject had the features of a classic beauty.

They moved her to a recovery pod, an automated unit controlled by a sophisticated AI to monitor and administer any alterations necessary to her various drips or gas lines while providing protection from a fully roused demon. Once she was lying down in the sectioned, temperature-controlled hydraulic bed, they carefully cinched her restraints. They double-checked each other's work, and Sunny inserted a central line while Bill draped the peaceful-looking patient with a refrigerated blanket. Once the line was in place, Bill closed the lid on the pod. Sunny hung two bags of saline and pushed serotonin along with their forty-third experimental antiviral cocktail. Sunny laid a hand on the pod and said, "You get well now."

09-22-36 7:00 PM PDT: ROYALLY FUCKED

WITH THE GEAR and the wings finally yanked away, the fuselage of the A400, carrying the lopsided weight of the 20-ton Ridgeback 6x6 and the 7-ton command vehicle, violently sought equilibrium. John cringed at the sound of scraping aircraft aluminum on tarmac and the shouts of success as the plane rolled to near level. The demons would hear that and come, sure as night follows day.

Two days to drain the plane's 16,000 gallons of Avgas safely. Another day to tear off the wings and the mangled undercarriage with cutting torches, hydraulic spreaders, and 20-inch circular saws. Everything made eardrum-shredding, bone-rending noise. Airframes and wings were perfect resonating chambers for the cacophony, which carried across the open taxiway and surrounding fields.

Each soldier not involved in tearing the plane open to give their vehicles a rough cesarean birth was on demon watch. The four Humvees, brand new ten days ago, formed a broad perimeter twenty yards from the ruined plane. Twenty yards beyond them, fifty-five-gallon containers of the afore-mentioned Avgas stood ready for an assault from the rabid, should it come to that.

Three days in, and they'd been lucky. The incursions were random and came from stragglers within the airport grounds.

They weren't as exposed as they'd been at the terminal. Their crash left them two-thirds down the runway, half on the taxiway. The terminal stood nearly a mile to the west. A quarter mile to the east, fenced off park land bordered the field.

There was a story John had heard of Cortez burning his ships when reaching the shores of the new world. It gave his men something to focus their minds on while Cortez explored the alien landscape. Each night, beyond that park, the troops had a fine view as Madre Pueda burned with so-far undiminished fury. The din of the demons, the new ruling class of the city, was enough to drive a man insane. It was, John reflected, the very motivation his troops needed. It kept them on task. If they wanted to get back to NTC, they needed to accomplish the work at hand.

As the engineers worked and the snipers kept watch for Ray-Ray, John had the rest of his team planning, preparing, and scavenging resources from the surrounding area. The weather forecast in Nunavut made it unlikely they would get another plane out. He didn't need Zoe or his Aurora to work that out. If a plane could get out, Thorne was fucked as a landing strip. The smaller strips were clear, but too short for the big birds. The only small aircraft in NTC's fleet were the Otters, which didn't have the capacity for 43 soldiers. If NTC could clear their runway, they'd be sending the transports. If they couldn't—it was a long walk to Nunavut.

The nearest airport that could handle the A400s was Sacramento.

So, that was the initial plan: a road trip to Sacramento International. Certainly, their Aurora network would be back up by the time they got there. If Zoe had been online, she could have arranged another ride with a few twinkles of fairy dust and some Oneiri juju. She'd have no intel on their situation since her data warehouse's contents ended three days ago. But she could still have placed a supply depot in some inconspicuous shipping container for them to retrieve. She could still save the day.

He missed her deep in his bones.

The fact that NTC's AuroraNet was down was climbing on his list of concerns. They used Aurora to communicate with their future-timeframe handlers, but they also used them as their primary means of communication. It was as if all their phones were down at the same time. Their implants still gave them the equivalent of a desktop workstation with lots of apps, but the power of Aurora was the network connection, and that was FUBAR.

"We've got Ray Charles performing at the eastern fence line," Emily Tran said over her walkie.

In Aurora's absence, the platoon had been reduced to old-school tech, but Emily didn't have implants, anyway. A small blue-haired pistol, Emily was one of the recent additions, a civilian, a refugee. John remembered her from the last days of SDS's Springdale office presence. She'd met with Mary Allan as his men were serving as stevedores. Tran had been a stringer for SDS intelligence, and Mary Allan made her rescue a first-tier priority behind the One staffers out in Crofton.

Oz and his squad had been assigned to rescue her from the Gallows a few nights back. They'd found her in hand-to-hand combat against three early-bird demons. Her police and military background made her a good fit for the Lost Boys, but an anti-authoritarian attitude put her at odds with everyone above PFC.

"How many?" Robin checked as he exchanged a glance with John.

"There are just a few at the fence now, but there's a herd of them in the long-term parking area south of the park. They're going to pick up the activity before too long." The mass of demons in the distance started stumbling toward the fence as she spoke. "I hate it when I'm right all the time."

Within a few minutes, the fence line began to shake with sputtering, shambling demons caked in days-old blood. Their guttural roars, hoarse and shaggy, were intermittent but growing. With demons, more always meant *more*.

"Specialist Goldstein, now that we've righted the plane, how long to get that door open and those transports out?" Commander Banks asked.

"Thirty minutes, sir."

"Get on it. You have fifteen."

"Aye, sir."

Goldstein and his engineers scrambled. John circled around the plane to get a better look at the fence line in the distance. Twelve feet tall, with two thin strands of barbed wire along the top—that wouldn't even slow the rabid down. John had seen demons tear an arm off, pushing their way through shattered glass doors.

At some point, the crowd size would push the fence over. There were, John guessed, about eight to ten-thousand in the swarm. It would hold if they weren't reinforced with new passers-by, but the swarm's bellowing was already attracting smaller packs.

"I don't want to waste ammo if we don't have to," John said as Robin joined him. "It would be great if we could avoid drawing more attention. Let's make sure everyone is using suppressors. Let's keep it quiet."

With a resounding clang, the A400's rear ramp dropped without warning behind them. They both jumped at the teeth-aching crash.

"Jesus fucking Christ, Goldstein!" John shouted.

The demons at the fence line surged as the speed of sound delivered the noise. After a quarter-second, their roars and inhumane hoots made their way back to the soldiers. Goldstein poked his head out the back of the plane with a look of shame and fear. John waved him back to work.

"The timing of that screw-up couldn't have been much worse, Commander." Emily's voice over the two-way was calm.

"Get anyone with a rifle up on that fuselage and wait for orders. No one shoots without a suppressor, and no one shoots without my order," John grunted at Robin. Mercer sprinted to round up the rest of their markspeople. Within a minute, the A400's fuselage was topped with a row of long guns.

"What do you think, Tran?" John asked into his walkie. "Is that fence going to hold?" He turned to look at her sixty feet away, atop the most beat-up Humvee.

"I'm no structural engineer, Commander," she said, then looked over at him. "But I wouldn't bet my life on it."

"I agree. Captain Mercer, give the shooters the green light. Suppressors on."

In unison, the rifle barrels flared with orange light, and John watched as demons began to fall. He backed up to the fuselage and looked in at the progress of Specialist Goldstein and his team of engineers.

"We're going to need to make an exit here soon, Chris," John said gently but firmly.

Goldstein nodded and looked to his team. "Are we good on the Ridgeback?"

"Yes, sir." Four soldiers responded in unison.

He jumped into the massive six-by-six, clicked on its lights, and flashed an OK sign to John. John waved him to pull it out, as the LT-powered vehicle surged forward with a whine of its brushless motors and out into the open.

"Get that command vehicle out now! Good job, Chris!"

Goldstein smiled, nodded, and ran back to his team, busily attacking the tie-downs and chocks in the plane.

"Commander, we have a problem," Robin shouted down to him.

He turned to the fence line and saw it immediately. As the demons were dropped, they formed a ramp for the succeeding waves. If they kept shooting, the bodies would pile high enough for the swarm to top the fence.

"Cease fire!" John shouted loud enough that all could hear, walkie-talkie or no.

It was too late. The surge was now grinding zombies under, smashing them into the chain-link, giving the swarm an easier climb. The fence swayed and bulged as a pair of the things made it over the top. One snagged and hung as if crucified on the inward strand of barbed wire. The other dropped onto its face and struggled for a moment before standing, broken and bleeding black goo. Then it was shuffling toward them. Tran dropped it.

Behind John, the command vehicle crawled out of the fuselage.

"Okay, you primates," John shouted. "Get those vehicles loaded."

The Ridgeback held a crew of eight, but they could cram in fourteen. The Command vehicle could hold four, but six would fit. Six each in the Humvees meant some fighters would have to jump on top and hold on. Emily Tran stayed put on the roof and took out a fourth and fifth fence topper.

"That fence is going to go!" she shouted.

"Don't watch the fence! Get your asses in the vehicles! Mount up!" John shouted to the soldiers, frozen and gawking.

Emily was proven right once again as twenty yards of chain-link collapsed. Three heavy, galvanized fence posts tipped suddenly to the ground, their concrete footings tearing through the sod. Across the distance, the sound of the fence ringing as it struck the ground reached them as the demons surged into the breach. That moved the troops to frenzied action.

"Katy, would you mind *barring* that door?" Tran asked calmly.

The horde surged over the fence, then increased their speed in unpredictable fits and starts. Some monsters could sprint, a lesson they'd learned over the last few months. As John hopped onto the running board on the driver's side of the command vehicle, the speedier infected made it across the tarmac and were bearing down on them. Robin was behind the wheel and gunned it, nearly dislodging John's grip and raising shouts from the soldiers on the roof. The Ridgeback followed as the first of the demons reached them.

"Light 'em up," John said into his mike.

Snipers with tracer rounds targeted the fifty-five-gallon

drums. The Avgas went up, creating a hundred-foot-tall wall of flame. The demons never slowed. With their clothes and skin ablaze, they kept coming.

A dozen more energetic runners slammed broadside into the Ridgeback. They flailed their arms wildly as they spun off the moving vehicle. Their black, viscous blood spattered the fenders and anyone holding on. Despite the trauma inflicted by the impact, despite the fire burning their tattered clothes to ash, the demons continued to snatch and snap at the soldiers. John watched helplessly as soldiers on the six-by-six grappled with the things. A soldier, a woman, lost her grip. A demon with four-inch horns covering her back clawed and tore. John couldn't get a line of fire. The soldier started to tumble. In sudden slow motion, he saw it was Maria Ramirez. He reached for her, even though he was meters away, but she was already gone, pulled under the wave of gore-covered rabid.

Then, three more monsters slammed into the hood of the command vehicle and started to climb.

John took out two with his service Glock as he held onto the mirror supports. The soldiers on the roof opened fire, dropping the third and a few more snapping and lunging at them. The roar of the swarm rose above the staccato sounds of the gunfire and the rattle and thrum of their off-road treads.

More infected swarmed through the fire line. The Humvees, all packed with soldiers like spam in a can, opened up with full automatic, unsuppressed weapons fire. By that point, even the fastest monsters could not keep up.

"Save your ammo!" John shouted into his mike, but no one in the last Humvee had a walkie-talkie. They'd all grown way too dependent on Aurora's instant, ubiquitous comms.

John replayed Ramirez's slow motion tumble.

Not Maria!

Maria was so bright, so vital. She'd been a joy to lead, and he'd led her to this. John was angry, wracked with remorse, and struggling to maintain the demeanor his troops needed if he wanted to get them home. If a violation had caused this, all he wanted to do was track it down and strangle whoever committed it. Then an intestine curdling thought tore through it all.

Could it have been Zoe?

He plastered anger into the hole in his psyche blown open by that thought. He clenched his teeth, screamed through them, and snapped back into the moment. The convoy was rolling, leaving their trashed plane, leaving the tide of demons. The sun had set completely, and the fires of Madre Pueda loomed to the west. Robin navigated out of Thorne's flight operations and cleared the terminal. It took some weaving around abandoned cars and a few lone, wandering demons, but within twenty minutes, they were on I-5, and Madre Pueda was just a glow on the horizon.

"I forgive you for my parents."

"What?" he asked. "What about your parents?"

"I forgive you. I'm going to lose you, but you'll find m—"

John woke with a jolt as Robin hit the brakes. The smell of nut-wood smoke made John's groggy mind think of barbecue—like hickory, but sweeter. The almond orchards north and south of I-5 headed into Yolo were all ablaze.

John thought of Zoe. He'd dreamt about her, and the dream was fading fast. Her voice still echoed in his bones. In the dream, they'd been in bed together. She'd nuzzled up to his ear and told him she forgave him for her parents.

Her parents? What did that *mean?* He shook his head and pulled a protein bar from the glove box.

The going had been slow. A three-hour trip had stretched into the early hours of the morning. The troops had to clear a cluster of abandoned cars every five miles or so. A few of the vehicles had passengers that had turned rabid. Demons weren't smart enough to open a car door or unbuckle a seat belt.

It sickened John that NTC might be sitting on a cure, but that it would be of no use to them until they had demons to test it on. Last week, demons were scarce. Now, the supply far exceeded the demand. But there was no way to send the demons bodily into the past for testing. With all the data gathered, the testing could only ethically take place after Downfall. It was the reason med teams had accompanied all the Borealis CSAR teams.

With a cure in hand, tested and verified, production teams could deliver at scale; but a cure had to come first, and so far, the eggheads at NTC would only say they were close. Meanwhile, his soldiers continued to execute innocent people.

The only way to move the cars with demons in them was to kill them. It was different from shooting them in a swarm. They were just people in cars—fish in a barrel. He made it clear to all his fighters that, though he couldn't stop them from referring to them as demons or Ray or any number of pop-culture nicknames, he wouldn't stand for them to be treated disrespectfully. So, half a dozen shooters went through and cleared the cars of demons before the engineers cleared the highway of cars.

He told his team to grab any maps they found, since Aurora and GPS were currently not an option. Somebody brought back a deluxe Rand McNally map that must have harkened back to the 1900s. John felt oddly nostalgic, leafing through the spiral-bound book. He felt like he was doing an imitation of his father. But the highways that mattered were the same—he'd found what he was looking for, a way to Sacramento Airport.

John had tried to grab some shuteye once the highway was cleared.

Now, they were back to fire. Fire was a repeating pattern now, a leitmotif. Four PFCs were asleep, curled on top of one another like kids on the back shelf. His window was open, and the roar of the burning trees was deep and filled with loud cracks and pops as green wood exploded from steam. He liked almonds. He wondered if he'd ever be able to eat an almond again. Did the botanists in B-Dome have a bonsai almond grove squirreled away that would supply humanity with almonds in the Arctic?

"It looks like Yolo is burning too, Commander," Robin said.

John leaned forward, peered through the bug-spattered windshield, then checked his map. He shook his head.

"Yolo isn't that big. We're looking at Sacramento on the horizon, beyond Yolo."

John tested his Aurora network connection. Nothing. Without their handlers, without a functioning Aurora network, everything took longer. Everyone was suffering withdrawal from instant gratification at their fingertips.

"Any contact on Aurora from anyone?" John asked.

Robin shook his head. His eyes were large and shiny and full of concern. "It's going to be like this *everywhere*."

John had never seen fear in Robin's eyes before. His chipper optimism was one thing he counted on over the last six years. Sometimes it was downright annoying. But John had more than once pulled himself out of a blue mood with Robin's sunny outlook.

"Maybe not," John said. "Oracle painted a bleak picture. We knew that."

"Yeah. Knowing and having it realized… it's like that old film of the blimp on fire."

"Dirigible. The Hindenburg."

"*'Oh, the humanity.'* I used to make fun of the emotion in that announcer's voice. But fuck me. I get it now. It makes me want to cry too."

"Captain, we have been on the road for one night. I expect before we cross into Nunavut territory, we'll see shit that will tear us inside out. But I need you to be solid for the souls we need to get home. And you need me to be solid, too. That's our deal. Between us. Can you make me that deal?"

"Sir, yes, sir."

"And that's the deal I'll make with you, Captain. *No sleep till Brooklyn.*"

"No sleep till Brooklyn, Commander."

John looked out at the dull red glow of Sacramento on fire.

He'd dreamt of Zoe. That much he could recall. Something about her parents. He wished he could go back to sleep and dream of her again. He'd grown accustomed to falling asleep with her: talking about nothing and everything, her humor teasing him when he took himself too seriously, or backfilling his confidence when he felt unequal to the task. She might not be his handler anymore. Without the database, would they reassign her? Maybe. But he could still talk to her, right? Yeah. That was almost certain. He would catch up when they were back online, he reassured himself. They'd be back online *any time now*.

09-23-36 7:00 AM PDT

Morning only existed on clocks. The skies around Sacramento were dark with blood-red haze from the fires. John's platoon wore bandanas as face masks, soaked in bottled water. It was impossible to see the sun through the evenly murky red dome of the sky. They had made it around Yolo and Woodland without a major demon confrontation. Small swarms were sighted to the north twice, but nothing to compare to the scale they'd encountered in MP.

But Sacramento had a population of 600,000. Twice the size of Madre Pueda. Even in the ruddy daylight, the fires lit the sky. Hell was here, too. Thankfully, Sacramento International was on this side of the city with plenty of open land and low population density. With any luck, an A400 would be waiting for them. Six years of having a time machine to manipulate his luck left him seeing future unknowns in terms of uncollapsed wave functions. He was Schrödinger's soldier. The plane would be there. The plane would not be there. Heads or tails.

Luck felt like an expression of humanity's need to account for reality's superpositions. And when he thought about their current situation, maybe luck wasn't something they should count on.

"I'm wondering if we killed an albatross somewhere in Madre

Pueda," John said to Robin as they peered out at the airport from the middle of the Sacramento River Bridge. They still had tele-photo vision, thanks to their lens implants.

"What's an albatross?"

"A bird? A big seagull-like bird?" John looked over at Robin, but his lens was still zoomed, and he saw nothing but his thick brown hair. He zoomed out. "Did you read *any* books in high school?"

Robin laughed.

"The Rime of the Ancient Mariner?" John asked.

"I sure as hell never read any poetry books in high school." Robin frowned sourly.

"Rime, not Rhyme—well, it IS a poem, but—never mind." John turned back to the airport. "Looks like something going on," —he checked his dog-eared Rand McNally—"Airport Boulevard."

"Yeah. There's a swarm and lots of cars," Robin confirmed.

"Once we get across the river, we can just cut across the farm-land." John squinted. "It's a straight shot over plowed fields. The Ridgeback won't even need to slow down on that terrain. You see an A400?"

"I do not, Commander." He squinted, too. "But we don't have a great angle. Their long runway is 34R, on the far side of the terminal."

"Back to being an optimist? Good." Though John knew it was hard to hide a bird of that size. "Let's find out."

The caravan made a quick trip across fallow farmland before a stop for Goldstein's team to pull down the chain-link fence marking the airfield. They rounded the terminal on the north side. There was no NTC bird to be seen. Instead, in the distance, a small swarm of demons gathered at the edge of flight operations and the private commercial terminal. John tugged on his canteen.

"Circle the wagons," he said, gesturing to the other vehicles. After the soldiers piled out of their rides, John barked, "Okay. Okay. At ease. Cop a squat and listen up."

The troops quieted down.

"So, there is no A400 NTC bird here. We've known the weather was headed for Nunavut since last week. This isn't a big surprise. It was a long shot." He noticed a cluster of shipping containers behind the Ridgeback as he spoke. "The fact that the Aurora network is still out means we're back to being soldiers without superpowers, but we are the Lost Boys!"

"Bangarang!" they hissed in whispered unison.

"I want to meet with the officers, and we'll map out our next steps. We'll need to resupply. We'll need more ammo. Thankfully, this is the US of A." They all chuckled. "Fnding ammo between here and home will not be a problem. But get your minds wrapped around this: there will be problems to solve between now and home. I know a lot of you have been in the suck. Well, here we are again. Yeah." He gestured to the red sky above. "The sky is a new thing. But anyone who's lived in the Pacific Northwest or Canada in the last twenty years has seen skies like this from wildfires. I was a fire chief before I died and came to heaven. This? This was what we called summer." He stopped as he looked closer at the containers.

They were stacked three high, in a twelve-sided circle. There were gaps between each stack filled with chain-link fencing all the way to the top.

"So, take a breather." He turned his attention back to the troops. "Grab an MRE. Keep an eye out for Ray-Ray. We will reconvene before nightfall with a plan of action. Dismissed."

The circle broke apart. John looked again at the containers. It seemed like a weird place and a weird configuration for storage. And they were marked by three hobo signs, spray-painted in white on the rusted red container in the middle. Above them was a bible verse. John 9:23. Per John's training, Borealis used hobo signs on all their doomsday prep storage sites. These were different.

The first sign was a picnic table seen from the side, with two eyes on either side. It meant *Safe Camp*. The next was a circle with an x inside. That meant *Handouts Inside*. The last was an arrow-head pointing down. That meant *Be ready to fight*. John had taught all of those to Stephen in Afghanistan.

John whistled to Robin. He sauntered over.

"Do you recognize those containers as part of our doomsday prep?"

Robin shook his head. They walked over to them together. As they got closer, John saw two smaller signs. No, they weren't hobo signs. There was a One Corporation logo and a small Bore-alis polar bear logo, both spray-painted with a stencil.

"You familiar with scripture?" John asked.

Robin shook his head. "John 9:23? Hold on. Auroras come with a dictionary, the complete works of Shakespeare, and all the holy books. No network required." His eyes lost focus, and after a few seconds, he quoted. "Therefore, said his parents, He is of age; ask him."

John shook his head. "That means nothing to me." But the Bible *never* spoke to him. Maybe it was a deep and meaningful passage.

They walked around the circle of containers. On the backside was a sixteen-foot, chain-link gate with double doors barred and padlocked. They looked at the interior space. It was the size of a pair of basketball courts. These were side-open units with doors facing into the enclosed area. A scaffold hung against every stack of three containers that allowed easy climbing access to the top. The gaps between each stack were bridged with reinforced chain-link and featured shelves strung between the roofs of the container boxes.

John thought, *It would make a good fort.*

"What's today's date?" John asked.

"The twenty-first? Twenty-second? Shit, I've lost track."

"September twenty-third." John smiled. "9/23. It's not scripture. It's a message for me. John. 9/23."

He walked to the padlocked gate and dialed in a quick combo from rote memory. The latch fell open. He spread the gate wide, and it banged open against the metal boxes with a clank.

As it did, they heard gunfire.

"GET THE MEN INSIDE! Big rigs too! Leave the HumVees," John shouted.

They sprinted around the makeshift fort to see the troops engaging a cell of thirty demons in a shambling run only twenty yards away.

"Get the bus. As soon as you're in, get snipers on top!" John slapped Robin on the back as he turned to the soldiers, picking off the incoming Ray-Ray.

Robin ran to the vehicle and got its crew moving. Oz popped out of the roof hatch of the Ridgeback with a machine gun and started laying down loud but effective suppressing fire.

"Move it, Lost Boys!! Oracle has given us a fort!" John ordered as he pointed back to the container enclosure in the shadow of the terminal. "Get your asses in the gate around back." He pulled out his Glock and started picking targets, dropping three before a smaller group of four surged to the right and surprised three younger soldiers. He was about to engage when Tran raced the Ridgeback forward, and Oz fired bursts of covering fire. John jumped onto the vehicle's side ladder to see past it as the soldiers joined the retreat, sprinting for the enclosure.

The larger herd, 200 yards away, took notice of the automatic weapons fire. Their grunts and howls echoed across the taxiway. John pounded on the six-by-six's rooftop.

"Let's go! Fall back to the containers!"

Tran gunned it, and they circled behind the fort as the rest of the platoon ran for the gate. The command vehicle was already parked inside. Robin and the snipers were atop the scaffolds and positioned on the ramparts. With suppressors on, they started casually picking off the lead demons in the swarm.

"Save your ammo until we know they're headed for us!" John shouted up. Robin nodded and relayed the order. John noticed he still had the padlock looped around the thumb of his left hand.

"Is everyone in?" He asked with his commander's volume.

The soldiers all looked around.

"I hope so," John said quietly as he pulled the gates closed, slid the bar into place, and clasped the lock through the hasp. He jogged back to the opposite wall and climbed to the top of the scaffold.

The demons were marching toward them, no doubt about it. His soldiers didn't have the ammo for a prolonged siege—or even a short one. He leaned back and shouted down, "Get these containers open. The combo on the locks should all be the same— 11-13-17. See if we've got ammo in any of these."

Everyone near a padlock grabbed it and started fumbling with the dial, surrounded by questionably helpful kibitzers. Robin looked at John.

"It was my combo in Afghanistan. Lucas cracked it. The first three two-digit primes."

Padlocks started popping open all around the circle. Doors swung back. The contents were arranged using Oz's packing system.

"MREs!"

"Water!"

"Ammo!"

"Way to go, Oracle!" John said to himself, then barked orders. "Start sorting and get the shooters refreshed!"

"Commander?" shouted a PFC.

"What?"

"There's an envelope here addressed to you!" the young woman hollered.

"Get it up here!" He turned to Robin and shrugged.

The PFC swung her way up the scaffolding's monkey bars as others started ferrying ammo boxes up to their snipers. She handed the large brown envelope to John. It was addressed to Commander John Banks, Borealis 1st. 9/23/36. He took a look out at the demon horde. They were nearing slowly. He leaned against the railing and opened the envelope.

LT,

Shit has gone sideways. Roberts' Rules violation—probably several. Winter arrived just before the Downfall refugee planes were hitting NTC Nunavut Field. As you read this, the fourth foot of snow is already piling on. They tried to keep the strips clear, but it was a losing effort. They're still trying to engineer skis for the A400s.

The NTC FTL network is toast and with it all Aurora traffic until they get the rules violation sorted. Every server is out, and new motherboards will need to be fabricated.

Walrus arrived safe and sound, thanks to you. But I provisioned his team for research, not production, so it will take a few weeks at best to get online again. He also can't fire it up until we've identified the violation. My fear is that you picked up an albatross along the way—a thing or a person whose arrival at the NTC would alter the sender's current reality. Someone ordered that pizza that was never delivered—and you and your team are the delivery drivers.

If we can't identify it, your efforts to get home will continue to fail. That could be something as simple as a flat tire or something more drastic. I could set my timeframe further into the future, but collapsing multiple wave functions will make my job a lot harder—

the big job of getting humanity back on a path out of all you see around you.

I set up this waypoint for you after my LLM flagged C-Dome's daily log. I serve as a handler for C Dome from my timeframe (it's how we got the idea for your handlers in the first place). But I don't have Aurora. I have Oneiri, a handful of desktop workstations, a holosuite, and a database that only has Pre-Downfall data in it. My resources out here in the wastelands are limited.

Like I said, I'm working through the NTC record seriatim to avoid collapsing wave functions. I used my imagination for what you'd be in for and packed these containers accordingly. I have access to your Aurora files. Keep a log like Captain Kirk on Star Trek. We have to be careful about creating more violations but, if you ever make it back, I can use AI to scrub your logs to help resupply you where I can. It won't be reliable. Without all the data sources, we can't be sure anything we put in place pre-Downfall will be there when you get to them in your timeframe. But it's all I can do.

I can't jump ahead, so I don't know what the violation is or how long the Lost Boys will be on the march. I don't even know if you'll be headed to Sacramento. But it's what I'd have done. I'm dropping similar resupply/battlements at all airports within a days journey from MP. When/If we identify the Roberts' Rules violation, I'll try to leave a sign you won't be able to miss. But you should be on the lookout for it, too. If you keep heading for home carrying a violation, your chances of reaching NTC again are zero. So figure it out, LT.

I know you'll get your soldiers home. You always do.
Climb to Glory!
Sgt. Stephen Lucas

It was his first direct communication with his friend in six years. His eyes shone with a welling tear. He blinked and smiled briefly before handing the letter to Robin.

"*He* knows what an albatross is," he said as he looked into the envelope and pulled out weather forecasts for the next ten days and a neatly folded map of North America with possible routes. The fallout zones of the three nuclear bomb sites were clearly marked. Two primary routes were highlighted that gave them a wide berth around the radiation danger. One went north and meant a cold march. The other went south, through the desert, a hot march. Ice or Fire.

He shook his head as the snipers started firing again. He turned to see the demon horde had grown, and the distance between the swarm and their position had shrunk. The individual demons could now be seen. Something about the rusty daylight made them seem even less human. Flipping on telephoto, John watched a waitress, with horns sprouting from her matted hair, stagger toward them in a blue frock and red-and-white-checkered apron, the order pad still in her front pocket. She had almost no bloodstains on her uniform, but the calf of her right leg had a large mouthful taken from it.

The earlier weapons' fire might have attracted them, but the platoon's retreat to the enclosure had hidden them from the swarm. Although they were closer, they were losing cohesion, ambling in no particular direction. With suppressors on the snipers' rifles, the sound from their shots—barely louder than a slapping a denim-covered ass—was quieter than the demon's footfalls and vocalizations. The crack of a headshot dropping a target was far louder to the nearby rabid than the silenced muzzle exhaust fifty yards away.

"Holy shit, Commander, this box has a full armory!" shouted a younger recruit. "*Fucking A! Grenades!*" Before John could respond, the kid pulled a pin and chucked the grenade over the ramparts. He had a good arm. He must've played ball in school. The M67 was about the size of a hardball and it arced up, over the containers and onto the tarmac midway between the circle of HumVees and their fortress. It exploded with a wallop that shook the chain-link and the scaffolds against the containers.

"You stupid son of a—" John yelled, but it was too late. The herd's chorus of howls and inhuman roars was a more eloquent reply to the kid's stunt than anything John could articulate. He watched as a demon sloppily sprinted from the swarm's main body. He felt its impact rattle the scaffold he stood on. Then another. Then another, until the impacts were coming in a constant barrage. The shooters took aim at multiple targets at the base of their fortress.

John scrambled to the top and looked down.

A high-powered rifle delivers a round at 3,000 ft per second. The pressure wave as the round moves through the skull and torso is more effective than any meat grinder humanity has ever conceived. Goal-oriented as ever and yearning for the humans atop the container, the rabid slammed into the bottom row of containers with arms extended and jaws snapping in the air. The snipers' hail of bullets turned the infected into ragged, half-exploded piles of shredded flesh and black, sooty blood.

And that horrifying pile was growing. John recalled the demons topping the fence in MP.

"HOLD YOUR FIRE!" John bellowed. Everyone stopped what they were doing and turned to look at him. Even the demons seemed to pause. "If we pile up bodies at the base of the containers, these fuckers are going to climb up the remains and top the ramparts. Aim for targets fifty yards out. Make a ring of bodies *out there*. Then they have to climb just to get in, and maybe we draw the close ones away if we keep it quiet in here. But either way, they won't get reinforcements so quickly."

"Sir! Yes, Sir!" shouted Emily Tran, and she returned to shooting. The rest of the soldiers followed her example. The tension that had been building since they'd retreated into the container fort gave way to a determination to outsmart the miserable creatures' base instincts. The shooters formed a ragged circumference of demon corpses fifty yards away. Within minutes, the herd within that circumference lost focus. The demons closest to the containers continued to throw their bodies against the metal walls. Those closest to the body line were drawn by the crack of the bullets hitting skulls and the motion of the bodies hitting the tarmac.

John turned to Robin. "Once they get a pile going, have them start another line further out."

Robin nodded.

John climbed down and found the kid who threw the grenade.

"What's your name, soldier?" He growled.

"Private, Jason Clark. Sir!"

John towered over him with barely concealed rage.

"Private!? Private?" John shouted. "For fuck's sake! I can't even demote you! Private Clark." He wiped the sweat from his face. "Do you get that you screwed up, Private?"

"I do, sir!"

John nodded. And dropped a large hand on his shoulder.

"Don't do that again."

"Sir! No, Sir!"

"Get your ass back to inventorying these containers, Private Clark."

"Commander!" Robin shouted down from the top.

Clark took the opportunity to be anywhere other than under his Commander's gaze.

John frowned and climbed back up.

There was a hush among the shooters. At the taxiway's edge, the massive super-swarm they'd first seen on the road had found their way around the terminal. They were still a mile off, but their trajectory was unmistakable. Their roar—it sounded like heavy traffic or an oncoming tornado—drew the attention of the closer demons, who moved toward the onrush.

"Cease fire!" John shouted. Then, more quietly, he said, "Let's see what they do."

The smaller, closer herd pulled back from the carnage at the base of their half-assed Fort Apache. They met the larger group on the tarmac a third of a mile away. People, normal humans, would stop, exchange information, and formulate plans. These were not people. The smaller herd was absorbed, only slowing the larger body's forward progress slightly. The demons on either side continued like two outstretched arms, reaching for the site of their last attraction.

Within minutes, their fort was surrounded by demons, sniffing and clawing at the containers' iron sides. It didn't take long, despite the soldiers' best efforts to stay quiet, before the rabid found the gaps between the stacks and the chain-link fences that filled them. The demons caught the blood scent and howled again.

They strained to reach through the links, pushed their hideous horned faces into it until it tore their skin and the black sludge of their blood oozed out. Their roars and hoots and barks increased in volume. The swarm pressed forward, crushing those in the front, in creepy slow motion that was, in every respect, more terrifying than the running, frantic demons. The soldiers were trapped among an ocean of monsters.

John had seen enough.

"All right, back to our original plan. Start stacking up the bodies at fifty yards," John stage whispered to his team.

The shooters didn't need to be told twice.

Within minutes, the pile encircling the fort stood hip-high. The incoming demons stumbled over them, often spilling backward. The snipers began forming another perimeter, 100 yards out. It took nearly half an hour before the demon corpses piled high enough to deter new arrivals. The pressure on the fort decreased. Demons within the concentric rings could now be dropped randomly without attracting more attention from those further out. But the super-swarm kept coming.

"Do you know of the Battle of Isandlwana?" Oz asked for any on the battlements to hear.

The sky was now a dark, blood-red above them. The fires of Sacramento to the east were just barely visible on the horizon. There was no way to tell the time. The swarm continued to flow toward them and around them. Shuffling rabid stretched as far as the soldiers could see. The soldiers continued to build grim perimeters of the fallen dead.

"You have probably seen it in movies about the British Empire being *heroic*. Let me tell you. It was a famous Zulu battle. Twenty thousand Zulu warriors armed with little more than spears and hide-bound shields lay siege to the vastly superior weaponry of 2,000 British colonizers." He took a moment to reload when fresh ammo was laid at his feet. "The Zulu victory was complete.

"Many military minds chalked the Zulu victory up to the sheer numbers. This was lazy thinking. The Zulu strategy was sound. They lured the British fighters away, separated them before the attack, approached them from the east and from the west, and encircled them. The colonizers had no chance against the cunning of the Zulu mind." He paused for effect, beamed a radiant smile, and continued. "I have told you, have I not, that I have that same Zulu blood coursing through *my* veins."

The nearby shooters groaned and rolled their eyes.

After listening to Oz's story with amusement, John leaned down and said quietly, "The Isandlwana was in South Africa. Nigeria is in West Africa. They're further apart than we are from Nunavut."

"Commander, I swear I am a descendent of *Shaka* himself," he declared and returned to sighting and firing. As John stepped onto the scaffold, Oz's face curled into an impish grin.

Optimistic attempts at humor eventually gave way to grim professionalism. Their task took six hours of nearly constant weapons fire, prompting complaints of cramping and carpal tunnel pain from the simple, repetitive act of pulling a trigger. They went through two-thirds of the ammo stores found in the containers. Weapons failed. New arms from the armory containers were pressed into service while support engineers cleaned and repaired the overheated guns. It was a brutal, nightmarish duty.

No matter how ruined the virus left the infected—the lunatic eyes, the viscera-strewn collection of horns, the tattered clothes caked with dried blood—there was no way to take that many lives without killing something in yourself. GGB-Z may have overwritten the firmware, but the hardware was still human. It was impossible to fill your gunsight with a human face and not project onto it a similarity to a friend or a family member, a coworker, or a cousin—before exploding those features faster than the speed of sound.

On and on and on and on, for six hours under a sky that looked like Lucifer could arrive at any moment to command his demons on to victory. But demons had no generals, no strategy. Demons only had blood thirst. The smell of uninfected human blood pounding in the soldiers' veins drew demons from hundreds of yards away and made nearby demons frantic. The blood of their own, with which the tarmac was slick, was of no interest. It oozed out of them like maple syrup or motor oil in winter. It made the heaps of corpses impossible to climb once they reached a meter or two high. Demons attempting to scale them rarely achieved the summit and only tumbled backward again and again.

Slapstick monsters.

But none of the soldiers were laughing, none were smiling. Overnight, the swarm thinned and moved on, apparently through their own sort of Brownian motion alone. A few snipers, notably Emily Tran, Oz, and Robin, stayed atop the ramparts til morning's orange-gray light. A northern wind was pushing the smoke away for the moment, and John surveyed their position.

The markspeople had done a good job of piling their targets in sloppy concentric rings. The inner ring was over two meters high. The outer rings were less uniform and shallower.

The overall effect left John with the impression of a ghastly dartboard with the fort at the center. Everywhere beyond their bullseye was that black-red, tar-like coagulated shit that oozed through the demons' veins. It looked like a pile of offal had been dumped on the target and hit everything but the center.

The smoke from the pecan groves combined with the pervasive odor of the corpses was oddly, nightmarishly, sweet. But John knew it wouldn't last; the flies would come, then the maggots, then the birds. The bodies would eventually fill with methane and expand like hellish Macy's Thanksgiving balloons.

John wanted his platoon gone by then. Buried under two feet of bodies, the Humvees were no longer an option. Getting them free of the guts would take days. No Humvees meant a march—and a march meant climbing that circle of bodies.

He walked to the scaffold and looked down at his soldiers. The engineers were still cleaning and repairing weapons. A few were distributing MREs and water bottles. All were staring blankly at whatever their eyes had landed on. Gone tharn. No one had slept. No one was talking. That was a bad thing.

"Listen up!" he shouted. "Look around." They looked at him with a uniform blankness. "*Do it!*" John ramped up his volume. "Look to your right. Now look to your left. Lay your eyes on all the *warriors* you serve with. Take a minute. Make eye contact!" John waited for the rifle team to move to the edge and look in. "Lost Boys!"

"Bangarang."

"Lost Boys!"

"Bangarang!"

"LOST BOYS!"

"BANGARANG!"

"There you go!" He leaned against the scaffold's rail. "I want you to acknowledge an undeniable truth. We *stood*. We held! The demon hordes laid siege to this proud fortress." He shook the scaffold, and the sound rattled around the containers. "And we *stood FIRM*. Because it's not the fort. It's not the battlements. It's not the weapons or the numbers." He looked around. "We stood *together*. That's what it's about. Look out there. Tens of thousands of them dead. Tens of thousands more fled.

"We stood. *We lost no one.*"

The soldiers looked around at each other. Some began to grin.

"There will be history books written about these times when the world went to hell. In a bright future, when the skies are shining blue again. They will write about this siege, and all your names will be written there.

"You're hungry. Eat. You're thirsty. Drink. You're tired. Sleep. Those are my orders. We're going to hunker here for 24 hours. My direct reports and I are going to plan our next destination. But for now, rest. Tomorrow, *we head for home.*"

There were no rousing cheers, but as he turned to look out over the ramparts, he could hear the conversations beginning and, after a bit, some laughter. That was a good thing. Perhaps now, some of them actually would sleep. Some might not even suffer terrible nightmares. Most would. John knew well enough how long a trauma stays with you and how often it comes to visit your dreams.

09-24-36 9:00 PM PDT

The day was quiet, thankfully. The sky ramped through a gradient of orange through rusty brown to deep scarlet before night fell. The starless sky was filled with low clouds lit in the east by the fires of Sacramento, renewed again by a southerly wind. Outside their fort, the dead had not yet begun to rot. The air smelled earthy and hot. Smoke made all the soldiers sneeze something fierce. The inventory team found a few decks of cards in one of the containers, and the platoon formed into smaller circles for poker, spades, and pinochle. Occasionally, a lone demon could be heard hooting in the distance.

"I vote north," Robin said.

"The cold path? Are you *mad?* I can never tell when Americans are joking," said Oz. "The south will be hot, yes, but it will be flat. Also, I have never marched through snow. Desert marching is nothing."

John rubbed his face. He'd have killed for a hot shower and a cold bourbon.

"If we go south," Robin pointed to the laminated map. "We have to go clear to the Mississippi before heading north. We'll hit the Ozarks and they ain't flat or sandy. Between us and the Mississippi, there are swamps and shit."

"If we go up the Mississip', we'll have fallout downwind, remember. Prevailing winds carry west to east."

"But the Mississippi has boats we can take north. A boat ride!"

"*Jesus.* Flip a coin, Commander." Emily Tran piped up. She wasn't an officer or enlisted, but always circled up with the leaders, anyway.

"I've marched in snow," John said. "I've marched in sand. I've marched in mountains and swamp, too. I hate 'em all equally. I hate a long sustained march. But I can do them all equally if it gets me home. If we can get more vehicles to replace the Humvees and don't have to hoof it all the way, we can make it to NTC earlier going north. Oracle gave us the ten-day forecast. It's snowing up in Nunavut, but the US border is expected to be warm for the time of year. If we can get geared for cold weather before we hit it, it won't be too bad. We do that."

"Oh my god." Oz shook his head.

"What's that, Specialist Osunyemi?" John said sharply.

"Good choice, sir!"

John smiled. "C'mon, Oz. If we go the desert route, these lily-white folks will burn."

"These white folks will be the death of me," Oz laughed long and hard. In the dark distance, a trio of demons echoed back his laughter as a series of rough barks. The officers all fell silent.

"That is fucking creepy," Robin said.

09-25-36 7:00 AM PDT

During the calm night, the carrion fowl arrived. The dull red sky was filled with turkey vultures, ravens, crows, and even seagulls circling in tight arcs above them. Goldstein and his engineers pulled the pins on the chain link gates and the platoon lifted them off their hinges.

The command vehicle was connected to the Ridgeback with chains and tow webbing. The smaller vehicle might not make it over the pile of guts, but the Ridgeback surely would, and it had more than enough power to tow it's smaller sister along. Robin hopped in, and the six-by-six eased out the gate. It reached the pile, found its footing after a few of its large tires spun a few wretched rotations in the slop, then it ground over and disappeared beyond, leaving almost no visible divot in corpse mountain.

Six soldiers carried the dislodged gates like pallbearers to the heap of corpses. They approached the base of the pile, raised the sturdy gate onto its narrow edge, and let it flop onto the top. It landed with a crunch of bone and a sickening squish. The team with the second gate climbed to the top on the ramp formed by the first. They dropped their gate down the other side, forming a twelve-foot-wide catwalk across the carnage.

John looked at his troops, many of them turning pale or green, and marched to the fore.

"Good morning, primates. I thought I would go for a stroll this morning. Thought I might stretch my legs! Who is with me for a morning jog?"

"Lost Boys are with you," a few murmured unenthusiastically.

"I didn't hear that." He cocked an ear toward his troops.

"LOST BOYS ARE WITH YOU, SIR!"

"EXCELLENT!"

He turned to Sargent Peck, a tough blonde girl from Houston, Texas. "Know any good dance tunes, Sargent?"

Lisa Peck smiled behind her bandana and shouted as she jogged in place. "LOST BOYS ARE MADE OF?"

The platoon snapped into a pair of columns.

"Greasy, grimy gopher guts!"

Peck tilted her head and began jogging toward the chain link ramps. "Mutilated monkey meat"

"Hairy pickled piggy feet."

"French fried eyeballs."

"Floating in some kerosene."

"And me without a spoon."

They marched awkwardly through the bodies as they maintained their cadence. Nearby crows eyed them cautiously but never stopped pecking at their protein bonanza. John took the lead, marching them up and over the ring of death. Once they were clear, the gates were lifted and moved to the next ring. This hundred-yard ring was not nearly as well fortified, however. The soldiers marched over and out, finding their footsteps more surely. The outer ring was incomplete, with many gaps. Once they cleared that and were onto the open, unstained tarmac, John peeled off and let his troops pass.

They were *all* green now, struggling to keep their MREs down, but they were out. He turned and looked back. It was as if a tornado from hell had circled around them and slowly dissipated, leaving all the mortal debris. But the fort had held. Stephen's time machine juju had saved their lives. Tonight, he would start a Commander's Log. On a long march home, every bit of juju would help.

He double-timed it to the head of the column and jogged alongside Sgt. Peck.

Peck nodded with a grim determination. "LOST BOYS ARE MADE OF?"

"Greasy, grimy gopher guts."

"Dehydrated dino dung."

"Mutilated mutant mung."

"Flaming ear wax."

"Bobbing in a bowl of barf."

"And me without a spoon."

09-25-36 10:30 AM EDT: DREAMLAND

"*WHAT* IS THE HOLDUP? Why are we *still* out of touch with the Borealis field units?" demanded Athena.

With John Banks incommunicado and the Critical Path's conclusion nine days in the past, the lead players in preparing for Downfall were suddenly in the position of making it up as they went. Mary Allan had plenty to do finding her recruits among the new arrivals and slotting them into existing and emerging enterprises. She also maintained a massive and growing list of unresolved personnel requests. There were literally millions of recruits left out in the fallen world that she still had hopes of recovering. The odds of their survival dimmed with every day they delayed in rescuing them—and the weather wasn't doing them any favors.

So, Mary had plenty to do.

Athena knew exactly what she had signed on for. She and her allies among the Inuit had built a miracle of modern civil planning and engineering. The domes were filled to their bursting points, but there was enough food, energy, and resources to provide for everyone, so long as no one wanted extravagances. Athena was a wartime leader, the first mayor of the post-apocalyptic era. It was up to her to manage the expectations of the citizens of the NTC. That was a challenge she was made for.

So, Athena had plenty to do.

The problem was, there was still plenty that needed doing beyond Athena's or Mary's portfolios. Some of these things fell neatly under the purview of Commander Banks' authority: managing the twelve-thousand Borealis military forces (of which two-thirds were now bivouacked here in M-Dome while the rest were out in the field without their comms), securing the last of the Oneiri prototypes (six of which had been returned on the same transport that delivered Walrus Roberts), and leading missions into the field to rescue those millions of vital human resources on Mary's database.

So, Banks had plenty to do.

If he was even *alive*.

The first wave of survivors had crashed on the shores of the NTC, and the structure, as meticulously planned by Stephen and his teeming minions, had held. There had rarely been a refugee relocation operation of this scale in humanity's long history of inhumanity.

At Stephen's instruction, Athena, Mary, and John had formed the NTC Steering Committee. Stephen had requested they be joined by his One Corporation right-hand woman, Marianne Crouch, a quiet woman in her fifties who had accepted the abrupt change to her life with impressive stoicism.

The topic of today's meeting? The NTC IT department's handling of the AuroraNet outage.

Les McBride, NTC's Chief Information Technology Officer, or CITO (or, as he pronounced it, "cheeto")—a man with an impeccable if somewhat inflated resume, unmatched self-assuredness, and a covertly fascistic leadership style—was briefing them on the Borealis AuroraNet outage. He was the rare hire that Mary Allan regretted. He was one of the seventy-three percent of NTC staff and citizens who were hired off the street, not resurrected by John's Lost Boys. The opportunities to resurrect a quality IT leader were rare. Based on his resume and a brief video conference, she'd signed off on his acquisition three years earlier as the NTC systems were coming online.

In the few minutes since this meeting began, Les had demonstrated nothing but arrogance and a dismissive attitude toward the women currently running the world.

"The sChips embedded in the Aurora implants connect via OneFTL network protocols in a peer-to-peer manner." Les gestured to the flow diagram that illustrated the network architecture. "However, each chip's MAC address is registered via a database managed by NTC-housed Borealis servers. To connect, the Aurora pings the Borealis server and receives the MAC address for their target."

Mary shook her head. "None of this tells us why the AuroraNet is down or why we can't establish contact with any of our field units."

"We've had multiple cascading system failures in the OneFTL server farms addressing the Borealis AuroraNet. As soon as we correct one, another unrelated system fails." Les said with a smarmy confidence that didn't reflect the urgency of the situation. "We're working the problem, I *assure* you."

"Commander Banks and his unit have been offline since Downfall. The pilots of the planes that made it out of Madre Pueda reported seeing a crash on takeoff," Athena nearly shouted with frustration. "Beyond the fifty or so of his troops in the Borealis First, we have a *third* of our military stranded in the field around the world. We need these system failures *identified, addressed, and corrected*. Do whatever you need to do to re-establish contact with the field units so we can assess Commander Banks' team's status."

Les prepared to inform the women of the complexity of the systems involved, to tell them they couldn't possibly comprehend the extent of his problems—but Marianne Crouch politely interrupted, "Have you consulted with Walrus?"

"I'm sorry?" Les asked.

"Walrus Roberts invented the sChip and wrote all the sChip's

FTL network protocols," she said firmly. "I'd think he'd be well suited to help diagnose your cascading failures."

Athena and Mary fixed Les with their unique death stares.

"Do *that!*" Athena said.

Les gulped and nodded on the outside; but, on the inside, he seethed at the perceived professional affront.

09-25-36 1:40 PM EDT

Walrus' orientation buddy was Brian Cosgrove. Brian delighted in taking the well-known genius through the NTC domes, partly because he was a big fan of Walrus', but mostly because he hadn't laughed so much since he was a teenager. Walrus was what everyone said he was: a big, friendly kid at heart. They spent over an hour in B-Dome alone. Walrus couldn't help exploring all of the bays and hydroponic stacks. "Smell this!" he demanded, shoving a root under Brian's nose.

The root smelled like super Root Beer. Brian had never smelled anything like it. It made his eyes roll back in their sockets. "Is this…what…?"

"Sassafras!" Walrus laughed and nodded. "Yeah, Root beer! Or Birch beer. They use it in filé gumbo powder. I could sit here and huff this stuff. When I was a kid, the vacant, wooded lot across the street from my house had this stuff growing alongside the paths. I used to pull it up by the roots and…." He filled his lungs with the smell and then laughed it all out.

Brian looked at his watch and wondered if he should even *worry* about time. Walrus was sort of E-Dome embodied. They would wait. Walrus wandered off to examine another hydroponics stack. Thirty feet wide at its base, the looping, plastic conveyor belts contained arrays of transparent, blue bubbles filled with nutrients. The rows emerged from the nutrient solution, and farmers methodically pushed root bundles into the bubbles. On the other side of the tower, harvesters pulled freshly grown onions about the size of Brian's fist from the gelatinous bubbles before they returned to the water bath. The plastic blisters kept the roots surrounded by nutrients while their leaves grew out and up toward the dome's ceiling. Each row made the round trip, from the optimized nutrient bath to the top and back, in four weeks. A basket of perfect yellow onions was filled to the brim at the end of the harvest row.

Walrus said, "With the temperature outside, you could see this being a prototype for…"

"A Mars colony?" Brian said.

Walrus laughed. "Okay, so maybe I'm being *Captain Obvious.*"

"It's the geodesic domes. They just look futuristic." He looked up at the awe-inspiring structure. "There were rumors in the early days. Some said that the technology center was just a cover story for a Mars mission, funded secretly by Stephen Lucas. I guess we were all being sold a bill of goods for our own benefit."

Walrus admired the structure before tilting his head toward Brian. "I think you'll find that's a *Lamella* dome." Walrus waved his hands at the dome. "They all are."

Walrus spent more time walking around C-Dome than Brian had *his* first time. Brian found all the admin stuff boring—logistics, schedules, and timelines. Definitely *not* his thing. However, Walrus spent a good ten minutes looking over shoulders at the multi-dimensional Gantt charts that all the admins worked on. Brian saw something like awe in Walrus' face as he stood silently. Perhaps this is the nature of genius, the ability to be compelled by the mundane. Finally, Walrus became aware of Brian waiting in silence. "Oh hey, Brian. I'm sorry, man. This is fascinating. This is taking what Stephen was doing at One to the next level. Orchestrating scaled Agile work streams across timeframes. Oneiri-empowered multi-threaded project management. Beautiful."

Brian looked puzzled. He'd always assumed C-Dome was just for paper pushers. He also puzzled over the term "Oneery." NTC had security clearance levels as strict as the Pentagon, he knew—and so far, he hadn't been granted access to a lot of the really woo-woo shit He tugged on Walrus' sleeve to ensure Walrus got to the main event, E-Dome, the current largest dome at the NTC.

———

09-25-36 3:00 PM EDT

There was cake. There were balloons. There was a sign that said "Welcome Walrus". The new labs were wrapped around the top level of the dome. The inner windows looked over a small lake and a waterfall. Perhaps an homage to the basement laundry. Workspaces for engineers wrapped around the green spaces. His entire One Corporation team had been evacuated, all two hundred of his researchers, engineers, and assistants. They were all in various stages of shock, amazement, grief, and confusion. All were now aware of how badly the world had crashed outside these domes. Everyone felt equal parts giddy hysteria, heart-swelling gratitude, and crippling survivor's guilt.

But there was *cake.*

Walrus took a forkful of yellow cake and sugary frosting and walked to the whiteboard like a tenured professor. The crowd quieted. He smiled and looked around. "So. I want to say thanks for the welcome from the folks here at NTC. Those of us who've just arrived had a front-row view of what's going on out there. I think you all know we witnessed something horrible, and I think we all suspect… we were spared the worst of the horror." His smiling face was sober for a moment.

"We're all amazed at what has been created here. It's like Dreamland. We're all humbled by how much these labs recreate our workshops back home. And so many brilliant new minds to work with! I think we can, for the most part, pick right back up where we left off before…." He was silent for a moment.

"I think I know why we've all been gathered here. Imagine what we can accomplish here. Over the next several months, we'll all talk about where we're going, together and one-on-one. But we have a home here. A safe space. I think we owe it to our new friends and our old ones to work to rebuild what was lost. I know that's what Stephen would have hoped, too."

He looked around at the shell-shocked faces of the new community members, all lit by tentative hope—the weak embers of optimism. He smiled his wide, gap-toothed smile. "Here's to Dreamland."

The festivities were waning, and Brian had promised to be home for dinner. He took one more lap around the welcome party and found Walrus in Workshop 4, inspecting the cabling on a rack of four devices Brian had never seen before. They appeared to be server blades. Each was intensely black, and around their base, a line of LEDs revolved, split, and merged like living things. Walrus looked up. "Hey, Brian! I was checking out the cabling back here. It's how my OCD rolls. I was happy to see these had finally made it through logistics. Commander Banks' *Mission Impossible* crew snagged them before they yanked me, I guess. This is just one rack. It seems C-Dome confiscated the other three."

Brian was about to ask what they were but decided, in the interest of time, he'd only say, "I'm heading home for dinner. You're invited if you'd like to meet my family. Lasagna?"

Walrus smiled and rubbed his belly. "Like Garfield, I do love me some lasagna. Thanks, man, but I'm going to ask for a rain check. I have some unfinished work I was doing before I was evacuated. I'm going to see if I can get up and running here before I call it a day."

Brian nodded. "Okay, man. It was great to meet you, a huge honor. I mean it, though. You have to see what we're doing down in 3D fab. It's going to blow your mind."

Walrus emerged from behind the racks and lifted Brian into a bear hug. "Tomorrow morning. I'm there. Can't wait to see your stuff."

Brian chuckled at the unexpected intimacy. "Okay, then. Have a good night."

"Later, man."

Walrus watched Brian walk down the long, curving glass walls. He found his way to his personal office space, walked to the glass wall, and looked out over the breathtaking view.

"In Xanadu did Kubla Khan a stately pleasure-dome decree," he said, and for one of the few times in his life, he was undeniably sad.

Walrus had deduced how such a place could have been made to order in the few short days since he last spoke with Stephen. A place this beautiful showed its designer's hand. He knew Stephen's work. It was not the sort of thing he could have done quickly, however, and Walrus wondered how many years Stephen had labored—would labor—into the future to see this vision through. A decade, two, more? They'd been friends since that day on the PE field in intermediate school when Stephen had stood up to Walrus' harassers. Once again, Stephen had come to his rescue.

Walrus was coming to grips with the knowledge that the world's downfall, the falling of this darkness upon the world, all came from Oneiri. Cliff had been a serial killer, a monster, and he and Stephen had put a time machine in his hands. Cliff somehow had used Oneiri to order the fall of civilization for immediate delivery… hold the anchovies, please.

Oneiri had been Walrus' discovery.

But Oneiri had been Stephen's tool in making *this* place, too. This safe haven, cleverly hidden from collapsing wave functions —Stephen had built a place that didn't exist in a place where no one would think to look. Who had ever heard of Nunavut before they boarded those cargo planes? It was a clever evasion of Roberts' Rules. It was a miracle of rare device.

Walrus smiled. He'd never even known there was a place on

the planet called *Walrus Rocks Island*, literally translated from the Inuktitut, Aaffaffak Qaqqaq. He turned away from the window and looked at his office. It was perfect. The dome was perfect. The staff was perfect. Stephen had designed the NTC as a tool with one purpose: to save human civilization. It was now up to Walrus to use that tool.

"It was a miracle of rare device, a sunny pleasure-dome with caves of ice."

Walrus owed it to his lifelong friend to make the most of the time Stephen had given him. He returned to the new Workshop 4, pulled the bottom-most server blade from the rack, and mounted it on the workbench. He grabbed a Torx driver and popped the case. It was 5:30 PM. Though the sun had been down since 3:00, there was plenty of daylight.

He tapped his mobile and said, "Hi. Concierge Service? Where can I get a twelve-pack of ice-cold double-caf RageColas?"

"They'll deliver," Athena Shaw said from his doorway.

"I understand you'll deliver?" Walrus turned around and nodded. The concierge replied, and Walrus cupped his hand over the mic. "Where am I?"

"5024E."

"5024E. Excellent. Thanks!" He closed his connection.

"E-Dome, level five, Office 24." She pointed to the plate on the door. "I know we covered that in orientation."

"You did!" Walrus laughed and offered no further defense. Athena found his lack of guile charming. People often said he was like a big kid, but Athena thought she sensed something deeper. He had a lot going on beneath the surface, even if that surface appeared childlike.

"Has NTC's IT director contacted you yet? Les McBride?" she asked as she entered his office.

Walrus looked skyward, thought, then replied, "I met a lot of people today. *Les McBride* wasn't one of them." He returned his attention to dismantling the Oneiri blade server.

"We've lost contact with Commander Banks and his unit—all

the field units that didn't make the last flight before the weather hit."

Walrus recalled the scenes driving through Madre Pueda. He'd only seen the beginning, but that was bad enough. He tilted his head. "How many in the field?"

"Commander Banks had forty-three on his plane. We've got units in Hong Kong, Brisbane, Cairo, and dozens of smaller stringer teams. 3,879 troops and intel agents all totaled."

"I wouldn't want to be out there without a connection to…" He paused. She could see him replaying some dark memory of his rescue. "I was going to say the real world." He looked up at the dome roof. "These domes are all there is. I guess the real world is out *there*." He looked back at Athena. "How can I help?"

"I'd like you to walk down to IT with me and talk to Les. See if anything seems obvious to you." She was certain something would. She'd known Walrus for less than a week, but she, like Stephen Lucas, could see that his mind was operating in another dimension. She'd sought power all her life, and here was a man with more power between his ears than any political wonk would ever yield, and his mind was as still as a windless lake.

"Well, *this* has room for improvement," Walrus said as he poked his head into the NTC's FTL server farm. The cabling looked like the Flying Spaghetti Monster's breach birth. Once he'd opened the door, he wasn't sure it would close again.

"We don't think the network issue is in that server room," Les said curtly.

Walrus turned away from the nightmare and took a breath.

Athena and Walrus had found Les working his way through his backlog of service tickets. Walrus looked with confusion for Athena, who'd made her introductions and beat a hasty retreat.

One Corporation had never had an IT team. Stephen wouldn't hire anyone who couldn't manage their own devices. Walrus was spoiled by Stephen. Everyone who worked at One was. He only hired the best. Walrus had only worked with savants who could build a system from the raw silicon blindfolded. People like Les never got past the front door.

"How long has the network been down?" Walrus asked.

"Four days."

"Four days? As in *ninety-six hours?*" Walrus' eyebrows raised. "And you still can't diagnose it?"

"First, we thought it was a breaker," Les said. "When we flipped the breaker, it would keep blowing. Then we started looking for shorts. We started turning off systems."

"And you never isolated the short."

"Correct."

Walrus nodded.

"The Borealis AuroraNet sChips are peer-to-peer once they're connected, but the entire system relies on Borealis servers to negotiate the handshake. Everyone in the field on all the missions around the planet is out of communication."

"Could they set up LANs?"

Les frowned and looked up for a moment. "Theoretically, they could be hacked to connect to a token ring topology." He shook his head in disdain. "I doubt the grunts in the field will know how to—"

"I don't know," Walrus said. "Stephen Lucas was in the service, and he could've hacked his system in a heartbeat. That's sort of how he got the idea to start One when he got home. Stephen and John Banks were buddies." Walrus never gave the impression he was being judgmental, mostly because he wasn't. He was just gathering data. "So, what did you do after the breaker blew?"

Les, however, projected his *own* perceived judgments. "We turned everything off, and the breaker stayed on. Then, no matter what device we plugged back in, it would snap the breaker again."

Walrus closed his eyes and smiled. "You know how I got here, Les?"

"By plane?"

Walrus nodded with genuine delight. In that one response, Les had revealed himself to be an idiot. Walrus unironically loved truly idiotic people. He could never tire of analyzing how their minds worked.

"I mean—*how* I got *on* the plane. I was at my house seven nights ago, and John—Commander Banks walked in my front door, waved hello, and triggered a pocket EMP device." Walrus pantomimed a small handheld device. "You know what happened? Every circuit in my mobile, all my desktop systems, my dishwasher, the toaster, my stereo—a beautiful vintage tube amp that I really, *really* liked—all fried in a snap." He snapped his fingers. "Then all my breakers blew! GRRRZZZT!" He laughed.

"The Borealis soldiers use those pocket EMPs on resurrection missions," Les said pedantically.

Resurrection missions, Walrus mouthed silently, as if the concept was new and delicious. "I think *I* designed those EMPs when I was back in college. Stephen had the plans for damned sure. The case John had was designed to *look* cooler. But I bet the PC board would be identical if I pried one open." He looked up at the ceiling and blew out through pursed lips. "Where do the Borealis soldiers train with the EMPs?"

"There's a proving ground out past M-Dome."

"And they never train or test in—what dome is this?" Walrus looked around as though he hadn't just been told this by Athena fifteen minutes earlier.

"E-Dome. E for engineering."

"Are they all assigned that way? Initial mnemonics?"

Walrus pulled a Torx driver out of his pocket and stepped over a tangle of cables to a nearby Borealis FTL server blade.

Les waggled his hands. "Ish. I think they found it restricting, and now it's sort of—"

"So, they never train or test anywhere near these blades?"

He checked the server was powered off. They all were.

"The soldiers keep pretty much to themselves out in—wait. This big CSAR operation has everybody all stirred up. I think some of the troops moved into F-Dome temporarily to make room for new arrivals." He pointed to E-Dome's exterior wall behind the server rack.

Walrus pulled the board from the server and held it up to the light.

"Holy shit!" he exclaimed. "I've never seen so many blown circuits on one board. It looks like ants were crawling around in here." He sniffed in the case. "Smell that toasted phenolic!"

Les' eyes widened. There was no hiding that he hadn't ever actually opened that server.

"Les, can you contact whoever moved the folks into F-Dome and find out where the soldiers were moved to?" Walrus eyed the damage. "I'll bet you'll find some of them were within a few hundred meters of this server room. And I bet you'll find someone had their pocket EMP in their back pocket. Some soldier probably butt-zapped this whole room full of servers."

He was already halfway done opening another server as he spoke.

"But that's not the *real* problem," Walrus said absentmindedly as he pulled another board and squinted at the fried circuits.

"It isn't?"

"Nope. Yeah, all these are fried too." He started opening another. "The *real* problem is, someone violated one of the rules for time machines, and this was just how reality chose to protect itself."

Les had been briefed on the Oneiri device. He had concluded it didn't matter to him, so he had assigned it to purgeable memory. It had been well and truly over his head, and he didn't believe half of it.

"So, if we fix all these servers," Walrus continued, "if we don't figure out what that violation was, there's just going to be another thing that goes wrong." His eyebrows raised gleefully as he pointed to the horrible cabling mess. "And the odds may be ever in the favor of that tangle of Category 6 cable back there."

Les' eyes narrowed in an expression that reminded Walrus of a Walt Disney cartoon rat.

―――――――

09-25-36 7:40 PM EDT

Alina checked herself through the assessment process for the second time that day. She'd had to welcome some new recruits and evacuees in the afternoon. She'd been heartbroken by the stories they told. The citizens of NTC were insulated from the rest of the world by design. The workers in V-Dome doubly so. There were very few televisions in the Domes. Sometimes, she would catch a news broadcast in the summer when they'd have a happy hour at The Blue Caribou, the island's only real diner in Broad Harbour. The evacuees made her selfishly glad she'd chosen to join the NTC. But she also felt a responsibility to the victims of the demon virus.

The evening attendant read the device readout. "You're good to go."

She pushed through the process of examining her suit. Her discipline would not allow her to rush. It was like packing your parachute. Your life was in your hands. She had eaten a delicious curry dinner and didn't want to stay in the trailer for long, but her patient was the first since their treatment had received the green light. It was an accelerated approval process to be sure, but the early successes were enough to be confident. Her patient had the interest of people so far up in C-Dome Alina was not cleared to even know their names.

She found Sunny entering some forms into her tablet. "Have you been here all day, Sunny?"

"Gotta get these RT forms entered for C-Dome."

Alina nodded. "How's our latest patient?"

"She started fighting her restraints once we got the temperature above forty-five. I pushed 33 of BetaTrank at 4:00 PM."

"Okay," Alina said as she walked back to the row of recovery pods. Her new patient's breathing had increased to twelve breaths per minute. Her hair had already grown nearly a quarter of an inch. Golden blonde. Her O2 saturation was coming up to 86%. As Alina watched, her patient's eyes fluttered and then opened. They were still dark, shot with blood, but clearing. Light blue irises were now easily discerned from the cornea. She struggled against her restraints. This was the moment Alina wanted to witness. She'd seen it a thirty-seven times now.

The woman stopped struggling and began to cry, elegant proof that the cocktail was defeating the GGB-Z virus. Human emotions were returning. Through the tears, her subject tried to speak. "Wh… Wh…"

Alina stepped closer. "Where are you?"

Her subject nodded stiffly.

Alina said, "You are somewhere safe. A hospital. We are making you better. You are healing, recovering from a severe viral infection." Her subject nodded and relaxed into the hydraulic bed. Alina asked, "Do you know who you are? Do you know your name?" The woman cried again.

"Ju… Jul… Julia…"

COMMANDER'S LOG 9/26/36 8:00 PM PDT

The troops are settling into a survivable rhythm. Up at 04:30. Light chow. Check the gear and submit inventory. From SMF, we marched to California State 99 and made good time. Goldstein and the engineers acquired three big 4x4 pickups to replace One Corp's fancy white Humvees. You can dig them out from under several feet of rotting meat if you want them back. The trucks are LT plasma and should get us the rest of the way home without too much expenditure of boot leather. Goldstein's tech ape, Johnson, devised a way to hook up our Auroras in a Token Ring Local Area Network. The procedure takes a half hour of entering machine code directly into the Aurora developer's terminal, and one wrong character makes you start again unless you type it into notes and then cut and paste. Some of the Lost Boys are better than others at that sort of task, but by tomorrow, we'll all be hooked up and won't need walkies anymore.

We'll be on the outskirts of Yuba City tomorrow around lunch. I thought we'd cut across Beal Air Force Base to see if any of the forces there survived. If not, we'll head on to I-80 and make for Reno.

The SMF resupply was everything we needed in terms of food, drink, and equipment. We walked away from that siege with as much ammo as we could carry. Now that we're rolling again, we could carry more ammo, I guess. With the trucks and the Aurora LAN, we'll be in good shape for now. The troops are tough and in good spirits, all things considered. The hangover from that siege is about what you'd expect. I'm trying to keep them talking. Keep them laughing.

I count myself lucky to lead them. It sure could be worse. It would be good to contact NTC to let them know we're alright and start coordinating the ride home. If we have to hike clear to Walrus Rocks, it is going to be a whole thing.

John Arthur Banks, CDR

Borealis 1st

Personal Log 9/27/36 2:00 AM PDT

Zoe,

You're out there somewhere in the future.

Will you read this? Did you commit the Roberts Rules violation that has us on this long march home? When Aurora is back, will I be able to reach out to you again, hear your voice in my head again?

Many questions. No answers.

I reach for you a dozen times an hour. I open realTime and click on your icon—like a rat pressing a button to get a dose of crack. Whenever there's a problem I rely on you to solve, a decision I count on your advice to reach, or just a thought I want to share—I turn to you, and you're not there. When I need a smile. When I need your laughter in my ears.

When will this be over?

When will I see you again?

I miss you, baby.

Commander's Log 9/27/36 11:45PM PDT

Today was a long, bad day. We need ammo.

Running low on:

7.62 x 39mm rounds

9×19mm Parabellum

AK Firing pins and rebuild kits.

More automatic weapons.

Grenade launchers

RPGs

Claymores

Anything you can think of that we can carry or mount to a truck.

We lost two soldiers today. I'm not writing about it now. Just getting the supplies ordered. We are hunkered down west of Reno. Where I-80 crosses the Truckee before the Floriston Historical Marker. Will go looking for container depots in the morning.

Fuck.

John Arthur Banks, CDR

Borealis 1st

Commander's Log 9/28/36 04:12 PM PDT

We took one on the chin yesterday. Rolled over a bluff, our little convoy of pickup trucks and fighting vehicles, and saw a sight that took us a while to resolve in our minds. We'd crossed into Nevada after a day of easy travel. It was starting to feel like an old-fashioned road trip, with our Aurora LAN acting as a CB and different soldiers competing to control the Aux.

So we had forgotten for a moment that we were driving through Cliff Price's newly minted Hell.

That was on me.

We rounded a bluff into the part of Nevada that looks for all the world like Kandahar. Ahead of us, in the low valley between Mogul and Lawton, we saw a cloud of dust. It was like watching a herd of buffalo back in the 19th century. It took us 20 minutes before we saw it for what it was. Demons on the move. A swarm of millions of demons crossing I-80, kicking up a dust cloud that hung in the red air. For 20 minutes, we drove at 70 miles an hour toward a nightmare of unimaginable proportions before our little pea-brains could piece it together. The scale was screwing with our ability to see the trees for the forest.

Robin Mercer saw it first. He asked, "That couldn't be a swarm of demons, could it?" Then we all saw it, and our vehicle's brakes locked up simultaneously. By that point, we were three miles away. We cut our engines, and we could hear their god-awful sound. It sounded like a cattle drive. The thunder of their shuffling, of their animal hoarse howls, like rhinos hooting in the distance.

My bowels went loose, I'll admit.

Before we could get turned around, an arm of the swarm came over the sandy rise to the north. We gunned it, but they had flanked us. The swarm was even more enormous than we could see. We'll never know how big it was. I'm pretty sure it would have shown up on satellite. We retreated as fast as we could, but the swarm kept coming. Gunners out every window with automatic weapons. As quick as they could clear the path ahead of us, the demons surged to fill it. I may have lost some hearing in my left ear from the roar of ordnance.

We couldn't keep the path clear on the highway and ended up off-road. The ridgeback took the lead and plowed the fuckers down. We drove over so many bodies. That's a sound, a feeling in your bones you never want to feel again. I'll never be rid of the tooth-loosening jolt of driving over a human body. Never.

We used so much ammo. So many grenades. The AK47s over-heated. Melted their firing pins in some cases. I didn't think that was possible.

We lost Private Scott Dominguez and Specialist Joseph John-ston—the tech engineer who showed us how to hack our LAN. The monsters jumped off an embankment and into the back of the trucks. The soulless monsters don't slow down, they don't think, they just throw their bodies at anything that moves, anything with a pulse—and they start gnawing and clawing.

So. we left MP with forty-two. Now we're forty.

Today, we resupplied. We honored our dead. We licked our wounds. We lost a lot of that optimism we left the Sacramento airport with. We're sobered up. That's probably a good thing. But the cost…

And we're still this side of Reno. We will head down to Lake Tahoe tomorrow and get south of the herd.

The M134 miniguns provided in the resupply container dropbox are mounted. That was a good addition. They'll be hell to keep fed, but they'll come in handy if we meet another swarm that size.

John Arthur Banks, CDR

Borealis 1st

09-28-36 8:13 PM EDT:
TEMPORAL ENFORCEMENT

LES MCBRIDE HAD A RULE. *Never* work angry. He was a man who had many rules, and though he often quoted them to his direct reports, he never followed them. He liked the impression his rules left with those in his organization that he was a *sage*. In truth, Les was *perpetually* angry about any number of perceived affronts, professional, personal, or, in most cases, imagined. For example, the no-vaping policy in the E-Dome was just the kind of horseshit that he was certain was tailored just for him. Les believed that the constant dosing of nicotine made him a more alert and perceptive manager and technician.

The connecting rings—inflatable donuts that kept the real weather out but weren't heated—were the closest place for him to dose up. So here he was, the CITO, for fuck's sake, in a parka, standing in the cold, dragging on his vape pen like a common junkie.

But *that* wasn't why he was pissed off. Walrus Roberts had waltzed in with the refugees and made him look like an idiot. Les' techs would have pulled those server boards, eventually. And, while he was thinking about it, *who* just walks into a server closet and starts pulling boards without an invitation?

The truth was that the failure was so massive that his team hadn't been able to isolate a single component causing the outage.

He'd never seen a situation where everything seemed to fail at once. Looking back, Roberts' hypothesis made sense. But who looks at that sort of failure and jumps right to EMP? No one is that insightful or smart.

No one.

Les had a plan, though. As soon as his nicotine serum levels were balanced, he was going to march into that FTL closet and replace all the boards in one of the servers and power it up—himself. What were the odds it would fail, too? Miniscule. The chance of one of the Borealis apes triggering another EMP would be nil. He'd power up the board, establish contact with the away teams, and lower the Mayor's blood pressure. He honestly didn't see the big deal. No one at NTC was impacted. It was just a few *soldiers*.

Les took a final drag, blew some impressive cotton in the frigid air, and trudged back into E-Dome. The forced hot air that usually warmed incoming workers was down for maintenance. He kept his parka on as he made his way to the FTL server closet. He closed the door and blew on his hands. He left his vaping parka on to warm himself up as he set to work.

He had the case open within a few minutes with his Torx driver, placing the cover haphazardly on the cluttered bench. The three main PC boards were PCI-bus components and could be removed after a bit of rocking. The sChip SOC had a ground line to the power supply that required a quick disconnect. The disconnect was stubborn, however, so Les traced it to the supply cover and pulled the Torx screw securing it. This screw also held the supply's cover on, and so he pulled that and tossed it on the bench with the rest. He leaned briefly with his hand on the grounded stainless-steel bench.

"That's all I need, Walrus Roberts as my OCD overseer, critiquing the artistic lines of my team's network cabling. That fat fuck can kiss my ass. No one ever died from some sloppy cables," he muttered to himself as he worked. He also made a mental list of every tech that he would happily tear new assholes for making him look bad. But now he got to work. He still knew more about refitting a server than anyone at NTC.

He pulled the replacement boards from their translucent metallic mylar pouches one at a time and clipped them into their places. Since he hadn't removed the ground cable from the old SOC, he forgot to pull it from the discarded board. This fell into the same memory hole as the power supply's cover, which remained detached and loose when Les snapped the case back onto the chassis.

"That should do it," he said as he flipped the power on the blade's surge suppressor. The system fan whirred on, and the display in front of him showed the first arcane booting process logs.

"Okay. Looks like we're back in business."

As he said this, the metal buckle on the right sleeve of his parka made contact with the stainless-steel case. This briefly formed a circuit allowing electrons to surge from the power supply's 400-volt mains, through the ungrounded SOC board—frying its more delicate circuits instantly—to the chassis, through the Torx screws, into the case, across the buckle, through the metallicized threads of his Dacron parka, and into Les' body through his expensive titanium smartwatch. From there, the circuit continued through Les' nervous system, through his heart, down his other arm, and out his clammy palms to the grounded bench he leaned on. The 400-volt current flowed at 0.1 amps, a sufficient charge to render Les unconscious almost instantly and, ever so briefly, to cause the Dacron surrounding the buckle to blacken, glow, and briefly ignite. The small flame was extinguished as Les' arm hit the floor. The volume of smoke produced was small but enough to set off the server closet's automated fire suppression system. Usually, the system's failsafe would have detected the closet was occupied through normal human body temperature. However, Les' parka was still cool from his vaping session, and it effectively masked his body heat. With no occupant detected, the system locked the door and flooded the server closet with halon gas.

With Les face down on the floor, the heavier-than-air halon displaced the breathable atmosphere in the small space, starting from the ground and rising. Within two minutes, Les' unconscious body suffocated. The whole incident was nearly noiseless and went unnoticed by his team. The first indication that anything had gone wrong was an alert on the NTC facilities panel in F-Dome annunciating the fire suppression system trigger event. In a room full of such alert panels, it wasn't immediately noticed. An automated text message was sent to Les' attention to investigate. It took nearly twenty-five minutes before anyone opened the door to the server closet and found the body.

The odds of Les' fate were astronomically small but not zero.

09-29-36 10:10 AM EDT

There was a structure in the stream that was *intoxicating*. The flow of data could have easily been dismissed as random hexadecimal characters matriculating down the screen in a cascade that looked like an ornate representation of *The Matrix*. But there was a structure. It was *not* random.

Walrus stood watching the endless torrent of values pour down the large holodisplay in his office, mesmerized as one might stare into a campfire.

Walrus had seen the elegant structure in the stream the first time he'd seen the Rashad Event in August. He shook his head. It blew his mind that it was only a month and a half ago. The Rashad Event had spawned two new breakthroughs that Walrus had barely been able to explore. The first, the one he'd shown to Stephen, was the time machine.

The Rashad Event had crashed the One Corporation's global OneFTL gaming network by accidentally sending a signal 1/3 second back in time. Stephen had found that to be as cool as

Walrus expected. That led to three weeks of furious hacking to make a prototype of the device Stephen dubbed Oneiri, the stuff dreams are made of.

And that fantastic device led to the end of civilization.

Within a week.

But the Rashad Event had revealed another feature of subspace that day. Much more interesting was this data stream the sChip produced when the Rashad Event was triggered. This was raw data streaming from the sChip's tunneling tensor arrays, an open channel to the subspace domain.

Whenever Walrus had a spare moment, he parked himself in front of a holodisplay hooked up to one of the rescued Oneiri server blades, triggered the Rashad Event and stared into subspace. He was training his unconscious mind to see patterns, slowly developing an organic feel for a phenomenon for which human evolution had no analog.

When a child is born, they must learn about elemental forces like water, fire, or gravity. The method they employ is play. A child can play with a bucket of water and a plastic cup for hours, learning how water works.

Walrus was learning through play.

This was how Athena Shaw found him when she came to deliver the news of Les McBride's death. She saw him standing stock-still before a holodisplay filled with random-looking, ever-changing characters. She stood at his door for a moment. It was clear he wasn't simply wool-gathering or zoning out. She looked closer at the display. How could anyone make sense of that? But occasionally, his head would nod, or his face would erupt in a smile, evident even from her vantage point.

"Walrus?"

He turned from the display, and his face looked as though she'd caught him meditating. She envied that serenity.

"Have you heard the news?"

"Hey, Mayor Shaw." He blinked a few times. "No? I don't know. What news?"

"Les McBride was found dead in the FTL server closet last night."

Walrus' eyes closed, and he frowned as if somehow unsurprised by the information.

"How? Do they know the cause of death?"

"He suffocated. The fire system…"

"Halon gas?"

Athena nodded. She moved past the threshold and leaned against his desk. "H-Dome has taken him for an autopsy, but they think it was the halon."

"He was fixing the servers to contact the away missions?"

"That's what his team assumes."

"I'd suggest you tell his team to stop any attempt to contact the teams in the field. You also ought to shut down any teams using the Oneiri device."

"What do you—"

"I'd suggest we gather all the Oneiri devices and lock them up. Or limit access to them strictly." His face, Athena noted, was downright handsome when he was serious like this.

"Wait. Walrus, what are you thinking?" He was looking at the floor. She had to duck down a little to force him to make eye contact. "What does Les' death have to do with Oneiri?"

"I just got here a week ago. I don't know how much or how little anyone knows about Oneiri and the rules that we've figured out that enforce reality's aversion to paradox."

"Roberts' Rules. All the senior staff have been briefed. All the Borealis teams. Most of C-Dome."

Walrus raised his eyebrows.

"The comms blackout with the field units, the away teams, whatever they're called, all the blown circuits in the servers, and Les' accident, these are the weird coincidental failures we found when testing Oneiri."

"But everyone has been trained to avoid Roberts' Rules violations," Athena said. "The SDS HR teams drill new hires and resurrections like lives depend on it." She shook her head. "I never really thought that they actually did."

"They actually do."

"Explain this to me like I'm twelve."

"The Oneiri allows you to send messages back in time. You can order a pizza that takes thirty minutes to be delivered, but send the order thirty minutes in the past, and—boom—your pizza arrives immediately. But, say you buy a new house, look out at your empty front yard, and say, I want an oak tree right in the middle of my lawn! So you use Oneiri to contact an arborist six years in the past to get them to plant an oak sapling. What's going to happen?"

"I don't know."

"Neither do I. But since there's no oak tree in your front lawn —why would you order a tree that's already there—what does the lack of a tree tell you about your order?"

"The order never went through?"

"Or it did, but maybe the sapling died before you bought the place. But if the order failed, why? What was the failure?"

"I don't know?"

"Neither do I." It was the first time since she walked into the room that Walrus smiled that warm, gap-toothed smile that Athena had already come to treasure. "Because it could be anything. A problem with the arborist's computer, a problem with your computer, a problem with the various ISPs between you and them, a power outage, maybe a server board fries. Maybe a squirrel jumped onto a power line and blew a transformer in the neighborhood of the arborist's web host server. Or, maybe an IT tech—like Les McBride—tried to fix a problem with the server and had a terrible accident."

"You think Les was killed by a Roberts' Rules violation?"

Walrus frowned. "I *really* regret that naming choice. It was just meant as a joke for our demo to the beta testers. I would like my name not to be associated with every tragedy caused by misuse of the Oneiri." He looked Athena in the eyes—a rare occurrence. "I think someone placed an order for something that they knew was never delivered, and Commander Banks, without his knowledge, is trying to make that delivery. He and his team's lives are in danger as long as he's got that item with him. If they're not dead already. Anything we do to try to get that team home is going to end in failure —and perhaps tragedy." He rubbed his bushy eyebrows. "It may be more than one violation. It feels like it might be more than one."

"Could you find the violation?" Athena asked. "Could you hunt it down, isolate it, and resolve it so we can get the teams home?"

Walrus tugged at his beard slowly as his eyes went to a faraway place.

"I'd need some help," he said after a few seconds.

COMMANDERS LOG 2

Made it to Mill City in good time today. Three stops to clear pile-ups. It's tragic seeing a demon in a car, trapped by its seatbelt, dehydrating in the heat. They look like people made of jerky. They keep on keeping on, though. The temperature would have killed these people before they were infected. Now, it just makes them greasy, dried living meat. Something that virus did gave them more than rabies. Still dangerous, still hungry for blood. It would be fascinating if it wasn't horrible. Sometimes, you can see their stories, who they used to be to the world. A single woman alone in her car before she turned. A salesman in a cheap suit. A dad with a backseat full of soccer balls. It's harder to see them as monsters, then. Easier to see them as victims.

I used to hope we could find a cure for these things. Maybe we will. Maybe V-Dome's cure will pan out. I sure hope so for Julia Swann's sake. But these dried fruit people, they're never getting cured, are they? Curing them would kill them. Nothing human comes back from what they've become. In a real sense, they are dead. Nothing left of what they were. A headshot becomes a kindness.

If that isn't the sickest sentence to commit to a log, what is?

Some of the troops are complaining about feeling shitty. Wind was blowing briefly from the east. Radiation? We'll need Geiger counters, dosimeters, blood tests, and shelf-safe Potassium Iodide or Prussian Blue. As we get north, I want to know what we're facing regarding the nuke zones.

We could use a doctor, but I expect that would be hard to store in a shipping container. A shelf-safe medical team.

John Arthur Banks, CDR

Borealis 1st

Commander's Log 10/01/36 11:25 PM PDT

First sign of survivors today. The container you marked for us had been broken into. I guess someone is out there with a lot of ammo, MREs, and medical supplies. Hopefully, it will make a difference. The lock clasp was cut off with a cutting torch. The container was completely empty. All the neighboring containers were opened, too. The cuts looked fresh-ish. No obvious rust. It gives me hope that our depots of Doomsday Prep were found and put to use. Still haven't seen any in-person survivors. We occasionally see signs of refugees—footprints in a straight line with adult and kid-sized feet. Demons don't walk in straight lines. And usually, they're in a herd when they're on the move. Maybe it's wishful thinking.

But demons definitely don't know how to use a cutting torch. So, reason for some hope.

Maybe from here out, mark the containers for us with UV paint. We can tune our implants to see it. Maybe it'll increase the odds of them being stocked when we find them.

John Arthur Banks, CDR

Borealis 1st

Commander's Log 10/02/36 10:40 PM PDT

More signs of survivors. A strange bit of graffiti. Spray-painted on a billboard:

FRANNIE!
HEADED FOR NONE-OF-IT!
GO NORTH ON 93
LOVE YOU!
HOPE YOU SEE THIS!
STU

It was hard to miss. The reference to None of it (Nunavut) was what got me. Took my breath away. It seems there's a post-apocalyptic rumor mill. We counted on gossip to spread the word about the Doomsday Prep containers. This would be evidence that the basic idea is working. We will see if we can locate some Doomsday Prep depots and see if they've been discovered.

John Arthur Banks, CDR
Borealis 1st

Commander's Log 10/03/36 11:40 PM PDT
Found containers marked with UV light. That worked a treat. Started radiation protocol. Everyone is feeling fine. I'll keep them off the iodine for now. We'll see what the dosimeters tell us.

Also found Doomsday Prep depots in Winnemucca. All opened and empty. That's another good sign that survivors are getting our help.

John Arthur Banks, CDR
Borealis 1st

Personal Log 10/04/36 1:12 AM PDT
Zoe,

Two weeks? I'm down to clicking on your icon three or four times a day. I can't shake the habit entirely. When there's a quiet moment on the road, I click on your @Once profile and look at your picture. That professional smile. The light in your eyes. I should have asked you for pictures. I should have squirreled away images of you, audio files of your voice. My brain is wired to yours and you? Where are you in this timeframe? Are you out there with your family in this wasteland?

The thought makes me ache.

You said you forgave me for your parents. That I'd find you. I have replayed that last sentence on an endless loop for two weeks. I have to let that go. When I talk to you again, I'll ask you what you meant—if I can. If it's not a violation.

I expect to see you around every corner. I expect to hear you in every quiet moment. If I didn't have these soldiers to get home, I'd be lost without you.

But I do.

I miss you.

───────

Commander's Log 10/05/36 9:25 PM PDT

The last few days have been brutal. We're taking a day to rest in Wells before starting up 93. We hit a traffic pile-up in Battle Mountain. Miles and miles of cars. Everyone from Reno suddenly hit the road for Salt Lake City, and folks from Salt Lake started out for Reno. They ended up in a twenty-mile tangle in the middle. The cars stretched from Battle Mountain to Elko. We never saw a living soul. Saw plenty of demons and plenty of corpses. I try to imagine the scene. Stuck in traffic for hours as people start turning. Nothing for miles around but the low, dry scrub. Nowhere to run. Maybe there are survivors out there. Where could they get to on foot? It doesn't look like many escaped. So many dead or undead.

A few of my troops got into close action with a small cell of them. Opened up a step van and out poured six of the things. Sgt. Murphy got a nasty bite. He was worried about turning, and we reassured him that the vaccine would prevent that. But the bite is bad, and we aren't prepared for any kind of serious infection. We pumped him full of antibiotics and cleaned and bandaged his wounds.

We've camped in a warehouse on the outskirts of Wells that looks like it was abandoned long before Downfall hit. I wish I'd logged an entry yesterday. This would have been an excellent place to drop resupply containers. We're low on ammo of all kinds, MREs, and bottled water. Also, antibiotics and tetanus shots for Murph.

Hey, if we could get some comic books. Anything but Archie. Comic books, Mad Magazine, anything like that. Maybe a portable chess board with magnetic pieces. You know how it is. When we aren't fighting for our lives or busting our asses, we're bored out of our minds. Sort of like baseball.

The dosimeters show higher than normal exposure, but nothing we need to worry about. Less than nuclear submariners. The wind has been from the mountains since Mill City a couple weeks back.

The troops are getting tired. Three weeks on the road. The sky isn't that deep red anymore. Mostly white. Certainly not blue. But the fires seem to have gone out. Can't see Salt Lake ahead, but neither can I see the glow of fires on the horizon. I'll take that as a good sign for now.

What's taking so long reconnecting the NTC Aurora net? We've been out of touch for a long time now. Has Walrus not been able to find a workaround? The NTC IT team? I met their director, and he sure seemed confident in his abilities.

While on that subject, I'd like to get a message to Zoe Chandra, my handler. I miss her counsel. Shit, I just miss her.

John Arthur Banks, CDR

Borealis 1st

10-05-36 06:12 PM EDT:
FINDINGS

"AS YOU CAN SEE, our team has narrowed the violation vectors from several hundred thousand to fifty-six probable sources." Priya Kumar stood before a holodisplay showing an enormously complex tangle of sources, platforms, and organizations networked via uncountable lines of connections and interactions, with a total of fifty-six of those lines highlighted in bold red. "All of them are connected to the Borealis field operative handler program." Her voice was quiet but carried well in the large C-Dome SCIF conference room.

Mary looked at Walrus with an arched eyebrow.

"I told you she was the best!" Walrus said with a smile that accentuated his more Sasquatchian qualities. It was his idea to assign the newly arrived staff from One Corporation's Software Quality Assurance team to the problem. He turned to Priya. "What was your methodology?"

"Prakanth trained a neural net using all communication files referencing Oneiri-capable programs—any incoming communication with an Oneiri client header in its metadata and any tickets added to the Oneiri request backlog. Machine Learning often finds patterns our minds skip past."

"And all of these fifty-six vectors are *handlers*," Athena repeated.

Priya nodded. "Also, all forty-three of the Borealis troops on the A400 that crashed on takeoff at Thorne International are or have been assigned to one of these fifty-six handlers."

"Tell me about the handler program," Walrus said, staring at the SCIF's ceiling.

"As with many of Stephen's projects, I have a list of position requirements for the team he's assembling. Beyond that, I have been kept at arm's length," Mary said. "The requirements include former intelligence agency experience, specifically field-asset handling but also including data intelligence analysts, logistics specialists, and field operations management. SDS presented Stephen with a list of candidates. I know I've seen a few of his picks among the names of the recent arrivals, but once Stephen had the list, he's held the project and its personnel closely to his vest."

"The construction team built several domes that are unlisted. They're not formally part of NTC," Athena added. "V-Dome was one of those, but there are three others. When I asked about them—"

"Per Stephen's instructions, there are several projects and staff that he's sequestered from this timeframe. Like V-Dome, some of their staff live among the main population, but they have instructions to maintain secrecy from this timeframe. I was not at liberty to even discuss those projects," Mary said without apology.

"That's about what she told me when I asked," Athena said to Walrus, with a nod in Mary's direction.

"The only reason I can discuss them here to this extent is because we're in a SCIF and… times being what they are…"

"But they haven't had *access* to the Oneiri devices or the Oneiri servers," Walrus mused. "Right? I mean, they just got here."

"The Oneiri server blades and seven of the cubes were retrieved in the final Borealis 1st CSAR mission. They were on the transport with you and Priya," Mary confirmed. "This is the reason for the Oneiri backlog ticketing system. SDS, now C-Dome staff," Mary nodded to Mrs. Crouch, "were responsible for generating Oneiri requests which will be sorted and addressed in a future timeframe. My impression is the Borealis handler program is still in its early stages."

"So, we couldn't shut down the handlers even if we knew for certain they were the source of the violation?" Athena asked.

"If we identify the violation, we can tell Stephen and he can handle it from his timeframe," Mrs. Crouch said quietly.

Walrus turned his chair.

"Have you spoken to Stephen?" Walrus asked with a sad smile.

Mrs. Crouch nodded. "He's tasked me to oversee C-Dome. He has—as you'll all understand—had to take extreme precautions to limit what he knows of the outcome of this entire project. If his perceptions of our reality remain unclear, he has more freedom to act. He struggles against collapsing wave functions enough as it is."

"How was he?" Walrus asked. "When was he?"

"He seems well." Mrs. Crouch nodded. "He looked... older. Nearly my age." She allowed a slight smile to reach her eyes.

Walrus' smile widened. He emoted sorrow and joy in one liquid expression.

"You know how he gets when he's working too hard," she said. "I have the feeling that he's *spinning a lot of plates,* as he used to say."

"*The ultimate man. He stands upon the high ground of history.*" Walrus quoted dreamily.

"Let's get back to the plot." Athena smiled, but she wanted a resolution to the problem. "It sounds like it's still on us to identify the violation. How do we do that? How do we nail it down for certain?"

Walrus chuckled. "Listen, I wrote the rules. But I don't think I could spot something that will cause a violation 100 times out of 100. Wave functions can collapse on things unexpectedly. Sometimes you observe some tiny feature of reality without knowing it. Sometimes, you look right at something and can't see it.

Humans have a malleable relationship with their reality. Much of Zen Buddhism exists to address that very problem. Observation of reality and awareness of what one observes are squishy concepts. Squishy, squishy, squishy." He suddenly wondered if squishy was an actual word.

"This is the first time you've had a major violation in six years of operation? That's a miracle!" He shrugged. "Stephen set up the handlers, trained them better than anyone could have hoped, and they got through six years before one of them committed a serious violation. Again, that feels like an impressive track record." He shrugged again. "But now, it looks like somebody ordered off the menu. One of these fifty-six handlers made a request of someone on one of those teams—probably on John's team—to bring back something that they had to know never made it."

"But that would be an obvious violation of the rules. I've dealt with many of the handlers personally. Zoe Chandra, John Banks' handler, is a real stickler. Jeremy Hall, Robin Mercer's handler, too. They're all pros. Stephen trained them to avoid just those sorts of things," Mary repeated.

"Sometimes, no matter how hard you train, something happens that makes you forget all your understanding of the rules," Priya interjected quietly. "Desperate people break the law all the time."

"Bingo," Walrus said. "It's a thinking versus feeling problem."

They all looked at him with confusion again. He laughed. He was used to it.

"Feelings can eclipse cognition. Most people can't think and feel at the same time. Intelligent people can color between the lines right up to the point where you make them sad, or horny, or afraid—then their IQ drops precipitously and their reliability drops with it. Anyone who's lost a parent, or a puppy is a mess for a while, right?"

Athena nodded. "Can we ask Stephen to assess the handlers from a timeframe in the future to see if any will have had a family crisis while on the job? Jesus wept. I need to consult a grammarian whenever I'm discussing different timeframes."

"It's future perfect tense for the most part," Mrs. Crouch said matter-of-factly. She was quickly becoming adept at her new position, overseeing initiatives in multiple timeframes. "My next meeting is my COB standup with Stephen. I'll add it to his backlog."

It was clear now, to all of them, that Mrs. Crouch was once again Stephen Lucas' gatekeeper.

COMMANDER'S LOG 3

COMMANDER'S LOG 10/21/36 9:25PM PDT

We had strong easterly winds all day. Dosimeters showed a visible increase throughout the day. Oddly, the skies showed bright blue for the first time on this trip. Today marks a month since we left Sacramento. We're starting on the Potassium Iodide tablets. That set off a rash of the skitters in the troops. Had to stop every fifteen minutes for troops to shit their brains out. It's made everyone a little cranky and irritable. Some of that is fear. Radiation freaks everyone out. My teeth hurt and my throat is sore. But we're still within acceptable doses if we keep up the pills... and if the wind clocks back to the west.

Haven't seen a lot of the rabid since Jackpot.

At least the troops have reading material to keep them occupied. The fiddle, squeezebox, and harmonicas were pleasant surprises. Sure makes the nights easier.

We're heading into the mountains once we get past Twin Falls. Idaho has been quiet. Still haven't seen a single live human. The demons in Idaho have been scattered and far off the way we like them. I was thinking, I haven't seen any other animals either. No dogs. It feels like the world has moved on.

Murphy is much improved. The antibiotics seem to have done the trick.

John Arthur Banks, CDR
Borealis 1st

———

Commander's Log 10/22/36 6:45 AM PDT

Sergeant Timothy Murphy died last night when we were
sleeping. It was sudden. When we found him, he was stiff and
blue, and his eyes looked blown out like the demons, but he
didn't turn exactly. He just died. The eyes had everyone unset-
tled. The vaccine kept him from turning, but his immune system
still had a battle on its hands? I don't know. V-Dome would have
probably liked to do an autopsy.

Thirty-nine.

We buried him with honors. Robin said a eulogy.

Murphy was one of the kids that resurrected me. He was a
dope. Always smiling. He deserved a better death.

I've got to get the rest of these soldiers home to NTC. Where
the hell is that AuroraNet connection?!

John Arthur Banks, CDR
Borealis 1st

———

Commander's Log 10/22/36 6:45 AM PDT

We ran into our first actual survivors today.

Figures they'd be assholes.

We saw them long before they saw us. Three pickup trucks
running diesel and "rolling coal." Blowing vast clouds of black
carbon as they gunned their guzzlers. When they finally laid eyes
on us, they cut across open farmland like a bunch of yahoos. We
were so happy to see other vehicles, other living souls, we didn't
hesitate. We gunned it and rushed to meet them.

Then they started shooting.

All three of the trucks were flying a Confederate flag. The lead vehicle was a no-shit monster truck jacked four feet off the ground with tires to match.

We held our fire because...well... because they were the first survivors we'd seen and because they were so far away. Their weapons fire was idiotic and sloppy. When one of their rounds actually hit the Ridgeback, I gave the miniguns permission to lay down some warning shots. That got their attention real quick. The BRAAP from those guns and the tower of dirt they threw into the air in front of their trucks were hard to miss.

They piled out of their trucks, shouting, waving their hardware, and flipping us off. They were just redneck kids. I went out into the field to meet them.

Their leader wore a red hat with the words "NEW SOUTH" embroidered in white Comic Sans. He said something to his men and walked out to meet me. They all laughed.

"Oh! Hey! Their leader is a nigger!" he shouted back to his goons.

I'd sort of forgotten what that felt like, to be called the n-word. Like a muscle I hadn't stretched in a while.

He rambled on for a while about the end times. I told him we were on a trip to the north. He nodded like he knew where we were going.

"What, is there a convention up north? Everybody we run across is headed north."

He said he'd seen folks going north for weeks. Called them easy pickings and acted like a jackass. He looked at our platoon and asked if we were Social Justice Warriors. I said we all fought for justice. Isn't all justice social justice? Isn't justice a good thing?

He said something I didn't understand. Something like, "Colonel Green is going to reckon with you. Colonel Green is going to reckon with all you mutants and sports. His reckoning will come right soon!"

I asked who this Colonel Green was, and the asshole just laughed.

Clearly, he didn't need us and we could get nothing from his gang of bullies. There was no common ground or common cause with these maggots.

They drove off, and we returned to our course.

That encounter left me down, not going to lie.

John Arthur Banks, CDR

Borealis 1st

Personal Log 10/23/36 1:43 AM PDT

Zoe,

Miss you. I'm feeling down and blue and I can't share it with the Lost Boys—not even Robin. I need to maintain a face of confidence, of certainty, and of strength. I have to play the hero. You only know how much I hate that role. We ran into some maggot dickweeds—some racist rednecks that called me racial names—the n-word and such. We have seen very little evidence that anything we did made a difference. I don't think any of my clever ideas to hide survivors from the future had any effect. I thought I was pretty sharp using epistemology as a strategy.

We may have saved a lot of people up at NTC, but I don't think that will be enough to save humanity when the rest of the planet is filled with assholes.

I'm feeling like a failure. I'm turning to you to talk me out of it, and you're not there. It was probably never right for me to burden you with my self doubt in the first place. I sure could use your laughter and your love right now.

Sure is hard to sleep on nights like this.

Miss you, girl.

Commander's Log 10/24/36 6:45 AM PDT

We are hoofing it. Encountered a good-sized swarm in Twin Falls. We couldn't get through the city on 93, so we hightailed it to the farmland to the west—Godwin, Clover, and Deep Creek. Crossed the Snake River on 30. The miniguns were the only thing that kept us from taking further losses. Twin Falls is a small town, but there seemed to be an outsized demon population. The main drag of 93 was Demon Central. All the parking lots were jammed with swarms, and they all coalesced as we entered town. We went through more minigun chains than I could count and the sound of four M134s all opened up like that was something else. We headed west and fought our way out of that berg. Once we were across the Snake, the demon density returned to something more manageable.

But our troubles weren't over.

We cut back to the east north of the city on 26 and headed north on 75 into the mountains. The highway was covered in a landslide north of Galena. We weren't going to pass, even with the six-by-six Ridgeback. So we recalculated, headed back for 26, and tried north again on 93. We got north of Dickey, and the road was again covered by falling rocks and boulders.

Well, fuck.

I sent the engineers up to inspect the canyon. They confirmed my hunch. It wasn't any earthquake. Someone set charges and closed the road on purpose. If I was blocking mountain passes, I'd block them all. We didn't waste any more time finding another way around. I ordered the troops to pack what they could carry and leave what they couldn't.

Oz worked out a sling for one of the miniguns, and I admit, he looks pretty badass. Whether he can carry it for days on end will be another matter, but we all sleep better knowing we have it. We left the vehicles with the key fobs hanging from the mirrors and were on the march again. It's good weather for marching while you're at it. Cools down when you stop. It's not winter here yet, but *winter is coming*, as Lord Eddard Stark liked to say.

This is the only way north. I'm not spending another month heading south and then trying to endure Death Valley. We're going north, and we're going to see who's alive up in the mountains. Simon Challis National Forest is a three-day hike.

I'd like to find the people that detonated those landslides. I hope they're not assholes. I think maybe the landslides were to keep the assholes out.

John Arthur Banks, CDR

Borealis 1st

Commander's Log 10/28/36 6:45PM PDT

We've made camp on Iron Lake at the invitation of some new friends.

John Arthur Banks, CDR

Borealis 1st

10-29-36 07:40 AM CST: THE PEOPLE

JOHN WOKE from a dream he could only dimly retain. Again, he had dreamt of James. As he lay panting on the ice, he turned back to look at his father's ashen face. This time, behind his dad, stood Maria Ramirez, Scott Dominguez, Joseph Johnston, and "Murph" Murphy. These were no specters or spirits. His soldiers stood as he remembered them, vigorous and hale but with solemn faces of doubt and betrayal.

He had saved no one.

He was no *hero*.

It pissed him off Stephen had ever called him that. He hadn't saved the world. As this road trip had shown, he hadn't set the world on a speedy road to recovery. The world had been swallowed up by Hell. There was no easy route, no straight and simple climb from perdition. He'd been playing at soldier and secret agent. When the actual feces collided with the fan, he'd only succeeded in getting good soldiers dead. His dream rubbed his nose in his failure.

As a result, he woke in a dark mood, but it was tempered by the smell of fresh coffee percolating over a campfire. He could see his breath. As he stirred from the hammock and sleeping cocoon his hosts had provided, he smelled fresh, buttery, scrambled eggs. Coffee percolating, the crackle of the wood fire, and the sizzle of the frying spam were the only sounds. Thank the universe for Captain Robin Mercer.

The sun had been up for a bit but hadn't yet risen above the tree line. John rubbed his face and joined Robin by the fire. The night had been cold; the morning was still bracing, but the fire was warm.

"Good morning, boss," Robin said as he poured a cup of coffee and handed it to John.

"Good morning, Captain Mercer. Thank you." He took a sip. It was hot, and he'd have liked a bit of milk, but it was the first cup of coffee he'd had in two weeks, and it was delicious. "Oh god."

"Yeah, thanks to our hosts, we have everything we need for a decent breakfast." He gestured to the deep blue lake and the pine-covered hills. "And the view is terrific."

John nodded. A few more nights like last, and that lake would begin to freeze by dawn. Robin dished up two metal plates of spam, eggs, and unevenly toasted bread, topped with scrapes of semi-melted butter. They ate with their hands wordlessly. Real food. Not an MRE or jerky or a power bar. When was the last time he had spam?

"The rest of the troops?" They'd arrived at the site in the dark.

"Their hammocks are spread out along the waterfront. A few got up early and went on a hike. Most are still racked out."

"The smell of coffee and spam will round them up soon enough." John looked up. "Jesus, look at that sky."

The sky was a deep, cloudless blue. A perfect blue that made the soul forget the world had been put through a meat grinder. Their days under the blood-red sky seemed like a mass hallucination. The blue was so fresh and pure that it hurt a little. It sapped his will to trudge onward. This could do fine. Why keep pushing north? John felt the urge to abandon any ambitions of seeing them through whatever horrors it would take to get home to NTC.

"Have our hosts made an appearance this morning?"

Robin shook his head. "No, but I was reviewing the supplies

they left for us. I didn't see this in the dark last night." He held up a small aerosol can with a blue plastic megaphone. The label read *Bear Horn* and it showed a ferocious looking grizzly roaring at the customer.

"I guess we ought to be on watch for Yogi and BooBoo. Let's not leave any spam and eggs around." John frowned at the prospect.

"Are you rethinking letting our hosts hold on to our weapons?"

John shook his head. "I wasn't going to start a firefight with 'em. They weren't armed, aside from the one with the badge—their sheriff. We'll get 'em back. They weren't like those maggots we ran into on the road." He looked out at the beautiful scenery. "I get the feeling this little campground is a quarantine zone for *us*. A place to keep an eye on us while they figure out if *we're* infected—or assholes."

"It makes sense." Robin nodded. "Closing the highways was a good move. Keeps the demons and the human scavengers away. These folks have their heads on straight." He mopped up the last of his eggs with a corner of the toast and popped it into his mouth as he stood. "Bus your plate?"

John handed him the plate and took a deep swallow of coffee. For a moment, the last flash of his dream slipped through his mind and was gone. Murph had been there. What had it been about? It was a bad dream, he was pretty sure. No. It was gone.

Robin took the plates down to the water's edge, rinsed them, and clanged them together.

"BANGARANG! Rise, Lost Boys, rise!" he shouted. "You want to sleep this glorious morning away?"

Groans of protest echoed back to him from hammocks in each direction.

The sun had risen halfway to its zenith when their hosts rode up, as they had when the Lost Boys had first encountered them, on horseback. John recognized the Sheriff, a short man with angular features, light-brown skin, and long black hair. He wore a leather jacket, a black cowboy hat, and a gold-plated badge. He thought the rest included some of the same riders they'd seen the day before, but he couldn't say for sure. They all looked like Native Americans or—*he didn't know*—Native American adjacent? The Sheriff dismounted and walked to their fire circle. John started to stand, but the Sheriff squatted, resting on his haunches.

"You the leader here?" he asked John.

John nodded.

"Thought so. They all treat you like an officer." He looked at the small group of soldiers gathered around them. "Military?"

"I was former army. Most of us are former this and that," John said. "But we're not U.S. Military."

"The U.S. isn't the U.S. anymore."

John nodded. "I guess that's so."

"We saw the nukes in the east. Then, the gas trucks stopped coming to fill the service station on the rez. When oil companies don't care if they get paid, well…." He spit into the fire. "That's when we knew things were broken."

"You all are Native Americans?"

The Sheriff did a thing with his eyes that might have been a smile. "You can call us Indians. We do." He gestured back to his companions. "We're what I guess amounts to delegates of the Confederated Salish and Kootenai Tribes." He turned back to John and looked him quietly in the eye. "This used to be the Flathead Reservation. Now it's the sovereign nation of Salish."

"I'm John Banks, the Commander of the Borealis 1st Division." John offered his hand.

The Sheriff looked at it. Then he shook it slowly. "I'm Matthew Walksfar. I'm the chief of the Flathead Tribal Police." He looked out at the lake. "*Borealis*. Where is that?"

"We're an organization that has been preparing for the… for

all of this." John gestured to the world. "We have a community up north, in Nunavut, Canada. A sanctuary from all the destruction."

"You *knew* it was coming?"

"It's hard to explain."

Walksfar nodded as he narrowed his eyes. They sat in silence for a while as John tried to decide if talking was helping his situation.

"Those vehicles on the other side of our landslide on 93." Walksfar changed the subject. "Those are yours? A couple of military vehicles. A six-wheeler and another. Three 4x4 pick-em-up trucks? All of 'em LT plasma?"

"Yes."

"Sorry about that. When things went bad, we wanted to keep the wendigoes out. So we dynamited the canyons."

"It was a good idea. We call them demons," John said.

Walksfar shrugged as if to say, *same difference*.

"What about the... the wendigoes among your people?"

Walksfar shook his head. "Wasn't a problem."

John frowned at that. What did he mean?

"You trying to get to this Borealis?"

"Yes. Nunavut."

"Just passing through?"

"Yes."

"Okay."

Walksfar stood and walked back to his companions without another word. He climbed into his saddle, and they rode away.

"Are they coming back?" Robin asked as he flicked a disc-shaped stone low across the lake's calm surface. It skipped once, twice, thrice, and submerged with a distant *plip*.

John shrugged and flicked a larger, flatter stone. It sailed further and skipped seven times.

"How the fuck do you do that?"

"It's all in the wrist," John said with a sly grin. The sun had passed its zenith and was creeping back down to the west. He looked at his Aurora to check the time. 2:06PM. "At least it warmed up. They sure don't worry about time here on the rez."

"I feel like I've been left by my parents at summer camp." Robin flicked another stone. Four skips. "What does that mean? All in the wrist? *What's* all in the wrist?"

John found a roughly round, roughly flat stone on the pebble-laden shore. He held it about knee height and angled it with his wrist. He showed how he could set the pitch and the roll of the projectile by angling his wrist before snapping it out over the lake with his long arm. The stone flew nearly parallel to the surface for twenty yards, then met the surface with a kiss and arced in another low, flat curve. Twice, three times, four, five, six, seven, eight, and before it skipped a ninth time, it was across the camp's small inlet.

"All in the wrist." John turned and headed back to the fire. The day was warm now, but the coffee was still good. "I got the impression we were put on hold. I think they'll be back before sunset." He poured the last of the coffee and found a nearby picnic table to sit at.

Robin tried to adjust the angle of his stone and flicked it out over the lake. It skipped six times.

"Hey! That worked!" As he turned to John, he saw their hosts riding up the camp road. There were more of them this time. John saw them, too, but he continued to sip his coffee. This time, the contingent rode right up to their camp. John guessed his team had passed the *no assholes* test. Sheriff Walksfar led them, but John was certain the rest were new additions. Seven riders were in nicer clothes. Three men and four women. The Sheriff dismounted, and the rest followed his lead.

"This is John Banks. He speaks for them," Walksfar said to the riders.

John waved. Robin joined them from the lake shore.

"Mr. Banks," a woman in her forties said, as she moved to the front of the group and reached out a hand to shake. She was tall, regal, with salt-and-pepper hair held in a tight bun with a beaded band. Her face showed a calm intelligence, and her eyes were graced with lines of laughter and thoughtfulness. "I'm Dr. Shiela Wolf. I'm the head of the Confederated Salish and Kootenai Tribal Council, CSKTC, for short."

John shook her hand as the rest stepped forward.

"This is John Star, Billy WhiteFeather, Jane Brand, Gary Chase, Sarah Billings, and Joyce WhiteFeather."

Joyce, a middle-aged woman with happy eyes and soft dimples, jerked a thumb over her shoulder at Billy, a younger man in a tan Stetson. "Wife, not mother," she said with spot-on comic delivery.

Billy snickered.

John shook all their hands, and Robin did, too.

"This is Captain Robin Mercer," John said.

"It's a beautiful afternoon. As you have seen, our solution to the rez's gas crisis has been to revert to our friends here," Dr. Wolf said as she patted her horse's soft nose. "We brought up some more camping gear and supplies. It might turn colder tonight, so we have a few tents. I hope you'll understand if we restrict you to this campground for a few days."

"Quarantine?" John asked.

"Yes. You should know that you're the first folks we've encountered from outside the rez that weren't infected."

"We've run into a few survivors on the road. What about your people?"

"I'm an MD. Besides serving on the council, I'm the director of the Flathead Reservation Medical Center. We received a bulletin from the CDC about the GGB-Z virus a day before everything went dark. Folks on the rez didn't have the same profile as the bulletin advised. We had the season-normal flu numbers, maybe a little higher. But our population wasn't presenting symptoms that matched the advisory."

John frowned.

"We had a few white folks, sixteen to be exact, who work on the rez. Ten of them turned. None of the tribal families reported any of the wendigo behavior." She must have noticed his glance to Robin at her use of the term *wendigo*. "Wendigo is an old Algonquin myth. They're cannibals, gluttonous things that stink of death and decay. Zombies, basically."

John nodded. "That's pretty accurate."

"We watched the reports on the streaming networks while the internet was still up and running. We saw things going bad, and then everything shut off."

"Some folks who did business in Twin Falls and Missoula let us know how bad it was getting," Billy WhiteFeather added. "And Gary has a ham radio license."

"GT98MD," Gary, an older, grayer man with lighter skin and a big white mustache, chimed in. "It was like Orson Wells' *War of the Worlds*. Every operator I knew went dark one after another over ten days."

"Have you ever reached as far north as Nunavut? Canada?"

"Yeah, I know Nunavut! North of Manitoba. I don't know of any Ham operators up there."

"Does NTC have a ham operator?" John asked Robin.

Robin shrugged.

"When Gary lost contact with the outside world, and we started seeing nothing but the infected coming north, we voted to close the highways," Shiela said. "We have farms and other resources on the rez. We decided there wasn't anything we got from the outside world that we couldn't live without until this blew over. But we're over a month in now."

"You're luckier than most," John said. "We came from Madre Pueda, California by way of Sacramento and Reno. Other than a gang of rednecks in southern Idaho, You're the first people *we've* seen who weren't demons. The first live ones, at least. The cities—MP, Sacramento, Reno, Twin Falls—all of them are gone. All of them were on fire."

"And the nukes to the east in Montana?"

"The winds have been westerly for you all?" John asked.

"The mountains almost never get winds from the east," said Joyce.

"I see your men wearing dosimeter cards," Shiela said.

"Yes, the winds clocked on us for a day or two on our journey. So long as the winds stay westerly, you should have no concerns. After a few weeks, the fallout danger drops to near zero. But you shouldn't travel east for… 30,000 years or so."

"We have some Potassium Iodide in stock if your people need it."

"We were resupplied with that, Prussian Blue, and activated charcoal." He raised his hand. "We're good."

His hosts exchanged glances. Clearly, the troops' adequate preparation for nuclear fallout raised questions.

"Matthew said you had advanced knowledge of all of this. That you prepared for it. Can you talk about that? Also, he mentioned you were from Borealis, in Nunavut? We have a lot of questions about that," Shiela said.

John gestured to the picnic tables and said, "Let's sit, and I'll try to answer all your questions."

By sunset, John had briefed the tribal council about much of the history of Borealis. Instead of telling them about the Oneiri time machine, he fell back on their stock cover story—predictive machine learning AI networks had been fed all of human history and all current events. The result of that was a probabilistic model that drove Borealis's preparations.

The tribal leaders commented that AI models always seemed to ignore the original nations' populations. John had to face the fact that none of the Borealis planning had even considered native populations, except the Inuit, and that had been an unanticipated result of placing the NTC refugee colony in Nunavut. In retrospect, it was a colossal oversight, a huge missed opportunity. The history of these populations was always ignored. They were a refuge of uncollapsed wave functions. Borealis could have partnered with them. Instead, they'd ignored them.

John wondered if, even with Stephen's help from the future—or perhaps because of it—they were still just making the same mistakes of a white-centric culture. He kept his own counsel on those thoughts. He missed Zoe suddenly and intensely. Zoe's check on his own personal, inherent bias was a resource he'd become dependent on.

As Shiela Wolf spoke, he saw similarities between her and Zoe. Her light brown skin and the silky black hair, of course, but also her self-assuredness and humor. Shiela was a good approximation of what Zoe might look like in ten years. Or in ten years from whatever year Zoe was operating from. Nothing was easy.

"We would be happy to consider a treaty with NTC if it means we have access to some important resources," Shiela was saying. "We're self-sufficient for the most part…barely. But we've been cut off from suppliers of things we've relied on. We've got meat, dairy, fruit, vegetables, eggs, a granary for bread."

"What about water and power?"

"Lots of clean, fresh water for our needs. We don't have enough wind generation—or solar at this latitude and this time of year—we depended on the Montana grid." She shook her head. "But it's a lot of little things that keep a population healthy. For example, we have no citrus and no *variety* of produce. We're going to have nutritional deficits that lead to illnesses like scurvy and rickets before long. And winter is coming on. We'll get through as a nation, but we'll need to re-establish supply lines."

"If you could open a magic box full of supplies, what would you ask for?"

"Medical supplies, vitamin supplements, LT Plasma power cores, winter weather clothing, diapers, formula—"

John held up his hand and smiled. Shiela laughed. It wasn't

Zoe's laugh, but it made John wonder if he'd ever see Zoe at that age. He wanted to. He yearned to.

"Sorry," she said, "I've been keeping a running list for a month and a half."

"Write that list down and give it to me. We might be able to help in the short term." He thought for a moment. "NTC can help with longer-term needs. It will be some time before we have a sense of what enclaves of the world are still... have survived—if any."

Shiela looked up at the sinking sun. "We have stores of drugs and pharmaceuticals, but they're mostly resupplied monthly. These aren't shelf-safe items. We might have three months before we lose people to simple things like diabetes and hypertension. Can NTC fill those needs?"

A month after Downfall, he was already running out of answers.

"Some of them we can. I'm not a medical expert, but I can commit to finding the answers for you. As soon as we re-establish our coms with NTC or make it back, I'll put you in touch with the Director of NTC; she's sort of like the mayor up there. She'd be better positioned to make formal agreements with the nation of Salish."

"Okay. I understand," she said. "So it's in our interest to get you on your way as soon as possible."

John was about to agree when four of his soldiers sprinted, out of breath, from one of the camp hiking paths.

"Commander! It's Clark, sir!" a panting Sargent Loomis shouted.

"What about Private Clark?" John said as he and Robin snapped to standing.

"He's dead, sir."

John and Robin exchanged glances.

"Don't worry about us, Commander," Shiela said. "Tend to your emergency."

THE LIGHT WAS DYING. The terrain was unfamiliar, fine-packed dirt with random roots stretching across the twisting path. Their soldier was already dead, without question. Yet John and Robin still ran the way parents do when their child's been injured. The three soldiers who had fetched them fell behind. Ahead, in the shelter of an outcrop of rocks, John saw Oz and Emily Tran. Tran was on her knees next to the body with her mobile device, lighting the scene and taking holos as if she was still a SFPD detective. John and Robin skidded to a stop at their side, panting. Jason Clark's body lay face up, but a large rock, roughly the shape of an anvil, lay where his head and chest would be. The rock was about three and a half feet across its shortest dimension. The part facing toward the darkening sky was as flat as if it had been machined.

"Holy shit!" Robin said.

"My words exactly," Tran said. She pointed her device's flashlight up at the outcropping. "It fell from up there."

"We were on a run," Oz said. "Just to pass the time out here. Clark was in the middle of the pack."

"I was right behind him, sir. Back about forty feet," said a private John didn't know by name. "One minute, Jason was running in front of me. I looked down at my feet for a second—

less than a second. I felt the ground shake and looked up. He looked like this."

"Anyone else see it?"

No one had.

"Okay. Y'all get back to camp. The Salish have brought us some tents and supplies. Go see to them for me, will you? Get the tents distributed and set up while there's still some daylight."

The other runners headed off, leaving John, Robin, Oz, and Emily to survey the scene. John tried to imagine the odds that this stupid kid would be right where he was when that boulder dropped. For Christ's sake, the thing looked like... it looked just like a scene out of a cartoon. Like Clark was Wile E. Coyote, and an Acme anvil dropped on him from a clear blue sky. The odds were not *calculable*.

"Thirty-eight."

He walked to the outcropping and picked up a handful of rocks. He stacked them on Clark's chest.

"Let's get him covered," he said, returning for more rocks. "We sure as shit can't move that boulder without a backhoe, and there's wildlife that will get to him if we leave him overnight." The others pitched in and ferried rocks from the hardscrabble to the body. It took them twenty minutes to dome a six-inch pile over the remains. The anvil-shaped boulder made a crazy-looking headstone.

As the rest were about to head back to camp, John stopped them. He dropped to a knee and bowed his head. They followed his lead.

"Our Father, who art in heaven,

Hallowed be thy Name.

Thy kingdom come.

Thy will be done on earth,

As it is in heaven.

Give us this day our daily bread.

And forgive us our trespasses,

As we forgive those that trespass against us.

Lead us not into temptation,

But deliver us from evil.

For thine is the kingdom, the spirit, and the glory,

Forever and ever. Amen."

He placed a large hand on the headstone. "Jason, you deserved better. You were a brave kid with a kind soul. I wish I'd had the opportunity to lead you just a little while longer. As it was, I was honored to serve with you…and I wish you well. The hard part is over, son. Now you're on the easy path."

They stood and walked back in the dark, in silence.

John couldn't shake the feeling that the boy's odd death made something clear. They were dealing with a Roberts' Rules violation. Someone on his team had participated in a violation. It might not even be a person. It could just be cargo they were carrying. If someone in a future timeframe had ordered a pizza knowing it wasn't delivered, the delivery would go sideways. What was the pizza that his soldiers were being prevented from returning?

If he could identify it and leave it here in Idaho, could he get the rest of the team home? Was the solution that simple? If he could identify that albatross that hung around their necks, perhaps the winds of fortune would give them a fucking break.

The tribal council had headed home, but this time, they'd left a police radio to contact them. His soldiers were all gathered around three fires near the lake shore. As John and the others approached, they stood. John gestured for them all to gather around the central, largest fire. John was silent for a moment until all the soldiers were quiet.

"We just buried Private Jason Clark. I can't think of a more beautiful spot to spend eternity. Though his death was sudden and random, we will remember him and honor his sacrifice." Then he repeated a tribute he'd formalized with the other five dead soldiers. "Let's pause here with a moment of silence for Jason."

He hated that this was becoming routine, but it was. He

bowed his head and remembered the look on Jason's face after he chucked that hand grenade over the containers. The kid was so pleased with his pitching arm. John imagined Clark's high school baseball career was worthy of the record books. He also remembered Clark's shame and guilt when John shouted at him. In John's mind, that was the mark of a good soldier. The bad ones just got pissed when you point out their mistakes.

"Thanks, Jason. You made us proud to be a Lost Boy. LOST BOYS!"

"BANGARANG!" they responded as one.

The simple tradition completed, John wiped his nose and held up a hand. "*Hold up.* Before you head off to your tents, a word. We've lost Maria Ramirez, Scott Dominguez, Joseph Johnston, Bryan Murphy, and now Jason Clark since we left MP in September. I know you all are trained up about Roberts' Rules. I trained most of you myself. Over the six years I've been on the job, we've been really lucky with violations. We've had a few, and they've usually shown up as blown fuses or shorts in circuitry. I want you to think long and hard tonight about anything you may have done or heard that may constitute a Roberts' Rules violation. If anyone asked you to carry something back to NTC that seemed weird or even questionable, let me know."

He looked out at all of their faces lit by the fire. They were all such good soldiers.

"Okay. Dismissed. Hit your racks."

He would have them strip down to their skivvies and leave everything behind at Iron Lake if he had to. One way or another, he would get rid of the curse hanging over them.

"*Commander? You sleeping?*" It was Emily Tran. As he was waking, his mind conflated her voice with Zoe's. He double-tapped the spot behind his ear to no effect. For a moment his eyes glowed in the dark as his Aurora awoke and painted its interface on his retinae.

"I'm up." Before he had raised himself up on one arm, he saw the flashlight playing on the dacron walls and reconnected with the world. He unzipped his tent and looked up at Tran, who was holding a flashlight on him. He gestured for her to lower it from his eyes.

"Tell him," she demanded of the other soldier. It was Chris Goldstein.

"Commander, um—" Goldstein stammered.

"You tell him, or I will."

"What's up, Chris?" John asked as he emerged from the tent in his skivvies. He towered over Tran and had six inches on Goldstein.

Emily handed John a metal canister. He squinted at it as Emily trained her flashlight on it. It was a dewar flask with biohazard markings, a cryogenic medical container. It was sealed tight and felt cool in his hands, heavy too.

"He also had these." Tran shoved a wallet filled with four-terabyte data cards. Each of them bore the logo of a different pharmaceutical company. "I haven't been trained in *Roberts' Rules of Order and Chaos*, but I know when someone's acting suspicious. He's been carrying that since Sacramento, at least. That's when I first saw him and the dead private, Murphy, arguing about it."

"It's not—Commander, it's not what it looks like," Goldstein stammered.

"Go sit at the picnic table by the lake. I'm going to put some pants on."

He set the canister and the wallet inside his tent and pulled on his jeans.

"Fucking narc," he heard Goldstein mutter as they walked away.

"I *was* a narcotics officer in San Francisco back in the day," Tran replied. "Most people miss that, but not you, Goldstein. Not you."

John joined them at the picnic table.

"Okay, Chris. You say it's not what it looks like." John said quietly. "It looks like you're smuggling drugs."

Goldstein's eyes widened. He realized it did look like that.

"It's for Penny's kid!" he said. "It's not—"

"Who is Penny?" John asked.

"Penny Hoyt, she's my handler. Not exclusively, the specialists and PFCs share resources. We can dial up our handler on an as-needed basis. She's great. Penny's the best. She saved my bacon a dozen times at least."

"And?"

"And her kid got sick… is going to get sick. She needs this drug that the medical teams at NTC can't manufacture. She told us about these kinds of drugs called *orphan drugs*." His earnestness was evident. "Penny's kid Sandy is going to be diagnosed with a kind of pediatric cancer. And NTC isn't going to have those drugs 'cause they're rare even before Downfall. Like one in ten million kids ever gets the thing. But those that do die without these rare drugs."

"And Penny's kid died without the drugs?"

"She did… she's going to, unless we bring the drugs back with us. Yes sir. We got 'em when we were in Madre Pueda. All the pharma companies have labs there. Penny asked her field officers to do her a solid. We got them while we were on stand-down —on our own time. The labs were all empty, and the people were all gone. It was a simple retrieval compared to some of our missions."

John was relieved in a sense. Goldstein had described the very definition of a Roberts' Rules violation. But his soldiers' complete lack of discipline and understanding of their violation was unbelievable to him. It was understandable. It was infuriating. They wanted to save a kid's life. But they should have recognized the violation after all their *god-damned training*.

"Chris, Penny's kid died in her timeframe. If she asked you to get the drugs to save her, it's a violation. Violations fail. 100% of the time, they fail. You know this!"

Chris folded up. His long, lanky spine curled, and his head drooped.

"Who else was in on this?"

"They're all dead now," Chris said sadly. "All of them. Am I next? Commander, am I next?"

"Ramirez?"

Goldstein nodded.

"Dominguez?"

"Yep."

"Johnston? Murphy? Clark?

"Yep. We all had Penny as a handler at one time or another."

Time had done a nearly perfect job of cleaning up the violation. Time was a methodical fucking serial killer.

"We're lucky it was just the conspirators," John said. "A violation could have been resolved by killing us *all* on the tarmac at the airport, Chris."

John stood up, returned to his tent, and grabbed the canister and the data cards. He walked to the water's edge and skipped the cards one by one into the lake. As his eyes adjusted, he could see the stars in the still water. He opened the canister with a stubborn twist. The cold inside spilled out over his hand. He heaved the thing as far as he could. It was a throw Jason Clark would have respected.

He walked back to the picnic table. Goldstein was grief-stricken, not crying but barely holding it together.

"Penny's little girl will die now." Goldstein moaned.

"There's nothing we can do to stop that. All that we could ever do is fail. Fail and die." John placed a hand on his shoulder. "It absolutely sucks. But now, at least, we have a chance to get home alive. Now get your ass to bed, soldier."

"Sir, yes, sir. I'm sorry, sir."

"We'll deal with repercussions later, Chris. Get."

Emily and John watched as Goldstein shuffled off to his tent.

"That's it?" Emily asked.

John shrugged. "No. He's in for some shit duty for a few months. He was feeling when he should have been thinking." John sighed. "I'm going to have to demote him. That won't mean much since he's the best engineer I have on this little hay ride, and a natural leader of the tech apes. But he's watched all his conspirators die. And then he watched me chuck the reason for their deaths into the lake. That'll do more to punish him than anything I could do."

"Where were you when I was in the Army?" she said with a smile.

"Fighting fires, I expect." He stretched and headed back to his tent.

"Good night, Commander Banks."

"You too, Emily. Thanks for being a good detective tonight."

"I *am* the best."

WALRUS SAT in the NTC FTL network server closet. A wooden push broom leaned against his knee. He'd spent the better part of a week cleaning, reorganizing, and rerunning cables. He'd rebuilt all the servers from the metal up. He'd purged every buffer of incoming, undelivered message data. He didn't look at it. He simply hit the keystrokes to wipe that data in case it held any requests or information that might, even in the most oblique way, violate any of his rules for time machines.

At least some part of his enormous brain was aware that what he was doing was one of the most dangerous things he'd ever done. Time's spooky enforcement mechanism had killed Les McBride quickly, quietly, and without warning.

The childhood memory of Adam Savage and Jamie Hyneman saying firmly, *"Don't try this at home! We're what you might call 'professionals'!"* surfaced. It was a reassuring memory because who, if not Walrus Roberts, was a professional when it came to this process of trying to re-establish coms via the NTC/Borealis Aurora FTL network? Nearly every board and most of the silicon were Walrus' designs.

And the flip side of spooky temporal enforcement was that what failed was what one could expect to fail. It played the short odds more often than not. Sometimes, it played the *really* long odds, but it played the short odds far more often. And, really, what killed Les was his own sloppiness and self-confidence. Self-assured and inept—*there* was a deadly combo platter if ever there was one.

No, Walrus was methodical and orderly as he reassembled the last blade server. Once the final component was snapped into place and the ground leads were connected, he paused, folded his hands over his belly, and sat quietly appraising the device before him.

Mrs. Crouch had delivered the goods. Stephen had identified the likely cause of the violations—plural. There were two. The first was that John Banks' handler, a woman named Zoe Chandra, had tried to communicate to Banks information about his future life that would have violated the third rule. According to Stephen, she'd filed a report immediately after her message was cut short, her last communication with Banks. Even as she was doing it, she knew she was violating the rule. Elegant evidence in support of the *feeling versus thinking* pickle.

The second violation was committed by a handler named Penelope Hoyt. Unlike Ms. Chandra, Mrs. Hoyt had never reported her violation. It was unclear that she knew she'd committed a violation, though most suspected she did. Mrs. Hoyt's daughter, three-year-old Sandy, had died—would die—of a pleuropulmonary blastoma, a cancer so rare that NTC's medical pros had never included the drug treatment among their extensive inventory of pharmaceutical stores. It was clear, though Mrs. Hoyt denied it, that she had enlisted a small team of Borealis soldiers to acquire the drug and all the available data to manufacture more.

It was a little heist movie within the larger operation that was the final week of Downfall.

Walrus felt some comfort in knowing they had identified the violation. Now, he hoped Commander Banks had been able to identify the violation on his end and remedy it in the month they'd been out of touch.

He finished his inventory and appraisal of the work he'd done assembling the device, attached the case cover with six Torx screws, and pushed his stool away from the server rack and the stainless-steel workbench. He'd already taken the precaution of disabling the fire suppression system—even disconnecting the small tank of compressed halon from its fire control mechanism.

The door was open, and several IT team techs stood watch with a portable defibrillator as he reached out with the wooden broom handle and rested it on the rocker of the UPS/surge suppressor's power switch.

"Here goes nothing," Walrus said.

Then, he pushed the switch to ON with the broom handle.

———

10-30-36 08:35 AM CST

John woke to a familiar tone playing in his head. It was an incoming voice message. He bolted into a sitting position and tapped behind his ear.

"Zoe?"

"Hey! Hey! Is this John?"

"Walrus Roberts?"

"Hey! We didn't blow the board or anything!"

"It is good to hear your voice, Walrus." John hastily threw on his jeans and shirt.

"You too! I honestly didn't expect this to work right off the bat. But let me tell you first, we found out the source of the violation."

"A handler named Penny Hoyt?" John smiled as he pushed his feet into combat boots.

"A handler named Penelope Hoyt!" Walrus' laughter was loud in his bones. "You figured it out, too!"

"We discovered the source last night and resolved the viola-tion." John stepped out of his tent and gestured to Robin, who was bent over the fire. "I didn't expect that would clear up our network issues so quickly. But I'll take it. I suspect if we hadn't, it would have blown your circuit board when you tried to contact me."

"Last night?" There was a moment of thoughtful silence on Walrus' end, then, "I suspect you're right! Hold on." There was the sound of small applause on Walrus' end. "Commander, can I call you right back? I'm going to let Athena, Mary and, and Mrs. Crouch know, and they'll want to—"

"Yep. I'm not going anywhere." John finished buttoning his shirt and took a cup of coffee from Robin. He walked out to the lake shore and paced a bit, waiting to be reconnected.

After a few minutes, a window popped up in John's HUD. Now, he could see Walrus in his lab.

"I've sent an invite to the steering committee. They'll be joining us in a second." Walrus' eyes widened with his smile. "How have you been holding up? Where are you?"

"We're in northern Idaho. A stone's throw from Montana. Hey Walrus? Will we get reconnected to—has there been any word from my handler Zoe Chandra? I—"

"Commander Banks!" Athena joined their conversation. Mari-anne Crouch joined a moment later.

"Director Shaw!"

Mary Allan joined.

"John!" her eyes were shiny with tears.

"Mary!"

They all laughed. It was a delirious moment for all of them as weeks of stress evaporated into jubilant relief. John had worked with Athena and Mary for years, but Walrus was a natural addi-tion to the mix. Mrs. Crouch was a quiet but happy observer. Robin looked on for a moment and then walked down to the water's edge to practice skipping stones.

"Where are you?" Mary and Athena asked almost in unison.

"I was telling Walrus, we're in northern Idaho, near Montana. Well west of the nuke zones. After DC went dark, the Flathead Reservation tribes—Salish, Kootenai, and Pend d'Oreille Tribes" —it had taken John some time to learn to pronounce the tribal names correctly, but now they rolled off his tongue trippingly— "have provisionally declared the area the nation of Salish. I don't think any federal or state authority is left to argue with them. The V-Dome folks will want to send a team out here. They had almost zero GGB-Z infections here."

The look on their faces was of shared amazement.

"I know, right?"

"So, you've been on the road since Madre Pueda," Athena said. "What have you seen? How bad is it?"

John rubbed his hands over his face. "How bad is the world? Worse than I had imagined all these years. Cities are gone. The bigger the city, the worse it is. It's all about population density. MP, Sacramento, Reno—all burning. Total losses. I doubt anyone survived. The demons are everywhere people were. You don't see any when you get out to the wilderness of the desert or the mountains. But you don't see any living people either. We saw a lot of farmhouses where it was clear the demons and the healthy members of the family fought to their last, with no one left alive. When you near a population zone, though…." He shook his head. "The swarms were ten miles across."

"Swarms of rabid?"

John nodded.

"Survivors?"

John shook his head and sighed. "We ran afoul of a gang of redneck teenagers. They were like Lord of the Flies with a heavy dose of Proud Boys. Perhaps that's redundant." He shook his head. "The Salish are the first community of survivors we've seen. You have to hand it to them. They've pulled together and made a lot of smart decisions." John found talking about the Salish was a balm compared to talking about the ruined cities or the assholes. Their survival, their general well-being in a world so completely fucked up, was the only thing keeping him from losing all hope. "They're going to need some help to get through, but they have met most of their own needs so far. I'm particularly impressed by Shiela Wolf, but the rest of the tribal council are also fantastic. They've got a ham radio operator, Gary, and we thought he might use it to contact you. But I had no idea if NTC had any kind of shortwave operators."

Walrus laughed. "Son of a gun! Old school! Everybody got used to Aurora, I'll bet. I can piece together a shortwave."

Mrs. Crouch made a note of this exchange in her moleskine.

"I think there are a few of the Inuit with ham radios," Athena said. "I'll check. We need to form an alliance with the Salish immediately. We can help them, trade with them. We'll be stronger together."

"I told them you'd want to talk," John said with a wide grin. "Dr. Wolf has expressed her eagerness to negotiate a treaty. I expect they'll be back this afternoon." John recalled their departure the previous evening. He rubbed his brow. "We lost a soldier last night."

"Oh, no!" said Mary.

"It actually led to our sussing out the violation. All told, that violation claimed five lives."

"Six," Walrus corrected. "We lost NTC's IT director to the violation."

"Les McBride?"

"Yeah."

"We started off from MP with forty-three souls. We're down to thirty-eight. It could have been far worse. Mary, I'll send a report. Also, my daily logs. I need to get those in the Oneiri ticket backlog. Stephen will need those to work some Oneiri magic that saved our bacon more than once."

"John, did Emily Tran make the plane?" Mary asked.

"She did," John said with a nod. "I can see why you wanted her saved. She's been a big help on this trip. Hell of a sniper and a hell of a detective."

"We hire the best." Mary smiled.

"Now. Let's get you home," Athena demanded.

"Yes, ma'am. What about a plane?"

"Planes are a no-go until spring." Athena shook her head. "But how would you feel about a boat?"

BOOK 3
THE FUGEES

"ALL RIGHT, you monkeys. Let's go get to know our new rides."
John climbed down the steps of the dusty yellow EV school bus,
and the Lost Boys followed in various degrees of excitement and
apprehension. The country-to-city ratio of the soldiers was about
fifty-fifty.

Twenty-five horses stood tied in a row to a long split-rail
hitching post, each saddled up and ready to ride. At the end of
the hitching post, their hosts had also provided a dozen fuel-cell
electric dirt bikes with a range of 700 miles on a hydro charge.
Their luck in finding their way to the Flathead still amazed John.
But then, there'd been bad luck to pay for it, he supposed.

Shiela finished up her conversation with a few ranch hands
and walked over to their school bus.

"Welcome to *Good Wolf Ranch*, Commander Banks."

"It's a beautiful place, Dr. Wolf."

"My husband will be happy to hear it. You're here on a beautiful day," she said. She pulled her hand out of a leather glove to
shake his. John thought she looked at home on this ranch more,
he expected, than in a hospital center board meeting. She was
smiling, and he noticed again that she had a practical, understated beauty. He also noticed that he'd had feelings for Zoe for so

long that he suffered from an unexplainable sense of shame for his appreciation of a woman in this timeframe. His life was *weird*.

The weather had turned warm for Halloween. Dates were feeling like a relic from a previous age. Before the morning's conference with the NTC steering committee, John had to check the Aurora display twice. October 31st. Being back online meant being back on the calendar. It also meant being back on the map.

Walrus and his engineers had successfully refreshed the GPS satellites after a couple of months of neglect. They had access to the military's dual-band system now. It would take a few weeks before their orbits were returned to true. But they were on the map again.

The big gray brindle turned, looked his way, and uttered a low nicker.

The mare was probably seventeen or eighteen hands, and as handsome as any John had ever seen. Brindles are rare, but this horse's coat was a fascinating mixed gradient of grays—from deep, lush dark gray to light, powdery gray, dotted with delicate whorls of white. All the horses had their winter coats coming in, but the big one was positively shaggy, and her long hair swirled like a Van Gogh night sky. Her mane was pure white, and she bore a white diamond on her forehead. It was love at first sight.

"These are some fine rides." John smiled.

"Not all of them." Shiela laughed. "But they'll all give you a good day's ride if you rest them and give them a place to graze. And you won't have to worry about charging 'em or filling them with gas or hydrogen."

"Nobody touches that gray brindle!" John shouted as the soldiers approached the horses. Every woman in his command turned and shot him a look, which they followed up with laughter and various mopey versions of *sir, yes sir.*

Sometimes, it was good to be the Commander.

"Good eye," Shiela said. "Are you a rider?"

John nodded. "My uncle Bill had a place down in North

Carolina. He taught me to ride, and I worked his place a couple of summers in college."

"I called in favors from all across the rez." She walked with him to the horse. "But these should serve you better for traveling off-road."

"And off-road will be safer. Roads lead to cities, and cities are demon territory." He cocked an eyebrow. "Those vehicles on the other side of the landslide aren't payment enough. You sure you can get them around the obstruction?"

"We know all the logging trails. Those LT plasma cells will light a few neighborhoods each, power our schools, and last longer than I'll live. These days that sounds like a fair trade. But if NTC can get us the medical supplies we need, you'll have more than repaid the ranchers that offered up their horses."

"Speaking of that—" John pulled out his notepad and drew three quick hobo signs. "After we leave, have your folks look for shipping containers placed somewhere on an abandoned lot around the rez. I submitted your list—"

"To the Borealis AI?" Shiela took the note and squinted at him.

"Something like that." They now knew each other well enough not to bullshit each other. He winked. "You should find some provisions stored in containers with those symbols on them, with our thanks."

"How could they have delivered these containers with our landslides?"

"If I told you, I'd have to…" He drew a finger across his neck and laughed.

The mare nuzzled John's hand as he raised it to her muzzle.

"She likes you, Commander," one of his soldiers said.

"I like her back." He turned to Shiela. "What's her name?"

"We call her Hera, but she's yours now. You can call her what you want. We never knew *what* to do with her. She just turned four back in August. She's a big girl, too big for most folks. Too big to race. She's built for speed, though, not work."

John stroked her winter down, and the gray brindle looked like swirls, like spiral galaxies.

"I'm going to call you Galaxy." He patted her long nose. "Is that okay?"

The mare nodded and snorted as she leaned her forehead against him. He laughed.

"It's like she knows you. That's a good sign, Commander."

"It surely is. Okay, Galaxy. Okay." He untied the reins and walked her to the dirt parking lot. He pulled himself up with rusty grace. Galaxy adjusted her stance to accept the large man's weight. God, she was a good horse. He clicked his tongue, gave a little shake to the reins, and they were off. Galaxy trotted at first, and John steered her toward the dirt drive. He leaned forward and said, "Haw!"

Galaxy burst into an easy gallop. John laughed and held on for dear life. Her size and strength were impressive. John saw what Shiela meant. She wasn't a racehorse, too big and too strong, but she wasn't a workhorse either. They rode out to the state road before John eased her back. He patted her neck. It had been too long since he'd been on a horse, and he'd never been on one like this. He was always a little big for his horses, but Galaxy was just the right size.

John walked her back to the barnyard to applause, hoots, and hollers from his troops and the ranch hands.

"Made for each other." Shiela smiled. "Big horse for a big man."

"I can't thank you enough," John said as he patted Galaxy's neck and stroked her shoulder, swirling the brindle into spirals. He looked up at the sun. "We should be getting on the trail."

She nodded. "You have a long way to go. I've spoken to our brothers and sisters on the Blackfoot Reservation. They'll meet you at the border. I expect their council will send representatives to talk. Then you'll be in Alberta, and it's 1,200 miles to Port Nelson. Like you said, stay clear of the cities." She shook her head.

"Galaxy will see us through," John said. "We'll get to the boat by December."

"Keep an eye on the weather. You won't always have weather like this. I wish you could call when you get there." Dr. Wolf gave his hand a quick squeeze. He liked this woman. *A lot.* Salish was lucky to have her leading them.

"Tell Gary Chase to keep an ear out for us on his shortwave," John said as he led Galaxy away. "I'll see you again, Dr. Wolf."

THE ENGINEERS all preferred the dirt bikes. John worried they'd hit their 700-mile limit and have a hard time finding a viable H2 station. Goldstein was determined to engineer an electrolysis still to make the hydrogen they needed. It sounded like a hassle, but the bikes were eerily quiet and kept a pace that matched the horses. If a still couldn't get made, John could train the gearheads to ride on the way. The course he'd plotted would probably cross more horse country than they'd traveled so far.

John took a dare that first week on the trail to see if the bikes or Galaxy had the better speed. Galaxy beat the bikes in the first hundred yards. She could spring from zero to full gallop almost faster than John could brace for. It took the length of a football field for the bikes to catch up, but beyond that, the bikes had the edge—but just barely.

Every day on the trail was an opportunity for John to find out what she could do. She was probably the smartest horse he'd ever ridden and easily the most affectionate. Their bond was immediate and deep. He thought maybe she saw him as a human made to her size specifications—that or she liked the Snickers miniatures Lucas had left for him in a supply container. John found he preferred to spend time with her over idle fireside chatter with the troops. But he made time for both.

He had a lot of time—too much time—to dwell on his memories of Zoe.

At the Steering Committee's request, Stephen had shut down the Borealis handlers to avoid triggering another violation. John had voted for the motion when it was proposed by Athena, but he regretted it. How could he explain any objection? Oneiri traffic was now limited to timeframes before Downfall. Any magic tricks from here on would be performed exclusively by Oracle..

He was forgetting her face, her slightly crooked nose, her laugh.

Their Flathead guides rode with them for a week through the Salish National Forest, out of the hills, and down into the Blackfoot Reservation. John was gratified to find the nation of Siksikaitsitapi nearly on par with Salish in terms of self-reliance and tribal governance. They, too, showed unexpectedly high levels of GGB-Z immunity. Something in the original people's genome protected them from the bio-engineered plague—an ironic reversal of the plagues brought by the European colonizers. Perhaps the arc of the karmic universe bent toward justice as well.

As she'd said, Shiela had been in contact with the Siksikaitsitapi tribal council since the beginning of Downfall. The two tribes treated each other as wayward cousins, but their bonds stretched back thousands of years. The Blackfoot border with Salish was a soft and unenforced boundary, but a team of four riders met them at Bison on the Salish side. John wondered if Sheriff Walksfar had relatives among the Blackfoot, as their escorts were all serious men in their twenties who spoke rarely and with little affect.

The riders camped the night on the shores of Buffalo Lake and let their rides forage and drink their fill. Their camp site could hardly have been less like Iron Lake. The water was clear and sweet, but the surrounding land was barren, windswept, and bleak. The weather turned cold overnight. They were grateful for their Salish-provided tents.

In the morning, they woke to approaching trucks. Apparently, the Siksikaitsitapi had more gas reserves, or had faith Big Oil would rise again. John met with their council briefly. Their leader, Joseph RedHawk, welcomed them. He confessed he'd taken on the Executive Director role on the tribal council only a few months before the troubles began. John felt Joseph was in over his head, had a lot of balls in the air at the same time, and was meeting with him out of obligation to Shiela. He quoted a bit of website copy about the history of the Kainai-Blood Tribe, the Siksika, the Peigan-Piikani, and Aamskapi Pikuni.

Joseph didn't see NTC as the valuable resource Dr. Wolf had—or, at least, didn't seem as eager to establish a treaty. But he was polite and went through the motions before wishing them well on their journey.

And that was fine. Now that he had a place and time to meet their ride to NTC, John felt itchy to hit the trail. They broke camp, headed out from Buffalo Lake by 10 AM, and made good time in the windy November sunshine. By sunset, they were crossing into Alberta.

11-16-36 02:32 PM EDT

The weather grew colder in the haphazard way it had since the Paris Accords had failed to hit their carbon goals back in the late 20s. Some days felt like late summer, and the traveling was happy and swift. On other days, the sun would disappear, and flurries would dapple the horses' winter coats. Then, the soldiers were quieter, and the daily mile totals would fall.

NTC eggheads had determined that the effects of global warming would take almost a century to balance out once human civilization had collapsed. The closest analog to Downfall they had was from ice cores that showed a drop in CO_2 after the western hemisphere had been discovered. In the century after Europeans hit the shores of the Americas, 90% of the continent's populations died of smallpox, measles, influenza, bubonic plague, malaria, diphtheria, typhus, and cholera. Wave after wave of novel new viruses had wiped out cities in the Americas the size and scope of London. The result was that the CO2 dropped enough to be significant and measured.

The NTC brains expected the loss of six billion would have a much larger global effect, eventually. That clock had begun ticking. John supposed the new era would need a name. They had said BC (Before Christ) and AD (Anno Domini) when he was a kid. Then they changed it to BCE (Before the Common Era) and CE (the Common Era). John never quite got the hang of that, but he saw the reason for it. Christ was a good dude and all, but Christianity wasn't as universal as the self-centered colonizers imagined. AD—After Downfall? BTSHTF and ATSHTF?

There were reasons military men weren't in charge of naming things. They ended up with acronyms like SNAFU (Situation Normal, All Fucked Up), FUBAR (Fucked Up Beyond All Recognition), or BOHICA (Bend Over, Here It Comes)—which, while useful and appropriate in the shit, were probably not the pinnacle of sophistication.

John guessed all that would sort itself out if they'd done their job. There was still no guarantee humanity *would* survive. John currently placed the odds at 70-30 against. All of their epistemology tricks, all their elaborate games played on the future, He had no evidence that any of them had made a dent in the universe. He'd thought he and Stephen had been so smart. More and more often, his mind swirled around his guilt at all the loss. He'd bet all of Lucas's unlimited time-machine-conjured wealth trying to hide billions of survivors from the future and none of it had paid off. The house always wins. The image of that family running for their lives on that last traumatic day in Madre Pueda —the look in that boy's eyes—haunted him.

Galaxy shook her head and snorted loudly enough to break him from his wool-gathering. She had a knack for that. John looked out at the team ahead of him. He liked to hang back and offer guidance to anyone slowing their collective roll. He crested a large grassy bluff to see Robin riding toward him at a gallop.

Robin usually rode point. He wasn't the best rider of the platoon, but he did all right for a city slicker. John said, "Haw!" and Galaxy bolted forward to meet Robin on the way.

"Commander, you're going to want to see this!" Robin shouted, trying to slow and turn his horse, Nightwing.

"What is it?"

"Survivors!" He finally got Nightwing pointed in the right direction.

John eased back on the reins and waited for Robin to catch up.

"Damn, that horse is *fast*," Robin said. "Up that hill. We positioned a lookout in that old tree. There's a slight valley beyond and a river. The Saskatchewan. We were planning on crossing on 41 further north."

John nodded, and they raced up the hill to the ancient box elder. Their horses munched on timothy below as three soldiers perched in the branches for a better view. John, atop Galaxy, had a pretty good view of his own. From the hill, they had a long, wide vantage point of the rural highway 41 as it diverged from the river and headed north into farmland. Groups of people on foot, on bicycles, and a few with horse-drawn trailers dotted the road.

John zoomed in. It was not an organized migration. They were not moving as one cohesive group. These were families, small parties of three or four. He could see some larger, looser bands of up to a dozen. There were no electric vehicles. John traced Route 41 south. These people were survivors of the nukes. Their EVs would have been fried by the EMP. LT Plasma cores were shielded, but the rest of the vehicle and its delicate computers would have been turned into useless plastic and lead. So they were on foot.

"They stretch as far as I can see. Figure five hundred?" John estimated.

"Easy," Robin said. "Where are they all *headed*?"

John shrugged. "Away from the bombs. They've been on the road, same as us, for a month or more." These folks didn't have Stephen Lucas as their guardian angel. No one was resupplying them. They'd be hungry and maybe sick from radiation. John didn't have to think it over.

"We're going to help them if we can."

"Sir, yes, sir," Robin replied.

"We'll wait for the rest of the team to catch up." John looked back at the stragglers. "Then I'm going to go down and talk to somebody. They don't look like they have a leader. I'll just figure it out as I go."

"I'm going with," Robin demanded. "You don't *know*, they might be armed. I'm *watching* your back, Commander."

John nodded.

———

"There were three of them. The one to the southeast was the brightest, but they all went off within a few seconds of one another. We were watching the news all that night because there was civil unrest breaking out everywhere in the world. The news streamers, all of them, left *and* right, were filled with scenes that looked like the zombie apocalypse. Anyway, we were just about to turn off the tube and hit the sack when the windows lit up like it was noon. Jeremy looked out first. He pulled back the curtain, and the neighborhood just looked like a normal afternoon—except it was twenty after eleven at night. The TV went dead, all our phones went dead. People walked out on their front porches in their PJs and robes. Jeremy asked our neighbor Glenn Russert if he knew what was going on. Glenn had that flu everyone had at the time, y'know? He didn't know what was going on. Nobody knew. Everyone was checking their phones for news. Nothing. The phones never worked again."

Greta Ellis told the story as if she'd rehearsed it, as if she'd told it a hundred times, which, in the intervening weeks, perhaps she had. Her son, Joey, a cute but malnourished golden-haired six-year-old, sat on her lap while her husband, Jeremy, added a few branches to the fire. Her other son, Caleb, an eager-to-please, eager-to-help nine-year-old, continued to forage for dry branches.

John had asked the family to sit with him as the sun set. He and Robin, two well-fed men with military-looking outfits and weapons riding in on horses from the west, attracted attention. As they built the fire, other families gathered. Soon, they had an audience of two dozen around the fire. More gathered as Greta spoke. All of those gaunt, road-worn faces. Their wide eyes reflected the fire, all watching with wonder, and fearing to hope.

"We watched the fireballs rising up. The sky turned from white to yellow and finally to red. The fireball dissipated and started to look like a gigantic jellyfish, getting bigger and flatter and slowly washing out just before sunrise. None of us slept that night. We live in a nice neighborhood in Havre. Jeremy works with the Border Patrol. I teach geometry and algebra at Havre High. We figured the government would tell us what the hell was going on."

Joey got up and walked to the fire. Greta snagged him by the back of his blue-and-white-striped OshKosh B'gosh overalls. He giggled and struggled against her attempt to keep him safe.

"The *government!* We never even saw a police car since that night. Jeremy went in to work the next morning, hoping they'd have some news. He's still driving an antique gas guzzler, thank God. By then, the demons were turning." Her pale blue eyes changed as if a switch had been thrown. John watched as the life drained from them. "We were having lunch when we heard the screams. I looked out and saw Glenn chasing after his wife, Rosa. I thought they were playing. But Glenn was covered in blood, and he was carrying... he was carrying an *arm*... a child's arm... it looked like a dolls arm, but it was no doll. They had girls. Glenn and Rosa had three girls."

Jeremy sat next to Greta and patted her arm.

"I found the same sort of scene all over Havre," Jeremy said, his eyes briefly rising to meet John's. He poked at the fire with a long maple branch. "Montana State was the first I saw them. It looked like another college protest from a mile away. But then—you know when starlings flock in a group at sunset and sort of whirl and turn together? The crowd did that the closer I got. People, uninfected people, were running from the infected. They'd head for open ground and run. Then the demons would see them and turn as a group in that direction." He shook his head. His eyes went dead, too, as if he suddenly wanted to sleep.

"Then I saw the blood. All of them were covered in fresh, red blood. Demons and healthy people. It didn't matter. This was right in front of the hospital on Thirteenth Street. The swarm poured across the field and onto the road. I turned into the hospital, and *that* was a mistake. I didn't see anyone alive that hadn't turned. Folks had been taking their sick there, and I guess it looked like the sick all turned. I barreled through the parking lot to Fifteenth and…." He went silent for a moment. John could see Jeremy replaying that portion of his memories. He shook his head quickly, eyes lost in the fire.

"I made it to work, to the Border Patrol office. No one was there. The armory was unlocked, open, and empty. But I was able to fill my tank, at least. The patrol has a pair of pumps out back. It took me an hour to get home. I hit more demons with my truck than I care to count. I passed the Exxon on Route 2. It was burning. I got home in time to see Glenn Russert tackle Rosa on the sidewalk. Her face got tore up by the concrete, but she didn't *really* fight as he ripped her throat open with his teeth. I never saw the arm."

"He *had* an arm."

"I *told* you I believe you."

Greta shook her head and looked up at the stars.

"We filled the truck with camping gear and the coolers with food and ice from the fridge," she continued. "It was still cold from the night before. Stopped at the IGA. The doors were open, and there were a few demons, but we had to have food and water. Jeremy was so goddamned *heroic*." She stroked his hair. "He went in and filled a basket."

"Remember Guy's Grocery Games?" A quick, sad smile.

John nodded and smiled back.

"Like that, with a lot of gunplay and blood."

"And we headed north on 232. I figured we should get where there weren't so many people."

"She's the genius in the family." Jeremy stroked her hair now.

"It was a good idea." John looked at the small gathering. "I expect you all made similar decisions."

There was a general sense of agreement.

"Otherwise, I guess you wouldn't be sharing our fire tonight."

Caleb came closer to the fire with an arm full of dry maple and hickory branches. He tossed them on the fire as Joey joined him and helped. John looked at their dirty faces. The kids were okay. *These* kids. How many more were out there?

"How did you lose the truck?" John asked.

Jeremy shrugged. Greta looked down.

"There were some bad guys. We stopped for the night at an old farm. It looked abandoned. There were two demons and three of their dead... victims. Jeremy shot them, and we parked out back. There was no power. We just needed to *sleep*," Greta said, as though in a trance.

"We woke up to three guys with more guns. They took our stuff. Took our truck. Said they were real sorry—but took it at gunpoint and all our kids' food and water. *Real* sorry. We've been walking since. At least we were clear of the town." Jeremy was running out of steam. "On the road, we heard the rumors. So we kept on heading north."

"Rumors?" Robin asked.

"That there was a safe haven up north in Canada. A place called *None-of-it*."

John raised an eyebrow.

"And that there were shipping containers filled with food and weapons if we could find them." He drew a crude picnic table with an eye on each side in the dirt. "They say, keep a lookout for containers with hobo signs. If you find them, you can open them with the combination *9-17-36*. We found one in Simpson. It had already been opened, but there were still a few bottles of Pedialyte. That saved our lives. We were badly dehydrated by that point. Found three more on the way, but they were cleaned out."

"There was one with those military meals?" Greta looked to Jeremy.

"MREs." He nodded. "Yeah. I almost forgot about that. We ate for three days from those."

John and Robin looked at each other. At least their doomsday prep work had some impact.

"We found one of those containers." Shouted a man in the back. "Saved our bacon, too."

"Us too," shouted a woman. "Same as he said. It was almost empty, but there were three cans of Enfamil."

"Us too!" shouted another, followed by a chorus of more. Nearly everyone gathered around their fire had been sustained at some point by supplies from the container drops. John was surprised by the lump that formed in his throat. He looked at Robin and found his eyes were wet, shiny, and bright in the yellow light of the fire.

John stood before another fire later in the night. This fire was circled with Lost Boys. He saw them now with fresh eyes. The dirt and grime of the long-traveled road covered their faces too. Though they were better fed and more fit, they too were exhausted, weary, and processing the trauma of a world gone mad.

They'd killed more people in the last two months than any of them thought possible. They'd all seen the way demons fed up close. It didn't take much talking to trigger memories that stole the life out of their eyes, too.

"We've all been on the road for a long time. By my reckoning, if things go the way they've been going, we'll all make it to that new deep-water harbor at Port Nelson by the first week of December." There were a few chuckles. "I know. *The way things have been going.*" They laughed with him. "Despite all the shit, I'm proud of the way you all have hung together as a unit. I'd march with you to the gates of Hell." He nodded and looked around. "But these survivors need to get where we're going, too. If we don't get them up to Nunavut, they'll wander around Canada until the winter kills them—or until they cross paths with a swarm of Mr. Ray."

"Right now, there are just over a million souls under NTC's domes. Except for us, the CSAR mission went exactly according to plan."

"Except for us! Yay!" Oz laughed. John smiled.

"They are within their projected capacity, and according to Mayor Shaw, last we spoke, they're doing fine. They'll be better when they add more domes in the spring. I haven't briefed her on my idea yet, but it doesn't matter. I'm going to do what's right. Athena will have to make room for a few more." He paused and jerked a thumb over his shoulder to the people in the distance. "Those are real survivors. All of us? The people in those domes up north? We survived because we were on Oracle's list. Or Mary Allan's database." He shook his head. "And God bless 'em. Many of the people we rescued were just people Stephen Lucas knew—including *this* Black man." He jerked his thumb at his chest. "But these folks aren't on a list. They weren't selected by Human Resources. They faced the demons and did what they needed to save themselves and their families.

"When humanity gets back on the good foot again, I want it to look like these folks."

His troops nodded.

"So here's what we're going to do. I'm going to split our little movable feast in two. I will lead a small group of volunteers to accompany the survivors. Captain Mercer will carry on to Port Nelson to meet that NTC boat in December. I'll get the survivors there at the best speed possible, which I estimate to be about half the speed we're making currently. That puts us in Port Nelson at the end of January." He let them imagine what it would be like in Northern Manitoba in late January.

"So. I'm only taking volunteers. Who wants to take the slow road home and keep these survivors safe? If you're with Cap, stay on down. If you want to head home now, stay down. If you want to freeze your genitals good and hard, stand up."

Emily Tran was the first to stand. Then Chris Goldstein. Then, three more stood in the back. Then, four more close to the fire. Then, in small groups of two or three, they all stood.

John shook his head in wonder.

"You all are *idiots!*"

They laughed.

"All right. All right." He turned to Robin. "I'm still sending you to meet that boat. Pick ten, and we'll figure out how to divide the gear." He turned back to the soldiers. "Okay, get your rest, you primates. We split up in the morning. Dismissed."

"TWO *THOUSAND* NEW ARRIVALS?" Athena said with steel in her voice.

"That was our final estimate," John confirmed. "But count on more. The stream from the States is constant. Albertan survivors have begun to join our little caravan, too. I can't imagine Saskatchewan will be much different. Somehow, they *all* got word of *None of it*. The rumor is fueled by hope. It's like the term *demons*. No one knows where it started, but it spread everywhere. Without a functioning internet, memes still spread, turns out. Everyone we meet calls the infected *demons*, except the Indians who call 'em *wendigoes*. But everyone knows the hobo signs we used on the storage units and containers, and everyone knows about *None of it*."

"It's *impossible* to manage a planned community when the influx of new arrivals is not planned as well," Athena said sternly. "NTC is busting at the seams. Even 100 unplanned arrivals would be a challenge."

The room and the Aurora feeds were silent for a moment.

"It appears we need a different plan," Mrs. Crouch said matter-of-factly. She didn't speak often in meetings, but when she did, it was always a bit of a show-stopper. "I worked with Stephen for twenty years. He is a genius and unbelievably creative. He is the best manager of creatives I've ever met." She paused. "But he relied on others to challenge his designs. He hired smart contrarians to tell him when his big ideas were fatally flawed. If this community can't accommodate waves of new survivors crashing on its shores, it's a design problem." She paused again. "Because that's what it's designed to do if I understand it correctly."

"Well said." John's voice echoed in the nearly silent room. "It's also a sign that some of our preparation worked. Every living soul on the trail with us is a life that might not be part of Stephen's final butcher's bill. It's a life *saved*. And that's been our job for the last six years."

To her credit, Athena saw the truth in John and Mrs. Crouch's brief lectures. "We're still faced with the facts on the ground. Nunavut has three feet of fresh snow on top of the three it already had. NTC is beyond its capacity. We have families sharing apartments already. We have protein sequencing shortages. B-Dome is at its limit of fresh produce. I don't know how to make more beds available."

"At the risk of channeling Captain Mercer—we might be surprised by the community." Mary Allan spoke up. "We *are* beyond capacity, and there *are* shortages, but morale is high."

"That happens when you've been saved from certain, horrific death," Walrus interjected from his lab.

"True, but the new arrivals have pitched right in," Mary continued. "The domes are a hotbed of innovation. It's worth getting out and touring all the domes and seeing their work. If we present this challenge to them, they'll dream up more solutions than we can use."

"Hell yeah!" Walrus said enthusiastically from the holoscreen. "I'm working on some new stuff that might bear some fruit. There are lots of new breakthroughs in 3D printing too."

Eddie Akkilokipok, the leader of the Walrus Rocks Inuit Small Business Council watched all of this conversation with an unreadable smile. "What about the storage farm?"

The room was quiet.

Athena shook her head. "What do you mean?"

"The storage container farm Borealis set up on the south end of The Rocks? It's twenty acres of storage containers. Until Downfall, as you call it, the dock sent a shipment out there every week. There must be ten thousand containers out there. My friend Karpok tells me about things like that. He says the dock-workers still keep the roads plowed according to a Borealis contract."

The committee looked at him, then at each other. Then they all started talking at once.

11-17-36 4:21 PM EDT

Mary shouted the combination to be heard over the polar winds.

The temperature on The Rocks was fifteen below zero Fahren-heit. The sky was a deep bluish-black, and the stars on the secret container farm were almost bright enough to read by. Mary, Walrus, and Athena wanted to see the container's contents with their own eyes, so they had bundled in their most rigorous winter gear.

The Borealis soldier clumsily spun the dial on the cold lock with her gloved hand. It fell open. She quickly pushed her hand back into her larger snowmobile mitts and pulled on the handle. Ice cracked and fell to the snowpack as the container's door opened.

"Holy shit!" Walrus laughed and pounded the air with his hands as LED lights inside the container winked on, revealing a thoughtfully designed, well-insulated, one-room apartment with bunks for four.

The steering committee filed in to get out of the wind. Once the door was closed, an electric fan in the baseboard started pushing heat. It was laid out similar to a recreational vehicle with a kitchenette, bathroom, shower, small living area, and curtained berths for sleeping.

Walrus could see evidence that Stephen had designed the instant living space. It would have taken him months to draft it up to this level of detail. How far in the future? There was no way of knowing. But it was further proof that his friend lived on and continued to enable their survival.

"There are over 1,500 containers with these markings. That will give us enough temporary housing to get through to spring," Athena said. "We should have them moved into the connector rings. It'll still be a chilly neighborhood, but they can't live out here."

"*If* John can get those survivors here," Mary said, blowing warm air into her hands. "They have a long road."

"About *that*," Athena said. "Before the first ship left for points south, I had them take on additional cargo."

11-25-36 02:12 PM CDT

"Galaxy is *tallll!*" Joey shouted as he rocked happily in John's saddle.

"That she is." John clicked his tongue, and Galaxy snorted as she moved from a walk to a canter. "She's fast, too. Wanna see?"

"This is fast *enough!*" Joey squealed and closed his eyes.

John laughed. "Okay." He clicked again and ever so slightly eased back on the reins. Galaxy slowed back to a walk. Two months in, rider and ride had merged. Whatever John thought, Galaxy did.

They'd been lucky, though John never said it out loud. The weather had been mild so far. There had been a few snowfalls, and the nights were usually below freezing, but the days had been short, sunny, and fine for overland travel. Goldstein and the tech apes continued to hope for a few LT Plasma 4-wheelers, but LT systems were rare in Canadian farmland to begin with and,

John imagined, anyone who had one or found one probably hit the road back in September.

Early on, John had tasked the engineers to cobble together a covered wagon design. The design specs required it to carry four adults, travel over rough terrain, and be easily pulled by a man, woman, or horse. Chiefly, it had to be built from parts they could scrounge along the way.

Goldstein used Aurora CAD apps to rough out the basic design overnight. He posted it to NTCGit and opened it up for E-Dome engineers to submit pull requests. There'd been a three-day hackathon to arrive at the Mark-1 design. The team found Ox-Acetylene gear in an abandoned service station and scavenged parts from three farms along their route. Once they had all the parts, the engineers camped out at a secure, abandoned barn and set to work. They built the first Mark-1 in two days, packed all their newly found gear in the back, hitched it to a horse, and rejoined the caravan by the end of the third. Dirt bike wheels and scrap steel could be found on almost any farm in Saskatchewan.

They spent the next few weeks cranking out a new wagon every other day, making design improvements on the way. Every new farm presented them with fresh materials for their hackathons. They were up to Mark-2.8 now. Every new wagon sped their progress as the slower walkers found rest and the horses made a better pace.

John circled back to find the Ellis family. They were still among the walkers. They were young and strong, and had adapted to the daily mileage well.

"Galaxy is *tall!*" Joey shouted to his mom.

"Yes, she is. Tall horse for a tall commander!" She reached up to take him as John lowered him down.

"Say thank you!"

"Thank you, Commander Banks."

"It is my absolute pleasure, Joey." He looked at the sky and asked Jeremy, "What do you think?"

"I think we get snow tonight." He squinted into the distance. "No later than tomorrow. We've been *lucky*."

John masked his cringe to make it look like a squint. He didn't like to use the L word.

"You all need anything?" he asked.

"A hot shower, a feather bed, and a pedicure," Greta said with a dreamy look in her eyes.

"All that and more in Nunavut." John tapped the brim of his hat and took off for the front of the pack.

The going in lower Saskatchewan was level and straight. They stayed off the roads as a matter of course—the roads had become dangerous. The guys with trucks (almost always gas guzzlers) were always assholes or worse. They were all LARPing *The Road Warrior*. Lots of black leather, tattered red baseball hats, punk-rock wannabes rolling coal in big trucks. They'd survived the demon hordes, and now they were acting out their alpha-male, incel fantasies. The roads were the domain of bullies, dicks, and rapists.

So they stayed off the roads. It was better than fighting their way across Canada. Besides, roads only led to cities and towns. Cities and towns were where the demons ruled.

But the great plains of Saskatchewan were flat, fertile and empty. When they saw demons, they were far away and isolated. The troops hadn't had to fire their weapons more than a few times. It was good hiking. They were making 15 miles a day. He'd like to go faster, of course. Greta Ellis wasn't alone in wanting a hot shower, a bed without rocks, and time to read by a warm fire.

What he really wanted was time to talk to Zoe.

John made it to the head of the caravan and caught up with Emily Tran and Sargent Ortiz, a serious young woman John had come to rely on since Robin had taken Oz with him to meet the NTC ship.

"Pony rides over, Commander?" Emily asked.

"They are, Lieutenant Tran," John said with a smile.

"I am still protesting this field commission, Commander."

"Protest all you want, LT."

"Looks like snow in our future, Commander," Ortiz said as she nodded toward the graying horizon.

"Jeremy Ellis agrees. Let it come. We don't get a vote in the weather," John said. "Check with NTC and see if they can get us fresh weather intel. There's a campground between here and our goal for today. Let's make for it if the snow looks tough."

"Sir, yes, sir," Ortiz said. Her eyes unfocused as she pulled open her maps app.

"LT, we need to get you implants."

"So I can be assimilated by the Borg, sir?" Emily raised an eyebrow.

"Resistance is futile."

"Yeah. That's never been *my* experience, sir."

THE DEMONS WERE STACKED up like cordwood.

Robin and his two tech apes were raiding a farmhouse for supplies to make one of Goldstein's Conestoga Mark3.2 wagons when they found the monsters piled up in the root cellar.

Robin counted 20, primarily adults but a few teenagers, and at least one small, girl-sized demon. It was hard to do a complete inventory because the pile was a jumbled, haphazard mound of torsos with legs and arms jutting out at odd angles. It looked like they all just collapsed into a mound together.

Their horns had continued to grow as autumn gave way to winter. Some of the older demons sported 8-inch crusty, curly projections that looked like goat's horns made from infected toenails.

"Well, that's about as creepy as things get," Robin said as he cautiously circled the heap of monsters. Wearing the same clothes they'd turned in over two months ago, caked with old dried blood and viscera, the demons appeared dead.

The thing was, when he looked closer, they *weren't* dead—and they were all breathing in sync. Robin pulled up his stopwatch app. He counted five slow, shallow breaths, made more observable by the combined height of the bodies. The stopwatch read 90 seconds.

"So, three-ish breaths a minute," Robin said to Specialist Moore. "They show zero signs they know we're here, but let's not take any chances." He motioned toward the exit, and Moore eased up the shallow steps and out the large cellar doors. Once outside, Robin found a rock the size of his fist under the sparse drift of dry snow near the foundation. "Be ready to run like hell if this wakes them up. Retreat to the barn if they swarm out of there."

He threw the rock at the pile like he was shooting a free throw. It landed on top of a large woman wearing what had once been a pink sweatshirt and sweatpants. The impact caused her to puff out a quick sigh, and then she rolled away from the door and curled into the fetal position.

"Shit!" Robin closed his eyes. "I forgot to get this on holo for V-Dome." He turned to Moore. "Did you find anything for the wagon?"

"We found an Ox-Acetylene rig in the barn with plenty of juice. Plenty of steel scrap. They started cobbling it together. Still need some bike wheels."

"Okay, Ron, keep looking. If you still need anything, move on to that farm yonder to the north. I'm going to shoot some holo of our demon Jenga tower and catch up with you."

"Yes, sir." Moore trotted off to round up Yousef and Jessup.

Robin opened his Aurora camera app, swiped to the HOLO option, tapped the red square, and began speaking. The recorded holo data streamed right from his implants to the file.

"The weather has turned cold here in Saskatchewan, and we stumbled upon a new demon behavior." He walked down into the root cellar. "At least this was new to *us*. Perhaps the folks at V-Dome can explain it." He turned to look at the pile of demons. "Looks like they broke the basement windows to get in. As you can see, the pile is three or four bodies high and five or six across its base. There's no organization, just heaped together. They're still alive, or undead, or whatever.

"They're breathing, if you watch closely." He held his view as steady as possible for a couple of minutes. "I estimated three breaths per minute. I know demons respirate slower than healthy people, and their heart rate is something like 20 BPM. The pressure of that goop that used to be blood is damn near nonexistent. But the breathing here is even lower than usual. It feels like they're *hibernating*, maybe?"

He backed out of the cellar and pulled out the small aerosol bear horn the Salish had packed for them on their first night at Iron Lake. It had proved helpful for calling the troops together from a distance. He tapped the trigger twice—two sharp, short *BLAATs*. The pile shuddered and wriggled as one before returning to their torpor.

"They're almost completely unresponsive. The *smell* is something. Sort of like the primate house at the Saint Louis Zoo combined with a neglected porta-john. Zombie movies left that part out. Zombies eat brains, right? Do they shit and piss afterward?" Robin slowly panned across the mound. "Smells like demons just let it rip and fill their pants.

"They all look emaciated. Not as bad as the beef jerky demons we found in traffic in the desert, but like starving people. Probably dehydrated. Their skin is all thin and leathery, and turning sort of grayish-red. They definitely look less human the longer they go. Check out these horns." He zoomed in on a man with several six-inch protrusions that had ripped through his grey flannel shirt. "The name *demons* just gets more accurate. I think Commander Banks is right. The GGB-Z virus seems to be cooking up more surprises for us.

"I'll wrap this up and send it off to V-Dome. It will be good if this is how they behave in cold weather. One less thing to worry about. If so, we'd be pretty lucky. Capt. Robin Mercer, Borealis 1st, signing off." He tapped the red square, addressed the holo file to V-Dome and John, and sent it on its way.

He found the tech apes in the barn welding a wagon frame together. Yousef had found some suitable dirt bike wheels, and he and Moore were tearing them down. Robin was pleased by their quiet progress and was about to commend them when his Aurora pinged with a realTime message from Oz. He accepted it.

"Hey, Oz—"

"The fuck's a nigger doing with a weapon like this?" An unfamiliar, angry voice shouting with derision and bile filled Robin's ears. Oz's Aurora was sending his audio-visual feed. It took a while before Robin could figure out what he was seeing. The field of vision was moving: bright white, then tan, then white again. It was the ground. Oz was being dragged by his arms with his head facing the ground.

"Oz!" Robin ran to his horse, Nightwing. He didn't stop to fill in his soldiers. He was up in the saddle faster than he'd ever mounted before.

"Captain! These dickwads got the jump on—" Oz mumbled before he was dropped onto the ground, face first. He rolled over, and Robin could see his assailants. Five, no, six men in black leather jackets or hoodies and red hats or bandanas leaned over him and kicked the shit out of him.

"No!" Robin shouted as he looked out through Oz's eyes. The Aurora showed Oz's GPS position, a heading east-north-east from his. His companions mounted up as Robin left them in the dust, galloping almost due east across the open farmland. He pushed Nightwing as fast as he knew how.

"These asswipes have the minigun, Captain," Oz shouted, but his voice was ragged, garbled, and full of fluid.

"Captain? Who the fuck are you talking to?" Their leader, an older asshole with greasy brown hair, smiled and stood back. He looked to have the rest of his band of dirtbags beat by thirty IQ points. His buddies continued to kick. They were all white, all young—from mid-teens to mid-twenties—filthy and full of hate. "JD, go in the barn and find us some rope."

"Okay, Donnie!" The youngest kicked one last time and jogged out of view.

"Not so *talkative* anymore!" Donnie said with a grin.

"Not so *talkative*, now!" the biggest of them, an apelike blonde, shouted as he delivered a massive right cross with a fist that looked like a country ham. Oz's Aurora feed quaked, then lost focus. His field of view turned, and Robin could only see white. Then, the image vibrated roughly. The feed filled with the sound of Oz's body dragged over the dirt. Robin wanted to link John into it, but what could his CO do from hundreds of miles away at this point? He just rode harder as tears streamed down his face.

The view through Oz's eyes showed a dark network of lines. He must have been unconscious because the lines didn't focus. It was, Robin realized, the branches of a tree. He was looking up at a big maple devoid of leaves.

"No. Oh, no!" Robin moaned, wishing he could switch off the feed, but he couldn't. "OZ! OZ, *get up!* Wake up, Oz! Fight! Get up and *fight Oz!*"

"JD! Where the fuck is that goddamned rope?" Donnie shouted. "It's time we truss this piggy up in the proper New South tradition!"

"OZ! God damn it! Wake up and fight!" Robin screamed from miles away.

Then, the lines came into focus. Oz regained consciousness and looked around at the tree, his captors, and JD arriving with a coil of rope. It looked like coarse hemp, the kind that tears your hands up.

"Grnn. Dick-ahds!" Oz was trying to cuss them out, but his speech was impaired. The right image, his right eye, was swelling shut. "Muhhfukers!" That was clear enough.

The blonde ape punched Oz again with a frightening hay maker. Robin had to hold on to his saddle as Oz's Aurora feed pivoted, falling backward to show the white winter sky.

"*Bura Ubanka!*" Oz spat these last words. No interpretation was needed.

The ape appeared over him, his face full of rage. He raised his boot and drove it into Oz's face. Robin heard bone breaking. The video feed went black.

"Miller!" Donnie's voice was distorted, muted. "You fucking idiot! I wanted to hang the fucker."

"Fuck that asshole!"

"Is he dead?"

The audio feed was weak. Finally, when the Aurora implant no longer detected a heartbeat, it broke the connection.

Robin was presented with a dialog box asking if he wanted to save the session. The file was less than four minutes long. Robin had to fight to remember what he'd been doing before he took Oz's call. It felt like a lifetime ago because it was. He tapped okay, forwarded the holo file to John, and added a voice memo as he rode.

"Commander, some assholes killed Oz. I am going to respond. Mercer out."

He sent the grim message and pulled his squad into a conference.

"Drop what you're doing and form up on me. Use my GPS coordinates. Weapons hot."

He turned around and saw Moore, Yousef, and Jessup charging along on Nightwing's tail a quarter of a mile back. It was his first awareness that they'd been following—or trying to.

"So, what's the *plan*, Captain Mercer?" he said to himself. Nightwing's ears turned back. He knew he couldn't go in steaming. That was how COs got their soldiers killed. He had to force himself to ease back on Nightwing's reins. Oz wasn't going anywhere. He felt like his eyes were blazing and only then realized he'd been crying. The wind from galloping had driven the tears back. He wiped his face and shut his eyes tight. How long since he'd last *blinked?* He slowed to let his soldiers catch up.

"What's going on, Captain?" Yousef shouted as he entered earshot.

Robin waited until all three had reached them.

"About two minutes ago, Specialist Osunyemi was captured and killed by some fucked up Road Warrior wannabes." Robin's face, usually smiling and friendly, was drawn into a somber mask of grief, anger, and command. He tapped his temple. "I saw the whole murder through his Aurora implants." The soldiers grimaced in unison. Robin looked at Aurora's GPS. "We're three miles west of his—the location of his remains. I had Oz scouting ahead. He went alone. I let him go alone. That's on me."

"He had that minigun," Moore said quietly.

"And now these assholes have it." Robin nodded. "If I recall correctly, he had a quarter of a belt hanging when he rode off. Maybe 200 rounds?"

"Oz is the only person I'd trust with that fucker, and he can barely control it," Moore said, unaware he'd referred to Oz in the present tense.

"Those dumbasses could run through 200 rounds before they get their finger off the trigger. If we're lucky, the assholes will kill themselves when they try to light it up," Jessup joked grimly.

"That would work for me," Robin said as he raised an eyebrow in thought.

"*Captain,*" John said as Robin answered his call.

"Commander. Listen, I'm sorry—" Robin began.

"I watched the holo file, Robin," John said, his voice deep with weariness. "You have nothing to apologize for. Have you got your feet back under you?"

"Sir?"

"You had the sound of a man riding off to get him and his men killed in your voice memo," John said with a gravity that couldn't be ignored.

"Yes, sir." Robin hesitated. "I believe I have my feet under me, sir. We've established a perimeter two miles from the crime scene."

John could hear the change in Robin's voice. Leaders who lose a soldier under their direct command are never quite the same again.

"Do you have a plan of attack?"

"Yes, sir."

"These feel like the Canadian cousins of the assholes we ran into back in Nevada. I didn't tell you they called me the n-word back then, did I?"

"No, sir." Robin frowned. "You just said they called you some names."

John went silent. Robin felt like there was a lot his CO wanted to say but didn't have the words.

"Yeah. Well, there are aspects of the Black experience that take a lot of Black experience to talk about effectively. The n-word is something… I never know how to judge its importance. It's a word with body dysmorphic disorder, right? I either see its weight as too big or too small. I can't look at it and see it for what it is. I can't get a *perspective* on it."

Robin nodded. It was the first time he'd seriously discussed race with his commander. He was on unsure ground and didn't want to appear insensitive. He ended up saying, "I get that."

John sighed as if to say he couldn't be sure if Robin actually could, but he appreciated the gesture.

"I just wanted you to hear this from me, Captain. Your priority is to get your men to that boat. *Meet the boat.*" He was silent for a moment. "But kill these mother-fuckers first."

"Sir, yes, sir."

They approached from the main road, three of the squad of nine —Robin and two sergeants. They rode in slowly, giving their quarry plenty of time to notice them.

"Moore, are you in position?" Robin asked over an open Aurora channel.

"Yes, sir."

"Jessup?"

"Ready."

Their Aurora rangefinders allowed them to halt precisely three-quarters of a mile from the site of Oz's murder. His murderers had cut the clothes from his body and tied his arms to the crossbeam of the farm's barn. Two of them were up close to Oz. JD held an armful of cans of spray paint as Donnie, the leader, stood on a step-ladder incorporating Oz's corpse into some fashion of apocalyptic graffiti.

The other assholes were listening to music and lazing about on the hood and in the bed of their truck. Even from this distance, Robin could make out the baseline and drums of Metallica's *Enter Sandman*.

After a few minutes, when the assholes didn't notice, Robin proceeded to the next step in the plan. He pulled out the obnoxiously loud bear horn the Salish had left him and let it rip. The deafening *BLAAAT* rang out and echoed across the frozen field. He held the trigger down until the can was empty, then tossed it aside. He fired his service Glock into the sky three times for good measure.

That roused the assholes.

They jumped into furious, disordered action. Each of them leaped to attention and ran about in almost perfect circles. A kid, Robin recognized him as JD, lifted the minigun from the bed of the truck and circled back behind it to Donnie. He appeared to ask permission to use the weapon, but the leader hopped down from the ladder, grabbed the gun, and knocked him down. JD scrambled forward to join the other four punks. The leader, sure as shit, didn't have a clear idea of the power a minigun possessed, nor of the concept of clear lines of fire. It took him a while to figure out how to operate the thing. When he worked it out, he aimed at Robin and fired.

Robin and his companions never flinched as they watched the barrels light up and heard the distance attenuated *BRAAAP* of the weapon. They'd stopped well beyond the range of the M134. As Robin expected, the minigun lurched up and to the right. Before Donnie could regain control, the barrage of rounds cut through two of his gang—JD and a tall, skinny, red-headed boy—like a fork through pulled pork. The three remaining assholes, seeing their friends turn into bloody meat before their eyes, dove for the cover of the truck.

"Jessup, looks like you were right," Robin said.

"Goddamn, sir!" Jessup said, awestruck.

In a herky-jerky pirouette, the minigun twirled Donnie around, and its bullets tore a jagged line from the truck's front fender to the driver's door. The force of the fire rocked the vehicle like a toy.

Then the gun fell silent but for the electric motor's whine and rotating barrels' whir, barely audible from their position. The leader dropped the weapon, looked at his friends split roughly in two, covered his mouth, and puked with a projectile force nearly equal to the minigun. Green vomit spewed between his black-gloved fingers.

"Fire at will," Robin said quietly.

The range of the minigun was about half a mile, but the range of Moore and Jessup's sniper rifles were well over a mile when steadied with a tripod, and their vision enhanced by their implanted lenses. The ape was the first to go. Within three seconds, the shooters dropped the remaining murderers.

Robin nodded, nudged Nightwing with a gentle tap of his heels, and rode in to cut Oz down from that goddamned barn.

———

Oz's naked corpse was covered with paint—metallic silver, Ford blue, and Kelly green—from head to toe. On the closed hay loft doors, the leader—no artist he—had painted inept bat wings roughly connected to Oz's shoulders and a crown of thorns over his head. Above that, in block letters, it said, "The New South

Rises!" On Oz's dark chest he'd painted, "Col. Greene's piggy." Robin lifted the body and sliced the ropes with quick slashes of his combat knife. His soldiers were there to ease Oz to the ground.

The earth was frozen and bitter, but Moore found some good shovels, three digging bars, and an adz. It was hard, sad work, and they all helped, but Robin really put his back into it. Once they got below two feet, the soil softened. Robin didn't climb out of the grave until it was six feet deep, and its sides were square and true.

The soldiers each donated a piece of clothing to replace Oz's uniform that lay in ripped and torn scraps at his feet, or tied as trophies around the necks of his dead murderers. His friends cleaned his body with paint thinner from the barn and ice cold water pumped from the well. They dressed him with care and lowered him into the grave. Robin was quiet for a while as they stood before the grave. Then he cleared his throat and sniffed.

"We stand here to honor Specialist Iniko Osunyemi, a soldier, a Lost Boy, a friend. Oz was the hardest-fighting, hardest-working, smartest, and funniest soldier I ever had the pleasure to serve with. He was on my team when we resurrected Commander Banks from the middle of a raging wildfire."

His soldiers were awestruck at that.

"He never blinked in the face of danger. Nope. Not Oz. Oz *laughed*. Oz made *us* laugh when we were up against it. He made the last six years, waiting for Downfall... It's like... We were bracing for a terrifying tidal wave, and he... like, Oz would be waxing his surfboard." He laughed a little as tears flowed. "Thank you, Oz. I was honored to serve with you...and I wish you well. The hard part is over. Now you're on the easy path."

He raised his arm in a salute, and his squad joined him. They stood in silence for a moment. Then they each grabbed a shovel and covered him.

Robin picked up a rag from Oz's uniform and Moore poured a bit of gas on it from the farm's equipment shed. The squad had heaped the assholes into the ruined truck's cabin and bed. Robin tucked the rag into the gas tank's vent tube and mounted Nightwing. He leaned down and lit the rag as his team headed toward the main road.

As he caught up to his soldiers, the truck erupted into a ball of bright orange flame in the dimming daylight. For the next several minutes' ride, they looked as if they were lit by the setting sun.

THERE'S *little in life that's so disheartening as constant cold.* Who had said that? John couldn't place it at first. It could have been Alexander Solzhenitsyn in the *Gulag Archipelago* or *One Day in the Life of Ivan Denisovich.* He guessed it might also have been Roland Deschain in Stephen King's *The Dark Tower.* John's mind wandered, his toes burned with the onset of frostbite, and his ass was stiff and deeply chafed in his saddle. He was cranky, hungry —probably malnourished to be honest—tired, and cold deep into his bones.

But he was on a solemn mission.

It had taken the refugees almost a month to pass to the north of Spruce Home, Saskatchewan, the site of Oz's murder. John left Emily in charge and took the time to deviate from the caravan's current course to pay his respects. A solo trip, two hours alone in the dim early dawn with Galaxy and the bleak landscape. Snow had covered the grave, but he knelt by it anyway. His soul was hollowed out, exhausted from the loss of good soldiers.

John led thirty-eight of his original forty-three. Of those, seven Black soldiers served under his command, including Oz. He made an effort to lead all of his soldiers without regard to race. It was a privilege that came with service in the military and CALFIRE too. Within the boundaries of those organizations, a man or woman could imagine that racism wasn't a thing—or at least wasn't a *big* thing. In service of the mission, racism had no place, and for the most part, in John's career, that had been the case.

NTC's recruitment had been guided by fairly strict DEI policies. If the only humans to survive were in those domes, the logic was, then those domes should be filled with all races. Stephen had built a world where there were no minorities. All races were equally represented in None of it. They'd built themselves a cocoon that was comfortably multi-racial.

He looked up at the spray-painted, misspelled obscenities on the barn. The faint outline of Oz's slumped body could be made out from its masking of the overspray. A sudden frigid blast forced him to pull his parka hood closed.

The world had not been cleansed of racism. Hatred survived out here. The future wouldn't be free of bigotry so long as it thrived in this wasteland. John didn't know who this Colonel Greene was or what this nonsense about the New South amounted to. But he hated the sound of it and what it meant for the rosy future Oracle was guiding humanity to.

He shook his head and looked at the rough, snow-covered ground beneath his feet.

"I'm sorry, Oz. You deserved better." He shook his head. "I'm sorry."

He stood, straightened his back, and heard a dull pop through his jacket. At least Oz's death hadn't been tied to a conflict with time.

"Thirty-seven." He said as he pulled himself up into Galaxy's saddle.

12–23-36 10:45 AM EDT

John returned to his flock by mid-morning. The stream of refugees that stretched from horizon to horizon was disordered and barely keeping it together. Snow fell in a dense, constant, fine powder. It was the kind of snow that John knew wouldn't slow any time soon.

He caught up to Tran, Ortiz, and Goldstein to find them squabbling over something too trivial to discern.

"Did you search every farmhouse, henhouse, outhouse and doghouse?"

"Tran, you ain't the boss of me," Goldstein said before he saw his CO approaching. "But yeah, we turned that farm inside out." He sat up a little straighter as John and Galaxy drew near. "Commander."

"Lieutenant Tran, Private Goldstein. Are you two playing nice?"

"Sir. yes, sir," they both responded—Tran with a wry grin, Goldstein with a frown.

Every one of his soldiers was fighting to maintain an even keel. It would have been understandable if they screamed and shouted at the refugees but, in no small part due to John's example, they maintained a professional and respectful demeanor almost universally. It wasn't simply because their CO was watching. They all knew that as bad as they felt, as tired as they were, the refugees, in almost every case, had it worse.

And they were months from Port Nelson.

"Let's see if we can tighten these doggies up," John said to Tran, Ortiz, and Goldstein over their open channel. "With this snow, if we don't keep them together, we might lose some families and not know for hours."

"Roger that, Commander," Tran said as she nudged her horse, Stella, into action. John was impressed with Emily Tran. She'd never ridden a horse before Iron Lake but turned out to be a fine rider. She was a quick learner in general and acutely, often sardonically, observant. Goldstein wasn't half as comfortable on horseback, but even he recognized they were better at covering long distances in these conditions than the fuel-cell dirt bikes. He'd had his apes looking for snowmobiles. It was the right country for them. But all the machines they found were drained of gas or showed decades of neglect.

John leaned forward and patted Galaxy's neck. She raised her head to push against his hand and snorted her acknowledgment. Her coat was thick now, downright woolly.

John watched his team slowly bring the doggies into a more cohesive line. Doggies. When had he begun to think of these people as a single entity? 3,268 men, women, and children marched on foot across Canada in winter. A few new stragglers joined every week. Athena would have a shit fit when she saw the refugees' latest tally. Hell, there had already been two births. Over a dozen had died from illness or old age. John only knew a handful of families.

The rest were just a line of bodies, some on foot, most in wagons. Plenty alternated between wagon riding and walking simply to stretch their legs and break up the boredom. Stephen had dropped plenty of container depots with food and supplies, but many of them had been found opened and empty. They were all tired of Borealis MREs and they could all use more protein, fruit, and carbs—and every one of them would have killed for a home-cooked meal—but hunger wasn't slowing them.

They were also well-shod for the hike. One of Oracle's containers along the way had been filled to the top with snow boots and gear for every age group. It hadn't been snowing when they first found that depot, but within two days, they were glad for his thoughtfulness. If they had to trudge through the snow, they were at least doing it in style.

That didn't keep them from complaining. John left that to his platoon to sort out. The soldiers would field the complaints, sort them into action items, and report them. It kept the griping to a minimum. When his soldiers displayed annoyance at their charges' whining, John pulled them up short and reminded them just how many miles these people had walked and just what they'd left behind.

Even so, he found himself referring to them as doggies and

treating them as one monolithic whole. Perhaps it was forgivable, but John struggled with self-forgiveness on the best of days. He was getting worn out, too, and there was no one for him to lodge his complaints to. There was no Zoe to check his worst tendencies. He was, among all these people, all alone.

The caravan made their way up a mile-long rise and looked down across a shallow valley. Everything was white with fresh snow. The ground, the sky, everything visible was nearly the same color as if the world had been drained of blood—a vampire world. The only dark lines were tree trunks on the far lip of the valley, but between where John sat atop Galaxy and that tree line, there were no structures or roads.

"Let's be careful of streams down there," John said as his soldiers moved down the slope. "Maybe a frozen lake in the center of that."

A chill ran up his spine, an unconscious ancient memory tied to the snow and the possibility of a hidden lake.

"We'll take her slow," Goldstein said as he guided the forward walkers. "Let me check the map." His Aurora gave him an overlay of the path to Port Nelson cutting across the valley. It showed a thin blue line indicating a stream. "Good call, Commander. But it's got to be frozen solid by now. Right?"

"Take it slow, Chris."

"Yes, sir."

John's hackles were raised until Goldstein and his mount were across and reported a small stream that had frozen solid. The only danger was slipping and sliding. He prompted Galaxy to follow down into the shallow valley.

Galaxy treated the ten yards of solid ice with a confidence that eased John's mind, though their combined weight produced a few deep thrums in the frozen stream. John continued to turn in his saddle to monitor the refugees until he was at the tree line, looking back at the last stragglers. Then he released a deep sigh.

"Not a fan of ice hockey, Commander?" Emily Tran appeared at his side.

"What?"

"The ice." She jutted her chin toward the frozen stream. "I watch people for a living. You hide it pretty well, but you've been spooked every time we've crossed over anything bigger than a puddle with ice covering it. This is Saskatchewan. There are a lot of lakes up here. Every time someone plots a path over a frozen lake, you make 'em change course."

John looked at her for a long time. He hadn't really thought that through. Only an idiot couldn't see the connection. He'd seen others carrying weird little leftovers after a trauma, little ticks, habits, or phobias. Here was a beam in his own eye. It was a wound so old he'd learned to look past it. Except for the dreams. His immediate reaction was to get pissed off.

"It's nearly Christmas. The ice is frozen solid now," he said with an even voice. "We should be okay."

Tran studied him and nodded. He hadn't really answered her question, had he? She decided not to push it.

"Snow doesn't show signs of stopping." She changed the subject.

"No," John said, turning Galaxy into the sparse forest. "Let's look for a motel or lodge or something out of the weather, something that will hold a crowd. Have Ortiz spend some quality time with her Aurora to find something Goldstein can work with."

He rode off to end the conversation.

Ortiz was genuinely beaming as the caravan rounded the turn on old Route 2. The ski lodge was massive, picturesque, and appeared abandoned. She had found the place by searching Aurora's onboard database, which wasn't nearly as informative as the internet had been before Downfall. Still, the Timberline Lodge was a four-star hotel with 300 rooms and an adjoining condo community that might hold 2,500. There was room to spare. Goldstein and his crew rode ahead to see if he could establish anything like heat or running *liquid* water.

John called out to the rest of his platoon and slowed the refugees' roll.

"LT, take a team and clear all the living areas."

"Sir, yes, sir." Tran gestured to a handful of soldiers she trusted and followed the tech apes down into the Lodge's parking lot.

John hoped the place would be suitable shelter from the relentless snow. There was already ten inches underfoot, drifting in some places to well over two feet. Those on foot were slowing down. Lifting one's foot to clear the snow added a motion to walking that made leg muscles fatigue unexpectedly. The doggies were panting. Everyone was tired and aching and cold, bone-weary *cold*.

As they approached, the entire lodge lit up in the dimming gray daylight, like a sudden display of Christmas lights. The refugees responded with cheer and rushed for the lodge. The golden light against the snow felt like magic. How long had it been since he'd seen electric lights? John looked down at the Ellises in the wagon next to him. Joey Ellis's eyes were filled with sparkling reflections. Greta looked up at John and smiled through fresh tears.

John wanted them to wait until Tran had cleared the rooms for certain, but there was no stopping the stampede.

"Looks like they're making a break for it. Let's expedite clearing the living spaces," John ordered over the open channel. "No one goes anywhere that hasn't been cleared by a Lost Boy. Don't try to stop them, but ride ahead all of you and help clear. Emily? See any problems?"

"It's a mess, Commander. But, so far, nothing to freak out over."

"Goldstein?"

"I guess you saw we found intact LT Plasma generators for the whole complex. There's one for lights, another one for the HVAC. Powering it up now. There's a big, old-school, oil-powered boiler retrofitted for LT Plasma, but there's a full tank of fuel oil, too. Give us four hours, and the place should be warm as toast."

"Hot water?" John asked as he looked down at the Ellises.

"Yes, sir. The place was in the off-season when Downfall hit, I guess. The plumbing was all drained, and"—John heard Goldstein flipping switches and opening valves—"we *should* be able to get water running through the heaters."

John nodded, and Greta Ellis clapped her hands in a joyful prayer.

———

According to Aurora, Chris Goldstein's assessment was nearly perfect. Four hours later, the plumbing system produced enough hot water for over three thousand road-weary people to shower. The percentage of those bathers who sobbed as the dirt and stench of a thousand hard miles were washed away? It was a *high* number. Scissors were found. Hair was cut. Beards were trimmed.

Greta Ellis, cheeks buffed pink, gathered a handful of foodies, searched the kitchen, and found enough pasta, olive oil, and preserved garlic to cobble together an epic batch of Agleo e Olio. Those who had not succumbed to the Lodge's four-star mattresses joined for an impromptu feast. Their carb-starved bodies interpreted the pasta as the sweetest meal they'd ever had.

Musical instruments were pulled out of backpacks—the Lost Boys provided fiddle and accordion—and, before long, there was actual singing and dancing—Christmas songs, folk songs, dance songs. The air in the central lobby was still barely above freezing, but it was filled with warmth and good cheer.

John marveled at the sight—over a hundred refugees celebrating a meager bowl of pasta, garlic, and oil. The world had ended. Still, people could find joy in each other, in food, and in music. The sight fanned that tiny ember of hope that rested in his weary heart. He wished Zoe were there. Then he wished he could forget her. Then he shook his head, watched the dancers, and smiled.

The Timberline Lodge felt, for the moment at least, like home. Faces that John only dimly recognized due to the lack of traveling grime, somber expressions of determination, and layers of wool hats and scarves seemed lit by something more than relief. They were alive. Joie de vivre. They had made it to a place that felt something like *civilization* again.

Someone noticed the massive fireplace and it took all of ten minutes before it was filled with tinder, kindling, and a pile of dried pine logs from a sheltered wood stand. The fire did an excellent job of sending the air toward a very comfortable room temperature.

John snuck out to the pole barn out back, where the riders had found stalls for their horses. Galaxy snorted as he entered, and he palmed a couple of sugar cubes he'd found in the kitchen. She leaned her head against him as she chomped them up. His girl was tired, too. He made sure she had plenty of hay and returned to the party.

It was after ten when he ducked back into the lobby, as parents were carrying their children to bed. The remaining couples pleaded for the musicians to play some slow music for slow dancing. A few of the single women looked like they were about to make their approach, but John smiled, steered a path toward the towering spiral wood staircase, and beat a hasty retreat.

He was happy to find the HVAC system had prioritized the guest's rooms. A good night's sleep in a warm bed seemed the ultimate luxury. He drew back the curtains to get a sense of the snow. It was coming down in blowing, blizzard conditions. In the light of the Lodge's parking lot lamps, he had trouble making out the road they'd come in by, and their Conestoga Wagons were already under six inches. By morning, it might be a foot or more.

He pulled up the NTC Weather Gang channel on *@Once*. He hadn't checked since noon, and the forecasters in Nunavut had updated their models. John frowned as he centered the map over Saskatchewan and looked at the ten-day forecast. The snow would continue for three more days, then take a breather for two, and start again. The temps were going to dive.

It was good they found shelter, but he would have to solve for food, or Agleo e Olio would be their last meal until the thaw. And the thaw might not come until March. Over three thousand mouths to feed, and all of the resupply depots would be covered under—what? Six feet of snow when the week was over? He had visions of the Donner Party and pushed them away. They'd find food. He needed shuteye before he solved these problems. He collapsed onto the pillow-topped mattress, and his eyes closed.

His Aurora pinged.

"Of course!" John laughed wearily. He saw it was Robin pinging him, turned onto his back, and popped open the channel. "Captain Mercer!"

"Commander Banks!" He was finding his way back from the grief of losing Oz. "I have good news, boss."

"Good news is all I have the energy for, Robin."

"We have arrived at Port Nelson, and the NTC ship is here. It's a beauty of an icebreaker. Plenty of room for all of us."

"Well, that's excellent, Captain." John peered out the window as a gust turned the dark world white with dense powder. "You should head for NTC as soon as you can. It looks like we'll be here in Saskatchewan for some time."

"Have you checked the NTC weather channel on *@Once*?"

"I have. We've bivouacked in a ski lodge in the middle of the province. There's plenty of room for the doggies and the horses. Goldstein even hooked us up with heat and hot water."

"I caught you as you hit the rack, didn't I?"

"That's a *big* affirmative, Captain."

"All right, I'll hold off on the full debrief until the morning. You're going to love it."

"What is it?" John groaned.

"It can wait."

"All right." John smiled weakly. "Good job getting to Port Nelson. Wake me up at Oh Six Hundred."

"Roger that. Goodnight, Commander."

John closed the connection and was asleep within two slow, steady breaths.

12–24-36 09:56 AM EDT

Wisps of snow whispered against the hotel window, whipped by a hissing wind. Every impact of a dry flake tinkled like crystalline pixie dust, like a magical musical instrument played just at the edge of human hearing. John woke to the sound, his eyelids in no hurry to open. He'd left the curtains drawn, and the room was bright and quiet but for the sound of the fine snow against the glass. The room was warm. Thank the universe for Chris Goldstein. He would have to re-promote the young man.

Finally, his eyes cracked open. He looked at the luxury room and shook his head. Atop a credenza sat his pack, drying from days of snow, caked with mud and a thousand miles of soil. His battle-worn AK47 hung nearby. It looked like he'd been using it as a sledgehammer.

It looked insane in the context of this upscale lodge. But it was the Lodge that was insane, wasn't it? Beyond these walls, beyond the snow, the world was still a smoldering wasteland. The Timberline Lodge, the Salish community, and the NTC were, to his knowledge, the only things that still looked and felt like the world that was.

He brought his hands up to his face and raked his fingers

through the tight curls of his beard. He hadn't felt compelled to shave as others had when he showered. Maybe when he reached NTC. He stood and looked out the window. The sky was bright light gray, nearly white, though the snow continued to drift down steadily. Their Conestogas were no longer visible beneath what John estimated to be fifteen inches of fine, dry powder. The road was drifted over and was indiscernible from the surrounding hills. He wondered how long it used to take for the plows to clear this place when there was still a civilization geared up to do things like that. Probably a week?

He'd have to task his soldiers to find some snowmobiles, start raiding any standing structure they could find, and maybe locate a container drop from Stephen. He strained to recall if he'd seen any stray shipping containers on the road in. That was the beauty of those things. You couldn't recall seeing them when you looked right at them.

Maybe they could resort to hunting. There were bound to be some deer or caribou or something out there in the surrounding forests.

His Aurora told him it was nearly 10AM. Robin had let him sleep. Good man. John decided to see if Greta Ellis had rustled up anything better than MRE dehydrated scrambled eggs. He dressed, sniffing at his clothes. If they had hot water, perhaps he could get Goldstein to get a laundry room functional.

As he walked down the lobby stairs, he was happy to see the temperature had continued to climb. It was well above room temperature, and the fire continued to be stoked and tended to. He walked through the restaurant to the kitchen and found Greta had indeed found a walk-in fridge stocked with eggs, bacon, and —praise Jesus—hash browns.

"You are a miracle worker, Mrs. Ellis," John said as she handed him a plate and a mug of hot coffee with sugar and creamer.

"So long as the miracles are limited to breakfast," she said with a smile. "We found a pantry in the back. A lot of canned vegetables, more pasta, tomatoes, potatoes. Enough to feed our people for a few days. We won't starve, but this bacon is the only meat in the walk-in."

"The troops should be able to get us some venison, eventually."

"Chris Goldstein says, according to the floor-plan, there's more storage downstairs and a laundry." She was eager to explore, obviously.

"Has Lieutenant Tran cleared them yet?" John asked, transfixed by the crispy, golden hash browns.

"Not yet."

"Safety first."

"Yes, Commander." She smiled.

John found a table in the restaurant and took his time enjoying the meal. He wished he had a newspaper to go with his coffee. The news of the day? Same as yesterday. *Demons rule the world.*

Emily Tran pulled up a chair and grabbed a slice of his bacon.

"Good morning, Commander Banks, sir!"

John watched her munch the pork strip like she was feeding it into a paper shredder.

"Good morning, LT. Have you finished clearing the facility?"

"Almost. No sign of any demon activity." She finished the bacon and started eyeing his hash browns. John moved his plate closer to his side of the table and frowned. "The recently demonified, as you know, tend to make a mess, what with the chasing and biting of other, non-demonified humans. Usually, there are unsubtle signs of struggle and blood spatter, of which we have, as yet, found none anywhere in the Lodge or the adjoining condominiums. Same for the pole barns and the equipment shed. We *did* find a small fleet of snowmobiles."

"Hey, now!" John said with a smile. "Tell me they're full of gas."

"They are all *LT plasma*." She nodded as she looked for nearby uneaten food. "Even better. This place was, I guess, a pretty swanky destination pre-end-of-the-world." She got up and ducked through the swinging steel doors to the kitchen, emerging with a plate of eggs and bacon of her own with a mug and a glass pot of coffee. She sat and poured herself a cup as John stole a slice of bacon from her plate.

"Greta Ellis says they think there's a laundry on the lower level."

"That's our next stop." She stopped to have a minor orgasm over the buttery eggs. "Thank god the apocalypse is not vegan." She found a pepper shaker and added a few grinds to her hash browns. "The only thing we've seen on our first pass was signs of vandalism. Looks like kids knocked out a few basement windows, throwing rocks. Aside from that, Ortiz found us a dream place to ride out this snowstorm."

John wished there'd been some bread for toast to mop up his plate, but he was actually almost full. That was a first since Iron Lake.

"All right. Finish your breakfast and get to that lower level." He sniffed at her shoulder as he stood. "We could all use clean clothes for a change."

Tran shrugged and shoveled a wad of eggs into her gob.

———

Joey Ellis was full of breakfast. It was the first time in almost three months that his belly was full and his hunger pangs were utterly absent. As a result, he was behaving like a holy terror in the Lodge's restaurant kitchen. He'd started by finding the biggest stock pots and their lids, along with a pair of long-handled ladles. He began to serenade the foodie brigade with a drum solo that could wake the dead.

That kept him occupied as the first hungry breakfast customers streamed through—many of whom had missed out on the pasta the previous night. As the later risers wandered in,

Commander Banks among them, Joey had moved from cook to cook, playing peekaboo until the adult became occupied by other things. Then, he would find another victim.

Greta, thrilled to have the run of the kitchen, was also doing an admirable job of keeping Joey amused or busy helping with simple tasks. As she figured out how to run the kitchen's industrial dishwasher, she found a latex glove, inflated it, tied it off, and bopped Joey in the head with it. He laughed and began playing soccer back in the hall to the pantry.

The other door in that hallway led to a concrete-block stairwell to the lower floor, an area off limits to guests and exclusively for the lodge's maintenance, housekeeping, cook staff, and servers. Joey found he could kick the inflated glove ball with its five blue fingers and bounce it off the wall. He imitated the ball as he kicked it, pretending it was kicking him back. The two of them rebounded down the hallway until he bounced against the stairwell door, which nudged open.

The smell that greeted his childish senses was one he knew as well as any adult. It was the odor of *poopy*. Someone down those white stairs had done a *job*. This was the type of thing a little boy wanted to investigate so he could report back to his mother.

He left the glove ball bouncing in the hallway and pushed the door open further. The lights in the stairwell blinked on. Joey did as his mom and dad taught him and held onto the handrail. He slid his hand down the yellow-painted metal rail until he touched something wet and gooey.

Was it poop?

No, it wasn't poop. It looked like a bloody booger smeared down the rail. He'd had bloody boogers from picking his nose in bed late at night. He wiped the booger stuff on his coveralls and kept easing down the stairs.

At the base of the stairs was a door that was propped open with a little rubber wedge. Beyond it stretched a long, dark hallway with three other doors. They were all open. Cold air was streaming from the hallway. The smell of poop was down that way, carried on the icy breeze. It wasn't as cold as outside when they were in the wagon. Joey walked beneath a ventilator grill, and warm air washed over him.

He snuck down until he could see in the closest room. The light from outside was coming from a high window, but all the glass in the window was broken and snow was filtering in. Then he saw the people—*lots* of people piled up beneath the window. They were all dirty and gross and had sharp, claw-like things sticking out of their skin.

And they all smelled like poop.

He stood in the doorway for a long time, just looking at the people in a heap. His thumb wanted to work its way into his mouth. He wanted to suck his thumb pretty badly, but he'd been a good boy for weeks. Something about these people reminded him of the day they left home when his mom and dad had been so angry and moved so fast. Mom had been breathing funny and shouting and even crying. And Mom was a big, grown girl. That had scared Joey. It had even scared Caleb.

And these people reminded him of the monsters…what did Dad call them? *Demonks*? These sleeping people looked like *demonks*.

As he stood looking at the demonks in a pile in the dim, cold light streaming from the window, a thing—a very skinny, dirty, man-thing with an arm that didn't look right—stirred. Its head rose up, and it sniffed the air as its arm hung at an angle arms don't usually hang. Its arm had an extra joint between its shoulder and elbow that was loose, blood-caked, and had a broken bone protruding from it.

The demonk's jaws snapped at whatever it was smelling. It pulled itself to a sitting position on the small pile it perched atop and turned its head as it sniffed until it faced Joey. Its black, animal eyes focused on Joey, and it continued to sniff, snort, and snap at the air.

Joey's bladder released, and, for the first time in years, he peed himself.

The demonk slid off the pile and squatted on its feet. It was wearing a dirty sneaker on one foot, and his other foot was torn and ragged flesh. Horns protruded from its legs, and its skin was mottled red and dark, veiny gray. Its head tilted like a dog's does when a high-pitched whistle is blown. Then it stood to its full, emaciated height and tilted back its head to let out three loud grunts.

The entire pile of demonks shifted in response.

One by one, the monsters pulled themselves to a sitting position and rolled off the mound. The first demonk focused again on Joey, who had begun to creep back out of the room. The demonk took an unsteady step toward Joey, then another, as if it was rusty at the whole walking thing. After a second step, it decided it had the gist of it and threw itself out the door toward the boy.

Joey ran, and though he had no relearning to do, his legs were only six-year-old-sized legs. He bolted up the stairs. By the time he reached the door at the top, the door to the kitchen, hot tears were streaming down his cheeks. He pushed—and the door stood solid. The grunts and the hoots of the demonks were getting louder, and Joey turned to look down the stairs as the first demonk entered the stairwell and croaked a series of breathy moans. It looked puzzled as it encountered the stairs. Then it leaped forward and fell on the steps, scrambling and scratching its way up a few feet at a time.

Joey pulled on the door—and this time, it worked the way he wanted it to. He ran into the kitchen hallway. His gloveball bounced out of his way. He ran to the dishwasher, but his mom wasn't there. He whirled and ran the length of the kitchen, head twisting to find her. Then he heard her laughter out in the restaurant and bolted through the swinging doors. She was talking to Commander Banks.

Joey wrapped his arms around her.

"What's the matter, Joey?" she asked, laughing. Then she realized he was crying. "Hey! Joey, did you wet yourself?" She pried his arms away and lifted him. She cast a confused look at the Commander. "He hasn't done that in months."

Joey locked both arms and legs around her tightly.

"Hey, little man, what's the matter?" his mother asked.

"*Monsters downstairs*," he whispered as he pointed to the swinging doors.

"ALL HANDS, converge on the lodge kitchen. *Not a drill*," John ordered into the Borealis 1st open channel.

He'd left his sidearm and AK in his room, a *stupid* lapse. Emily had her Glock, and they moved toward the kitchen's swinging doors as all hell broke loose inside. The foodie brigade fled in random batches, flinging the doors into their faces as they approached. They pushed open the doors and saw Jerry Oldaker, a firefighter from Montana, struggling with a tall, skinny demon with a badly broken arm, wearing a single Adidas sneaker. Emily dropped the demon with a quick single headshot. Jerry grabbed his arm and ran out as the hallway to the pantry burst forth with fresh demons.

John pulled a stout cast-iron skillet down from its hook on the wall and waded in. Emily continued to drop targets but marveled at the big man with the pan swinging away. His long arms and the heft of that skillet were enough to nearly knock the heads of the monsters clean off.

The stairwell door opened as they pushed the demons back to the hallway, and a flood of frenzied infected pushed through. John turned back to her and motioned for her to retreat.

They pushed through the swinging doors to find a crowd tending to Jerry, who had collapsed just outside the restaurant's exit to the main lobby. John shook his head and was about to tell people to back away when Jerry *turned*. Eyes mottled and dead, the man bounced to a standing position, eyeing the possible meals. He leaped onto the nearest helper and began tearing at her clothes, trying to get to her flesh.

Jerry's wife ran to him, trying to reason with him, and he dove for her neck.

The kitchen doors behind John and Emily flew open, and a stream of demons poured into the restaurant. Refugees bolted for the exit, only to stumble over Jerry slurping up the blood of his wife, who was already beginning to seize.

"Get to your rooms! Lock the doors! Shelter in your rooms!" John bellowed as Emily methodically put a round into the skulls of Jerry and Mrs. Oldaker.

The refugees within earshot ran for the stairs to the upper floors.

"Did you hear that, you primates!?" John bellowed into his Aurora channel. "Get the civilians into their rooms and make them lock their doors. No one in or out until this facility is *cleared!*"

Emily bristled with a resentful pang of guilt, decided it was deserved, and proceeded to take it out on the demons spilling out of the restaurant. John continued to swing his cast-iron skillet.

"And can someone get me a weapon?" he shouted.

"On it, Commander!" an anonymous voice said in his ear.

From the far end of the lobby, the garbled hoots of demons rang out as a crowd of civilians turned back toward the main lobby and bolted with plenty of shouting and screaming. The stairwell doors feeding that wing swung open, and a fresh stream of rabid gave chase in their halting, shambling run.

"They found the other staircases," John said as he dodged the screaming refugees. He steered them toward the spiral staircase, and he and Tran headed to work. A young private appeared with an AK47 and a service Glock for John. "Thank you, Private…"

"Jones, sir."

"Thank you, Private Jones." John took the guns, handed her the skillet, and moved toward the open staircase door, dropping targets as he went. Jones and Tran flanked him.

The demons were squeezing out of the doorway too quickly to keep up with, filling the lobby wing within a few seconds.

"Do I have anyone on the top floor?" John asked.

"Herschel and Benner here, Commander," a young voice responded. "We're on six."

"Okay, you two take the stairwell and work downward. They can't go up as easily as you can go down. Make your way down and clear any climbers. I want an armed guard at every stairwell entrance!" John ordered. "So long as they're limited to the stairs, we have the advantage. Once they get out into open space, it becomes anybody's game."

He turned to Jones. "I need someone to fetch ammo. You're it."

"We set up an armory in the gift shop," Lieutenant Tran shouted over her weapons fire. "Chock full of munitions in there."

John nodded to Jones, who ran off to the gift shop. Emily and John marched forward, making a fair amount of noise and drawing the attention of the crowd of demons who quickly left off, chasing the fleeing civilians. Now, the rabid formed a single solid phalanx the width of the lobby's wing and five or six deep. The stairwell door was still open, and more joined the party with every passing second.

"There seems like an endless supply in the lower level," Emily shouted to John. "Why *now?* Why was it quiet until now?"

"We warmed them up. They were hibernating until Goldstein got the furnaces up and running. Once the temp reached demon temperature, they woke up?" John mused as he fired with careful discipline. He tapped Goldstein's channel. "Chris shut down the HVAC. Shut down the heat."

"It's going to get cold pretty quick, sir."

"Yep. That's what we want." John affirmed. "When it gets cold, I'm hoping these things will go back to sleep."

"Sir, yes, sir."

"Commander, I figure these things broke those windows in the basement," Emily said. "Maybe we could cut the supply from outside."

Pvt. Jones returned with a pack full of AK and Glock clips.

"Thanks, Private. You get upstairs and guard the civilians."

Jones nodded and sprinted up the staircase. Eight soldiers appeared from the kitchen. As he reloaded, John instructed four to keep the lobby demons contained and took another four with him and Lt. Tran. They double-timed it out the back double doors and down the snow-covered steps.

When the heavy doors closed behind them, the sound of gunfire and the inhuman screeches and grunts of the demons were quieted. The winds and the snow silenced everything within the lodge, creating a surreal, muted contrast. Emily led them past the massive covered deck and along the base of the back wall. Ten four-foot-long, eighteen-inch high windows lined the foundation as it rose above sparse boxwood shrubbery. All of them were broken open. Five rooms in all. John looked up and saw the restaurant kitchen exhausts just above them.

The soldiers approached the window and found the dark rooms filled with recently woken demons milling about groggily. The basement must have been full of them. There were dozens left in each of these rooms alone.

"Open fire."

The soldiers switched to full auto and, with controlled bursts, eliminated the demons visible through the windows. They knocked the remaining glass in, added suppressors to their weapons per John's orders, and rolled through the openings. Here and there, they had to finish the job and place a headshot with their service Glocks, but these rooms were clear.

John led them through the lower level, quietly dropping any demons that hadn't streamed up through the stairwells. It was a brutal, disgusting business dispatching headshot after headshot. The sounds of the soldiers' suppressed fire and the sound of the demons' death struggles were minimal compared to the continued mayhem taking place in the stairwells. John could hear the unsuppressed weapons fire from above echoing down the concrete shaft. The hellish hoots and snorts and shrieks of the demons and the sound of their bodies bashing against the doors or each other was a constant roar.

Once they'd cleared all the visible spaces and the floors were wet with thick, black demon blood, they moved from room to room, opening every door, every closet, cabinet, and laundry bin. Only when John was satisfied that the level was cleared did they split into pairs and enter the stairwells, moving up to meet the teams moving down.

The demons were not a formidable foe for anyone with an automatic weapon. Their largest threat was their numbers. A swarm could be relentless. It was essential to conserve rounds and fire short, controlled bursts. Most of his team followed John's example and switched to semi-auto.

The demons crawling over each other to climb the stairs were graceless and uncoordinated. Whatever cognitive tools left to the victims of GGB-Z, stair climbing was not included. They stumbled up stairs, falling face first and heaving themselves up a few steps at a time. Doors were more demon-friendly, so long as they could open them with a push or a pull. They were never going to figure out how to use a doorknob. But the rabid had no trouble when John's teams approached from behind and below. They hurled themselves down the stairs with something like a war cry.

It was a bit like shooting skeet, John reflected as they littered the steps above them with demon corpses. Before long, the dead made their upward progress impassible. It didn't stop the demons from trying to get down to them, however, and they spent several minutes in a grim shooting gallery.

The battle sounds above were diminishing.

"We're cut off down here," John said into the open channel.

"We've cleared up to the third floor on the south stairwell," Tran replied.

"Coming to you." John motioned to his soldier, and they exited the stairwell.

The basement now felt quiet as they found the south stairwell and climbed to the lobby. The fighting was over. Carnage and the stench of the dead demons were everywhere. John circled the soldiers.

"Okay, we don't know who was bit, scratched, or wounded. I need you all to go room-by-room through the civilian's quarters and do a status check." He pointed to his eyes and back at them. "I want your eyes on *every* living soul in those rooms. Roll up sleeves. Look for wounds. I'm not letting any of them out until we know they're *clear*."

He considered leaving them in their rooms for the duration, anyway. It would be safer for everyone. The soldiers trotted off to follow his orders. As he walked to the staircase, he saw one of his soldiers among the dead. He knelt down and turned the body over.

It was PFC Jones, the fresh-faced girl who had gotten him his weapons and ammo. Her eyes were shot through with hemorrhaging. Her upper leg had a fist-sized bite taken out of it. Her mouth was full of blood and gore. There was a 22-caliber hole in her temple and an exit wound behind her ear the size of a golf ball.

She'd been bit, turned, and bit another. And she'd been *vaccinated*. John's legs gave out, and he fell onto his ass next to her body.

"How did this happen?" he asked no one in particular—he asked the universe.

A soldier stopped and approached.

"She came down from the upper level." Corporal Hart—or was it Hanks—pointed to the top of the wooden staircase. "She was turned when we saw her."

John nodded and sent him on his way. He reached down and closed Jones' eyes.

"I'm sorry, kid," he whispered.

After a few minutes, Emily found him.

"That sucks," she said. "Billy was a good one."

"Billy?" John asked as he stood.

"Wilhelmina Jones. Yes, sir." Emily nodded.

John sighed. The thing about command was you knew everyone and no one. Everyone acknowledged you and saluted you. You saluted back and offered a few platitudes or a smile. But often, you never knew their details. That is, until they were dead and you had to write a letter to their folks.

"Billy." He took a deep breath. "Thirty-six."

The battle was over. It was just past noon. He looked out the lobby's back doors. Their tracks were already under three inches of snow. He looked back at the lobby and the restaurant. There wasn't a single square foot that wasn't splashed with that molasses-like blood or draped with a corpse. Last night, they'd been dancing right where Jones' body now lay.

"Did Greta Ellis and her kid... Joey... did they?"

"They're okay. Up on three."

"Good."

"If we're going to stay until this snow melts," Emily looked around. "We're going to need a cleaning detail."

John nodded. As they looked around in their post-battle stupor, the lodge's strange, snow-blanketed quiet was undone by a low drone. At first, they both thought it was the moan of a victim or a fresh onslaught of demons. But it was longer, more mechanical, and it was growing louder. It was coming from outside, beyond the front door. The first-floor windows were nearly covered with snow. John and Emily bounded up to the stairs and looked out.

A line of ten big snow cats, NTC's snow cats, approached from the south on Route 2. They watched with a strange, somber blankness as the machines raced toward the lodge. John's Aurora pinged.

"*Merry Christmas, Commander!*" Robin said with a cheerfulness that stood in stark contrast to the morning's events inside the lodge. "Does anyone here need a ride?"

They could see him now in the lead cat, waving happily in the fresh white snow.

John raised his hand, still ruddy brown with Billy Jones' blood, and waved back.

———

01–08-37 08:12 AM EDT

"Don't go filling up on all those oats," John said as he leaned his chest into Galaxy's neck and stroked her mane. "There's plenty of hay."

Galaxy shook her head and pushed against him, her enormous eye regarding him. She could feel his sadness and knew, in that way that animals know, that he was saying goodbye. Galaxy was, of course, a little cranky about it. She reared up slightly and stamped her hooves into the frozen soil.

"Give me a break, girl." John laughed gently. "It's not like I want to leave you. I just can't fit you into that snowcat, and I can't take you on that icebreaker." He smoothed the coat on her nose and unhitched the reins. "Okay, Galaxy. You be good, now. I'll see you in the spring. I promise."

He was not ashamed at the tears welling in his eyes nor surprised by them. He patted her haunches and turned. The snow cat was waiting. It was the last bus out of Manitoba. It had taken twelve trips over two weeks to deliver everyone to the NTC ship in Port Nelson. Six hours each way for the ten NTC people movers. Thank the universe for Athena Shaw's resourcefulness. It was her idea to load the machines onto the ship before they sailed. Without them, the caravan wouldn't have made it home til spring, most likely.

While Robin and his team ferried survivors from Timberland Lodge to Port Nelson, John set out to find a horse farm with a big pasture and a winter's supply of hay. He really was looking to spend time with Galaxy—equine therapy. The sudden, brief battle to clear the infestation in the Timberline Lodge had drained him in a way only a few days on horseback, trodding through the fresh snow could refill.

The Aurora research genius, Ortiz, found the perfect spot seven miles east of the Manitoba line. Two hundred acres of rolling, grassy farm. The barn was open so the horses could shelter in truly bad weather or roam on their own. There were six horses left behind. The owners were found hibernating in the root cellar—at least the ones that had turned. Their turning had been a long, messy affair, judging by the state of the farmhouse.

But the barn was stocked with a beautiful array of saddlery and tack to die for. They'd laid in enough bales of hay to feed an army of horses. The barnyard had an automated solar-powered oat dispenser backed up to the corral. It was the only thing Galaxy had shown any interest in once John had coaxed her into the corral. Galaxy liked her some oats almost as much as she liked a snickers before bed.

As John climbed up into the passenger cabin of the snowcat, Galaxy walked to the pasture's edge. He waved to her. She snorted so loud he could hear it over the engine. Then she rose up on her hind legs, whinnied, and galloped into the hills.

"I'll see you in spring," he said quietly.

He took his place next to Emily Tran, and Robin gunned the cat into motion. The cat followed the fence line east and, at full throttle, could hit forty-five miles an hour. Fresh powder blew up and over the windshield like a speedboat's wake.

"Check this out, boss!" Robin shouted as he pointed to their left. Galaxy was charging along at full gallop, pacing the cat perfectly. John's eyes glistened as he watched her. *God, what an animal!* He placed his hand on the plexiglass. Galaxy reared up again, in an almost cliché, *high-ho Silver* tableau, and then stood and watched them continue on.

"I'll see you in spring," he whispered.

JOHN IS DREAMING. *Submerged, looking up at the sunlight shafts, sinking. He is forty-two.*

Wait.

Rewind.

He's in a snow globe.

He stands in the middle of Sandy Lake. It's quiet. The snow swirls around him and James is there. James is grown up. James is thirty-seven? He looks so good! He looks like Uncle Bill.

They smile at each other for a long time.

"Johnnie. John," James says. He has a beard. He is shorter than John. Softer. Sweeter. John suddenly imagines the life James could have had and the times they could have had together. James smiles and shakes his head.

"Why do you have to do me like this, John?"

"What?"

The sound of the four-wheeler can be heard approaching from the shore. Twelve-year-old James is behind the wheel and seventeen-year-old John is chasing. Jesus, John is so young. He is a child no matter how tall he is. Dream John, old John watches as his younger self catches up to the four-wheeler. He's running so fast. It's a miracle he ever caught the thing. He tugs on James' coat. It's a heroic effort. Just as it looks like he might succeed in getting his brother free, they're out on the lake ice.

John's feet lose traction and he flips into the air before falling on his back. James' coat flies out of his hand. Every cubic inch of air is knocked out of John's lungs. He struggles to reopen airways collapsed by vacuum. He regains his feet as the four-wheeler reaches the center of the lake and falls through the ice.

Dream James, old James, stands and watches his younger self disappear, watches the slabs of 4-inch thick ice rock back into place, concealing any evidence that anything has happened at all. John starts to run out onto the ice, but his father has arrived and stops him, fights to keep him from following out onto the thin ice. John is crying. John is screaming.

James looks around at the snow covered frozen lake.

Young John and his father are gone.

"Is this all you remember of my life?" He gestures to their surroundings. "I was more than this. You've turned me into a ghost. A demon. Your demon. That's not who I was." He shrugged in his winter jacket. "I'm tired of just being this to you. I was once alive to you. Remember my jokes? Remember my drawings?"

John smiles sadly.

"You want to save me? Tell the world about me." He points to the ice at their feet. "This lake was the end of my story. But, in my short time, I lived my whole life. I was more than this."

"Do you forgive me?" John whispers.

"Johnnie, I forgave you before my air ran out." James smiles and shakes his head. "John. Don't you remember? Did you not just see how hard you fought to save me? I looked up to you. You were always my hero."

John walks closer to his brother. With every step, he feels the deep thrum of the ice breaking beneath his feet. Every step he grows heavier. He reaches for James and, for the first time in all of his endless dreams, John falls through the ice. The water is biting cold. John's breath is stolen from him. He plummets through frozen blue as the surface refreezes above him and the slabs of ice float back into place. There is just a mere shadow of James on the surface and soon that is gone as John sinks into the darkness.

John is under, submerged, the currents have him spun around and he's unsure which way is up, which way to the surface. He panics. He looks for the light, for James, for anything....

———

01–08-37 2:48 PM EDT

"James!"

"Commander?"

John woke with a start that shook through his long, stretched-out frame. Emily Tran was touching his shoulder and peering under the brim of his hat. She had a look of non-ironic concern. John sat up and pushed his hat back. The other passengers were watching him with various expressions of curiosity and concern.

"Bad dream?"

"Yeah. I'm all right." John rubbed his face, wiping away tears. He was not sure how long he'd been asleep. The sun was lower than it had been. His Aurora said it was almost three.

"Who is James, sir?" Emily asked.

"I guess I was talking in my sleep?"

"Sir, yes, sir." There was her ironic concern again.

"James was my younger brother, LT. He died when I was in high school."

Emily nodded. She looked at him for a while.

John looked out past Robin's shoulder through the windshield. The world was still clean and crisp and white. Robin had found the path they'd been following for two weeks, one well-packed by the treads of the ten snow cats. It stretched out before them like an illustration of the vanishing point, straight and flat. John turned and noted the hills were behind them now. The land was ridiculously even and level. As he looked, it occurred to him how truly flat the terrain was.

His heart skipped. He could physically feel it move in his chest. They were driving across a lake. He looked around at the snowcat filled with people, and wordless panic crept up from his bowels. His breathing sped up, slowly but steadily. His hands found the edges of his seat cushion and gripped them tight. He felt every bump and vibration, interpreting them all through an imagination that was spiraling.

He was a moment away from ordering Robin to stop, to turn around, or to let him out—or, perhaps, from leaping from the snowcat himself. He was about to scream, to shout that they were all in danger. Mortal *fucking* danger. His eyes were bulging with pressure. He had to get the fuck out.

"So, John!" Emily said as she slapped his knee with a big shit-eating grin. "We never talk anymore! Your brother was named James, huh?"

John nodded. He could barely make sense of her words, but she'd got his attention. He felt like his brain was starved for oxygen. Like he'd been drowning.

"I was an only child. What was it like having a kid brother? Tell me about James."

"He was… um," John fought to think. "He was, you know, younger. Not as athletic as I was. He was smarter, though. More creative. Um… funnier." Some part of him now knew she was trying to reach through whatever was fogging his brain. She recognized a panic attack when she saw one. His mind was divided against itself. It could not stand being perceived by Tran. But he wanted to escape the thoughts that were racing, swirling.

"Funnier?" Emily said. "What's the funniest thing he ever said? Tell me one of his jokes."

"They were stupid. They were stupid." He thought. His face was blank. His hands were slick with unwanted perspiration. From where? He didn't know. He struggled to think of James. "This won't sound funny, but here goes. 'Why do women wear makeup and perfume?'"

"Dunno. Why?"

"Because they're ugly, and they smell bad."

Tran looked stunned momentarily, then her eyes widened, and she bent over laughing. John's face curled slowly into a smile.

"You are the first person I ever told that joke to who

laughed." John felt the snow cat hit the shoreline, and the engine's pitch lowered as it churned up the sloping ground. They were leaving the frozen lake behind. His mind felt the panic attack lift, and his body felt cool from the evaporating perspiration.

"Tell me another one!" Tran shouted.

"Okay. Knock knock."

"Who's there?"

"Tennish."

"Tennish Who?"

"*Tennis shoe?* I thought we were doing knock-knock jokes!"

01–08-37 7:35 PM EDT

John watched as the ship's crane lifted the last of the snow cats to the deck. The Lost Boys patrolling the dock loosened the inch-thick lines, cast them off, and filed ahead of him onto the NTC vessel *Prudence*. The ship had been a U.S. Coast Guard service ship that Stephen had bought at auction in 2031. It had been refitted with LT Plasma steam turbines that provided more than enough power to barrel through the arctic ice of Hudson Bay.

The survivors, *all 3,253 of them*, were there, standing by the ship's rails and cheering as he made his way up the gangway. He thought the cheers were the crowd's delight at being underway, but finally realized they were cheering *him* when he stepped onto the ship. They *all* applauded him.

He felt confused and embarrassed. He nodded and found his way to the ship's prow, where Robin and Emily stood waiting. They, too, were applauding him.

"What is this? What the hell are they applauding me for?" John asked honestly.

"He's *totally* serious?" Emily asked Robin.

Robin nodded.

"You saved all their lives, boss. You're their hero," Robin said as he turned John to face the crowd.

"We *lost* so many good people." John shook his head.

"But you *saved* so many good people!" Emily shouted. "Give 'em a wave."

John waved.

3,253 people saved. He had hoped to save billions with deception and Oneiri-assisted sleight of hand. Epistemology. He felt like an asshole. The crowd applauded and shouted their respect, their admiration, and their heartfelt thanks. He struggled to accept their praise because to do otherwise would disrespect them. Even this, he did for them.

01–11–37 03:45 AM EDT

The Prudence churned the seamless ice asunder, breaking it into table-top-sized slabs that slipped back along the hull. The sound from the conning tower was a satisfying rumble. On their two-day voyage, John enjoyed leaning against the railing and sipping coffee. He was blissfully unaware that the thought of all that ice breaking beneath them would have brought about a whirl of unconscious anxiety just a few days earlier.

The ship moved through a thick fog, and the forward lights only penetrated a quarter mile or so. Suddenly, the ship emerged from the fog bank, the air cleared, and John could see lights on the horizon for the first time since they'd set out. Walrus Rocks—probably Broad Harbour—alone in the dark.

As the fog dissipated, the darkness became more profound since the running lights had nothing to reflect them back. The night sky faded into view, and John saw, for the first time, the northern lights illuminating the frozen world. The cold mist receded in their wake. The boreal spectacle looked like an elegant neon sign, a hint of an arrow pointing to NTC. The Captain shut down the forward lights. The pale light from above was enough to guide them home.

"HOW'S THE RE-ENTRY BEEN?" Julia asked.

"This, our couples therapy, has helped." He laughed. Then he thought about it more seriously. "I am feeling the itch to be out there. More every day." She watched his eyes lose focus as he checked the weather in his Aurora. Or perhaps he was checking the tower feed from NTC Nunavut field. It was the Aurora equivalent of checking his phone. John did it discreetly, but she'd learned his tells.

"John," she said as she set her chai down. "You know this isn't really therapy we're doing." He looked up at her. "I mean, sure, there have been some therapeutic benefits. For both of us. So much more of my memory has returned. I'm back to work." She paused and considered how to move forward. "But I'm not a therapist and neither are you. I go to therapy twice a week. NTC has some truly gifted psychologists on staff. You resurrected a few of them."

John smiled and the evening light traced a blue line across his battle scar.

"I think your trip across the north was incredibly valuable for you because it made you aware of your... well, there's no other word for it but trauma. All of us have been traumatized by

Downfall. All of us. But you know now that your trauma goes back at least as far as James' accident."

He frowned and looked out at the dimming dome below.

"It's time for you to process that trauma. I mean with a pro. It's helped me. Unprocessed trauma leads to bad shit."

John thought for a minute.

Julia let him. In the last almost four months, they'd become good friends, close friends. He'd told her things he'd never told anyone, even Zoe. She waited for him to find his words.

"I think you're right. I think you're right." He was talking to himself as much as he was talking to her.

That was a kind of closeness Julia had come to appreciate. When someone includes you in their inner dialogue, you are truly friends.

"My trauma does go back to James. Also, to Afghanistan. Also, to more than a few terrible wildfires right up to the one that ended my first life. These last six-and-a-half years have been tough. The constant drumbeat of the approaching disaster was… something. The last year, watching it unfold…."

He went quiet for a bit. Julia watched. It was so much like that time she and…. Who was it? Some date…had dinner in that little place. A French restaurant. Whoever it was…struggled with trauma and when he did, he spent a long time searching for words.

"I'm afraid of therapy." John continued. "I'm afraid I've become so comfortable with my trauma that I don't know who I'd be if I parted with it. It is a companion I've carried with me for so long."

He smiled.

It was a smile that Julia knew concealed an enormous body of fear, sorrow, and doubt—but it was mostly his old friend guilt.

"That's bullshit, John. You know—"

"I know. Julia, I know." He held up a large hand. "I hear you." He tapped behind his ear and pointed to his implant. "I can do therapy via Aurora. And I promise you I will look into that."

He stood.

She stood. She walked to him and wrapped him in her best hug. He hugged her back, enfolding her slight frame in his massive arms. There were tears in both their eyes.

"You are an idiot," she said.

"Every day of the week and twice on Sunday," he said. "Thank you, my friend."

It was the last time she saw him for over five years.

———

Later that night, Julia returned to her A-Dome apartment with a reusable hemp-plastic shopping bag full of single woman groceries. She had a box of instant B-Dome chai, a box of B-Dome potato crisps, and a box of B-Dome wine. She had accepted her ration of eggs and chicken breast—real eggs and real chicken breast, not protein sequenced. Bacon was the only sequenced meat she really liked. The NTC lab rats had absolutely killed the bacon.

As she put her replenishments neatly into her cupboards and fridge, her mind was turning her conversation with John over and over. It was a strange sort of ear-worm that had been replaying since they said their goodbyes. She could just see the NTC Nunavut field from her office. The snow had been thinning noticeably for the past three weeks. Julia knew it wouldn't be long before Commander Banks was on one of those big troop transports. Off to save the world, a never-ending battle—because the battle wasn't with Afghani Taliban, it wasn't with wildfires, it wasn't even with the Pentacula or the demon hordes. John Banks' battle was within. It didn't take a psychologist to see that plainly.

John Banks would be fighting to save the world until he made peace inside that enormous heart of his.

He was just like Stephen in that regard.

Julia stopped. She nearly dropped the wine glass she was about to fill.

John was just like Stephen. That was the thought she'd had in their session. That's what her mind had been spinning away in its memory jukebox.

John's loss for words whenever he was reliving trauma was just like Stephen's!

And the dam broke.

She and Stephen.

The whole of her hidden memories of their short but powerful relationship opened like a trapdoor and in she fell.

She recalled the tiny shard of titanium business card found in the waste processing station in Madre Pueda, the phone call to Stephen with butterflies in her gut like a teenager. She remembered meeting with him to confirm that it came from a One Corporation business card… and… and he asked her out!

The dinner had been amazing. A beautiful little French restaurant, a hide-away basement dining room for two. They talked, she flirted, he flirted right back. He told her about John Banks in that same halting, inarticulate way he and John shared. She'd slept with him on that first date. She NEVER did that.

She laughed and smiled a wicked little smile as she filled her glass.

But the sex had been… *great*. Stephen was a sweet, thoughtful, conscious lover. Their exploration of each other's bodies had been tentative, then increasingly passionate. That first time hadn't been as wild as they were capable of. That came later. *God,* the sex had been great.

She took a sip of the wine. B Dome made a decent red. She sat on her couch, looking out at the darkening dome. The community was still active late into the night, but Julia barely perceived them. All of John's stories helped illuminate her memories. She remembered the Cliff Price case. John had left Price to be consumed by the demons. Good. That was justice.

She recalled her own mission to save Stephen from Price. It

had a sepia-toned, dreamlike quality, as if the memories belonged to someone else. The fire. *City on fire. City on fire.* But she was probably sick by then, right?

She had a last flash of brief memory. She was in an elevator, and Stephen had his hand behind her neck. His face, his beautiful face, was shredded and bloody, with just a red rag of velour to stop the bleeding. He looked into her eyes. His eyes were so sad, but so determined.

"I love you."

The elevator doors closed, and he was gone.

She cried then, quietly at first. Soon she was sobbing, and each exhale produced a high-pitched moan. The memories cascaded and flowed, flooding her with details of her last few months with Stephen. She loved him, too. Had she ever told him? The question turned up the intensity of her cries.

Like a soap bubble popping, her mystery had been solved. She was here at NTC because Stephen had created NTC to save her. He needed all of this—the domes, the engineers, the virologists, the scientists and doctors—all of it to be ready to save her life once those elevator doors closed. Stephen Lucas had designed all of it to rescue her and used his time machine to prepare it, hidden from history.

Now the tears came in sheets. The sobs were wracking, loud, hoarse wails.

It took the better part of an hour before she found a way to control her body's reaction to her sudden loss. When she finally got her breathing under control, her ribs ached, her eyes felt inflated, hot, and raw. Mucus flowed from her nose in a steady stream.

She poured another glass of wine and swallowed it in a gulp. Slowly, she fell into a calm stillness. After washing her face to remove the last of her streaked make-up, she returned to her living room and picked up her device. She didn't have an Aurora yet. She was scheduled for next week. A few taps and her device's holo filled with the blue-haired Aurora avatar of Emily Tran.

Detective Tran was the newest addition to her team. Julia liked the little pistol right away. She reminded her of Frankie a little. But she really knew her better through John's storytelling. He clearly respected her, too—more than that, he relied on her.

"Chief Detective Swann, to what do I owe the honor of your call?" Emily said. She just couldn't leave a little wise-ass out of her voice, even when talking to her new boss.

"I have a new case I want you to work with me, Detective Tran. Are you up for it?" Julia said.

"Is it more interesting than finding out who left the lid off the trash compactor in A-Dome?"

"It is."

"Hit me."

"I want to locate Stephen Lucas."

WALRUS AND BRIAN followed the convoy of push carts and hand trucks as it left the assembly room in E-Dome, down the circular pedestrian ramp to the passageway to C-Dome.

"Why are we setting up our radio shack in C-Dome?" Brian asked.

Walrus shrugged with a slight grin. Brian wasn't sure if his response was an expression of ignorance or dodging the question.

"Mrs. Crouch wanted comms with the outside world to be in a SCIF," Walrus said as they passed under the air gate into C-Dome's gigantic cubicle farm. It was like walking into a library, moving from the hustle and bustle of the engineering labs to the quiet, scholarly pursuits of the C-Dome analysts. When people spoke between cubicles, it was in hushed tones. Everywhere was the whispered clickety-clack of keyboards.

"SCIF?" Brian asked.

"Secure Compartmentalized Information Facility," Walrus answered.

"Am I cleared for that?"

"You are now."

The convoy took a right at the dome's central crossroad and proceeded to the pedestrian ramp to the third level. One of the push carts' casters developed a noisy wobble but straightened itself out as they arrived at suite S-3334C. The double doors were open, but next to them, built into the wall, was a palm scanner, a keyboard, and a flat panel display. The walls, Brian noticed, were nearly a foot thick. They were treating this little operation with strict security precautions. Once the equipment and all the techs were inside, an NTC security goon locked the doors behind them.

The techs got right to work unboxing the equipment and placing them on the long bench-like desks that surrounded the space. Twenty-four brand-new ham radio transceivers, assembled in the past week from printed circuit boards designed by Walrus and cases designed by Brian. The E-Dome ZeloofCo fabrication suites had been grinding for two weeks to make the chips. Brian had to divert printers from other production tasks to crank out the cases, dials, microphone stands—everything mechanically necessary for the devices. E-Dome cobbled together a ninety-foot, high-gain antenna tower from a construction derrick in the hard-scrabble adjacent to E-Dome.

By eleven, each call station was set up with a transceiver, mic, scope, power supply, and a pair of cans. The techs filed out and handed in their temporary lanyards. As they left, Mrs. Crouch arrived with three men in winter coats and toques.

"Walrus, are we ready?" Mrs. Crouch asked.

"I think so," Walrus said.

"Walrus Roberts, Brian Cosgrove, I'd like you to meet Johnny Anawak, Atka Umiak, and Joseph Nanuq. Johnny, Atka, and Joseph graciously agreed to help out on recommendation from Eddie Akkilokipok. The five of you represent the sum total of ham radio operators on Walrus Rocks."

The men all shook hands and nodded as they repeated each other's names. Johnny, the oldest of the three, pulled off his jacket and hat and slung them over a nearby chair. He looked at the equipment with a judgmental eye.

"You made all this equipment out here? In your domes?" he asked.

Walrus nodded. "RadioHub stopped delivering back in September."

"How does it work?"

Walrus smiled. "We were hoping you'd help us find out."

Johnny nodded.

Mrs. Couch handed Johnny a piece of paper. "Here's who we want to contact as a test."

"GT98MD. Gary Chase. Montana? That'll be a good test," Johnny said with little emotion. "What's our call?"

Mrs. Crouch pointed to each call station. "NV01BOR through NV24BOR."

"So, this station is NV09BOR?"

She nodded.

"Okay. It says Mr. Chase hangs out at 14.215.00. Let's see if he's home."

Johnny flipped the power supply on, gave it a second, then powered up the transceiver and dialed in the frequency. He put one earpiece up to his left ear, leaned into the mic, and pulled the trigger on the stand.

"CQ. CQ. CQ. This is November Victor Zero Niner Bravo Oscar Romeo. CQ. CQ. Looking for Mr. Gary Chase. Comeback. Over." Johnny's radio voice was deeper, louder, and richer than his speaking voice. Walrus and Brian's eyebrows rose in appreciation. "CQ. CQ. CQ. This is November Victor Zero Niner Bravo Oscar Romeo. CQ. CQ. This is Nunavut. Looking for Mr. Gary Chase. You got your ears on Mr. Chase? Over."

Johnny's head tilted, and he reached forward and flipped a switch, directing the audio to the unit's speaker.

"…eight Mike Delta. Hell yes, I got my ears on! Nunavut! It's sure good to hear you! We've been wondering if Commander Banks and his team made it home! Over."

Johnny looked up at Mrs. Crouch.

She nodded with a smile.

"Mr. Chase, that's a big roger. Commander and team here in Nunavut. Over!"

"Yahoo! Over."

Johnny turned to his associates and nodded. Then he turned to Brian and Walrus. "Your equipment is good."

They both smiled as Atka and Joseph took off their coats and hats and found a station.

John and Robin walked through M-Dome's central parade ground. Drill sergeants were putting new recruits through hell. A good number of the *Fugees*, as the NTC's newest citizens were often called, had volunteered to join the Borealis fighting forces, and they needed to be trained up right. As they passed, everyone, noobs and veterans alike, paused to watch.

Robin chuckled. "You have achieved legendary status, Commander Banks."

John smiled and shook his head.

"Nobody deserves it more than you."

"Part of leadership, Cap, is going along with the fraud."

"Fraud!?"

"Yeah."

They continued on to the mag-lev station and hopped in. The train accelerated through the underground tunnel.

"I'll play the hero. NTC, Borealis needs a hero," John said as he watched the layers of concrete blur past. "But..." He paused. "I really thought we'd have saved more than three thousand refugees. It's hard to swallow that hero label with those results. I thought our epistemology tricks would pay off. That we'd save millions. Billions even."

"I wouldn't want you judging the Olympics, Commander." Robin laughed. "That's a steep curve. I don't know anyone who sneezes at saving three thousand people."

The train pulled into the airfield terminal, they hopped out and each donned a pair of dark aviators.

"It feels weird getting on a plane and heading back to the wasteland in clean fatigues." John changed the subject.

"Sir, it feels weird getting on a *plane* again, considering our last takeoff experience."

"Yeah," John said.

He thought, but didn't say, *It feels weird going on a mission without Zoe.*

But, he'd made a realization in all of his sessions with Julia Swann.

He'd see Zoe again.

He was now quietly confident of that. She'd be younger. She'd be a stranger, for her it would be their first meeting. But he'd meet her again. He didn't know where. He didn't know when—perhaps that information was the cause of the Roberts Rules violation that crashed the AuroraNet. But he knew she was out there and one day He'd find her. John smiled at the thought.

They strode in the brisk Nunavut April sunshine to the giant Airbus. Their team and pilots awaited.

04–03-37 09:12 PM EST

"CQ. CQ. CQ. This is November Victor One Three Bravo Oscar Romeo. CQ. CQ. Looking for survivors of Downfall. Over," Atka Umiak said into his mic.

The SCIF was loud and chaotic as the five operators scanned the frequencies, seeking contact with the outside world. It had started slowly at first. Their audience was, perhaps, unsure of the risks of responding. But they reached their first survivors shortly after 1:00. A community of 1,200 souls on Star Island in New Hampshire. Then, another enclave of 700 in New Jersey. Then, another 4,000 survivors in Maryland, outside of Baltimore.

Walrus stood up and stretched his back before bending over and touching his toes. He handed Mrs. Crouch a few pages of notes.

"Over 5,000 new survivors. Oshkosh, Wisconsin," he said with a tired smile. "We're going to need a bigger boat."

Mrs. Crouch nodded.

"I hear Commander Banks and his team took off for points south this afternoon."

"That's correct."

"If it wasn't for his team, most of these communities of survivors wouldn't have made it."

She nodded.

"He's going to find out about this, right?"

Mrs. Crouch didn't respond.

"How many survivors have we reached just since noon, just the five of us?" Walrus asked.

"Current tally is two hundred and twenty-three thousand."

"Holy smokes."

"And, yes, every contact we make, the story is the same. Doomsday prep provisions, containers full of food and supplies, or some other Borealis magic trick, made the difference between survival and… the other thing." She paused. "We'll brief Commander Banks. Once we know what the numbers look like."

Walrus nodded. He started to say something, then stopped himself.

"What is it, Walrus?"

"Mrs. Crouch, you can't tell Stephen about these survivors." He winced at the thought. "Right? We have to hide these successes from him."

She nodded slowly. "Why do you think we're in a SCIF, Walrus?"

"Epistemology."

"Correct."

EPILOGUE

09-17-36 01:52 AM PDT: ORACLE

THE TRIP HAD TAKEN seven hours so far. Only the first hour or so required a constant lookout for demons. Once he made it to the highway and got onto I-80 headed northeast, he could imagine the world was spinning along in greased grooves as it always had. The fire behind him in Madre Pueda said differently. So too did the fires in Sacramento, though Sacramento hadn't really caught as quickly as MP had. The end of civilization was just getting rolling. Reno was ahead. Reno was a shit show, even in the best of times. Before long, people would flee the cities and he'd need to off-road for a few hours. But, for now, GPS was still working.

He was tired, his face throbbed, and every bump in the road made it worse. Just before the Nevada border, he had to leave the road to a horde of demons streaming out of Mystic. He took the time to stop and more adequately dress his wound. He pulled into a sheltered CalTrans sandlot and opened the back gate. The Hummer had been packed to his specifications by SDS operatives before it had been placed in the abandoned lot behind Grady Castle. The first box he opened was filled with bandages and several bottles of Betadine. He stripped off his black cotton button-collared shirt and carefully peeled the stiff velour rag from his face. His wound gushed blood all over again, but he was ready with a large wad of surgical gauze soaked in Betadine. He poured the disinfectant on his face and over the gauze. The nasty liquid crept into the corner of his mouth, and he gagged. He had to spit the shit into the sand. He stood and caught a look at his reflection in the back window.

His face was shredded.

He found the appropriate bandage and covered one side with antibiotic gel. In a quick move, he pulled the gauze away and applied the bandage. His head swam, and tiny pin-pricks of light filled his vision. He sat on the back gate and just held the bandage in place, hoping he wouldn't pass out.

With his head tilted back, he could see the stars—it took a moment to realize they were the actual stars. Out here in the boondocks, they shined so brightly. It felt like the first time he'd taken a breath since… when? He and Julia had been up at 5:00 the previous morning, and they had been off to the races almost immediately. He took the time just to breathe and gaze at the stars for a few minutes. He had to slow down, or he'd explode.

He found the surgical tape with his free hand and tore off strips six inches long. Betadine had dried enough that he could secure two edges of the bandage reasonably well. The other two were more of a hack job, as they had to be stuck to the area beneath his eye. His cheekbone was torn to hamburger. The edge along his nose was also a challenge. He tore off two longer strips to finish the job.

His face still ached. Further rummaging in the neatly packed boxes produced some ibuprofen gelcaps, and he swallowed three dry. Now that his eyes were accustomed to the night, he could see the fire on the horizon. He dimly recalled driving past the almond orchards. Here and there, they'd been burning like the cities. Without firefighters to respond, they'd burn for weeks. They'd burn until their fuel was spent. It didn't matter. In the long list of ongoing tragedies, the fate of almonds ranked vanishingly low. The thought made him feel insane. He found a bottle of water and sucked it nearly dry.

He wanted to get into Nevada before daylight.

He pulled to a stop at an intersection that had no road signs. There was one stop sign for the four directions and it was simply leaning against a fencepost. He pulled onto the desert by the side of the pavement and walked to the center of the crossroad. He held his device in his hand and shielded it against the sun's glare. For the last two hours, he'd been getting random GPS errors. The constellation of LEO satellites, without human correction some-where across the globe, had slipped out of carefully maintained precision. Within a few days, GPS would be a thing of the past. One more human institution claimed by his Oneiri beta test.

He made a mental note to find a fix for that and filed it into his growing to-do list.

He peered down each spur of the intersection with his golden, predatory eyes—seeing nothing. He was tantalizingly near his destination, or so he thought. It was, to some extent, a good sign that there were no signs. He had reached the edge of civilization. If he could find the place, he could get back to work without fear of collapsing a single wave function of future events.

His Maps app blinked and then said in a quiet voice, "Proceed to route."

The map drew a green line telling him to turn left and drive three miles to Fausts Bluff Flats. He got back in and pulled the LT-powered four-wheeler back onto the broken, neglected asphalt. The Hummer's gruff, synthesized growl fell flat on the desert scrub. This was nowhere, he thought. It was perfect.

GPS held firm for the rest of the trip, another five minutes. He found the small ranch entrance and drove up the half-mile gravel and dirt drive. There was a large and shiny corrugated steel Quonset hut to the right, in front of an older storage building and a garage. The drive looped in a circle past the metal building to three nicely maintained wooden houses that looked to be built in the late twentieth century. There were covered walkways between the buildings, and their angled roofs were covered with solar cells. Behind the garage, where the desert gave way to shallow hills, an egg-beater-like windmill churned lazily in the paltry desert breeze.

It was exactly to his specifications.

He pulled into a parking stub and got out. It was already dry and hot, and he wasn't dressed for it. He unbuttoned his shirt to reveal brown Betadine stains and dark, dried blood. As he explored, the door of the smaller house—a cabin, really—opened, and a young woman who appeared to be of Mexican descent walked down her porch steps. He wondered if he'd taken a wrong turn.

"Mr. Stephen?"

He nodded. "Stephen Lucas."

"Good. I am glad you found it."

She was short and dark, and her face was friendly. She looked a little troubled by his appearance.

"I'm fine. It looks—well, it looks about as bad as it is. But I'm okay for now."

He reached tenderly to find his bandage was now stiff with dried blood as well.

She nodded. "Miss Allan said you'd be injured. I can dress your wound. I have training."

"Are you here alone?"

"My husband, Hector, went out to help some friends." She looked troubled. "Everything is falling apart, just as Miss Mary said it would."

"Mary Allan?" Stephen asked.

"Yes, Miss Mary Allan with Standard Data Systems. She hired us six months ago. We've been getting everything ready. I hope you find it to your liking. We worked very hard to make it exactly as she asked."

Stephen felt an overwhelming sense of relief. His instructions to Mary had been hastily considered, but he thought he'd come up with a plan that could be modified if everything was done according to his initial instructions.

"Do you want to see your house first, or the workspace?" She gestured to the quonset hut.

"The workspace, please." He stopped himself. "I'm sorry. This is all so—I'm Stephen Lucas. And you?"

"Maria Esparza." She couldn't have been more than twenty-four.

"Pleased to meet you, Maria. Yes, please show me the workspace." He stopped and thought. "Just one second." He opened the passenger door of the Hummer and grabbed his duffle bag. "Okay, lead on, Mrs. Esparza."

Maria opened the large, shiny padlock with a bit of effort. They both slid the door on its track. Everything was new. The galvanized siding, the door's hardware, the padlock—all of it was less than a few months old. The inside of the metal structure was huge, dark, and cool. Air conditioner units hummed on either end. The look of the building would lead one to expect to find it filled with tractors or an old biplane, but instead, there was a modern office space equipped with holographic workstations. The walls were lined with 96-inch holodisplays, and the back of the space housed a state-of-the-art holosuite that enclosed a pristine white office and a conference room. The whole interior could have been cut and pasted from the campus at One Flat Circle.

It was a big space for one man, but it gave him ample room for multi-tasking.

He walked to the nearest workstation and rummaged in his bag. Pulling out two heavy, black cubes, he placed them each on the desk. Two Oneiri cubes. One was his. The other was Cliff Price's. They both acquired the Wi-Fi network and logged on. Immediately, their thin white LEDs began to swirl and dance along their dark bases. The only way to tell them apart was the splash of blood on Cliff's.

"I'm going to get to work," Stephen said.

"Will you let me dress your wound, Mr. Stephen?"

"I will when the day is done. It's fine for now. Before dinner, if that suits you."

"Okay." Maria looked troubled, but she knew better than to argue with her new boss. "I will come back at 5:00, then?"

"That sounds fine, Maria."

Stephen had already found a seat before one of the workstations and connected to Oneiri. He heard the metal door close behind him.

He dialed the timeframe back to 2029.

John Banks

will return in

THE ATLAS OF HUMAN STRUGGLE

Book 3 of The WalrusTech Universe Series

IF YOU ENJOYED *THE AURORA'S PALE LIGHT* WE HOPE YOU'LL FOLLOW THE LINK BELOW TO RATE AND REVIEW THIS BOOK TO HELP INTRODUCE IT TO OTHER FANS OF SCIENCE FICTION AROUND THE WORLD.

ACKNOWLEDGMENTS

Thanks to my editors Elisa Faison and Victoria Straw for working their magic on this second novel. They continue to make me appear smarter than I actually am. Thanks also to my sensitivity reader, K.S. Dunigan for providing her perspective, insight, and wisdom.

Thanks to all my beta readers: Nick, Dan, Jake, Jason, Mary, and the other Dan—just to name a few. Thanks for volunteering to be my guinea pigs. Your input was vital.

Thanks to Allison Gunn, my critique partner, the blue-haired Shirley Jackson of her generation. Without her critical eye, her writer's vision, and her thought provoking notes this would be a very different book. Her debut novel, *NOWHERE* (Atria, March 2025) is available for pre-order now. You should get it.

And a final thanks to my parents, gone now over four years. If I have a way with words, it was inherited from them and sharpened to a fine edge at our family dinner table.

A book is not written, nor published, in a vacuum. To all of the above and to all of the many people who offered encouragement, advice, and the occasional "there, there"— This is where your good wishes took me.

ABOUT THE AUTHOR

Born to a self-taught artist and an electronic engineer, E.W. Doc Parris has always had one foot in the world of fine art and the other in the world of technology. He pursued a Bachelor of Arts in Acting at the Webster University's Sargent Conservatory of Theatre Arts before starting a family. A self-taught software engineer, he's worked as a graphic designer, art director, creative director, photographer, animator, video editor, web developer, and iOS developer. When he isn't writing he can be found rehabbing his 40 year-old colonial in the foothills of Virginia's Shenandoah Mountain.

You can find him on the following social media.
Mastodon: @ewdocparris@writing.exchange.
Instagram, Twitter, BlueSky: @ewdocparris

Milton Keynes UK
Ingram Content Group UK Ltd.
UKHW031908201124
451474UK00001B/25

9 798987 388983